Lifelong romance addict **JO** break from her career as a j a family and found her calling as a Mills & Boon author instead. She now lives in New Zealand and finds that writing feeds her very real obsession with happy endings and the endorphin rush they create. You can follow her at jcharroway.com, and on Facebook, X and Instagram.

USA TODAY and *Wall Street Journal* bestselling author **Janice Lynn** has a Master's in nursing from Vanderbilt University and works as a nurse practitioner in a family practice. She lives in the southern United States with her Prince Charming, their children, their Maltese named Halo and a lot of unnamed dust bunnies that have moved in after she started her writing career. Readers can visit Janice via her website at: www.janicelynn.com.

THE MIDWIFE'S SECRET FLING

JC HARROWAY

FLIRTING WITH THE FLORIDA HEART DOCTOR

JANICE LYNN

MILLS & BOON

First published in Great Britain 2024
by Mills & Boon, an imprint of HarperCollins*Publishers* Ltd,
1 London Bridge Street, London, SE1 9GF

www.harpercollins.co.uk

HarperCollins*Publishers* Macken House, 39/40 Mayor Street Upper,
Dublin 1, D01 C9W8, Ireland

The Midwife's Secret Fling © 2024 JC Harroway

Flirting with the Florida Heart Doctor © 2024 Janice Lynn

ISBN: 978-0-263-32180-7

12/24

MIX
Paper | Supporting
responsible forestry
FSC™ C007454

This book contains FSC™ certified paper
and other controlled sources to ensure responsible forest management.

For more information visit www.harpercollins.co.uk/green.

Printed and Bound in the UK using 100% Renewable Electricity
at CPI Group (UK) Ltd, Croydon, CR0 4YY

THE MIDWIFE'S SECRET FLING

JC HARROWAY

MILLS & BOON

To my mum.

CHAPTER ONE

EARLY BOXING DAY MORNING, Zara Wood parked her car and left the cosy interior for the sub-zero temperatures outside. Craving a hot shower and a decadent five hours of uninterrupted sleep after her night shift at the hospital delivering babies, she pushed open the front gate to her Derbyshire cottage.

This early, the village of Morholme was quiet as people slept off the excesses of Christmas Day. Zara sighed; no matter which way she looked at it, working on Christmas night had sounded desperately lonely. But unless she counted watching her five-year-old son, Zach, sleep, something she still enjoyed, she'd had nothing better to do. Besides, most of the other midwives had families and partners, and Zach had been so excited for a sleepover at her mum's, where he'd no doubt eaten too many treats and stayed up late.

As she headed for the front door of the end-of-terrace cottage she'd inherited from her late father, a noise—the metallic scrape of the squeaky side gate—grabbed her attention.

Zara peered around the side of the house to see a strange woman disappear down the lane that ran between Zara's cottage and that of her neighbour. Zara raced into the garden, confusion turning to panic. Had she been burgled while she'd been at work? She'd spent six months renovating the basement rental flat while also working full-time to support her son single-handedly. Had the stranger broken in using the key Zara had hidden under a flowerpot for her new lodger—a man visiting from Australia—who was due later today?

With adrenaline ramping up her pulse, Zara yanked open the gate, outraged that someone had taken advantage of all her hard work. But by the time she'd made it into the lane, the woman had vanished.

Indignant, she entered the rental with her master key, fearful she'd find the lovely cosy accommodation she'd slaved over on her days off while Zach was at school completely ransacked, but everything appeared undisturbed. Even the television and portable speaker, the only items of real value, were still present. Perhaps the woman wasn't a thief at all, but a squatter.

Zara sighed, her five hours of sleep dissolving. She'd need to wait up for a locksmith to change the locks. Her mood worsened as she moved to the bedroom, finding evidence that the squatter had indeed spent the night. The bed Zara had left immaculately made for her lodger with clean luxury sheets and a cosy duvet was all rumpled and had obviously been slept in.

Just then, she caught the sound of the shower door closing in the en-suite bathroom. Her pulse soared. There were two squatters. And one of them was using *her* hot water and *her* luxury body wash. The cheek of people!

Melodic humming came from behind the closed bathroom door. *Male* humming. With a sudden chill of fear spreading through her veins, Zara grabbed the nearest heavy object—a ceramic candlestick from the mantel. She should probably call the police, but first, this guy was going to get a piece of her mind.

The bathroom door flew open. A stark-naked man appeared. On seeing Zara, he came to an abrupt halt in the doorway, his expression registering shock, which quickly morphed into a hesitant smile.

'I come in peace,' he said, holding up his hands in surrender as he nervously eyed the candlestick she'd menacingly raised. 'But if you're going to use that, do you mind if I cover myself first?' His eyes darted to the nearby towel rack.

'You can't be here,' Zara said, too strung out to place his accent, but it was clear he wasn't local. She yanked an expensive Egyptian-cotton towel from the rail and tossed it at his naked chest.

He caught it with one hand and quickly wrapped it around his hips. 'Why don't you put down the candlestick before someone gets hurt?' he said, one side of his mouth kicking up, a playful edge to the nervousness now.

'There's nothing funny about breaking and entering,' Zara said, inflamed that he seemed to find this situation amusing. 'You're trespassing. If you don't leave immediately, I'll call the police.'

How dared these people take advantage of all her hard work? Renting out the newly finished flat would help subsidise her wages so she could give Zach everything he deserved in life, given that she'd never received a single penny of support from his father, a man Zara considered the biggest mistake of her life.

He held up his hands again now that the towel was securely tucked. 'Hey, there's no need for the police,' he said, as if she were overreacting. 'Let's just chill out for a second.'

'No, you chill out,' she volleyed back. 'And while you're at it, get out.' Thanks to this freeloader and his lady friend, she'd have to spend valuable time that she could have been sleeping fixing up the flat for the arrival of her lodger.

'I'm not trespassing,' the stranger said with amused patience, his inquisitive stare taking in Zara's creased midwife's uniform. 'Are you Mrs Wood? I'm Conrad Reed.'

At the mention of his name, Zara sagged with relief, her adrenaline draining away.

'It's *Ms* Wood, actually. I'm not married,' she snapped, feeling stupid. 'So you're Conrad Reed...from Australia?' There'd be no need to use the candlestick, call the police or change the locks, because *this* was her lodger, the man who'd signed a month-long lease and was supposed to be arriving that afternoon.

'Yep,' he said, his smile widening as he stuck out his hand. 'Good to meet you. If I'd known you were going to let yourself in, I'd have put on some clothes.' Humour flashed in his eyes.

Reluctantly, she shook his hand, her face flaming at the misunderstanding. But was everything a joke to this guy? Perhaps Aussies were just naturally easy-going thanks to all that sunshine and surfing. His accent was so obvious to her now, she cringed at her eagerness to jump to the wrong conclusion.

'Sorry,' she muttered. 'I thought you were a thief, or a squatter.' She lowered the candlestick to her side.

'Nope. But you weren't really going to use that, were you?' He eyed her makeshift weapon doubtfully.

'I don't know...' She narrowed her eyes and stood a little taller. 'Maybe.'

He laughed then, but she couldn't join in or see the funny side. She was too tired.

'I hadn't thought it all the way through,' she continued. 'I just know that I worked hard to single-handedly renovate this place, and I've just got home from work after a night shift, and I have to pick up my son in five and a half hours so I was looking forward to some sleep and—'

She took a breath; she was waffling. This man didn't need her sad life story. And now that there was no need to evict him, she couldn't help but notice his attractiveness. Dirty-blond hair still damp from the shower. Piercing grey eyes, sparking with amusement. Tall and tanned with a muscular physique, his broad chest dotted with water droplets. Helpfully, her brain chose that moment to remind her that she'd seen him naked, even if she'd been too scared and outraged to enjoy it at the time.

But Conrad Reed's smokin' body and roguish good looks were irrelevant. Since a holiday fling six years ago had resulted in her precious baby, and after Zach's biological father had declared he wanted nothing to do with Zara or his son, her sole focus was taking care of Zach so he never once felt the loss of a positive male role model in his life. What with her shift work and her five-year-old, there was no energy left for members of the opposite sex, not even an exotic one with a drool-worthy body and a charming smile that came far too easily and made her think of all the things she'd denied herself since that pregnancy test had turned positive—partying, dates, *sex*.

'Hold on a second… You were meant to be arriving later this afternoon?' she reminded him, her voice pinched with fresh annoyance. She hoped her very first lodger, as hot as he was, wasn't going to be problematic.

'Change of plan. I took an earlier flight.' He gave a casual shrug, one hand pushing his wet hair back from his handsome face so his biceps bulged.

Zara grew hot, all too aware that it had been almost six years since she'd been intimate with a man, and that, but for her Egyptian-cotton towel and a cheeky grin, he was stark naked and impressively endowed.

'I did message late last night to let you know I'd arrived,' he said. 'Thanks for leaving out the key, by the way.'

'I don't check my phone when I'm working,' she said tightly, desperate to get away from his male confidence and amused curiosity. He was making her feel like an ancient, uptight freak.

'So is it too soon to joke about this yet?' he asked, flashing her the kind of smile that had probably rescued him from many a tricky situation. 'It's one hell of an introduction story.'

Zara raised her chin, feeling foolish for her part in the misunderstanding. 'Yes, I'm afraid it is.' He, on the other hand, seemed to find everything amusing. 'I'll...let you get dressed,' she said, wishing he were wearing more than a towel, his tall, lean body tauntingly on display.

She flushed hard. She was clearly exhausted; she wouldn't normally be susceptible to a guy's sexy confidence and charming smile. She turned for the bedroom door and then froze. The rumpled bed, the steamy bathroom, his freshly showered appearance finally registered, the pieces falling into place. Obviously her new laid-back lodger had entertained female company last night, and the mystery woman sneaking out of the side gate had not long left his bed. Or, more correctly, *Zara's* bed. Ignoring the sudden flare of irrational loneliness—her own nocturnal activities were non-existent by choice, despite her friend Sharon's constant urging she *have a little fun*—she fisted her hands on her hips and spun to confront him once more.

Having clocked the name badge on her uniform, Conrad had been about to mention that he'd taken a locum position at the same hospital, when she spun around, her lush mouth pursed with suspicion.

'Wait…' She frowned, her big hazel eyes taking another sweep of his naked torso before she met his stare. 'I just saw a woman leave here, but the lease was for you alone. Single occupancy.'

She looked embarrassed to mention it, but clearly wasn't scared of a little confrontation. And she clearly hadn't finished confronting him. At least she hadn't decked him with that heavy-looking candlestick…

'It *is* just me. Don't worry, she won't be back.' Conrad shrugged. What was a single doctor a long way from home supposed to do?

She flicked a glance at the unmade bed, her lip curling with disapproval as she slowly nodded. 'Oh, I see… So that woman isn't your girlfriend?'

Her stare returned to his, and then shifted over his chest. Ever since she'd decided he posed no threat, she couldn't seem to stop checking him out. And the curiosity, the attraction, was mutual. Zara Wood was a complete bombshell— petite, brunette, her body boasting the kind of curves that made him think of bikinis.

'Nah.' He shook his head, not in the slightest bit embarrassed to have been caught in the act of the morning after. 'I met her on the train. She gave me a lift from the station. It was just a one-time thing. No big deal.'

But from the way his feisty landlady was looking at him, he could tell she wasn't impressed.

'A one-night stand on your first night in town,' she said with a disbelieving slight shake of her head. 'Impressively fast work.'

Conrad smiled wider, wondering exactly what her problem was. She was only in her twenties, too young to be a prude. She had a son. Surely she must have had a one-night stand before.

'Is that not allowed?' he asked, fascinated by her prickly attitude. 'I don't recall anything in the lease agreement I signed that prohibits your tenants from having casual sex.'

'No problem at all,' she said, flushing but raising her chin defiantly. 'You can have as much casual sex as you like as far as I'm concerned. Who am I to judge?'

Conrad folded his arms over his chest, chuckling to himself when her stare dipped there once more. 'And yet you sound as if you're judging.'

His curiosity sharpened. Who was this intriguing woman and why was she so...uptight? He could understand the whole intruder misunderstanding, but she was acting as if she'd never once let her hair down.

'I'm not,' she bluffed haughtily. 'Your sex life is none of my business.' She blushed furiously, looking away.

'Well, I'm glad we've got that cleared up.' Conrad nodded, smiling to himself.

'However...' Zara thrust the candlestick at him, so he took it with an incredulous snort of amusement. 'I do have a small son, so, as your landlady, I'd appreciate it if your, um...*guests* could limit themselves to your half of the garden.' She backed away towards the bedroom door as she spoke, as if she couldn't wait to get away from him now that she had him pegged as some sort of player.

'Of course, no worries,' he said with a shrug and a non-threatening smile. 'With this weather—' he glanced point-edly at the window and the grey skies beyond '—I don't think it will be an issue. It's hardly barbecue season. But I'll be sure to let you know of anyone else sleeping over. I don't want my *guests* bludgeoned in their sleep.' He held up the candlestick, his lips twitching with amusement. She was fascinating, formidable and so sexy.

'There's no need for that,' she said, appalled, the pitch of her voice rising. 'I don't need to know every time you have casual sex.'

'Are you sure?' he teased, unable to resist coaxing out the fiery sparks of challenge from her eyes. 'It's no prob-lem to flick you a message.'

He should stop antagonising her and let her get some sleep, but, for some reason, he really wanted to see her smile.

'I'm positive, thanks.' The smile she offered him was frustratingly tight and insincere. Then she glanced down and muttered, 'I don't want to be inundated with messages.'

'What's that supposed to mean?' he asked, his stare nar-rowing. For someone with a son and no husband, she was acting fairly high and mighty. She'd obviously made some snap judgements about him, when all he'd actually done was arrive at a property he'd legally rented half a day early. Perhaps he and his landlady weren't going to get along after all. Shame, given they were most likely going to be work colleagues. But he wouldn't drop that bombshell now, not when his every move seemed to infuriate her.

'It means you clearly enjoy being single.' She smiled brightly. 'I know the type.'

Conrad sighed. They'd clearly got off to a terrible start and, by the sounds of it, she didn't think much of men.

'Anyway,' she went on, 'I need some sleep. I'll leave you to it.' She backed towards the door, practically vibrating with nervous energy, so all he could do was watch her, bewildered. 'It was…good to meet you.'

'You too.' He replaced the candlestick on the mantelpiece and followed her from the bedroom into the kitchen, where she made for the front door as if the building were on fire.

'And merry Christmas, for yesterday,' he said as she yanked open the door, letting in a blast of frigid air that made him shiver.

'Merry Christmas,' she said, on a nervous squawk before she kept her stare lowered and fled up the path to her part of the house, leaving Conrad to scratch his head and wonder if he and his wildly sexy English landlady could be any more different.

CHAPTER TWO

A WEEK LATER, on his third shift as a locum obstetrics registrar, Conrad strode onto the labour ward at Derby's Abbey Hill Hospital, his footsteps slowing to a halt. Up ahead at the nurses' station stood his incredibly sexy but uptight landlady, Zara Wood. Internally, he groaned, his heart sinking. To say they'd got off to a bad start last week was an understatement. He'd never met anyone as wary as her, and she clearly thought him some sort of philandering creep. Sadly, that hadn't stopped him wondering about her incessantly, knowing this day, when their paths would cross again, would come. But if they *had* to work together, it made sense to clear the air.

Expecting their reunion to be as frosty as the English winter weather outside, Conrad hesitantly approached, watching Zara, who wore a harassed expression as she stabbed at the computer keyboard in frustration.

'Do we actually have a registrar working today?' she asked her midwife colleagues, Sharon and Bella, whom Conrad had already met. 'They don't seem to be answering their pager.'

'We certainly do,' Sharon said with a knowing smile as she wiped patient names off the whiteboard behind the desk. 'Haven't you met our locum?' She winked suggestively at Bella, who chuckled and rolled her eyes.

'Oh…are you in for a treat,' Sharon continued, with her back to Zara. 'In fact, I think he's single. I know I sound like a broken record here, and I know that you "don't need a man"…'

Clearly Zara often threw around this argument.

'But for him,' Sharon said, 'it might be worth finally breaking your long dry spell.'

Conrad hid a smile, his ego posturing as Bella fanned her face dramatically. 'Right…that accent,' she said to Sharon, 'the body, those eyes. I certainly wouldn't kick him out of bed for not emptying the bins. Makes you wanna move to Australia.'

Conrad crept closer on softened footfalls so he could eavesdrop for a little longer. He worked hard at keeping in shape. It was good to know that his efforts at the gym hadn't gone unnoticed. He was only in town for another three weeks, and, after past events in his personal life he was trying not to think about, it had been a long time since he'd felt in a relationship kind of place. That didn't stop him wondering what Zara Wood really thought about him though.

'Wait,' Zara said, rounding on her colleagues, her back to Conrad and her hands on her hips so he had an uninterrupted view of the gorgeous outline of her figure. 'Did you say Australian?'

Bella nodded and Conrad froze, wondering if Zara would make the connection.

'He's not tall with grey eyes, is he?' she went on. 'A smile that could melt off your clothes?'

His lips twitched as he forced his stare from the curve of Zara's hips, although she'd certainly checked out his nakedness a week ago, before she'd torn a few strips off him and almost kicked him out of the flat he'd legally rented. But it was good to hear confirmation that their attraction, their chemistry, was mutual.

'Yes, that's the one,' Sharon said as she wrote new names on the board. 'Dr Reed.'

'Oh, no…' Zara muttered, her shoulders sagging.

'So you *have* met?' Sharon turned to fully face Zara, a delighted smile on her face. Then the older woman caught sight of Conrad in the background, her eyes widening with surprise and a flicker of guilt.

'Good afternoon, ladies,' he said, announcing himself with a straight face. 'Did I hear my name mentioned?' He came to a halt behind Zara, who seemed to freeze, her shoulders tensing.

Zara spun on her heel, her expression impressively innocent considering how they'd just been gossiping about him. 'Of course you're a doctor here…' she muttered stonily. 'I suspected as much when I saw your stethoscope hanging by the door last week.' Her voice was clipped with annoyance and accusation, telling him he was in trouble again. But at least she wasn't wielding a weapon this time.

'That's right. A locum.' Conrad smiled and dropped his voice, unable to resist teasing her again. 'But at least this week I've got my clothes on.'

Despite trying very hard to look busy, the other two midwives were obviously shamelessly eavesdropping, because they gaped excitedly and then hid stunned smiles.

'You couldn't have mentioned that you worked at *my* hospital when we met?' Zara said, ignoring the delighted, slightly impressed mirth of her colleagues. She grabbed one of the ward tablets from the charging station and glared his way, clearly still furious with him.

'I had planned on bringing it up when I saw your name badge,' he said, his lips twitching as he glanced down from her green-brown eyes to where she clutched the device the way she'd gripped that candlestick—with malicious intent. 'But my fight-or-flight response got in the way. You looked menacing wielding that candlestick.'

Zara sighed and glanced at her colleagues, who were pretending not to listen. 'It's not what it seems.'

Sharon and Bella looked up, innocently.

'She's right,' he added. 'It was just a simple misunderstanding.'

'Okay, okay, don't protest too much. We believe you,' Sharon said, eyeing Zara with an impressed and questioning look. Clearly Sharon *didn't* believe them and wanted all the juicy details. In trying to smooth over their misunderstanding, he'd only made it worse.

'I thought he was a squatter,' Zara exclaimed to the other women, 'so I accidentally confronted him getting out of the shower. He's renting my basement flat, although he's one infringement shy of being evicted.'

Zara returned her glare to Conrad and the other two midwives chuckled and trailed away, back to work.

'As we're housemates as well as colleagues...' Conrad said with his most charming smile. How had she described it? Capable of melting off clothes? He could work with that. 'I take it you won't mind me calling you Zara?'

Her eyes narrowed with suspicion. 'As you're *finally* here,' she said, pointedly, 'I have a thirty-three-year-old primip who's been in second-stage labour for forty-five minutes that I'd like you to examine.' Without further preamble, she marched down the ward, heading for one of the delivery rooms as if he were an obedient dog who would come to heel.

Conrad followed, setting aside the invigorating friction with his prickly landlady for now, although it was certainly helping him to forget why he'd as good as run away from Australia to hide for a while in deepest, darkest midwinter England.

He paused outside the delivery room to wash his hands. 'I take it the foetal heart rate is stable? No sign of distress?' he asked, his mind now on work.

'It is, but mum-to-be is pretty exhausted. She's been labouring for eighteen hours.' She pressed her lips together as if Conrad were to blame for her patient's predicament.

'Have the membranes ruptured?' he asked, tossing the paper towels in the bin.

'Yes, and the neonatal registrar is on their way,' Zara replied, pushing open the door and nodding to the other midwife in the room before addressing the patient.

'Angela, this is Dr Reed, the obstetrician. I've asked him to examine you because you've been pushing for a while now and this baby doesn't seem to want to be born.'

As another contraction took hold of their patient, Conrad observed the foetal heart monitor for signs of distress and pulled on some sterile gloves.

'Angela,' he said, 'on the next contraction, I just need to examine you, okay?'

The woman nodded, bracing herself as another wave of pain struck. Conrad quickly examined the birth canal, felt the baby's head and the fully dilated cervix before meeting Zara's stare. 'The baby is right occiput-transverse,' Conrad told her.

Zara nodded, a flash of relief in her big expressive eyes.

'The baby is absolutely fine,' Conrad explained to Angela and her partner, a concerned-looking guy with round glasses and dark curly hair. 'But its head is a little rotated. He or she needs a little bit of help coming out, so, if you agree, I'm going to use the ventouse suction to help things along.'

Angela nodded weakly, her grip tightening on her partner's hand as another contraction took hold. Zara set up the instrument tray for the delivery while the second midwife assisted Angela through her contractions and her breathing. The neonatal registrar arrived, the small delivery room filling up with bodies. While the baby seemed fine at the moment, instrumental delivery could be a traumatic experience and the newborn would need checking immediately after birth.

'Okay,' Conrad said to all concerned. 'Let's get this little one delivered.' He slipped on fresh gloves and set up the instrument, while Zara positioned herself at his side, the second midwife and the partner holding the patient's hands.

'On the next contraction, Angela,' Zara instructed, 'Dr Reed is going to straighten the baby's head and apply suction, okay? You keep pushing until we tell you to stop and soon you'll have your baby.'

With that familiar surge of adrenaline in his veins, Conrad attached the suction cup to the top of the baby's head and applied gentle traction while rotating slightly to reposition the baby's head. He never tired of the thrill of helping to welcome a human being into the world. He loved his job, and it was immediately obvious that so too did Zara. At least that was one thing they had in common.

With the baby's head in the usual position of occiput-anterior, the next contraction delivered the baby's head.

'Okay, Angela, pant now,' Zara instructed, watching his every move.

Conrad quickly removed the cord from around the baby's neck, becoming aware that Zara was tightly gripping his shoulder, as if fully invested in the safe delivery of her patient's baby.

In the pause between contractions, Conrad glanced up and met her stare, a flicker of respect blooming in his chest. Given they'd be living together and working together for a few weeks, it made sense that they try and get along. Life was too short for disagreements and misunderstandings.

'Just one more push now,' Zara told the mother, releasing Conrad's shoulder with a slightly embarrassed shrug, 'and you'll meet your baby.'

Now that the hardest part of the delivery was over, Conrad shifted sideways to make room for the feisty but fascinating midwife. As an obstetric trainee, he'd soon learned how midwives could be very possessive of the babies they delivered. Where midwifery specialised in normal pregnancy and birth, Conrad was only really required when things weren't going to plan. That said, the specialities depended on one another. Everyone involved in obstetrics was there for the same reason: to ensure the safety of both the mother and the baby.

The baby's shoulders were delivered with the next contraction, followed by the rest of the newborn, a baby boy with a lusty cry and a full head of dark hair just like his father. Conrad detached the suction cup from the baby's head and wheeled his stool aside to allow Zara close enough to lift the newborn onto his mother's stomach.

'You have a son,' Zara said. 'Congratulations.' Her eyes

shone with emotion as she supervised Dad to cut the umbilical cord.

Conrad smiled to himself, glad that the situation was so easily resolved. While the tearful couple met their baby, Conrad assessed the woman's birth canal for damage. 'Just the placenta to deliver now, Angela, then I just need to give you a couple of stitches and we're all done.'

The woman nodded her consent, too in awe of the new life in her arms to worry about the business end of things, so Conrad got to work. The room emptied of the now redundant extra bodies—the neonatal registrar and the second midwife—leaving Conrad and Zara alone with the new family.

'I'll bring you some toast and tea,' Zara said to Angela as Conrad finished up the sutures and pulled a blanket over Angela's legs.

'Congratulations,' he said, taking a second to glance at the contented newborn, who, after all the excitement, had dozed off to sleep, before leaving the new family to get to know each other.

He found Zara in the ward kitchen, making toast.

'I feel like we got off to a bad start last week,' he said, slouching against the door frame and watching her brusque movements with fascination. 'We should probably try to get along, seeing that we're not only working together but also living in the same house, don't you think?'

She shot him a sideways glance. He raised his eyebrows expectantly, his pulse bounding with excitement, because he'd been right earlier: their attraction was clearly mutual.

'Did you have to mention the lack of clothes in front of my colleagues earlier?' she said, eyes narrowed with suspicion. 'It sounded bad.'

'I'm sorry. I didn't mean for them to hear. And I was just teasing you. I hoped to coax out a smile after the misunderstanding of our first meeting.'

'It seems everything's a joke to you,' she huffed. 'But you should know that it's hard to keep a secret around here.'

'That's a bit harsh,' he said, wondering exactly how he'd managed to get so far under her skin. 'I take my work very seriously. And I did overhear you all talking about me behind my back earlier. Why don't we call it even and call a truce?'

His apology, the reminder that he'd been the topic of some pretty unprofessional conversation, seemed to appease some of her indignation, but not all of it, because she went on. 'I know you seemed to have charmed everyone else here with your... This...' She waved her finger in his general direction.

'With my *clothes-melting smile*?' he offered, enjoying the sparks in her stare. But he rarely clicked with someone this strongly and instantly.

Her scowl deepened. 'But, just for the record, you're wasting your time trying to charm me. I work and take care of my son. That's all I have time for.'

'Noted,' he said, his expression serious. 'It can't be easy being a single parent. I take my hat off to you.'

Ignoring his comment, she looked up sharply. 'So you understand that I'm not interested in being your next casual conquest?' She shot him a pitying smirk, even though *she* was the one rumoured to be stuck in a prolonged dry spell. But his first impressions had clearly been spot on. Zara Wood obviously had no time for men. And despite finding his landlady incredibly attractive, Conrad hadn't dated seriously for over six years.

'Of course I do. But from what I've seen of Morholme,' he added about the village just outside Derby where they both lived, 'we seem to be the only two residents under the age of sixty. I'm only in the UK for another three weeks, but it makes sense for you and I to at least be friendly, don't you think? After all, life is too short for drama.'

Sadly, he knew that first hand. His brother's violent death six months earlier had been sudden and shocking. A man he'd loved and looked up to, there one minute and inexplicably gone the next when all he'd been doing was his job. It had made Conrad all too aware of the fleeting nature of life. You could lose what you loved in a split second.

Conrad dragged his thoughts from his still fresh grief and watched Zara set her features in an unreadable expression. 'I don't have much time for friends, so don't get your hopes up.' She smirked. 'You might want to consider other forms of…entertainment.'

Of course, by entertainment she meant sex. Because she'd obviously picked up on his casual attitude to dating, something he'd perfected over the past six years, since he'd moved too fast and been dumped.

'I understand,' he said with a smile, desperately trying to work his charm. 'But I was really just talking about a friendly coffee between two colleagues.' It was her mind that had turned immediately to sex. 'I don't want any awkwardness between us; that's not my style. Do you have a break coming up?' he asked, gratified to see her flush.

If they didn't have to work together *and* live together, he'd have given up trying to win her over by now. But there was something about her he couldn't seem to ignore. Despite their misunderstanding and their other differences, she, like him, was a straight talker. After the betrayals of his past from the one person he'd trusted more than anyone else, his late brother, he instantly respected that about Zara.

'I'm due a break in ten minutes,' she said, placing the buttered toast on a tray with two mugs of strong tea. 'I'll finish up with Angela and meet you in the staff canteen.'

'Great,' he said, his heart banging as if he'd won an epic victory. 'Coffee is on me.'

She raised her chin. 'I can buy my own coffee, thanks.'

Feisty and fiercely independent... 'Got it.' He sighed. What was it about Zara Wood that intrigued him?

'I'll see you later.' With an inscrutable glance, she picked up the tray and passed him, the sway of her hips as she walked down the ward his only reward for bravely extending the Anglo-Australian olive branch.

CHAPTER THREE

TEN MINUTES LATER, in the cafeteria, a flustered Zara took the seat opposite Conrad. What were the chances that her Australian lodger was also the new obstetric locum? If only she'd asked him what he did for a living that first day instead of shamelessly ogling him and judging him for being young, free and single, she might have avoided further embarrassment.

'Thanks for coming,' he said, all easy charm, those grey eyes of his smiling.

Zara shrugged, still mortified that he'd overheard her comments on his attractiveness earlier. But at least he hadn't gloated too much. She unwrapped her sandwich, although her stomach clenched with nerves. She blamed her colleagues on the delivery ward. The minute Sharon and Bella had discovered she was meeting the new locum doctor, who also happened to be her tenant, for a coffee, they'd shrieked like a couple of silly excited schoolgirls. Matchmaker Sharon, who was always encouraging Zara to *live a little* and *have fun*, had even fussed with Zara's hair and tried to persuade her to put on some lip gloss. As if...

'So, what brings you all the way to the middle of England from Australia?' she asked, trying her best to be friendly. 'As you pointed out, it's not for our barbecue weather,' she scoffed.

Outside, it was another dreary, grey and bitterly cold winter's day. But no matter what the state of the weather, she couldn't seem to forget she'd seen him stark naked. That was what six years without sex did to you.

'I finished my registrar training back in Australia, but I didn't want to apply for a consultant post yet.' Conrad smiled that killer smile, shrugging casually as if his easy-going personality was natural and in no way contrived. 'So I applied for a locum position and here I am.'

He took a sip of his coffee and she forced herself to take a bite of the sandwich, knowing from past experience she should take the opportunity to eat while she could. But despite all her tough talk, despite blaming Sharon for her nerves, there was something about Dr Reed that made her edgy.

Maybe because they were opposites, chalk and cheese. Maybe because he was the first Australian she'd ever met. Maybe because he was the only man in six years she'd found attractive enough to make her wonder if Sharon was right when it came to dating and sex and relationships: Zara *was* selling herself short. And she had to reluctantly admit that, whatever his other faults, he seemed to be good at his job.

But she didn't suffer fools. She'd meant what she'd said. His charisma, the good looks, the hot body—all irrelevant. She'd fallen for that kind of charm offensive once before. Zach's father had been one of *those* guys—avoiding commitment or being tied down, simply out for a good time. Her mistake had come with consequences for the most precious person in her life: her son.

'I actually like the contrast,' he said, still referring to

the weather. 'Where I'm from, winter temperatures rarely drop below twelve degrees Celsius.'

Zara sneered, wondering again why he'd come all the way to the middle of England in the winter. She couldn't imagine that Derby, or even Morholme, would be anyone's choice of travel destination. Looking at his light tan, the sun-kissed ends of his hair, the laughter lines around his eyes and mouth, Zara imagined the exotic heat and golden sand beaches of Australia, a place of surfing and picnics and laid-back vibes. A place she'd never been.

'Where in Australia are you from?' she asked, thawing to him a little, not that she wanted him to know she'd spent the past week daydreaming about her sexy new tenant or furtively hoping for another glimpse of him leaving the flat. When Bella had mentioned the new doctor was Australian, she'd even secretly hoped him and her lodger, the only Australian she knew, were one and the same.

'Brisbane,' he said, watching her intently as if, to him, she was equally exotic. 'Well, the Sunshine Coast to be precise.'

Zara rolled her eyes disbelievingly. *The Sunshine Coast...?* That sounds like a dreadful place to live. No wonder you prefer sleepy, freezing-cold Morholme.' What on earth was he doing there?

He laughed, his smile lighting those gorgeous grey eyes that seemed to bore into hers. Zara couldn't help but smile back. It had been a long time since she'd clicked with a man or found a shared sense of humour, not that this mild flirtation could go anywhere, of course.

'Have you ever been to Australia?' he asked, something in his laid-back attitude surprisingly intriguing now that she knew he took his work seriously, something she could respect.

Zara shook her head. 'No. I've always wanted to visit. It's on my list.' She didn't want to tell him the last time she'd been abroad she'd been a twenty-year-old student midwife. She'd saved up for a friends' holiday to Spain, where she'd fallen for a handsome Spanish waiter, had a dreamy holiday romance and come home pregnant. She already felt pretty unworldly compared to Conrad Reed.

And the last thing she wanted to think about in front of him was her youthful naivety and how, even after all these years, there was a part of her that blamed herself for Zach's situation. Holiday romances never lasted, and she didn't regret having her wonderful boy. But she wished she'd chosen a better father for him, one interested in knowing him, even if he and Zara weren't together.

'Holidays for me are usually a rainy week in South Wales.' She shrugged, her face heating. 'Or a road trip to Chester Zoo, but I wouldn't change a thing, obviously.'

She pressed her lips together, experiencing the familiar sharp ache of rejection on Zach's behalf. Spain wasn't that far away from England, and if Lorenzo had asked, she'd have brought baby Zach to meet his father. Instead she'd learned just how little she'd meant to the Spanish waiter, who probably had a different fling with a fresh holiday-maker every two weeks. A man like that, just selfishly out for a good time, had no use for a kid cramping his style.

'So, how old is your son?' Conrad asked, seeming genuinely interested.

'Zach. He's five.'

Conrad raised his eyebrows, his smile filled with satisfaction. 'Same age as my nephew, James.' Something shifted over his expression—pride, longing, a flicker of sadness, gone before she could be sure of it. 'Is he at school?'

Zara nodded, instinctively sensing that Conrad and James were close. She recognised the adoring look on his face. 'He goes to Morholme Primary School.'

'So how do you juggle shift work and childcare?'

'I'm lucky to have my mum living close by. She often picks Zach up from school while I'm at work. And, depending on my pattern of shifts, has him for sleepovers, which he loves.' In many ways, she had a great life: a good job she adored, a secure home thanks to her father, a son who made her smile, every day. No wonder she couldn't find the energy to bother with something as dissatisfying as dating, not when, in her experience, men were so unreliable.

'So is your nephew in Australia?' she asked, curious that they seemed to have the love of a five-year-old in common. Would she need to revise her first impressions of this man?

'Yeah, in Brisbane. I miss the little guy.' He glanced down at his coffee, telling her he didn't want to say more on the subject.

'It must be quite a culture shock for you coming here,' she said. 'Derby isn't exactly a cosmopolitan city and there's literally nothing to do in Morholme unless you're into pensioners' bingo at the village hall.'

He laughed again, meeting her stare. 'Morholme is very quaint, I guess. But you've done a beautiful job with the flat. It's very comfortable.' His expression was full of warmth and curiosity that left Zara aware of his observation to the tips of her fingers and toes.

'Thank you,' she said, his compliment bringing an unexpected ache to her throat. 'My father left me the house, so Zach and I are lucky.'

'Your father has passed?' he asked, with a frown.

'Yes, five years ago, just after Zach was born. He had pancreatic cancer.' Why was she telling him this? She barely knew him. But he was right; life *was* short. Her father's untimely death was proof of that. Not a day went by where she didn't miss her dad. She owed her parents so much. She could never have finished her midwifery training and established herself at the hospital without the support from Pam and, thanks to her father, she and Zach would always have a roof over their heads.

'I'm sorry,' he said, simply. 'I understand what that's like. I've lost someone, too.'

Zara blinked away the sting in her eyes. 'Then I'm sorry, too,' she said, feeling awkward and wondering if the real reason he'd left Australia was to mourn.

'So what *do* you do for fun, *Ms* Wood,' he asked, pasting on a bright smile and changing the subject, 'if it's not pensioners' bingo at the village hall?'

Zara smiled, grateful that they could shift back to lighter topics. 'Well, nothing as exciting as I'm imagining you do on the Sunshine Coast, perhaps barbecues and beach walks.' If only he knew how mundane her life was—not that she needed his pity. She and Zach were fine.

She smiled a genuine smile, thinking about her son. 'After a week of juggling childcare and shift work, the highlight of my week is usually feeding the ducks at the village pond on a Sunday, followed by a trip to the playground.' There was nothing better than spending time with her little boy, the centre of her world. If her own personal life lacked a certain…sizzle, it was a small price to pay for Zach's happiness and security.

'So no New Year's Eve party lined up for tonight?' he asked. 'Perhaps a hot date?' His stare glittered with that curiosity that told her their attraction was obviously mutual, even if they had no intention of acting on it. 'I heard mention of a dry spell earlier, so I just wondered…'

Zara blushed furiously. She couldn't even recall what a *hot date* felt like. In fact, she'd barely had a couple before having Zach. But she was going to throttle Sharon. 'No, no date tonight.' And she'd already declined an invite to drinks at Sharon's house.

'Really?' he asked with flattering astonishment. 'But New Year's Eve only comes around once a year. You're too young and too interesting *not* to have a date tonight.'

Zara shrugged, abandoning the rest of her sandwich, because her appetite had vanished. While his comments were flattering, she felt the need to defend herself. 'I'll probably have an early night, actually, given I have the early shift tomorrow and Zach spends every Friday sleeping over at his grandma's. She has a little dog he adores, and she spoils him. But I don't mind.'

He nodded, and she continued her justifications. 'Besides, I've kind of had my fingers burned in the past. I've raised Zach single-handed. My spare time is precious. I'd rather give it all to my son.' And having made one mistake with her holiday romance, having exposed her innocent baby boy to his father's rejection, she just couldn't face the effort of meeting some stranger who'd most likely do a runner as soon as she mentioned she was a single mum.

'Of course,' he said with a guilty wince. 'It must be a lot to juggle.'

'What about you?' she asked, desperate to change the subject back to Conrad. 'Any kids of your own? A wife or girlfriend back in Australia? Or maybe both?'

She needed some nugget of information she could give to Sharon and Bella when she returned to the ward. Her colleagues would be hungry to know what she and the hunky Australian had talked about, and Sharon would go ballistic if all Zara had done was talk about why she was so sworn off relationships.

He shrugged, looking mildly uncomfortable for the first time. 'I've dated in the past, but, you know, nothing serious in recent years.'

She sensed there might be more to the story, but, like her, he obviously didn't want to talk about his past relationships. 'You're just having a good time, right?'

Why was she poking at him this way? She wasn't normally rude. But there was something about him that was forcing her to revise her first impressions and messing with her head. She blamed Sharon, who'd acted as if Zara were going on a real date, when in reality *she* wouldn't know a good time if it came up and kissed her senseless.

'You don't think much of me, do you, Zara?' He smiled, holding her eye contact for a long while, making her squirm.

'I don't know you,' she said, all bluster now that he'd called her out. 'But I think you're a good doctor. You paid your rent on time. The rest is none of my business.'

He laughed and Zara couldn't help but smile too, glad to pretend she'd been joking, because, otherwise, she'd sounded like a bitter old shrew who judged every man she met against her disappointment with Zach's father.

But now that she'd met this sexy Australian with such a different outlook from hers, the huge hole in her personal life gaped open. If she didn't know better, she'd think he'd been sent there to shake up the life she'd assumed she had under control and make her restless for something more. She'd just cast that ridiculous thought out of her head when Conrad's pager sounded an urgent tone.

'It's Labour Ward,' he said, looking down, abandoning what was left of his coffee and jerking to his feet.

'I'll come with you.' Even though she had fifteen minutes of her break left, Zara grabbed her bag and they both started running.

The alarm led them to one of the delivery rooms. Sharon glanced up as they entered, her expression sagging with relief, but Zara's blood froze. She and Sharon had been looking after this woman together, before Zara had gone on her break.

'This is Jane Phillips,' Zara told Conrad. 'A twenty-eight-year-old multiparous mum on her third pregnancy.'

More help arrived: the obstetrics SHO, Max, and a crash team anaesthetist.

'Normal vaginal delivery four minutes ago,' Sharon added in a panicked voice, her stare flicking to the newborn in the arms of the father, who was looking on anxiously. 'Sudden post-partum haemorrhage following third stage,' Sharon continued, reaching to the wall behind the new mother to adjust the flow of oxygen to a mask she fitted over Jane's face.

Conrad grabbed a wide bore cannula and a tourniquet, quickly introducing himself to the patient as he sited the cannula in her arm.

'We need cross match. Four units,' he said, extracting a blood sample and passing it to Max.

While Sharon set up an infusion of intravenous fluids,

and Zara drew up syntocinon, a drug that would contract the uterus and hopefully slow down the bleeding, Conrad placed a hand on Jane's abdomen, manually massaging the uterus.

'Start the syntocinon transfusion,' Conrad told Zara, his alarm obvious in the clipped tone of his voice. 'Was the placenta intact?' he asked Sharon.

'I thought so.' Sharon nodded as the woman's blood pressure dropped, the alarms sounding once more.

With panic and fear in charge of her heart rate, Zara took over the compression of the uterus while Conrad examined the patient.

'There's no obvious tear,' he said, meeting Zara's stare. 'The bleeding is coming from high up. Keep massaging.' He reached for a second intravenous cannula and sited it in the woman's other arm, the sense of urgency in the room building. Catastrophic post-partum haemorrhage was fortunately rare but life-threatening, and every midwife and obstetrician's worst nightmare.

'If we can't get the bleeding to stop,' Zara explained to the alarmed couple, who hadn't had a chance to enjoy their newborn baby, 'you might need to go to Theatre.'

'Get a second bag of fluids up, please,' Conrad told Sharon, who rushed to do his bidding. 'Zara, can you draw up some prostaglandin?' asked Conrad as they nervously watched the blood pressure monitor, willing the drugs to work and the bleeding to slow.

Zara reached for the second line drug as Conrad took over with the uterine massage, their efforts coordinated, their differences and misunderstandings forgotten as they worked as a team.

Zara injected the prostaglandin into the muscle of Jane's thigh and looked to Conrad for guidance.

'Blood loss isn't slowing as quickly as I would like,' he said, addressing the patient and her partner. 'Do you consent to surgery?'

The couple nodded, wide-eyed now with the same fear Zara was desperately trying to control.

'Call Theatre,' Conrad told Sharon, clearly reaching the limit of his composure. 'Tell them we're on our way.' He unlocked the wheels of the bed and nodded to Zara. 'Take over here with uterine compression and, Max, get the blood sent round to Theatre.'

Leaving Dad and the baby in Sharon's care, she, Conrad and the anaesthetist steered the patient out of the delivery room and rushed towards the lifts that would take them straight to the operating suites.

Inside the department, Zara handed the patient over to the waiting theatre staff, her job for now done. 'Keep me posted,' she told Conrad as the doors swung closed.

He gave her a determined nod. Of respect, of thanks, of promise. Then he disappeared out of sight, racing to surgery with their patient. Zara headed back to the delivery ward, her adrenaline draining away to be replaced by concern. She hoped for their patient's sake, for Jane's newborn and her husband, that her instincts were right: that Conrad *was* a good surgeon. For now, all she could do was wait.

CHAPTER FOUR

LATER THAT NIGHT, back in Morholme, Conrad knocked on Zara's front door, nervous excitement making his heart skip a beat. He understood how Zara's alternating shifts created issues with childcare, but he hated the idea of her being alone on New Year's Eve. He waited in the freezing pitch black. Days were dark when he arrived at work in the morning and dark again by the time he left the hospital in the evening. It made him wonder if he'd ever again see the sun.

The door opened and Zara appeared, her expression one of surprise. Warmth flooded onto the doorstep from the house. She looked relaxed and sexy in her jeans and sweater. She'd been on his mind all day since their talk in the cafeteria and the emergency they'd dealt with together.

'Hi,' he said, trying to keep his voice serious. 'I wondered if you could point me in the direction of pensioners' bingo? I hear it's the most exciting thing that happens around here.'

Her laughter lit her eyes and raised his sun-starved spirits, so his smile widened. There was something about her laugh, her sense of humour, that mocking challenge in her stare, that took his mind off his own troubles. She'd admitted she'd had her fingers burned when it came to dating, and he wondered how far her trust issues went. That would be another thing they had in common, although Conrad's own sense of betrayal was complex and snared up with his grief over losing his brother, Marcus. It was hard to be angry with a dead man, especially one Conrad had always looked up to, the one person he'd thought he could trust.

'Actually,' he went on, keen to change the direction of his thoughts away from his late brother, and his reasons for leaving Australia so he'd had space to think and grieve, 'I'm going to try out the local pub, and wondered if you'd like to join me, seeing as you're alone tonight and we're probably the only two non-retired people in the whole of Morholme.'

A moment's hesitation flicked over her expression. 'Um… I have to be up at five.'

'I know, but it's New Year's Eve. We don't have to stay long, but I hear there's live music,' he cajoled playfully, switching on the smile she found charming, 'a buffet, and, if you need further convincing, even a meat raffle donated by the local butcher! How could you possibly resist?'

She laughed again, her refusal clearly waning.

'We might have a good time,' he urged. 'I don't know about you, but after today, I could use a few laughs.'

At mention of their emergency, she seemed to change her mind, to his relief. 'Sure, why not? Although I can't promise I'll make it to midnight. And I hope you like your beer warm and your sandwiches curly, not a barbecued prawn in sight.'

'They're my favourite, as it happens,' he joked, elated that he'd managed to persuade her and draw her a little more out of her shell. Today, he'd revised his opinion that she was prickly and uptight. She was smart and funny. She was clearly a dedicated midwife and was understandably devoted to her young son. When she let down her guard, her attractiveness shot through the roof. When she laughed with him, he didn't miss Australia quite as much.

'I'll just grab my coat.' She disappeared for a second, reappearing wearing boots, a puffer jacket and woollen hat with a furry pompom. They set off on the short walk to the Miner's Arms, side by side.

'So how did the surgery go?' she asked. 'Thanks for texting me to say she was out of Theatre, by the way.'

'You're welcome. I'm not going to lie, it was stressful,' he said, watching a small frown of worry tug at her mouth. 'I found some retained placental tissue that was causing the bleeding, so she lost a lot of blood.' Post-partum haemorrhage was one of the worst emergencies he ever had to treat.

Zara glanced up at him with obvious concern. 'You were still in Theatre when my shift ended, so I've been worrying about the outcome. Will she be okay?'

Conrad nodded. 'I hope so. I had to transfuse three litres of blood and her renal function went off a bit. So she's recovering on the high-dependency unit for now, but I hope to transfer her to the postnatal ward in the morning, as long as she's remained stable overnight. How was the baby?' he asked, recalling how emotional and exhausted the husband had been when Conrad had spoken to him on HDU.

Zara's frown eased slightly. 'He's well. Perfectly healthy. So that's one good thing.'

'Yeah.' He dragged in a deep breath. 'Sometimes it's hard to leave the job behind, isn't it?' There was something very attractive about Zara's dedication to her patients. It spoke of loyalty and compassion, two very attractive qualities in Conrad's book.

'It is,' she agreed. 'It can be emotionally draining.'

'That's why I'm so glad I could persuade you to come for a drink tonight.'

She smiled and some of the tension around her eyes eased. 'Why did you choose obstetrics?' she asked, eyeing him with curiosity as they crossed the deserted road towards the quintessential English pub, which had brass carriage lamps beside the door and climbing ivy growing along the stonework.

'Well, my mother is a midwife,' he said, pulling open the door to the pub for Zara to enter first, 'and, believe it or not, I like the happy endings. If we do our jobs right, we not only help the patient, but we also send her home a mother to a healthy baby. That's pretty cool in my book.'

'I agree, it is,' Zara said, her observation intensifying as if she'd warmed to him since their earlier chat in the hospital canteen. And the feeling was mutual. Faced with an evening alone with only his ruminations on why he was there in England, Conrad had remembered Zara say her son was spending the night at her mum's place. The idea of getting to know her a bit better, a woman who'd pretty much been on his mind since the day they met, had galvanised him off the sofa.

Inside the Miner's Arms, the antiquated theme continued with low ceilings criss-crossed with wooden beams, old guys in flat caps propping up the bar and a roaring log fire in a massive blackened grate.

'What can I get you,' he asked over the sound of the band, who were playing popular classics no one was dancing to.

Zara removed her hat and unzipped her coat, her cheeks rosy from the cold. 'I'll have a pint of Chatsworth Gold ale, please.'

Conrad nodded, impressed by her drink of choice. While Zara smiled at a few locals and wandered off to find them a table near the fire, he ordered two pints of Chatsworth Gold, his attraction to his landlady building. He wasn't looking for a relationship. He was only in the UK for another three weeks. But Zara Wood was exactly his type: stunning, smart, funny and clearly dedicated to her work and her son.

Wondering again about her dry spell and what it meant for a harmless bit of flirtation, he joined her at the table and took a seat.

'Cheers,' he said, raising his glass. 'To the end of a busy week and the end of another year.'

'Cheers!' She smiled and clinked her glass to his, taking a sip.

'Oh, that's good,' he said, the hops and honey blending on his tongue.

'As good as your Australian beer?' she asked, her hazel eyes twinkling in the glow from the fire.

'Better,' he said. 'And perfectly chilled too. You promised me warm beer...'

'Well, warm beer is the house special,' she teased. 'You have to ask for it with a secret handshake.' She winked. 'I'll teach it to you.'

Conrad laughed, delighted that she seemed to be enjoying herself. 'Obviously beer drinking is how you Brits manage your seasonal mood disorders,' he countered. 'Is winter always this dark? I literally haven't seen the sun for days.'

'Don't be such a baby,' she said, laughing at him.

Conrad basked in the sound, his curiosity for this woman building to an unreachable itch. 'What made you change your mind about joining me tonight?'

'It's a woman's prerogative,' she said. Then she shrugged, mischief in her eyes. 'Actually, I think it was your willingness to eat curly sandwiches, or maybe what you said earlier about life being short and New Year's Eve only coming around once a year. As you might have overheard this morning, Sharon is always trying to fix me up with single men, although dating is the last thing on my mind. Don't tell her about this, by the way. She's a dreadful matchmaker. If she finds out we had an innocent drink, she'll have us married by next Tuesday.'

'Your secret is safe with me.' He smiled, something she'd said earlier niggling at him. 'So, is Zach's father in the picture at all?'

At his mention of her son's name, she looked surprised, as if she hadn't expected him to listen or to remember.

'Nope,' she said, with a shake of her head. 'It was a holiday fling. He's Spanish. When he found out he was going to be a father, he declined the offer to stay in touch.' She shrugged, her eyes darting away as if she was embarrassed. 'And can you really be called a father if by choice you've never met your son or contributed to his life in any way?'

'I guess not.' He winced, appalled on Zara and Zach's behalf. 'So he doesn't even support Zach financially?'

She shook her head again, looking uncomfortable. 'But I see to it that Zach has everything he needs.'

Conrad nodded, the steely glint in her eyes highlighting the fierce independence he both admired and wondered if it masked more vulnerable feelings. 'I'm sorry,' he said. 'That's his loss.'

She glanced at him sharply, as if he'd caught her off guard in return. 'It's fine. My son doesn't need a male role model like that.'

'So is he the reason you don't date, even if you had time?' he asked, cautiously, wary of crossing the line and upsetting her again. He hated that someone with so much going for her had closed off that part of her life. She was in her mid-twenties, way too young to have sworn off relationships, although these days, he too took things slow.

Zara flushed, shifting in her seat. 'Don't get me wrong, I like men, well, the dependable, responsible ones, that is.' She shrugged. 'I guess I've had to learn to rely on myself and it's become a bit of a habit. And I go out of my way to ensure my mistake doesn't define my son or allow him to suffer in any way.'

'Fair enough.' He nodded because he'd made his own mistakes, rushed into a relationship with the last serious girlfriend he'd had, like the proverbial fool, and lost her. Of course, the heartache he'd experienced when she'd broken up with him was nothing compared to the sense of betrayal he'd known later when she'd moved on to his brother. It seemed he hadn't in fact lost her because he'd moved too fast. Tessa just hadn't wanted Conrad.

'So what would New Year's Eve in Brisbane look like?' Zara asked, drawing him away from thoughts he always seemed to get snagged on: how the brother he'd loved and looked up to could have deceived and betrayed him like that.

'Definite beer consumption,' he said, smiling through the flicker of homesickness pinching his ribs. 'Parties in every bar and restaurant along the river. Fireworks at midnight.'

She looked wistful for a second, before she blinked the expression away. 'You must miss home?'

'I miss some things.' Conrad paused, taking another swallow of the delicious ale. 'Family, obviously—my parents, my nephew. The weather…' His smile stretched, and he realised he was already pretty addicted to drawing out Zara Wood's brand of throaty laughter. First impressions aside, they actually shared quite a bit in common.

'Tell me about James,' she said. 'You two are obviously very close.'

'We are.' Conrad swallowed, his chest hollowing out with a sudden rush of sadness. 'Although I haven't seen him for a while, but he loves dinosaurs and anything with wheels, particularly trains.'

'Don't you live close by in Australia?' she pushed, her stare shifting over his face as she tried to figure him out.

'I do,' he admitted, reluctant to spill the complexities of his past, despite feeling relaxed from the beer and the warmth of the fire and already pretty confident that Zara was a loyal person. 'But… Well, the person I lost recently was my brother, James's dad. Six months ago.'

She gasped, her hand coming to rest on his arm and her stare full of that compassion she shared with her patients. 'I'm so sorry; that's terrible.'

He shrugged, still getting used to saying the words aloud. 'Obviously my sister-in-law, Tessa, is still in a pretty bad place. She's grieving, and you know how hard it is to raise a child alone.'

Of course, his relationship with both Marcus and Tessa had already been strained, before Marcus's death. How could it not have been, given that Conrad and Tessa had once dated, way before she'd slept with Marcus and fallen immediately pregnant with James. Not that it was *her* betrayal that stuck in Conrad's throat. His romantic feelings for Tessa had been long gone by the time she'd hooked up with Marcus. But his brother had owed him some consideration and loyalty and an explanation. Instead they'd sneaked around behind Conrad's back.

'But she's not alone,' Zara pointed out. 'She had you and your parents, right?'

'Yeah.' He nodded, glancing away. 'But since the funeral, Tessa has kind of withdrawn from our family out of grief, taking James with her, obviously.'

'I'm so sorry,' she whispered.

Conrad shrugged. 'When James was born, I promised my brother I'd always look out for him. But after he died, I obviously overdid the concern. Tessa told me to back off. So I figured I'd get away for a few weeks so we all had some space to grieve for Marcus.' And, of course, his and Tessa's history had also clouded the issue.

'So you chose a locum position in the UK?'

He nodded. 'I understand that Tessa is dealing with a lot,' he went on, 'but I miss James. I just hope that when I return to Brisbane, she's ready to let us back into his life.'

'I hope so too, for your sake and for your parents.' Her frown deepened and he could have kicked himself for killing the mood. But he was still trying to get used to talking about Marcus's senseless death without his voice breaking, still trying to make sense of it all.

'It's…complicated,' he said. In more ways than one. 'But the last thing we want to do is push Tessa further away.'

'Do you mind me asking what happened, with your brother?' she whispered when he looked up. 'It's fine if you don't want to talk about it.'

'I don't mind talking about Marcus.' Conrad took a gulp of beer, preparing himself, focussed on the uncomplicated time when Marcus had simply been the older brother he'd looked up to. 'He was amazing. There was only a year between us, so, growing up, we were best friends.'

And that had made the breach of trust harder to bare. He didn't blame Tessa and Marcus for falling in love. But he hated that his brother hadn't come to him straight away, that he'd kept it a secret until discovering Tessa was pregnant, until he'd been forced to come clean. Marcus had tried to heal the rift, and Conrad had been forced to swallow down his sense of betrayal and confusion for the sake of family harmony. But his absolute trust in his brother had been broken, the issue for Conrad going unresolved as life moved on.

'Marcus worked as a paramedic,' he continued, blocking out how he'd felt backed into a corner back then, before James was born, as if his feelings didn't matter because there was a baby coming, a wedding to plan, a sister-in-law to welcome into the Reed family. Then Marcus had died. Conrad's grief was compounded by those lingering feelings of betrayal he'd never quite dealt with. He knew he should let the past go, but he was stuck somehow with no hope of a resolution now that Marcus was gone.

'One day, he attended a call—a case of domestic violence.' Conrad gripped his pint glass, his knuckles white. 'The perpetrator had pushed his wife down the stairs and then called the ambulance. Marcus arrived before the police. He could see from the front door that the woman had a head injury, was lying unconscious and needed urgent help, but he probably should have waited for support. The guy was armed with a knife. He was smart enough to know he was going to jail, so he became belligerent, tried to justify what he'd done. Things escalated when Marcus tried to treat the casualty. He stabbed my brother in the neck before the police arrived. Marcus died later in hospital.'

'That's so terrible.' Zara swallowed hard, her eyes shining with tears. 'So senseless. I'm so sorry.'

Conrad nodded, shocked by how much of the story had come pouring out. But Zara really cared about people. She was easy to talk to.

'Sorry,' he said, drawing a line under the conversation. 'I didn't mean to bring down the mood. It's meant to be a party. It's New Year's Eve.'

'It's okay,' Zara said, her eyes full of empathy. 'I shouldn't have been so curious.'

Conrad eyed their near-empty glasses, eager to pack away his complex feelings for which there seemed to be no end, just an infinite loop. 'I'll um…get us another drink.' He pushed back his chair and stood. 'Unless…' He glanced at the band, who were doing a valiant job considering nearly everyone in the pub was ignoring them. 'Are you up for a dance?' He held out his hand, determined to get the party mood back on track.

Zara frowned at his abrupt change of pace. She looked around the pub, self-consciously. 'Dance…? Really?' She hesitated, eyeing his hand with uncertainty.

Admittedly the place was pretty dead, by New Year's Eve standards, but the band were reasonably good, the tunes catchy and recognisable.

'Definitely,' Conrad said, desperate for her laughter over her pity. If only she knew the other half of the story… 'I've let things get too heavy. And who cares what the old farmers think of us?'

'Okay.' Her eyes glowed with excitement as she put her hand in his, the decision made. Conrad pulled her to her feet and led her to the small carpeted area in front of the make-shift stage, glad to move his body after the serious turn the conversation had taken. With his heart pounding, he scooped his arm around her waist, holding her close, spinning her, making her laugh. The sound shifted the heaviness in his chest to a muted throb he could easily ignore.

Within minutes, another couple had joined them dancing and then another. Zara lost that self-consciousness, throwing herself into enjoying the music as if she hadn't danced in a very long time.

'Now it's a New Year's Eve party,' he said, dipping his head close so he caught the scent of her shampoo, felt the heat of her body, heard the exhilarating catch of her breath.

'It's been a while since I've been to one,' she said, blinking up at him with the same excitement he felt at her closeness. Could she feel this chemistry too? Was she, like him, torn between acting on it or pretending it didn't exist? Whatever happened between them, friendship or more, could only be temporary given he was headed back to Australia in three weeks. But they didn't need to trust each other to have a good time.

'Then I'm glad I persuaded you to come,' he said, simply focussing on enjoying the moment, her company, the building atmosphere, the fact that they were young and alive and on the cusp of a brand-new year.

'Me too.' She smiled and he believed her.

CHAPTER FIVE

'THREE...TWO...ONE. Happy new year!' Zara yelled at the top of her voice as Sid, the normally gruff owner of the Miner's Arms, fired a confetti cannon into the air and gold glittered down on the biggest crowd Zara had ever seen in the village pub.

Conrad scooped her into a big bear hug, his smile infectious. 'Happy new year, Zara,' he said, his warm breath tickling her neck, and the yummy scent of him making her head spin faster than the effects of the alcohol and the party vibe combined. 'I hope it's a great one for you and Zach.'

With her throat choked that he'd included her son in his well wishes and before she could overthink the foreign impulse, she hugged him back and pressed a brief kiss to his cheek. 'You too,' she said, laughing up at him as all around them people hugged and kissed and raised their glasses in toasts.

Conrad grinned. The sexy Aussie was surprisingly great company, effortlessly bringing her out of herself with his sense of humour and his laid-back personality. She'd danced as if no one was watching, laughed at Conrad's improbable tales and drank more beer than she should have drunk given she had to be at work in seven hours. She'd even thrashed Conrad in a highly contested game of England versus Australia darts.

'Wanna head home?' he asked, his hands sliding from her shoulders. 'We both have work tomorrow, and you said you have to be up at five.'

Zara nodded, knocked sideways by his thoughtfulness and by their chemistry that had been simmering away all night. Despite her first impressions of him as a Jack the Lad, he hadn't once crossed the line. There'd been plenty of touching while they'd danced, some flirtatious looks, lots of laughter. But now she wondered if she'd imagined his interest. She was so out of practice when it came to members of the opposite sex. She almost wished Sharon were there for advice. Perhaps he didn't fancy her the way she fancied him. Perhaps he just needed a friend.

Zara blinked, sobered by the memory of his grief earlier when he'd told her about his brother. Now his locum job there, so far from home, made sense. There must be a part of him running away from the pain, the memories, the grief. But those realisations brought more questions, like why he didn't date and why his relationship with his sister-in-law was so tense.

At their table, they collected their hats and coats before spilling out of the pub into the sub-zero temperatures. 'That was so much fun,' she said. 'Thanks for dragging me along. I can't remember ever having such a good time at the local pub.' Despite her earlier reluctance, part of her didn't want such a great night to end.

'You're welcome,' he said. 'All we need now is the fireworks.' He looked up at the clear night sky dotted with stars, before flashing her a cheeky grin that set her pulse aflutter and left her wondering if her life did indeed lack a certain spark. 'Although I guess that's expecting a bit too much.'

'I think so,' she agreed with a chuckle.

They walked in silence for a few minutes, their breath misting the cold, damp air, close, but not too close. After all the touching on the dance floor, the 'happy new year' hug, the way he'd helped her into her coat, Zara missed the contact. Through her own actions, she'd been starved of intimate touch for over five years. As Sharon often pointed out, she'd shut herself off from relationships. Because they were a low priority? Yes. Because she'd had her trust damaged? Probably. Because she was desperately trying to make up for her mistake by being everything Zach needed, mother and father? So what if that was the case? It harmed no one.

'You okay?' he asked as they arrived at her cottage.

She nodded feeling as if his casual flirtations, his thoughtfulness and sense of humour had brought her back to life. He was ridiculously hot, a nice guy too, once you looked beneath the surface. Behind those dreamy bedroom eyes of his, the laid-back, good-time attitude hid more complex emotions, but even that called to her. Glancing over at his handsome profile, she'd never been more aware of what she'd denied herself since Zach was born—good times with someone her own age, connection, sex. But she should probably think of him as off limits. Kiss him goodnight and leave it there... So why did that idea send her stomach to her boots?

Conrad pushed open the garden gate and stepped aside. 'After you.' He even pulled out his phone and switched on the torch so she could see the path that bisected the lawn and led to her front door.

This was it. Decision time. Give him a peck on the cheek and say goodnight or go for it? She was so confused. And a bit tipsy. And turned on.

They'd barely made it two or three steps inside the garden when he reached for her arm. 'Wait—I think I saw something move.'

Zara froze, peering into the shadowy blackness of the back garden, her fear muted by the heat from his touch and the protective way he stepped forward, putting his body between hers and danger. It had been so long since someone other than her mum had cared and looked out for her, and this was different somehow. Sexier. Gallant.

'It's probably just a fox,' she whispered, trying to pull herself together. 'We get lots of those here.' She needed to calm down. He was just being considerate. Just because he was sexy, funny and charming and a dedicated doctor, didn't mean she seriously wanted to take flirting to the next level, did she? Could she even remember what the next level was? Perhaps that was exactly why she needed to live a little. Sharon was right…

'No, it was smaller than that,' he said, keeping a protective hold on her elbow as they crept further into the garden.

Zara released a tipsy giggle, enjoying that this urbane Australian who most likely didn't even own a pair of wellies was willing throw himself into the path of whatever beast was lurking in the dark. Then her blood ran cold as realisation struck.

'Billy Boy,' she whispered, her panic instantly full-blown.

'Is that an ex of yours?' Conrad said, standing taller as if fully prepared to face up to some thug in her honour.

Zara shook her head and pressed her lips together as another giggle threatened. But an escaped, much-loved pet was no laughing matter. 'No, it's Zach's pet rabbit. He's always escaping. He has a death wish.' She gripped Conrad's arm. 'We have to catch him before a fox does. Zach will be devastated if anything happens to Billy Boy.'

Stepping cautiously onto the frosty grass, Zara walked underneath the house's security-light sensor, triggering a blinding halogen beam that flooded the garden in light. From the corner of her eye, she spied a flash of movement, a blur of grey against the greenery.

'There.' She hurried towards the rabbit, cornering it behind a bush. Conrad stood at the opposite end of the hedge, his stare alive with excitement and amusement, as if he was enjoying himself as much as when they'd danced and played a very competitive game of darts.

'Don't laugh,' she chided, her own lips twitching. 'We need to catch him before he escapes into the fields, or my life won't be worth living.'

'Right.' Conrad nodded, his expression falling serious, which somehow made Zara want to laugh even more.

'Ready?' Zara shook the branches of the hedge to flush Billy Boy out.

The rabbit hopped sedately from his hiding place, utterly unaware of the dangers out in the dark. Zara crouched low, her hands out in front, ready to intercept the fluffy bundle. But before she could get within grasping distance, Conrad dived onto his stomach, his arms outstretched like a rugby player landing a try. His hands closed around thin air. Billy Boy hopped away, evading them both.

Zara burst out laughing, her mirth momentarily outweighing her concern for the pet. She fell back onto her backside with laughter, the dampness from the grass soaking through her jeans.

'What was that?' she asked, tears running down her

cheeks as Conrad climbed to his feet and brushed the wet grass from his front.

'I've never caught a rabbit before,' he said, seemingly delighted that he'd made her laugh so hard. 'They're a pest in Australia. Farmers shoot them.'

'Shh,' she hissed, scrambling to her feet. 'He'll hear you.' With her hand on Conrad's arm, they followed the rabbit deeper into the recesses of the garden.

'This time, stay low but nimble,' she instructed Conrad, impervious to the cold because she was enjoying herself so much. 'I normally have to catch him all by myself with Zach too busy giggling to help out.'

Conrad nodded, mock serious. 'So what's the plan this time? Do I catch him while *you* giggle?'

Zara held in another bubble of laughter. She liked that he could laugh at himself, and she'd pay good money to see this tall, sun-kissed Australian catch a pet rabbit in the dark, muddy garden alone. Suddenly his attractiveness tripled.

'I'll flush him out,' she said, trying to be serious, 'and one of us just grabs him. He's not actually that fast because he's a bit over-loved and overfed.'

Conrad limbered up by bouncing on the balls of his feet and shadow-boxing like a like a prize-fighter. Zara rolled her eyes and hid another smile, picking her way silently to the far side of the rabbit hutch. She crouched down to find Billy Boy happily munching on a patch of dandelion leaves that had somehow survived the cold. She tried to reach for him but he was already spooked by Conrad's unorthodox belly-dive. He darted away, Zara's fingertips grazing his fur, but he hopped straight into the waiting hands of a very smug Conrad.

'Just like catching a baby,' he said as he stood, a triumphant smile stretching his sexy mouth.

Zara breathed a sigh of both relief and longing. He was far too gorgeous and confident for his own good. And now that Billy Boy was safe, all she could think was how much she wanted to kiss him. Properly.

'Well done,' she said. 'We'll make a rabbit wrangler out of you yet.' She looked away from his victorious expression, his eyes dancing with merriment and something else she wasn't sure she was ready to see: desire.

Did she really want anything to happen between them? Would sleeping with him be reckless? Or just a safe, fun way to explore something she'd denied herself for far too long?

Ignoring the excited flutter in her stomach, Zara opened the hutch and grabbed a handful of fresh straw, shoving it inside Billy Boy's bedroom. While Conrad placed the bunny back inside and closed the door, Zara inspected the cage, finding a corner where the chicken wire had come loose. She stretched the wire over the makeshift nail she'd hammered in the last time the bunny had escaped, reclosing the gap. Tomorrow, after work, she'd dig out a hammer and repair the hutch properly.

'So it's not just pensioners' bingo that gets pulses racing around here,' Conrad said playfully as they headed towards the door to his flat.

Zara smiled up at him, her own pulse still leaping at the power of his sexy smile and the awoken urges pounding through her body. 'We only bring out the escaped bunnies for people who are rubbish at darts,' she said dryly.

He laughed, tossing back his head. Smiling at each other, they paused under the security light beside his door.

'Thanks for tonight,' she said, her voice a little croaky with lust. 'It will be a long time before I'll forget that hilarious rugby dive.'

'You're welcome.' He grinned wider. 'It's nice to see you laugh; you should do it more often.'

Zara stilled, embarrassed by how right he was and by how much she'd neglected her own needs to focus on Zach. No, that wasn't fair. It wasn't Zach's fault. It was fear that had held her back. Fear to be vulnerable with another man after Lorenzo. Of course her son would always be the most important person in her life, but maybe the universe was trying to tell her that it was okay to act her age and have a good time. And she didn't have to be vulnerable with Conrad, not when it could be for just one night.

'Well...goodnight, Zara,' he said when she stayed silent and unmoving for too long. 'Any time you need help catching Billy Boy, just give me a shout.' He leaned close, gripped her shoulder and pressed a cold kiss to her cheek.

Zara's breath trapped in her chest, her heart bounding as his lips lingered on her skin. It was now or never. If she didn't do something right that second, she would always regret it. Before he pulled back, she turned her face and grazed his lips with hers in the merest brush of a kiss.

Conrad peered down at her intensely, his hand on her shoulder still holding her in place. They stared, one second stretching into another, a loaded moment of possibility.

'Sorry,' Zara whispered, uncertain after being so rusty at flirtation for so long. But something had shifted between them, a crackle of awareness. Surely he'd felt it too, this chemistry between them, there all night, just waiting for one of them to acknowledge it? If she was going to put herself out there again, Conrad was as safe a bet as any.

He knew her situation, her priorities. Like her, he wasn't looking for a relationship, and he'd be going back to Australia in a few weeks.

'Are you?' he asked, simply, his voice husky and his stare unwavering. 'You shouldn't be.'

She shook her head. 'I'm not really. I'm just aware that I'm seriously back-pedalling. This afternoon at work, I said I wasn't interested in being your next casual conquest. I kind of regret that now.'

She tried to smile and he cupped her cold cheek, his thumb grazing her cheekbone. 'I don't recall that conversation. And life is too short for regrets.'

She flushed, nodding because he was right. 'You can probably tell I don't do this very often...' She couldn't make her feet move away, but was this, kissing him properly, perhaps sleeping with him, a stupid idea? With them practically living together and definitely working together, there'd be no escaping him for the few weeks he was in town. But it was only one night. Just casual sex. What had he called it that first day they met? *No big deal?* If only she was brave enough, it could be the perfect end to a New Year's Eve party unlike any other.

'You haven't done anything yet,' he pointed out, his stare dipping to her lips, as if he wanted more. 'No one is keeping score, Zara. I fancy you. If you fancy me, we could have a good time, nothing serious. Just for tonight if you like.'

He made it sound so easy. She *did* fancy him, and right then 'a good time, nothing serious' was *all* she wanted, *all* she could think about. 'I do want that,' she whispered, her body dragged down with relief and lust.

With an intense stare, he cupped her face in both his hands. 'And I've wanted to kiss you all evening.'

With a jolt of action on both sides, their lips collided in a rush. Conrad wrapped his arms around her and dragged her body flush to his. His lips parted, coaxing her mouth open, and their tongues touched. So turned on she thought she might pass out right there in the frozen garden, Zara kissed him harder, deeper, her hands finding and gripping his hips as she surged onto her tiptoes to keep their lips in contact.

He crushed her mouth under his, a sexy little grunt sounding in his throat as their tongues slid together, back and forth. Zara shut down her thoughts, closed her eyes and surrendered to the hormonal rush. The uninhibited excitement of feeling attractive again, kissing a sexy man who treated her with respect and made her laugh. She spent her every waking moment caring for other people—Zach, her patients, the babies she delivered. She deserved something that was just for her, didn't she? To start the new year off differently from the previous five—with a promise to take better care of herself and her own needs going forward.

Conrad pulled back, his hands still cupping her frozen face, his fingers restlessly sliding into her hair. 'Come inside. It's freezing.'

Zara nodded. He put the key in the lock, ushering her into the cosy, warm flat she'd worked hard to renovate. Before he could speak again, perhaps to offer her a drink or take her coat, Zara turned and kissed him once more, now drunk on the idea that tonight was about sex. He was used to that. Probably good at it, too. And she'd been without it for far too long, as if punishing herself for that one mistake in recklessly choosing Zach's father.

But she wasn't a naive twenty-year-old any more. She

was a woman. She knew what she wanted and what she didn't want. And she wanted Conrad.

With his lips on hers, Conrad removed her hat and pushed her coat from her shoulders. His kisses drove her wild and made her forget her responsibilities and the habitual way she kept men at arm's length. Zara caressed his tongue with hers, unbuttoning his coat and reaching for his belt, frantic now that this was really going to happen.

'Are you sure?' he asked when he'd yanked his mouth from hers, his breathing ragged as he pulled her close.

Zara nodded, abandoning his belt buckle as another moment of doubt crept in. 'Although I haven't done this in a very long time, but you've heard about my famous dry spell.' She shrugged, smiled, trying to keep the light playful vibe between them going, because it was a major part of her attraction to him.

'Should I ask how long?' he said, his eyes searching hers while his hands slid restlessly up and down her arms as if he couldn't *not* touch her.

'Since before Zach was born,' she admitted, her high from their kisses dimming slightly.

'Really?' he asked, incredulous, cupping her cheek. 'You're so sexy. It's hard to imagine you're not beating off Englishmen with a stick.'

Zara chuckled, grateful that even now, when part of her was besieged by nerves, he could make her laugh. Then she sobered. 'We should probably keep this between us, though. No one at work needs to know, right?'

Zara didn't want her night with the sexy Australian doctor to be gossip fodder on the maternity ward, not when she was so famously single. Sharon, in particular, would read far too much into it, and it was just one night…

'I hate secrets,' he said, his eyes hardening slightly, 'but this is our business, Zara.' As if sealing the promise with a kiss, he tilted her face up and lowered his lips to hers.

She had no time to wonder why he hated secrets, because this kiss was different, slower, deeper, more determined and thorough, as if it was leading somewhere she definitely wanted to go. Thank goodness she'd shaved her legs in the shower earlier, although her underwear was decidedly practical and no frills, but hopefully it wouldn't be on long enough that he'd notice.

When he slid his lips down the side of her neck and scooped his arm around her waist, pressing her restless body to his hardness, she couldn't hold in her moan. Then they were on the move, her hand clasped in his as he strode to the bedroom. Zara took a split second to notice that he'd changed the sheets since last week, these ones dove grey, not the original snowy white ones, before she gave herself fully over to the thrill and heat of their chemistry.

'You are *so* sexy,' he said, dragging her close once more, his hands in her hair. One hand slid under her jumper to the small of her back and she shuddered under his deep, drugging kisses. 'I promise I'll make this good for you, given you've waited so long,' he whispered against her lips, not that Zara was in any doubt. This was already the best sexual experience of her life and he'd barely touched her yet. But where Lorenzo had been a boy, barely out of his teens, Conrad was a man.

'Okay,' she said, pulling at the hem of his sweater until he yanked it off and threw it aside. His bronzed and defined naked torso called to her hands, so she indulged herself, sliding her palms over his abs, across the mounds of his pecs and the rounded muscles of his shudders. He was indeed all man. Strong and lean. Making her feel small.

Her fingers slid into his hair, and she craned herself up on her tiptoes to kiss him again, her desire flaring to an inferno of need she had no hope of fighting. They kissed, stripping, laughing at a stubborn jeans button and a welded-closed bra clasp. Even the serious business of getting naked was somehow fun with Conrad.

When they stood before each other in just their underwear, he scooped his arms around her waist and tumbled them both onto the bed with a chuckle that turned into a groan.

'I'm so glad you wanted this as much as me.' His hands skimmed her body, his lips, the heat of his breath, trailing over her skin. 'After our first meeting when I thought you seriously meant me harm, it could have so easily gone the other way.'

Zara smiled despite the way his touch inflamed her entire body. 'Never mess with a mama bear defending her den.'

'I wouldn't dream of it.' He slid her body under his, limbs tangled, his body heat scalding, his hands in her hair as his tongue surged against hers. 'And you are one seriously hot mama bear.'

Zara sighed, completely surrounded by and immersed in him, his sexy scent on her skin, the rasp of his facial hair against her chin, encircled in the flexing strength of his toned body. Finally she could relax and surrender, safe in the knowledge that they only wanted this from each other. No relationship, no feelings, no consequences.

He cupped her breast, his thumb rubbing the nipple erect, and she gasped, holding him closer, hooking one leg over his hip, her pelvis bucking against the hard length of his erection.

'Conrad,' she moaned as he dipped his head and captured the same nipple with his mouth. She was insane with want, scorched with heat, already so close to climaxing. Frantic to have more of him, Zara shoved at his boxers and slid her hand between their bodies, wrapping her fingers around him so he groaned into their kiss. He pulled back, kneeled beside her and removed her underwear, reaching for a condom from his jeans and tossing it onto the bed.

He gazed down at her naked body and Zara had a moment of self-consciousness. She wasn't a tanned, toned pin-up like him. She was an English rose, pale, and had stretch marks, her boobs less perky thanks to breastfeeding Zach. But Conrad didn't seem to care. His stare moved over her nakedness as an art fan admired a Constable. He cupped her breast, slid his hand over her waist and hip and then stroked between her legs.

Zara gasped at his slow, thorough touch. Her heavy stare latched to his as he watched her reactions, learning what made her moan and gasp and reach for him. When he lay beside her, Zara turned to kiss him, her hand finding him once more so they pleasured each other, face to face, hot breath mingling in between heated kisses.

But Zara had waited too long for this degree of intimacy to hold out. His touch infected her entire body in a wave of heat and longing and paralysing bliss that she welcomed, craved, needed.

'You're close,' he said, brushing his lips over hers, his fingers moving between her legs as he peered down at her with that confidence she should find arrogant but only found wildly attractive.

She nodded, impressed that he knew, moaned louder as he captured one nipple with his mouth and sucked. Lights flashed behind Zara's eyes, but then he shifted on top of her and handed her the condom. She tore it open, desperate to have him inside her. She rolled it onto him, fumbling in her haste because he continued to kiss her and stroke her, driving her closer to the edge.

Finally, he scooped his arm around her waist and hauled her under him. Zara panted, parted her legs and then he was kissing her and pushing inside her, so all she could do was cling to him and hold on tight as wonderful pleasure consumed her.

'You okay?' He paused, staring down at her as he pushed her wild hair back from her flushed face and brushed her lips with his.

'Don't stop,' she said, begging, gripping his broad shoulders, her fingertips digging into his steely muscles. Zara crossed her ankles in the small of his back and he sank lower, started to move, watching her reactions in between deep, drugging kisses as if ensuring she was there with him on this journey to oblivion.

'Yes,' Zara said as he gripped her hip and thrust harder, faster. She tunnelled her fingers into his hair and met the surges of his tongue in her mouth with her own, her body pure sensation, her every nerve ending alive, poised on the brink of ecstasy.

Then she was falling, shattered, her body awash with heat and wave after wave of pleasure as her orgasm struck, and she cried out his name in confirmation of the best sex of her life.

Conrad groaned as he picked up the pace, his hips jerking erratically now as he chased his own release. Zara kissed him once more, desperate that this be as good for him as it was for her. With a final jerk, he tore his lips from hers and crushed her tighter, his body taut and his groan muffled against the side of her neck.

She lay under him, panting, coming to her senses. Finally, he rolled sideways, each of them staring up at the ceiling and laughing, while they caught their breath.

'I can't believe I put that off for so long,' she said, her voice full of wonder and euphoria. Had she denied herself sex all these years because she'd been determined to make good on her mistake and be the best mother she could possibly be? Because she was scared to be vulnerable with another man in case she was, once again, rejected? But sex with Conrad was different. Freeing. Truly strings-free.

'That was something else,' Conrad said, tugging her close to press his lips to her temple. '*You* are something else, Zara Wood.'

Zara propped herself up on one elbow, beyond pleased with herself. 'So is this part where you kick me out and I do the walk of shame?' She grinned, enjoying that there was no overthinking to do, no bone-deep trepidation that he might not want to see her again, that he might not want a relationship with her, because *she* didn't want one with *him*.

'You can leave if you want.' He smiled, pressed a kiss to lips and then climbed from the bed and stalked naked to bathroom to take care of the condom. 'But if you give me a few minutes,' he said, casting her a cheeky wink over his shoulder, 'I'd like to do that again.'

'Okay,' she said, watching his toned backside disappear into the en suite before falling back against the pillow with a delighted chuckle.

'Happy new year,' she whispered to herself, hugging

her secret close. One day, when Conrad had gone back to Australia, she'd confess to Sharon that she'd finally broken her dry spell. And it had been totally worth the wait.

CHAPTER SIX

ON MONDAY, Conrad arrived at the hospital's outpatient department for an antenatal clinic, his stare scanning the name board for which midwives were present that morning. Seeing Zara's name, he felt his pulse bound violently with anticipation.

When he'd woken up New Year's Day morning, Zara had gone, leaving behind only the scent of her perfume on his pillow. Thanks to their differing shifts, and a series of emergency surgeries that had kept Conrad away from the wards and in Theatre, he hadn't seen her since. But a little distance was a good thing. A chance to process what had been, at least for Conrad, an unexpected and seriously hot night.

Entering his designated clinic room, he logged on to the computer and brought up his list of patients to take his mind off Zara. He'd just started to read the notes of the first patient on his list when there was a knock at the door.

'Come in,' he called, looking up from the computer.

The door opened and Zara appeared. Before his instantaneous smile had formed, before he could open his mouth to speak again, the urge to kiss her slammed into him and stole his breath.

'Hi,' he said, his heart rate going nuts. 'Good to see you.' If he'd thought she was sexy before, now that he knew how hot they were together, he really wanted to see her again. They had a great time together. They shared a career and understood the demands of each other's jobs and neither of them wanted a relationship. For him, it didn't get any better than that. But now wasn't the time to raise the possibility.

'You too,' she said, sounding detached. 'Do you have a second to discuss a patient?' She made eye contact but he could tell her guard was back up as if New Year's Eve hadn't happened.

'Of course.' He stood and beckoned her inside.

She entered and left the door ajar, telling him this conversation would definitely be patient-related and in no way personal. 'I've just seen a thirty-four-year-old primip following her twenty-week scan,' she said. 'The placenta is low lying, and she has type one von Willebrand's disease.'

Conrad nodded. 'Thanks for bringing this to my attention. It sounds as if I should see her myself today. She'll need repeated scans,' he went on, outlining an action plan. 'The placenta previa might correct itself as the baby grows, but the bleeding disorder certainly complicates the risks for the mother.'

Placenta previa, when the placenta blocked the opening of the uterus, was enough of a risk of haemorrhage without adding in an inherited blood-clotting disorder in the mother.

'Yes, that's what I thought,' she said, her concern obvious. 'I'll warn you now, before you see her—she's keen to have a home birth.'

'That complicates things.' Conrad winced. This pregnancy definitely qualified as high risk. 'Okay, let's go examine her.'

In Zara's clinic room, he introduced himself to her patient, Helen, and quickly examined the woman's abdomen to confirm the foetal growth matched the scans and corroborated the baby's due date, but everything seemed in order.

'Okay,' he said as the patient adjusted her clothing. 'As I'm sure Zara has explained, your scan shows that the baby is healthy and developing normally. But the scan also shows that the placenta has attached in a low position, near the internal opening of the womb.'

Helen frowned, worry tightening her mouth as she looked between him and Zara. 'What does that mean for my birth plan?'

Conrad drew in a deep breath, preparing to offer the patient news that might be poorly received. 'Well, the first thing we need to do is monitor your pregnancy a little more closely than we normally would. Sometimes, as the baby grows and the uterus grows too, the position of the placenta can elevate. I'd like you to have another scan in ten weeks' time.'

'Okay,' Helen said, looking relieved.

Zara shot him another meaningful look, full of encouragement, and Conrad nodded, their silent communication telling him they had the same concerns. Part of their job was to try and facilitate the patient's choice when it came to the birth of their child, but their job also involved explaining all of the potential difficulties.

'That being said,' he continued, 'the main risks of a low-lying placenta, which, by the way, affects one in every two hundred pregnancies, is premature labour and haemorrhage, which would obviously be complicated by your inherited bleeding disorder. If the placenta stays where it is, blocking the birth canal, the baby's exit route, I'm afraid I'll be recommending a planned caesarean section around thirty-seven weeks for your safety and that of the baby.'

Tears built in Helen's eyes. Zara passed her a box of tissues, nodding at Conrad in emotional support.

'I understand it's a lot to process, right now,' Conrad said, hating that he'd made the patient cry, 'but no decisions need to be made today. As I said, the situation could change. Do you have someone you want to call, to meet you here? A support person?'

Helen shook her head, sniffing into the tissue. 'My husband is working in Scotland at the moment.'

Zara rested a comforting hand on the woman's shoulder. 'What about a friend or other relative?'

'My sister actually works in this hospital as a medical secretary,' Helen said, looking up at them.

Conrad nodded encouragingly. 'Why don't you give her a ring? Maybe she could meet you in the café upstairs. They do a wicked scone, and the tea is strong.' He smiled, and Helen laughed through her tears.

'Thank you, Doctor. Thank you, both. I will call my sister. A cup of tea and a scone sounds wonderful.'

Zara shot him a grateful smile he enjoyed way too much.

'Remember,' Conrad said to Helen in parting, 'the most important thing is that the baby is healthy and growing well. Our job—' he glanced at Zara, including her in his statement '—is to present you with all the information so you're aware of all the options and to help you deliver your baby as safely as possible.'

Before he left, his own list of patients calling, Zara looked up from comforting Helen. *Thanks*, she mouthed, her stare glimmering with respect.

He smiled, grateful that that night hadn't altered their

working relationship. They were so attuned, so professionally supportive. He'd never worked with anyone quite like
Zara. Surely she couldn't ignore their chemistry? Surely she
still wanted him the way he wanted her? If not, he would,
of course, respect her decision. But with a busy clinic to
get through, he'd have to bide his time to ask the question.

Mid-morning, Zara had just added hot water to her instant
coffee in the outpatient's break room, when she grew aware
of someone at her side. She looked up to see Conrad smiling down at her.

Their eyes locked, and her stomach knotted with giddy
anticipation, the same feeling she'd carried since waking
up in his bed in the early hours of New Year's Day. Since
then, she'd lived on tenterhooks, craving the gorgeous sight
of him like a drug but scared to run into him on the ward
in case anyone, mainly Sharon, noticed something was different between them.

'Hi, again,' she said, stepping aside to allow him access
to the kettle.

'I thought you might like to know that I transferred Jane
Phillips to the postnatal ward from HDU last night,' he
said, reaching for a spare mug. 'I'm pleased to say that
she's doing much better.'

'That's great news,' Zara said in a breathy-sounding
voice, nervously glancing over her shoulder, only to discover they had the break room to themselves. 'Thanks for
keeping me updated.'

He was such a good doctor, dedicated and compassionate. That he knew she'd be worried about their post-partum
haemorrhage patient and wanted to reassure her also spoke
to the kind of man he was—caring, intelligent and funny.

Now that she knew him better, she saw so much more than a hot guy out for a good time. She saw the doctor who struggled to break bad news to patients because he obviously cared. She saw the man grieving for his brother and missing his young nephew. She saw someone perhaps hiding from something and wondered how she could help him the way he supported her.

'So, how are you?' he asked, his voice low. 'We've managed to somehow accidentally avoid each other since New Year's. But I've been thinking about you.'

'I'm good. Just busy,' she said, stirring her drink with a trembling hand. 'Never a dull moment around here...'

'True,' he said, that intense interest in his eyes, as if she might be the only woman in the world. 'But I wasn't talking about work. I wondered if you're free for lunch, after clinic? I think we should talk about what happened between us.'

'Talk?' she said, her pulse flying. What was there to say? That she couldn't stop thinking about him either? That she couldn't forget their night together.

'Yes, talk.' He smiled, and she lost her train of thought. 'I'd like to know if you had a good time. Make sure you have no regrets. I don't want us to tiptoe around each other for the next few weeks.'

'I don't have any regrets,' she said, her stare drawn to his mouth. He was awesome at kissing. 'What about you?' Her question emerged as an embarrassing choked whisper.

'None whatsoever, Zara. In fact, I'd like to see you again, perhaps when Zach next sleeps over at your mother's place. I thought we could explore Derby, maybe go dancing. Plus I've been dying to know if Billy Boy is okay after his escape.'

At his mention of the rabbit, Zara laughed, her nerves

settling. 'Zach's with my mum Friday, but... I don't know, Conrad. It was supposed to be one night. Zach is still my priority.'

She glanced at the door, worried they'd be interrupted. Worried that someone would be able to tell they were no longer just colleagues. But she was sorely tempted to say yes. They could extend their *nothing serious* into a temporary fling until he left for Australia. What better way to get her confidence back? After all, she wasn't looking for a relationship right now, but she didn't want to be alone for ever.

'Of course he is,' Conrad said with a casual shrug. 'I wouldn't expect anything else. As you know, I'm heading back to Australia in a few weeks. I'm not suggesting we date. I don't really do that any more.'

'Why don't you date any more?' Had someone broken his heart? She'd assumed he was running away from his grief, but maybe it was heartbreak that had chased him from Australia.

He glanced away, looking uncomfortable, and Zara shook her head. 'Sorry, forget I asked. It's none of my business.'

Just because they'd developed a close, supportive working relationship, just because they'd had sex, didn't mean he owed her anything. And the hospital was the last place they could talk.

Conrad inhaled deeply. 'Maybe I'll tell you some time, away from work. Look, I had a good time New Year's Eve, that's all. I got the impression you did too.'

'I did.' She nodded, her body turning instantly molten with that thrilling need he'd brought back to life on New Year's Eve.

'So, if you wanted to have some more good times, nothing serious, same as New Year's, I'd be interested.' He smiled and she got lost in his eyes for a second. 'I enjoy your company. You have a great sense of humour. It's been a long time since I could laugh with a woman.' He shot her a hopeful smile.

'I enjoy your company, too,' she said, still hesitant. 'But I'll have to pass on lunch, I'm afraid. One of the midwives on the delivery suite today has gone home sick, so I'm heading upstairs after clinic to cover.'

A small frown of disappointment tugged at his mouth. 'Okay, but make sure you grab something to eat. We've had a busy morning down here, and it sounds like you're headed into a busy afternoon.' He looked at her in *that* way. As if, in that moment, she was all he saw.

'I will.' Zara nodded, touched that despite being busy, despite their one night being nothing serious, he cared about *her*. It had been a long time since anyone had put her first. She even put herself last, although she couldn't blame anyone else for that. 'And about Friday...' She glanced at the door, still balanced on a knife edge of indecision. She could almost hear Sharon yell, *Go for it, woman!* And it wasn't as if it could go anywhere. He was leaving in a few weeks and neither of them wanted a serious relationship.

'No pressure,' he said. 'You don't have to answer now. Just think about it.'

Just then Sharon bustled into the room, complaining to no one in particular about the shortage of midwives on duty. Zara stepped away from Conrad, taking a guilty gulp of her scalding coffee and desperately trying to act normal in front of her friend.

'Hi, Sharon,' Conrad said, picking up his own drink. He

shot Zara one last glance she prayed Sharon hadn't seen and then left the break room.

'What were you two whispering about?' Sharon asked, flicking on the kettle. The woman never missed a trick.

'Nothing. Just discussing a patient.' It wasn't a lie, exactly, more of an omission. 'Jane Phillips has been transferred off HDU.'

'That's good. How was your weekend?' her friend asked, pouring hot water onto a teabag in a mug. 'Did you do anything for New Year's in the end?' Sharon had invited her to a party at her house, but she'd declined, knowing there would most likely be some single man there that Sharon would tactlessly thrust upon Zara.

She flushed, kicking herself that she hadn't anticipated questions and planned answers that didn't come with revealing blushes. 'Not much. I was working New Year's Day.'

'You should have come over to ours,' Sharon said, stirring her tea. 'Rod invited some people from work. One of them is a lovely guy your age. Smart. Good job. Works in the IT department.' She took a sip of tea and watched Zara over the rim of her mug. 'Want his number?'

'Sharon…' Zara sighed, busying herself with adding another splash of milk to her coffee to cool it down. Perhaps she should take the guy's number just to shut her friend up.

'Don't give me that,' Sharon said. 'It's not healthy always being alone.'

Zara tried not to think about New Year's Eve and Conrad. 'I'm not alone. I have Zach.'

'You know what I mean.' Sharon huffed impatiently. 'You're twenty-six, Zara. You should stop putting your needs last and take better care of yourself. Most people your age are at it like rabbits.'

Zara snorted and flushed again. She'd waited five years to let a man close enough for intimacy, but now that she had, all she could think about was Conrad and his mad bedroom skills. And he wanted to see her again...

'It's not the sex that puts me off,' she admitted. 'It's just—'

'I know. You've been hurt, so you struggle to trust men.'

Zara looked up sharply. Her friend wasn't wrong. What would she say if she knew Zara was denying herself more casual sex with the department hottie, just because, since Lorenzo, ignoring men had become a bad habit?

Sharon's expression brimmed with sympathy. 'Not all men are selfish and irresponsible, you know.'

'I know that,' Zara said, wondering how, despite all her tough talk and fierce independence, she'd allowed Conrad to charm his way under her defences.

'I know that you're focussed on raising Zach. I know you want the best for him, as if you're making up for his lack of a father, but it's important that you're happy too.'

'You're right.' Zara nodded, unable for once to argue. She had been putting her own needs last. And if Conrad was willing to wait for her, to snatch chances to be with her when Zach was at her mother's, she'd be a fool to pass that up, wouldn't she? 'Would it make you feel any better to know I've made a new year's resolution to take better care of myself going forward?'

A brief fling with Conrad was a perfect temporary situation, as if the universe had dropped a sexy, single toy into her lap. She should take what was on offer—a good time, nothing serious—and simply enjoy a long-overdue sexual adventure.

'Yes,' Sharon said, scooping up her mug and following Zara from the break room. They needed to get back to work.

'Then stop worrying,' Zara said, pausing outside her clinic room to shoot her friend a reassuring smile. She was going to do it, to see Conrad again. And now that she'd made up her mind, Friday seemed a long way off.

CHAPTER SEVEN

CONRAD HAD JUST finished seeing his final patient of the morning, when there was another knock at the door. 'Come in,' he called, looking up to see Zara poke her head through the opening.

'Zara!' Their eyes locked. 'Come in.' She had her bag over her shoulder so she was obviously headed up to the ward.

'I just wanted to catch you,' she said breathlessly, her eyes bright with excitement. 'I've thought about it and my answer is *yes*.'

Conrad stood and came around to her side of the desk, unable to dampen his smile. 'That's fantastic. So we can do something Friday?'

She nodded and stepped close, her pupils dilating. Realisation dawned, his heart rate spiking. She had *that* look in her eyes. He reached for her at the same moment she hurled herself into his arms. Their lips clashed. He scooped one arm around her back while the other tilted her face up to his deepening kiss.

'Thank goodness you caved,' he said breathlessly after tearing his mouth from hers. 'I've wanted to do this for the past two days.' His lips found hers once more and he pushed her back against the closed door.

'Me too.' Zara gripped his waist and dragged him close.

'But no one can know about this, okay? The gossip would be unbearable.'

'Okay…' Conrad frowned, his mind blanking when she pulled his lips back to hers. 'Although I'm not a fan of secrets.' But his desire for her outweighed everything. And besides, he was only in England for another couple of weeks so did it really matter?

'I know, but if Sharon finds out about us, she'll want to play cupid. The woman is relentless. She's even tried to fix me up this morning with some guy who works with her husband.'

A sudden flare of possessiveness heated his blood.

'And it's not like this can go anywhere,' she continued. 'Neither of us are looking to date and we live in different countries.'

'I can't argue with any of that,' he said. And he couldn't. He cupped her face and brushed her lips with his. 'So you'll meet me Friday, when Zach is at your mum's? Give me something to look forward to.' He kissed the side of her neck, his hand cupping her breast so she sighed, her body sagging against his.

'I'll meet you Friday,' she said, shuddering. 'But it's just sex, agreed?'

Conrad didn't play games. He wasn't making her any promises, but Zara knew what she wanted and, more importantly, what she didn't want. And so did he.

'No arguments from me.' He smiled, reeling when she gripped the lapels of his white coat, pressed a kiss to his lips and then shoved him away.

'I have to go. Until Friday.' She straightened her uniform and reached for the door handle.

'Zara,' he said as she swung the door open. 'I can't wait.' He adjusted the knot of his tie, his heart thumping wildly.

She grinned. Suddenly, it was as if they were transported back to that moment in the garden when they'd laughed together over the escaped rabbit and then kissed, their passion for each other burning quickly out of control.

With a final flirty look, she left. He dragged in a deep breath. It was going to be a very long week.

By nine p.m. Friday, Conrad had just about given up hope that Zara would keep her word, when there was a rap of knuckles on the door. He leapt off the sofa with the eagerness of a kid on Christmas morning and swung open the door, his pulse frantic.

'Hi. You look lovely.'

'Hi.' Zara smiled and hurried inside out of the cold.

No sooner had he closed the door behind her than she hurled herself into his arms, her lips meeting his in a desperate kiss. After days of restless anticipation, of secret looks on the ward and pretending she was just another midwife, her desperation resonated deeply with him.

'That was the longest week of my life,' he said when Zara let him up for air. 'How's Zach, by the way?'

'He's fine. He loves his Friday sleepovers at Grandma's,' she said, shrugging off her coat and immediately tugging at his shirt buttons. 'I want you.' She trailed her lips seductively down the side of his neck, making him groan.

He nodded in agreement, his desire for her as acute as their first time thanks to the build-up. 'What about Derby… dancing?' he asked, half-heartedly putting up a feeble fight.

'Who needs dancing?' she said, her demanding hands everywhere at once: inside his shirt, in his hair, tugging at his neck to bring their lips back together. 'I'm making up for lost time.'

Absorbing every kiss, Conrad stumbled into the nearby lounge where they collapsed onto the sofa together. Truth was, he didn't care one jot about Derby. What could the city really have to offer to rival Zara, naked and playful in his bed? He'd never wanted anyone as much as he wanted her right then.

'Your famous dry spell?' he said with a smile as she sat astride his lap and removed her sweater. Conrad's brain short-circuited at the sight of her amazing breasts clad in the sexy black lace of her bra. He sat up, capturing her lovely lips once more so she shuddered in his arms.

'I can't believe I ignored this side of myself for so long,' she said on a sigh as he popped her bra clasp and leaned forward to capture one of her nipples in his mouth. 'Seeing you at the hospital and not being able to kiss you has been hell.'

'I know,' he said when she tugged his shirt overhead and reached for the button on his jeans. 'I spent the entire week walking around the hospital, looking for secret places I could lure you. I found a large cleaning cupboard outside the postnatal ward that looked very promising.'

Zara laughed, smiled down at him indulgently. 'Hold that thought. You never know when it might come in handy.'

His laughter died as she shoved him down on the sofa and traced her lips down his chest and his abs, moaning as she unzipped his jeans. Conrad froze, recognising that wicked look in her eyes. When she freed him from his underwear and took him into her mouth he almost passed out, so sharp was the ache of pleasure in his gut. She drove him crazy, the yearning and waiting a sick kind of sensual torture, so that now he was on edge, his stamina shot to pieces as he watched her pleasure him with her mouth.

Then he sprang into action. 'Let's go,' he said, standing and pulling her to her feet. In the bedroom, they stripped off the rest of their clothes with unhurried determination, their stares locked. When they were naked together on the bed, he kissed his way from her lips to her breasts, from her stomach to between her legs. He couldn't seem to get enough of her, or stop touching her, kissing her, relishing her every moan and sigh.

'Conrad.' Zara gasped, her fingers twining restlessly in his hair as she looked down at him, the way he'd watched her. His name on her lips did something to him, something primal and possessive. He wanted to hear it over and over.

'Do you want me as much as I want you?' he asked in the pause for the condom.

'Yes,' she said. 'I tried to fight it, but I don't know what you've done to me. It's as if you've flicked a switch to my libido. I'm suddenly addicted to sex.'

Satisfied, he smiled and lay on top of her, kissing up her cries and moans as his fingers moved between her legs. They were obviously intoxicated by each other. When he finally pushed inside her, the hunger he'd tried to ignore since New Year's Eve consumed him so he had to close his eyes for a second against the rush of desire.

'This is the best sex I've ever had,' she said, pulling his lips down to her kiss, her hips moving against his.

'Me too,' he said, entwining their fingers and pressing her hand into the mattress as he moved over her. She stared up at him with arousal and wonder and joy. He could get used to putting that look on her face, just as he couldn't imagine tiring of the way she made him feel, almost as if he'd been waiting his whole life for a woman like her. But that was crazy and just lust talking. Sex that good could mess with your mind.

He kissed her more thoroughly, moving slowly inside her, drawing out the pleasure until their skin was slicked with perspiration and they were both so desperate for release they finally came together, their mingled cries filling the darkened room. As their hearts banged together, Conrad pressed his lips to hers, struggling to withdraw from the heat of her body and struggling to abandon the dizzying high they generated together. It had been years since he'd felt this connected to a woman, but maybe it was simply because they had so much in common beyond sexual chemistry: their grief, their work, her son and his nephew.

Finally, he rolled onto his back and pulled her under his arm, pressing his lips to her forehead. 'You are the hottest midwife I've ever met. I'm so glad you wanted more than just one night.'

She laughed. 'You, Dr Reed, were simply too much temptation.'

'I've created a monster,' he said, smiling, drawing her lips up to his.

When she laughed, he couldn't help but kiss her again.

Afterwards, Conrad switched on some chilled music and padded through to the kitchen naked, returning to bed with two large glasses of red wine.

'Do you mind that we didn't go to Derby?' Zara asked, taking one and placing it on the bedside table.

'Of course not.' He joined her in bed, tilted up her chin and brushed her lips with his. 'I seriously doubt there's anything in the city that's anywhere close to as great as what we just did.'

'You're not wrong.' Zara chuckled, her laughter turning to fear when he reached for her hand under the duvet. Holding his hand felt way too natural and somehow more intimate than all the other things they'd done. But relying on each other at work, supporting each other emotionally through the tricky cases, made this connection between them understandably intense. It didn't mean anything. It couldn't.

'Can I ask you something?' she said, to distract herself from those confusing thoughts.

'Of course,' he said, slinging his arm around her shoulders.

'You said you don't date any more. You said you'd tell me why,' she said, snuggling into his side. 'Did someone break your heart?'

He stilled and sighed, giving her a glimpse into his feelings on the subject. 'I was in love once, a long time ago. But I moved too fast and she didn't feel the same way, so she broke up with me. Since then, I've kept things casual.'

Zara pressed a kiss to his chest over the rapid thump of his heart. 'I'm sorry you were hurt, Conrad.'

'Don't worry.' His arm tightened around her. 'I'm over it. What about you?' he asked, switching the focus. 'You're twenty-six and a complete bombshell. Did Zach's father break *your* heart?'

Zara laughed and looked up, her ego preening. 'Bombshell, eh? I'll have to remember that compliment next time I'm cleaning out Billy Boy's hutch in my wellies.'

Conrad smiled softly, clearly waiting for a real answer.

'I wouldn't say he broke my heart as such. His name was

Lorenzo,' she said, her stomach twisting with embarrassment. 'I was so young when I met him, and very naive. It wasn't a great love story, just a holiday fling—exciting, intense, exotic.'

Her heart raced, her discomfort soothed by the rhythmic slide of Conrad's fingers up and down her arm. 'He said he loved me, but I didn't really believe him,' she went on. 'He worked as a waiter at the Spanish resort where me and my friends were staying. I knew there'd been other foreign girls before me, and there would be more after me.'

'So you weren't that naive, then,' he pointed out. 'Just young and enjoying yourself. There's no harm in that.'

Zara shrugged, dragging in a deep breath, the next part of the story sure to resurface the humiliation she'd felt after her final phone call to Lorenzo. 'When I came home, I'd accepted that we probably wouldn't see each other again, even though we'd swapped phone numbers. Then a couple of weeks later I found out I was pregnant.'

Conrad nodded, urging her to continue.

'I was still in shock myself when I called Lorenzo,' she said, her breathing shallow as she relived the difficult emotions. 'I didn't really know what I expected from him, but it was more than the nothing I received. I figured he might want to come to the UK to meet his child, or ask me to bring the baby to Spain, even if he and I weren't going to be together. But he did none of those things. He got angry when I refused to consider a termination. Said I was a stupid, immature girl and hung up on me.'

Conrad's harsh frown distorted his mouth. '*He* sounds like the immature one, if you ask me. So he let you both down? You and Zach?'

Zara shrugged, feeling a little sick as her protective urges for her son flared up. 'I was upset in the beginning, obviously. I didn't understand how someone could know they had a child in the world and not want to meet them.'

'I couldn't do it,' he said and Zara pressed her lips to his, instinct telling her his assertion was genuine. Where Lorenzo had been a boy, Conrad was a real man.

'Me neither,' she added, wishing she'd made a baby with someone more like Conrad. 'As my pregnancy progressed, I thought he might change his mind once he'd had time to come to terms with it, call one day out of the blue. But he didn't. After a while, I stopped waiting for the phone to ring.'

'I'm so sorry that you had to go it alone. That must have been hard, especially in the beginning.'

She shook her head, brushing aside his empathy. 'I had both my parents for support initially. And once Zach was born, I focussed on being his mother, on making sure he didn't pay for my recklessness, for a mistake in choosing the wrong father for him.'

Conrad glanced at her sharply. 'Maybe the mistake was Lorenzo's, not yours. After all, you're the one who's been there for your son, every day from before he was born. You carried him, delivered him and raised him, doing the work of two parents.'

Zara shrugged, dismissing his praise, but her heart swelling with maternal pride. 'I'm so lucky. He's a great young man.'

'Maybe it's because he has a great mother,' he said, refusing to allow her to brush him off. 'You know, just because you consider you made a mistake, doesn't mean you need to pay the price for ever. We're allowed to be naive and daring when we're young. To get carried away by our feelings and have intense romances.'

She frowned. Had she decided that raising Zach alone was some sort of penance for making a mistake with Lorenzo? Was that why she'd ignored her own needs for so long?

'You sound like Sharon,' she said, a fresh flutter of anticipation in her stomach. This fling with Conrad had certainly whet her appetite for sex.

'I guess I'm saying that you definitely don't *need* a man,' Conrad continued, turning serious, 'but one day, you might want a relationship. Don't close yourself off to that possibility or put yourself last. You're young. You still have so much living to do, and your happiness is as important as Zach's.'

Zara held her breath, torn. She liked that he cared about her well-being. But she'd spent so long going it alone, she didn't really know how to let someone, a man, that close. Maybe when this fling was over she'd be ready to start dating, for real. But could she find someone who not only wanted her, but also wanted to help her raise Zach? The way her stomach pinched with worry, that seemed like a pretty tall order.

Rather than admit those deep fears, Zara wrapped her arms around Conrad's neck, drawing his mouth down to hers. 'You are such a romantic, Dr Reed.'

'Am I?' he asked, seeming genuinely puzzled.

Zara nodded, wondering anew at the mystery woman who'd broken Conrad's heart. 'Let's hope, one day, we can both move on. Meeting you has certainly shown me that what I really need right now is a wild sexual adventure, the kind I missed out on by becoming a mum relatively young.'

'A wild sexual adventure?' He perked up. 'And that's where I come in, is it?' His expression turned to playful delight as he wrapped his arm around her waist, dragging her under him for a passionate kiss.

'It is.' She nodded and giggled. 'Feel up to the challenge?'

'Oh, I think so.' He grinned, brushed his lips over hers. 'Any time you want secret, late-night sex, you know exactly where to find me.' His hand skimmed her hip and her waist, cupping her breast where his thumb teased her nipple.

As Conrad set about proving that he was indeed the man for the job, Zara lost herself in their playful passion, forgetting all about their exes and past heartaches. As he'd said, life was short and so was this fling. Best to enjoy it while it lasted, because the last thing it could be was for ever.

CHAPTER EIGHT

IT WAS THE start of the following week before Zara saw Conrad again. Her weekend had been filled with the usual mum duties and domestic chores. She'd arrived at work that morning with an extra spring in her step, excited that their paths might cross once more. But there was no time now for goofy grins or sexy daydreams.

Zara had paged Conrad to urgently review an inpatient he'd admitted the day before. The woman, who was at thirty-five weeks' gestation, was being monitored following premature rupture of the membranes, or PROM.

As he marched onto the maternity ward with his SHO, Max, in tow, Zara sighed with relief and quickly intercepted him.

'Dr Reed,' she said. 'I need you to review Mrs Hutchins, the patient you admitted yesterday with pre-term PROM.'

The barely perceptible flicker of heat and recognition in his stare was, of course, gratifying, but it became quickly shrouded in concern and professionalism. They might be very pleased to see each other after days apart, but their patients always came first.

'What's going on?' he asked, pausing outside the patient's room to hurriedly wash and dry his hands.

'Her observations have been stable,' Zara said, bringing him up to speed. 'No sign of labour or infection and she's had her steroids. But this morning, after showering, the patient reported she felt something prolapsing internally. I think it's the umbilical cord. We've confined her to bed and placed her in the head down position to relieve any pressure on the cord.'

Conrad pulled on a face mask, his stare etched with the same concern for the patient that Zara felt. 'How's the foetal heart rate? Any signs of distress?'

Zara shook her head. 'It's stable, too. No bradycardias to report.' But they both knew the risks with premature rupture of the membranes. Infection, premature labour and foetal distress were serious enough compilations. But umbilical cord prolapse or compression could be life-threatening, especially for the baby.

'Okay,' Conrad said with a decisive nod. 'You did the right thing in calling me.' He met her stare, his conveying reassurance and faith. 'Let's take a look.'

They entered the room, where Sharon was with the patient. After greeting Mrs Hutchins, Conrad pulled on sterile gloves. 'I need to examine you, Mrs Hutchins.'

Zara waited nervously, trying to keep her concerns for the patient and her unborn baby from her expression. When he'd finished his examination, Conrad glanced at Zara and gave her a worrying nod of confirmation. 'You're right. It *is* the cord.'

Zara swallowed her fear. She'd never personally come across a case of umbilical cord prolapse before. She'd never been more relived that he was there.

Conrad turned to the patient. 'Mrs Hutchins, that feeling you have of something prolapsing inside is the baby's umbilical cord. It's slipped down outside the uterus. There's a risk that if we leave it, the blood supply to the baby could be compromised. I'm afraid we're going to need to deliver the baby with an emergency Caesarean section today.'

The patient nodded tearfully, her stare full of understandable alarm, but Zara was so grateful for the calm authority in Conrad's voice. She'd found it reassuring, so hopefully the patient had also.

Zara took Mrs Hutchins' hand. 'Try not to worry. The baby is fine at the moment. We just need to deliver him or her quickly and safely, okay?'

'Have you called Mr Hutchins?' Conrad asked Sharon, tossing his gloves in the bin and pulling out his phone while Max took some blood from the patient's arm in preparation for surgery.

'Yes,' Sharon said. 'He's working in Manchester today, so he might be a while. But he's on his way.'

From the corner of the room, Conrad made a quick but hushed call to the obstetrics theatre and the anaesthetist, glancing Zara's way with a concerned stare. She knew what he was thinking: there was no time to wait for the husband. Any shift of the baby's position could compress the cord and interfere with the baby's blood supply.

Having hung up the phone, Conrad addressed the patient once more. 'I'd be happier if we deliver this baby right now, Mrs Hutchins. I don't think we can wait for dad. Better for him to meet the little one safely delivered. Do you agree?'

The woman nodded, and Conrad unlocked the wheels of the bed. Seeing the grip the patient still had on Zara's hand, he met her stare. 'Zara, are you up for a trip to Theatre?'

She shot him a grateful nod and turned to the patient. 'I'll stay with you until your husband arrives.'

'Then let's go have this baby,' Conrad said, his own expression impressively calm as, together, they wheeled the patient towards the lifts and headed for Theatre.

With relief pounding through his veins following the emergency C-section, Conrad placed the healthy newborn baby girl onto her mother's chest for some immediate skin-to-skin contact.

'Congratulations. You have a daughter.'

As the neonatal nurses hovered nearby, ready to whisk the pre-term baby away for some initial checks and to be weighed, Zara and Mrs Hutchins stared at the newborn in wonder. Conrad's stare met Zara's over the tops of their theatre masks. Tears shone in her eyes, a raft of emotions shifting there—relief, gratitude, respect. Conrad lapped it up, his heart beating wildly that he and Zara could share this special, professional moment.

In a short time, things had gone from terrifyingly urgent to the happiest outcome, the kind their work was renowned for: a safely delivered and healthy baby. But today, maybe because Zara was there with him in Theatre, the rush he normally felt was amplified tenfold.

Yes, this was his job and he and Zara were just having casual sex. But ever since his brother's violent and untimely death, Conrad had become increasingly aware of how quickly life could change. You could lose what you cared about in a heartbeat.

Focussed on the fundal massage of the uterus and the delivery of the placenta, Conrad quietly guided Max through the surgical closure of the uterine incision while Zara and neonatal team cared for the mother and baby. With surgery complete, he removed his gloves and gown and spoke to the patient, who was now cradling her sleeping baby adoringly.

'We got there a little earlier than planned, but it looks like she's doing really well.' He smiled, loving this part of his job—the end result. 'I hope Mr Hutchins isn't too upset that we started without him.'

'Thank you for delivering her safely, Doctor,' the patient said, her eyes shining with tears as she rested a hand on his arm. 'She's perfect and I'm so grateful to you and the whole team.'

Conrad swallowed, her gratitude catching him off guard for a second, maybe because Zara was present and listening, watching on with shining eyes.

'I'll come and check on you back on the ward,' he said. Before he moved away, he glanced at Zara, who was looking at him every bit as adoringly as Mrs Hutchins. A moment of silent communication and emotional support passed between them.

You did a good job. I couldn't have done it without you. Thank you.

Did she trust him the way he trusted her? It seemed crazy given they'd only known each other a couple of weeks. But maybe the feast or famine nature of their fling, the stolen moments of intimacy they snatched when they could, made every moment, together or apart, more intense. Maybe that explained their building connection.

Reluctantly, he left Theatre, tossing his face mask and disposable hat into the bin before washing up. He was just about to head for the coffee room, where he hoped some much-needed caffeine would settle his thoughts, when he spied Sharon.

'How did it go?' she asked, her frown easing as he nodded his head.

'All good. A textbook C-section. The baby is a bit small, but otherwise seems healthy. Zara is still with them.' He glanced back towards Theatre, as if reluctant to leave without Zara.

Sharon chuckled. 'There was no way Zara was letting go of that woman's hand. She hates not being able to see a delivery through to the end. I swear if she didn't have Zach to care for, some days she probably wouldn't go home at all.'

He nodded. 'She's a great midwife.' And an amazing woman and mother. He hadn't come to England looking for a romantic relationship. He'd come to forget about the twisted love triangle he'd been dragged into by Marcus and Tessa. To grieve for Marcus without the constant reminders of the betrayals of the past. To give Tessa the space she'd requested when he'd tried to be there for James. But there was something about Zara he couldn't help but allow close. Closer than he'd allowed anyone since he'd learned the truth about his brother and his ex.

'She is. I keep telling her what a catch she is,' Sharon said. 'But Zach's father really let them down.'

He smiled, non-committal. He'd been surprised by how much Zara had shared with him last Friday night about her feelings of betrayal, rejection and humiliation. Maybe she was starting to trust him. And like Sharon, it really bothered Conrad that Zara blamed herself for a youthful mistake, when Zach's father had simply walked away without taking any responsibility for his son.

'Are you enjoying working here?' Sharon asked, switching subjects.

'It's great,' he said, with genuine feeling. 'I'm getting lots of experience and more surgical time than in Brisbane.'

'Maybe you should keep your eye open for a consultant post here. There are a couple of older obstetricians who are close to retirement age.'

'Maybe I will,' he said. 'But I'm not in any rush. No point applying for a consultant post until I know where I want to settle.' For now, he couldn't really think beyond going back to fix things with his brother's wife. They were both grieving, but now that Conrad had seen Zara's devotion to Zach, he could understand why Tessa had told him to back off. Perhaps he *had* been overprotective of James at a time when he was still processing his own grief for Marcus.

'See you later,' Sharon said, turning and exiting the department, leaving Conrad wondering how he was going to walk away from Zara when the time came.

Conrad was about to head for a nearby stairwell, when he heard his name being called. Zara caught up with him, wordlessly widening her eyes and tilting her head in the direction of the stairs. With his heart bounding, he followed. The door swung closed at his back, and Zara hurled herself into his arms, her lips clashing with his in a breathy kiss that almost knocked him off his feet.

'That was amazing,' she said, after pulling back to look up at him, her hands gripping his face. 'You are amazing. Thank you for letting me be a part of that delivery.'

Euphoria rushed Conrad's blood. He didn't need her praise, but it felt good to know their professional regard, their trust, was mutual. 'It was a team effort. I couldn't have done it without you, and, as it happens, I think you're amazing, too.' Now his feelings of closeness made sense. Their relationship *was* intense. How could it not be? They were sleeping together, essentially living together and working together.

She smiled, kissed him again, and, despite them being at work, despite the fact that they might be discovered, Conrad couldn't help but kiss her back. He slid his tongue against hers and pressed her up against the closed door as desire hijacked his system.

'How can I want you all the time?' she said, when they came up for air, her body shifting restlessly against his, a reminder of how she felt naked in his arms, her passionate cries ringing out.

Dopamine flooded his brain, swiftly followed by a sense of panic, a desperation to be alone with her once more. Not Friday night, but now.

'Can I see you tonight?' he whispered against her lips in between her desperate kisses. Suddenly, Friday seemed like a long way off. Too long. Clearly his physical need for her had reached uncontrollable levels, otherwise he wouldn't be risking discovery by kissing her at work. But in a couple of weeks, he'd be flying home to sort out his personal life. In the meantime, he wanted as much of Zara as he could get.

'I can't,' she said, with a sigh. 'It's a school night. I... I don't want to confuse Zach.'

Conrad's stomach sank, even though he understood. 'Of course not. I totally understand. I don't want that either.' He'd always known that Zach was her number one priority and he respected her for putting her son first. 'You're a great mother, Zara. I hope you know that.'

He was desperately trying not to judge Tessa's parenting, but a part of him couldn't help but worry that her withdrawal from the Reed family wasn't in James's best interests. Surely the boy needed his father's family, now more than ever. But maybe Tessa needed time to build new routines for her and James, in the same way Zara protected Zach.

'I just can't seem to get enough of you,' he admitted, pushing the hair back from her face and brushing her lips with his, one last time. Then he reined himself back under control as he stepped back, put some distance between their bodies.

'Me neither,' she said, her teeth snagging her bottom lip in a very distracting way. 'Unless...' She hooked her index finger into the V-neck of his scrub top so he couldn't step too far away. 'I could text you once Zach is asleep.' She blinked up at him playfully. 'Perhaps you could tiptoe up for a sneaky glass of wine.'

His pulse went crazy, his need for her outweighing his dislike of *sneaking around*. But he understood her reasons and it wasn't as though *their* clandestine activities were hurting anyone.

'I'd love to, but only if you're sure,' he said. 'Honestly, no pressure. I respect your boundaries. The last thing I want to do is make you feel uncomfortable or confuse Zach.' Not that Zara was ready to introduce the boy to some strange man.

'I'm sure,' she said. 'I'll text you tonight. I'd better get back to Mrs Hutchins.' She smiled, her stare sweeping over him in a way that was full of promise. Then she pulled open the door, blew him a cheeky kiss and disappeared.

Conrad dragged a ragged breath, stunned by the force of his addiction to Zara Wood. But he needed to be careful, to keep his emotions in check the way he'd done since rushing things with Tessa. He couldn't get carried away by their harmonious working relationship and great sex. He didn't want to hurt Zara or get hurt himself, and, as he'd said to Sharon, his life was back in Australia. His one comfort was that Zara seemed to know what she wanted, and it wasn't a real relationship.

CHAPTER NINE

THE NEXT MORNING, as soon as Conrad opened his eyes, a grin stretched his mouth, his first thought of Zara. She *had* texted him last night, once Zach had fallen asleep. They'd shared a bottle of wine by the fire, whispering like a couple of teenagers up late without parental knowledge. Wine had led to kissing, kissing to nakedness after Zara had sneaked him into her bedroom and covered his mouth with her hand to dampen any noise as they'd climaxed together. The clandestine nature of their desperate coupling had made it somehow hotter. Although Zara was almost too hot to handle, just as she was.

Conrad stretched out his body after a great night's sleep and headed for the shower. Given that he was covering the on call that coming weekend, he had today off, but he couldn't just lie around thinking about his favourite midwife. Perhaps he'd go for a walk. Head into the hills around Morholme, get some fresh air and think about what he would say to Tessa when he returned to Australia. Just as he respected Zara's boundaries, he would respect Tessa's, but he still wanted to be a part of James's life.

When he emerged from the bathroom ten minutes later, he heard squeals of laughter from outside. He quickly dressed and opened the curtains. The unexpected sight that greeted him forced out a bark of delighted laughter.

The garden, the fields beyond, the surrounding rooftops were all blanketed in a thick layer of snow.

Conrad's pulse picked up with excitement. Aside from a few skiing holidays in New Zealand when he was a teenager, he had little experience of snow. He'd certainly never lived anywhere with cold enough winter temperatures for snowfall.

Just then, a little boy he assumed was Zach ran past his window, his cheeks ruddy from the cold and a pair of multi-coloured gloves dangling from the sleeves of his coat by string. Conrad smiled at the boy's infectious joy, imagining how James too would love to play in the snow. A flood of sadness swamped him for all the moments in his son's life that Marcus would miss. It made Conrad all the more determined to patch things up with Tessa when he returned home so he could be there for James, not as a substitute father, but as an uncle who would be there if needed.

Zara appeared and, just like that, Conrad's sadness lessened. She chased after Zach, her hair caked with powdery snow and her breath misting the air in front of her as she laughed. She hurled a snowball, striking Zach in the back.

Conrad smiled wider. They were obviously having a snowball fight and, with a direct hit to head versus one to the torso, Zach was clearly winning.

In that second, Zara looked up and spied Conrad at the window. He raised his hand in a wave, his pulse galloping as usual as their eyes met. He prepared to move away from the window, reluctant to interrupt their fun. But before he could step back, Zara scooped two handfuls of snow from the ground, formed a tight ball between her palms and threw the snowball in his direction. It struck the window with a thump, right at Conrad's eye level. But for the pane of glass, it would have been a direct hit to the face.

Triumph gleamed in Zara's stare as she laughed, delighted with herself. 'Afraid of a little snow?' she called, beckoning him to join them at the door to the flat.

Conrad headed through to the kitchen and pulled open the door to a rush of frigid air and the crisp scent of fresh snow.

'Conrad,' Zara said, from his doorstep, 'this is Zach.' She looked down at her son. 'Conrad is from Australia.'

Conrad shook the boy's hand. 'Good to meet you, Zach. Looks like you're having a fun time and it seems you're better at snowball fights than your mother.'

'We're building a snowman,' Zach said proudly, stooping to grab another two handfuls of the irresistible powder.

'That sounds awesome. I've never done that.'

'Really?' Zach asked, looking up at him with astonishment.

'I don't think they have snow in Conrad's country,' Zara explained, her eyes full of pitying laughter.

Conrad smiled, pleased to see her, given she was supposed to be at the hospital right now. 'You didn't go into work?' he asked.

She shook her head. 'It's a snow day. School's closed, and the roads out here are impassable. But don't worry, they'll be out with the gritters soon. They'll have the roads cleared by tomorrow. Best to enjoy it while it lasts.'

'Do you want to help us build a snowman?' Zach asked Conrad. 'It's going to be so cool.'

'Good idea.' Zara nodded and ruffled Zach's hair.

Conrad hesitated, reluctant to gatecrash their precious family time. 'Are you sure?' he asked, respectful of her boundaries.

'Definitely,' she said, with a smile. 'Come and play.'

'Okay, thanks, Zach.' Conrad reached for his trainers, which were near the door. 'I'd love to help build a snowman.'

'You'll have soggy feet in seconds wearing those,' Zara said, glancing at the trainers.

'I only have these and my work shoes with me. I didn't pack for snow.' He looked at her feet. She and Zach were wearing gumboots.

'I still have my dad's wellies in the shed.' Zara smiled. 'They might fit you. Let me go grab them.'

While Conrad quickly donned his coat, Zach wandered off to retrieve his yellow plastic spade, the kind you'd take to the beach for building sandcastles. Within seconds Zara returned with boots. Conrad shoved his feet into them and stepped outside. The snow was inches thick, blanketing the entire garden, even the path. He stepped gingerly to avoid slipping, the rubber soles of the boots squeaking against the compacted snow.

'Come on,' she said, urging him to her and Zach's half of the garden where they'd already made a good start on the body of the snowman, a mound taller than Zach.

'Now we can make him even taller, Mum,' Zach said, excitedly patting handfuls of snow onto the mound. He looked up at Conrad. 'How tall are you?'

'I'm six foot two,' Conrad said, reaching for two handfuls of snow. 'Let's see if we can make him taller than me.'

'Yeah,' Zach cheered, enthusiastically piling snow higher and higher as Zara cast Conrad a look full of gratitude.

They threw themselves into the challenge, laughing as the mound grew taller and taller. Within seconds Conrad's fingers were frozen and the cuffs of his coat were damp, but he was having too much fun to care.

'Let's make a giant snowball for the head,' said Zach to Conrad, running to the far end of the garden where the snow was thick and undisturbed.

'Careful, mate, it's slippery on the path,' Conrad called out before he could stop himself.

Zara cast him an amused and curious stare. 'He's fine. Don't worry—he's English. He's made of tough stuff.'

Conrad winced. 'Sorry. I just wouldn't want him to fall and whack his head.'

'Thank you for looking out for him,' she said, her expression softening.

Conrad shrugged, adjusting his thinking as he joined Zach, who was rolling a snowball through the snow to help it grow. Of course, Zach wasn't *his* responsibility, but he couldn't help but be protective of the little guy, who reminded Conrad so much of James he experienced another pang of missing his nephew. Fresh guilt rushed him, because his overprotectiveness had upset Tessa, had contributed to pushing her and James away. He knew that. It was something he would need to fix.

By the time he and Zach returned from their trip around the garden, the snowball head was five times the size of the one they'd started with.

'Ready to put the head on top?' he asked Zach, who nodded and looked up at his mother expectantly.

'Is it okay if I put him on my shoulders?' Conrad asked Zara. 'You can pass him the head and he can crown the snowman.'

'Of course,' she said, smiling when Conrad lifted Zach, and the boy squealed with delighted laughter.

'It's the tallest snowman ever,' the boy said, his impressed stare wide. 'Thanks, Conrad.'

When Zach rushed off to grab some fallen branches for arms, Conrad glanced over at Zara. 'Thanks for inviting me,' he said, knowing that she wouldn't have taken the decision to introduce him to Zach lightly.

'Thanks for helping,' she said, tilting her head towards the snowman. 'We couldn't have made it that tall without you. My son clearly thinks you're the coolest thing since sliced bread.'

Conrad smiled, a lump in his chest. For an unguarded second, he could so easily imagine himself a part of this little family. He hoped he and Zara would keep in touch when he returned to Australia. Perhaps she'd even visit him there, given it was on her list. But whether they stayed friends or not, the day he'd built his first snowman with her and Zach would be one he'd always remember.

CHAPTER TEN

LATER THAT EVENING, Zara sipped her wine, a shudder of contentment passing through her like an electric current, bringing her to life. The surprise day off had been magical. After the snowman, she'd invited Conrad to join her and Zach for lunch—cheese on toast and soup—then an afternoon movie, followed by board games and pasta for dinner.

In the armchair by the fire, Conrad read Zach his favourite bedtime story. Her son was totally smitten by the lodger, who'd shown him some of Australia's native animals and taught him how to say, *G'day, mate.* When Conrad had once more lifted Zach onto his shoulders to crown the head of the snowman with an old bobble hat belonging to Zara's dad, she'd wanted to cry at the look of uninhibited joy on her son's face.

Now that all the excitement of the day had died down, icy fingers of doubt once more crept down her spine. She was taking a big risk with Conrad, blurring the boundaries she'd previously never needed to enforce because she'd always kept men at arm's length and away from Zach. Today, the snow had somehow helped her to justify her out-of-character behaviour. She kept telling herself that Conrad was different. Temporary. Risk-free. But the day had left her both happy and unsettled.

Maybe because, for a blinding second, as they'd played

together in the snow, she'd imagined the three of them were a family. Conrad would clearly be an amazing male role model.

'Right, time for bed, young man,' she said after Conrad finished the story and closed the book. Her boy looked exhausted from the day's excitement, and it would be business as usual tomorrow for them both—Zach back to school and Zara to work.

Zach dutifully hopped off the chair. 'G'day, mate,' he said to Conrad, offering him a final fist bump—another wonderfully exotic thing Conrad had taught him—before he dashed off to clean his teeth.

With her stomach churning with both fear and longing, Zara tucked Zach in, kissed him goodnight, and rejoined Conrad, who was picking up plastic blocks and jigsaw pieces from the floor.

'Thanks,' she said, taking a seat on the sofa. 'You don't have to do that.'

He tossed the blocks into the box. 'Thanks for including me in your day.' He grabbed her hand and raised it to his lips, placing a brief kiss there, his stare intense. 'I know how wonderfully protective you are of Zach. I'll always remember building my first snowman with you two.'

Because Zara wanted to hurl herself into his arms and couldn't, she reached for her wine and took a massive gulp.

'I should go,' he said, hesitantly.

Zara shook her head. She should let him go, but that other side of her, the woman, not the mum, craved a little more of his company. 'Stay for a while,' she urged, patting the sofa beside her and topping up both their glasses. 'Finish your wine.'

'Okay.' Conrad folded himself onto the sofa and stretched his arm along the back.

'Zach's completely exhausted,' Zara said, desire and gratitude making her sigh. 'We don't usually pack that much excitement into one day—snow and an exotic new friend, teaching him Australian words and cool fist bumps. Thank you.' Her throat ached anew with fear that Zach was missing out on a positive male influence. Suddenly, she felt jealous of James on Zach's behalf. The poor boy had lost his father, but he still had an amazing uncle, whereas Zara was an only child.

Conrad smiled indulgently, his stare shifting from her mouth to her eyes and turning intense in that way he had of making her feel seen. 'He's a great kid. I don't know if anyone has told you lately, but you're an incredible mum.'

'Thanks for saying that.' Zara swallowed the lump in her throat and looked away. 'It's a good job you'll be leaving soon,' she added with a teasing smile. 'A normally frazzled working mother could get used to those kinds of compliments.' And after the lovely day they'd spent together, after seeing how good Conrad was with Zach, she desperately needed the reminder that this sexy Australian with a big heart wasn't going to be around for ever.

In the beginning the temporary nature of their fling had been a huge part of his appeal. But after today, she couldn't help but wonder what might have been if he lived in the UK. A dangerous thought.

'You shouldn't doubt yourself,' he said with a frown, his fingers slowly stroking the nape of her neck in a way that turned her on.

'Sometimes, it's hard not to,' Zara admitted with a shrug that was part shudder from his touch. 'I think all parents worry that they're doing a good enough job. Parenting is the hardest thing I've ever done. Sometimes, I worry that I've ruined Zach's life by choosing the wrong man to have a baby with. I'm dreading the day he blames me because he doesn't have a father like the other kids.'

Would her boy one day resent her for her mistake? She'd always told him that his father lived in a different country, insisting she could take care of Zach as much as a mum *and* a dad combined. But those vague explanations wouldn't cut it for ever. Zach was a smart kid.

'That day may never come.' Conrad took her hand in his. 'It's like you said—you see to it that he has everything he needs. I hope my brother's wife does half as good a job with James. Man, I wish he'd been here today. He would have loved the snow and loved Zach.'

She met his stare, her pulse flying from his words and the way he looked at her, as if she was something special. Or maybe she was just seeing things because Conrad was addictive, their fling the most fun she'd had in years. But just because it had started out as nothing serious, didn't mean it wasn't…intense.

'You really love James, don't you?' she said, recalling the way he'd been protective of Zach earlier, understandable after what had happened to his brother.

'I do, of course.' He stilled, growing pensive. 'Kids have that way of making you love them.'

She understood the highs and lows of how it felt to love a child. The moments of sheer joy interspersed with the concerns that your parenting might not be up to scratch.

'You're right, they do.' She nodded, choked, because Conrad would be a wonderful father, the kind that Zach deserved. Whoa…that was an unrealistic leap.

'I was thinking about all the days, all the milestones and celebrations that my brother will miss.' His expression darkened with pain and Zara squeezed his fingers to silently let him know she was there for support.

'When Marcus made me promise that I would always look out for James after he was born, neither of us imagined that Marcus wouldn't be around to fill that role himself.' He glanced at their clasped hands, his fingers restless against hers so she guessed there was more he wanted to say, more he was feeling.

'Of course not.' Zara understood grief, and how it could come from nowhere when you least expected it. 'Are you worried about fulfilling your promise?' Since his brother died, Conrad had clearly become a more prominent male role model in his nephew's life.

'I guess.' Conrad looked up as if she'd hit the nail on the head. 'My relationship with Tessa is...complex.'

'Why?' she asked, her pulse buzzing in her fingertips with anticipation.

He watched her for a second then seemed to come to some sort of internal decision. He held her stare, doubt shifting across his expression. 'Because we used to date.'

Zara frowned, his words jarring. 'You and your sister-in-law?' That was the last thing she'd expected him to say.

'Yes.' He nodded, winced, glanced away.

Stunned, Zara fought the jealous twisting of her stomach. 'Tessa is the woman you loved? The one who broke your heart?' The one who'd left him because he'd come on too strong, too soon? Only she'd left him and turned to his brother, of all people. How confusing for Conrad.

'We'd split up long before she got together with Marcus,' he said, sounding defensive, as if he was trying to minimise how he felt about the situation. 'But as you can imagine, there's always been this kind of tension between the three of us. And it's only worsened since Marcus was killed.'

'Of course, it would be…awkward,' she said, still reeling and struggling to find the right words. Instinct told her that, for Conrad, *tension* was an over-simplification, but she could understand why he'd focussed on casual relationships since. There must be a part of him that had felt betrayed.

'Were you over her when they got together?' she asked, a hot ball of envy lodging in her chest. Was he still in love with this woman? After all, this Tessa was the reason he didn't date.

'I was. I hadn't seen her in months. Then one day, Marcus invited me out for a beer and told me that he and Tessa had hooked up one night after running into one another at a bar. They'd been seeing each other in secret, behind my back, and Tessa was pregnant.'

Zara hid her shocked gasp. No wonder he hated secrets. No wonder he'd needed space and distance in order to properly grieve for his brother.

'How did it make you feel?' she asked, her throat aching for Conrad, who must have felt humiliated and confused and horribly torn.

He laughed, the sound mirthless, not quite meeting her gaze. 'How I felt about it didn't really matter. By the time he'd confessed it was a *fait accompli*. Tessa was having Marcus's baby, and he was going to marry her. I had the sense he'd only told me then because he knew he'd have to come clean soon, before she started showing.'

'I'm sorry,' she whispered. 'That must have been so hard on you.' Watching Marcus date Tessa, knowing that they'd gone behind his back, feeling as if he *had* to be okay with the arrangement.

His head snapped up as if she was the first to acknowledge his feelings in this complex triangle. 'I was shocked, obviously. Marcus and I were close until then. I trusted my brother more than anyone else.'

'Of course you did.' And that brotherly bond would have made the betrayal worse for Conrad. Zara waited, stroking his hand. He was downplaying it, maybe because he'd been forced to accept it.

'I didn't want to make a big deal of it,' he went on, 'or make them feel bad because they'd fallen in love. I had no lingering feelings for Tessa, so why shouldn't the two of them be happy together, especially as they were going to be parents?'

'Feelings aren't as straightforward as that,' she said. 'Your trust had been damaged. And there's an unwritten rule about exes. There must have been a part of you that felt let down. Confused. Maybe even trapped in a situation out of your control.'

No wonder he'd stopped dating seriously.

Conrad kept his gaze downcast so she knew she was close to the mark. 'I didn't want to cause a family rift or put my parents in the awkward position of having to choose a side, choose a son. They were understandably excited about the birth of their first grandchild, as they had every right to be. And then there was a wedding to plan. Everyone else just accepted it and moved on.'

'So you felt you had to do the same. As if *your* feelings, *your* hurt and betrayal didn't matter.' Zara's heart clenched painfully. He'd swallowed down his feelings for the sake of family harmony and because he loved his brother, but he obviously hadn't fully reconciled those feelings.

He shrugged, evasive. 'With time to get used to the idea, I moved on.' His mouth twitched into an approximation of a smile but it didn't reach his eyes. 'I was genuinely happy for them when they got married and James was born. They were obviously in love, and James, like Zach, is a great kid.'

Zara nodded, choked by longing. He was so kind and honourable and dependable. And he'd been forced into unhealthy coping mechanisms—setting his feelings aside, keeping his relationships casual—by circumstances brought about by the actions of others.

'Did you ever talk about it with Marcus? Tell him how you'd felt betrayed that they'd sneaked around behind your back?' she asked, hoping that, for Conrad's sake, they'd resolved it before Marcus died.

He lifted one shoulder. 'We skirted the issue a few times. I think he knew how I felt on some level. He always seemed a little guilty whenever he looked at me after that. But then life moved on. He became a husband and a father. It seemed pointless to drag up the past.'

Only now, she saw how Conrad seemed stuck in that same past.

'I'm in no way minimising your feelings, or excusing what Marcus did,' she said, 'but he must have felt guilty for hurting you and torn between his feelings for you, the brother he loved, and those for Tessa. People say we can't help who we fall in love with.'

Or was that a myth? Marcus and Tessa hadn't been forced to act on their attraction.

'I agree,' he said, meeting her stare so she saw the pain and vulnerability he hid with his 'out for a good time' persona. 'Although there must have been a moment, early on, when they both consciously crossed that line. They both chose to ignore my feelings, to sneak around. But it was Marcus that I trusted.'

And Marcus had let him down and then died.

'So it never really got resolved?' she asked, her heart breaking for the wasted opportunity. For Conrad's damaged trust and bottled-up emotions and how they held him back, even now, years later.

He shook his head, his shoulders slumped with regret. 'No. We patched over it, but it was always there like a festering wound between Marcus and me or whenever the three of us were together. I guess a part of me figured that, one day, we'd resolve it, but now it's too late. Marcus is gone. I had to bury all the things I hadn't said to him the day we buried my brother.'

'I'm so sorry.' Zara wrapped her arm around his shoulders and held him close, their hearts banging together. 'But he would want you to be happy, just like he wanted you to be a part of his son's life, because he loved you. You can still say the things you wished you had. You can talk to him and let go of the past. It's never too late to forgive him.'

'I have forgiven him.' He pulled back and peered at her, his stare full of sadness. 'No point holding a grudge with a dead man.'

Zara nodded, uncertain if that was really true. She hoped so, for Conrad's sake. She didn't want to push him, but she was wired to care. She couldn't help but wonder if, on some level, he was stuck in the past, trying to untangle the threads of his mistrust and betrayal from his grief. He'd run away from the mess, after all.

As if he wanted to draw a line under his confession,

he leaned in and pressed his lips to hers. He cupped her face, and she shuddered, relaxed her body against his and kissed him back.

'Thanks for listening to me vent,' he said when they paused for breath. But the vulnerability was gone from his stare, replaced by the desire she'd grown used to seeing whenever they kissed. 'You are a very special woman, Zara Wood.'

'Thanks for confiding in me,' she said, touched that he'd trusted her enough to open up.

But no matter how close she felt to him, no matter how much she trusted him, otherwise she'd never have introduced him to Zach, she had no right to try and fix him. This wasn't a relationship, just sex. And she had her own problems to work through. It was one thing to embark on a temporary fling with a sexy colleague who was passing through town, a whole other scenario when it came to dating someone seriously. Finding a man she could, not only trust with *her* feelings, but also risk making a permanent fixture in her son's life, would be no easy task. That was why she'd put it off for so long.

'I think Zach must be asleep by now,' she whispered. 'Do you want to stay a bit longer?' She needed to remember they were just having a good time. No matter how wonderful Conrad was with Zach, no matter how much she craved both his company and his touch, no matter how much she might wish he were sticking around, this was still nothing serious. It couldn't be.

'I'd love to.' He cupped her cheek and smiled, the flare of heat in his eyes telling her that, for now, they seemed to be addicted to each other. Time was running out. They'd be foolish not to snatch every opportunity to satiate that hunger.

Trembling inside after such an emotional day, she stood and drew him to his feet, leading him silently to her bedroom. With every footstep, she reiterated how this was temporary. Conrad would soon be heading home to the other side of the world, to his loved ones and a consultant job. She couldn't become sidetracked by his confusion and fears and trust issues. She should simply focus on this sexual journey that had begun just for fun.

She didn't want to have regrets, but nor did she want to be hurt. And if she wasn't careful, she'd confuse the professional respect and sexual connection they shared with feelings. This fling had never been about feelings, because they both had trust issues. She understood that clearly, now more than ever before.

CHAPTER ELEVEN

As he moved inside Zara, Conrad's heart thudded so hard he was certain she'd feel it and understand he was caught at the centre of an emotional storm. The minute he'd opened up to her about Marcus and let her close, he'd wanted to bury himself inside her and chase away his demons and doubts with pleasure. And after such a fantastic and unexpected day spent together, part of him wanted the night to last for ever. But their chat, the way she'd effortlessly seen things he'd been reluctant to admit, perhaps even to himself, had left him feeling raw and exposed. How had she understood that being betrayed by the one person he'd trusted most in the world, his brother, had left him questioning exactly who he could ever possibly trust?

'Why is this so good?' she whispered, wrapping her legs around his hips, crossing her ankles in the small of his back, staring up at him with desire and faith as if they'd forged a new stronger bond because of their shared trust issues.

The minute they'd touched, slowly and silently stripping each other in the dim light of the bedside lamp, Conrad's urgency had turned into fierce longing he couldn't explain. He felt so close to her, he knew he would never forget his time in England. But he couldn't pretend that the relationship that had begun for fun was still under his control.

Now, with his stare locked with hers and their fingers entwined, he couldn't seem to get close enough to Zara. He couldn't breathe. Couldn't bring himself to think about the ticking clock or the time, in the not too distant future, when this would end.

'Because you're so sexy,' he said as he unhurriedly rocked his hips, refusing to think beyond the here and now. It was good because it was casual and temporary. But if he was honest, the full picture was far more nuanced. And terrifying.

Their connection was rare. She maybe didn't know it because she'd avoided casual sex since her Spanish fling, but *he* knew. It had been many years since he'd felt so in sync with a woman. Around her, his problems seemed smaller. Losing himself in their passion chased his doubts and regrets from his mind. Spending time with her, both in and out of work, put other areas of his life into sharper perspective and made him feel as if anything were possible.

'Or maybe it's because you make everything fun, even sex.' She smiled up at him and then moaned when he captured the other nipple in his mouth. 'Part of me wasn't living before you, before this.'

He groaned, moved by her admission. He'd always known that this was temporary. He would soon be heading home. He couldn't get used to the way one glimpse of Zara, one smile, brightened his day, because he'd have to leave her behind. But right then, in that moment, maybe because he'd opened up to her about Marcus's confusing disloyalty, he couldn't imagine walking away without feeling…regret. As if some part of him had been merely surviving before Zara.

'Conrad,' she moaned, wrapping her arms around his shoulders, bringing his lips back to hers, sliding her tongue into his mouth so he forgot everything but how she made him feel physically. He drove them higher and higher, moving faster and faster, nearing the point of no return, a place where he could ignore how she seemed to have changed him, the way she saw straight through him.

Her orgasm crested with a cry. He reared back, watching her fall apart, her pleasure snapping his restraint so he followed her with a groan, holding onto her tightly until the body-racking spasms died away, leaving them both spent. Panting hard, Conrad buried his face against the side of her neck and breathed in the scent of her hair, still yet to come back down from the incredible high, more aware than ever of how different this seemed. No longer just sex.

What was she doing to him? How could every time they slept together be better than the last and somehow more meaningful than any experience he'd had in years? Because he trusted *her*. That was why he'd shown her the broken version of himself tonight. He hadn't let anyone that close in a long time. But for Zara, maybe because they'd learned to trust each other at work or because she'd introduced him to her son today, or because he was leaving anyway, he'd felt safe to finally open up.

'Are you okay?' she whispered, skimming her fingers up and down his back.

'Hmm,' he mumbled, trying not to freak out as he withdrew from her body. He was far from just *okay*. He was both rejuvenated and confused. Euphoric and scared. As if, in letting her so close, some crucial part of him would never be the same. 'I've just never told anyone else what I told you earlier…' Conrad rolled onto his back.

Zara propped herself up on one elbow and watched him

with a concerned frown. 'If you ever need to talk, I'm here. And I want you to know that your feelings *do* matter.'

'Thank you,' he said, too conflicted and choked to say more or even to look at her. She was too wonderful, a great listener who really cared about people. She saw him far too clearly, and part of him was desperate to keep this light and fun, nothing serious, the way it had begun.

'I know he hurt you,' she said, touching his arm. 'But I don't think your brother would want you to be emotionally stranded.'

'You never met him,' he said, even though he knew she was right. Sometimes, alone with his endlessly looping thoughts, he felt stymied. Marcus was gone. It was too late to tell him how he'd felt disregarded six years ago, but nor could Conrad seem to move on from the fact that he'd been deceived by the one person in the world he'd thought he could trust. But he wasn't ready to hear what Marcus might think or say.

'I know.' Her frown deepened with hurt. 'But he obviously loved you. I don't need to have met him to know that he wouldn't want you to be alone for ever because he'd damaged your trust in people.'

'I'll get over it,' he said, scrubbing a hand over his face and then sitting up.

'What would you say to him now, if you could?' Zara pushed, her hand on his back.

Conrad closed his eyes, part of him regretting that Zara understood him so well because he'd lowered his guard. 'I don't know.' But he'd imagined versions of the conversation a hundred times.

'I think if he hadn't been killed, you two would have worked through your issues in time. I think your relationship would have healed, because you're brothers who loved each other. I think when he asked you to be there for James, he was showing you how sorry he was and how much he respected you.'

'Maybe you're right,' he said, his throat choked and his skin crawling, because she was forcing him to examine the mess more closely. 'I'd like to be able to remember all the good times we shared and not just the one time he let me down.'

Maybe he did have unresolved feelings of betrayal that were stopping him from grieving properly. Maybe that was why he'd acted so overprotective of James. He'd never had the chance to make things right with Marcus. He didn't want to risk that he might have regrets when it came to his nephew. Maybe Zara was right: it was time to talk to his brother as if he were in the room and say all the things he'd wanted to say.

'I should go, let you get some sleep,' he said, standing. Padding to the bathroom, he tried to pull himself together in private. What was this woman doing to him, peeling away his layers like that? Yes, he felt as if he could tell Zara anything, and *he'd* been the one who'd chosen to open up, but they weren't in a proper relationship. Neither of them wanted that and even if they changed their minds, it was a dead end. She lived here and he came from the other side of the world. It would clearly take a lot for Zara to overcome her own trust issues and allow a man into Zach's life. This *had* to be temporary. He *had* to go home and sort out the mess he'd left behind. He couldn't make Zara any promises or rely on her emotional support while he tried to grieve for his brother.

He returned a little more composed, pulling on his jeans

and sweater, the act of dressing like donning a much-needed suit of armour.

'I'm on the early shift tomorrow,' she said, her expression still hurt as she climbed from the bed, covering her nakedness with a fluffy dressing gown. 'I might see you on the ward.'

Guilt lashed him. She'd opened her home and her family to him today and he'd repaid her by spilling his guts and then shutting down. But she'd made him see that he'd never actually processed that damaged trust he'd felt, and now it was all tangled up with his grief over Marcus, the issue resurfacing. How was he supposed to work through all of that with Marcus gone?

'I have a ward round tomorrow,' he said, scared that by confiding in Zara, something that had come so naturally at the time, he'd failed to keep her at arm's length. But if he'd let her in, that was *his* problem, not hers. He gripped her shoulders and brushed a kiss over her lips. 'Thanks for today. I'm so honoured that you introduced me to Zach. He's a wonderful boy. You should be very proud.'

She nodded, her eyes shining with emotion as she blinked. 'You're welcome. Thanks for helping out with the snowman.'

Because he sensed she wanted to say more and he needed to collect his thoughts after such an emotional day, he moved towards the bedroom door.

'Conrad,' she said, stalling him, her breathing fast and her stare searching. 'Will you be okay?'

Conrad pressed his lips together, the urge to rush back to her and hold her in his arms until he felt his usual self almost overwhelming. Instead, he gritted his teeth, offered her his best approximation of a smile and nodded. 'See you tomorrow.'

Whatever the hell was going on inside him, whatever it was that explained his restlessness, he needed to pull it together away from Zara. Because the way she looked at him, as if she understood him and cared about his feelings, was seriously messing with his head.

CHAPTER TWELVE

THE FOLLOWING DAY, while trying to put his feelings from the night before behind him, Conrad was halfway through his ward round on the postnatal ward when he became aware of a raised male voice. He looked up in alarm, spying Zara at the other end of the ward. Some man, obviously someone's relative, was yelling at her, his face puce with anger.

With a surge of adrenaline, all of Conrad's protective instincts fired at once. He abandoned his ward round and marched in their direction.

'I don't care if it's normal,' the belligerent relative said to Zara as Conrad approached. 'It's your job to do something.' He pointed a meaty finger, aggressively. 'My wife is very upset.'

'I understand that, sir,' Zara said, casting Conrad a quick glance before standing her ground against the hulk of a man. 'But baby blues are very common, especially after a difficult delivery like the one your wife has been through.'

The man gritted his teeth in frustration and Conrad fought the urge to put his body between Zara and this angry guy. 'What's the problem here?' he asked, coming to Zara's defence whether she needed him or not because, just as she cared about him, he cared about *her*.

'No problem, Dr Reed,' Zara said, flicking him an impatient stare. 'I was just explaining to Mr Hancock that post-partum distress and sadness is a perfectly normal hormonal reaction to giving birth.' She kept her voice impressively calm as she addressed the man, whereas Conrad was in full-on fight-or-flight mode, and Mr Hancock was one infraction away from being marched off the ward.

'The best way to help your wife,' Zara explained soothingly, as if Conrad weren't there, 'is with plenty of reassurance and affection. The crying will pass.'

How could she be so calm, when he was genuinely scared for her safety? He couldn't stop himself from butting in. 'We don't need raised voices,' Conrad said pointedly to Mr Hancock. 'This is a maternity ward. Your wife isn't the only woman here who's just had a baby. Your outburst might be upsetting other patients. If you can't moderate your tone, you might want to go outside for some fresh air.'

'Thank you, Dr Reed,' Zara said impatiently. 'I've got this.' She had that same pitying look on her face that she'd given him as he'd left her place the night before.

Conrad baulked, feeling as if he were unravelling. He wished he could bite his tongue and not interfere. It was obvious Zara didn't need or want his help. She was an experienced midwife who valued her independence. But he couldn't help but feel protective. She was half this guy's size. If things turned physical, she could be seriously hurt.

'If you or your wife have specific concerns about the care she's receiving,' Zara went on calmly when the man stubbornly stood his ground, 'we can talk those through. Dr Reed is doing his ward round at the moment, so he'll soon be in to review your wife, but, as I said, the best medicine is love and reassurance.'

Finally, to Conrad's relief, the man ducked his head,

looking sheepish. 'I'm sorry,' he said to Zara, his colour high. 'I've just never seen my wife that upset. I...don't know how to help.'

Unlike Conrad, who was slow to forgive such an unwarranted attack, Zara softened, her head tilted in sympathy. 'Why don't you make her a cup of tea?' she suggested, indicating the ward kitchen a few doors away.

Mr Hancock nodded, his body deflating. 'A cup of tea... good idea,' he said and shuffled off towards the kitchen.

Conrad stared after him, his fear still a metallic taste in his mouth. He was half tempted to drag Mr Hancock back and make him apologise to Zara again. In fact, the way he was feeling nothing short of a formal written apology would do.

'Can we have a quick word?' Zara said, her mouth tight with annoyance. She headed for the office, knowing he'd follow.

'I know I shouldn't have interrupted that second time,' he said, closing the door behind them and wishing he could drag her into his arms until he was able to breathe easy once more. 'But I just didn't care for the way he was talking to you.'

Zara watched him for a few seconds, a small frown tugging down her mouth. 'Maybe you should have allowed me to handle it from the start,' she replied, her voice clipped with frustration. 'I had the situation under control. In fact, I think your presence made him worse. I think you overreacted, Conrad.'

'Overreacted?' He gaped, his heart rate still thundering away. 'Did you see the size of that guy? He seemed angry enough to get physical.'

'He wouldn't have laid a finger on me,' Zara said, with

a dismissive shake of her head and a lengthy sigh. 'He was just upset because his wife has been crying non-stop since her emergency C-section, that's all. Some men, often the big gruff ones actually, hate feeling out of control. They don't know what to do with themselves.'

'I'm not too fond of it myself,' Conrad muttered under his breath, because last night he'd let Zara too close and now it felt too late to claw back control. It was making him second-guess everything. 'But that's no excuse for raising his voice at you.'

Just as it had for Mr Hancock, Zara's expression softened with sympathy. 'I've experienced worse, Conrad. Look, I understand why you're overprotective, why you see risk everywhere, but I had the situation in hand. If I'd needed you, I would have called for you.'

Now it was his turn to frown. Of course she didn't need *him*. She didn't need any man. Not when she preferred to rely on herself. But was he hypersensitive to danger?

'I don't see risk everywhere,' he muttered, dismissing the idea that he cared too much. The last thing he wanted was to feel vulnerable and out of control like Mr Hancock. 'Of course I'm still trying to process such a senseless act of violence against my brother, a man who had just been doing his job, a man who, like you, had been trying to help someone. In some ways, I'll never understand what happened to him.'

She nodded, another of those pitying looks on her face. 'Anyone would struggle to make sense of that,' she said, her voice soft with empathy.

'And just like paramedics, hospital staff get assaulted, both verbally and physically, all the time.' He couldn't help but want to shield her. He cared about her and her son.

How could he not after everything they'd shared these past weeks? But maybe he *did* care too much. He'd let Zara close, opened up to her about Marcus, and now he couldn't seem to stop the tide of emotions. Whereas Zara was still coolly keeping men, including him, at a distance, the way she'd done since Zach was born.

'But I wasn't assaulted,' she said, quietly but firmly. 'I was dealing with the situation, and I know all about the risk-assessment procedures on the ward.'

Faced with her calm logic, he felt his stomach roll. He felt made of glass. Suddenly this fling felt way too serious. How had they arrived there so fast? Had he pitched it wrong again? Been too eager? Allowed her too close and rushed into something that wasn't reciprocated? He tried to breathe slower, dismissing the need to panic.

Zara sighed, looking at him the way she'd looked at Mr Hancock, with patience and empathy. 'I can't help but be concerned about you after last night. Perhaps your over-protective feelings—for James, for Zach, for me—are a symptom of your grief, Conrad. Maybe if you processed some of the betrayal over what Marcus did to you, maybe if you truly forgave him for hurting you, for going behind your back and making you feel that your feelings didn't matter, you could start to properly grieve for him. Otherwise how are you ever going to move on and trust someone enough for another serious relationship?'

Conrad stiffened. She was right about his unresolved feelings, ones he was still trying to untangle so he could return to Australia with a clear head. Did his concern come across as overprotectiveness? Tessa had accused him of the same thing, after all.

He sighed, scrubbing a hand through his hair. 'Maybe

you're right, but I'm not the only one struggling to let go of the past, Zara. It seems it's okay for you to want to help me, but not the other way around.'

Had he blurred the line between them, confused sex with feelings? He'd started to trust Zara after all, not just professionally, but personally too. Why else would he have confided in her last night? Why else would he feel so off balance since?

'That's not true.' She frowned.

'Isn't it? You're so independent. It's one of your great strengths. But it's okay to let people help you. To allow people to care. That doesn't make you weak.'

'I know that,' she snapped, her eyes darting away.

'Do you? You don't always have to go it alone, you know. Or are you so busy punishing yourself for your mistake that you push people away so you don't have to trust them?' Conrad had assumed she'd started to trust *him*. Now he wasn't so sure. 'How are *you* ever going to have a real relationship if you won't let anyone close?'

They faced each other, stares locked, breathing hard, their accusations echoing around the room.

'I need to get back to work,' she said after a moment, her voice flat. 'I guess we're both still scared to trust for our own reasons. Going it alone has become a habit born of necessity for me. Trusting someone means letting them close to my precious boy, so you can understand why I'm protective.'

'Of course I can.' Conrad exhaled, feeling depressed. Where he'd started to imagine they might have a future, she still wasn't ready for a relationship. And even if she were, he was leaving anyway. He wasn't making her any promises. Not when he needed to return home, to work through his grief and patch up his strained relationship with Tessa so he could be there for James and keep his promise to his brother.

'I'm sorry that I interfered with Mr Hancock,' he said. 'I won't do it again.'

She raised her chin. 'I'm sorry that I offered unsolicited advice about Marcus. What do I know about relationships? At least you've had real ones before, even if you're no longer interested.'

Her words jarred, stabbing at his ribs. She wasn't wrong: he wasn't ready either. He and Zara were similar, both scared to be gullible, scared to trust, to open their hearts to something real. But last night as he'd lain awake for ages, trying to sleep, he'd tentatively wondered if, because of Zara, he might be ready to move on and start trusting people again. He'd imagined a scenario where he and Zara lived in the same country, where they might have a chance at a real relationship, be a real family with Zach. But now that she was still intent on going it alone…his doubts roared back to life.

'I'll let you go,' he said, his heart racing. He hated the distance, both physical and emotional, between them. 'I need to finish my ward round.'

'Maybe we can talk again after work?' she suggested, heading for the door. 'Once Zach is asleep.'

He nodded and tried to smile. Then he watched her leave.

As he strode back down the ward, he couldn't shake the feeling of foreboding. Somehow, he and Zara had strayed from the casual good time they'd set out to enjoy. Even if they both wanted something real, they'd each spent years avoiding relationships. Even if they lived in the same country, there would be no guarantee that they could make it work.

He *did* care about her, that much was obvious. He just needed to keep a lid on the depth of his feelings. He'd been out of sync with a woman before when he'd dated Tessa. He'd rushed in and she'd held back, and when he'd confessed he'd fallen in love with her, she'd ended it then moved on to his brother. It wasn't that she hadn't wanted a serious relationship, she just hadn't wanted Conrad.

Resolved to double down and re-erect the barriers he'd let Zara slip past, he restarted his ward round. After all, he *had* to go home. His life was in Australia. He had to resolve things with Tessa and see James. And the panic that came whenever he thought about leaving the UK and leaving Zara behind? Clearly, that feeling wasn't reciprocated, so he'd need to do his best to ignore it.

CHAPTER THIRTEEN

LATER THAT NIGHT, Zara lay naked on top of Conrad, her face resting on the slowing thump of his heart. She'd invited him up after Zach had fallen asleep so they could talk after their earlier fight. But somehow, they'd barely apologised before they'd reached for each other, kissing voraciously as they'd stumbled towards the bedroom, shedding clothes. It was as if they each understood the futility of arguing, given that their time was running out. Instead, they'd communicated by touch, his regret left over every inch of her skin by his kisses and hers conveyed via their locked stares as he'd moved inside her, their passion for each other an all-consuming fire of which neither of them seemed to be in control.

Now, Conrad's fingers trailed up her back. Zara lay still in his arms as her mind raced and shivers of doubt raised goose pimples on her skin. She was in trouble, despite all her tough talk and independence. Addicted to his touch that made her feel alive, his secret smile that showed her his inner vulnerabilities, drawn to the way he cared deeply about people, including Zara.

And she cared too. How could she not when he'd been so horribly betrayed by the one person he'd thought he could always trust, his brother? When he had so much to offer but was scared to move beyond casual, scared or even unable to allow himself to be loved in case he got hurt again? It seemed like a vicious circle. She wanted him, more and more with every passing day. But since they'd been snowed in and he'd truly opened up to her, all the reasons this could never be anything but sex seemed glaringly obvious.

'You were right about me,' she whispered, needing him to know that, despite her earlier accusations and denials, he wasn't the only one struggling to let go of the past. 'I have been keeping people, well, men, away.'

She still carried doubts that she was ready for a real relationship. But since their closeness had deepened by working together, since she'd witnessed him interacting with her son, since he'd opened up to her about his ex and his brother, she'd begun to imagine that, with the right man, maybe she could trust her instincts again and open up her heart. Maybe she could risk letting another man, the right man, close to Zach.

His fingers stilled against her skin. 'I know. It's like you said, we've both had our trust damaged.'

Zara's throat burned with fear. Despite the way they touched each other, as if their sexual adventure was no longer just about having a good time but something more, Conrad was as broken as Zara. Whatever her feelings and imaginings, *he* couldn't be the right man. He didn't want a serious relationship, because he'd been betrayed. And he had another boy, James, to love and protect, far away in Australia.

'Perhaps I have been punishing myself,' she said, needing to be as brave as she'd urged Conrad to be. 'I've hid behind the need to put Zach first, when, really, I was just scared to trust my instincts, because they've steered me wrong before with Lorenzo.'

Scared to believe in feelings she'd had little use for these past six years while she'd put her own needs last to focus on motherhood. Scared to open her and Zach's life up to someone who might hurt them all over again.

His heart raced under her cheek, his body still as if he was holding his breath, waiting.

'But I'm also protecting Zach. I have to be careful who I allow close to him. I don't want him getting attached to someone who isn't going to stick around. For me to let someone close, I'd need to be really serious about them.' By definition, she and Conrad were *nothing serious*, and he wasn't sticking around.

'Of course,' he said, saying no more.

Recalling how he'd shut down her attempts to talk about moving on the night before, recalling their fight earlier, she felt her doubts multiply. In spite of his feelings of protectiveness, attraction, respect for Zara, he was obviously struggling with that unresolved betrayal, hiding his trust issues behind casual relationships, stuck because Marcus had died before Conrad could properly forgive him. How could he ever want a serious relationship again, when he'd been forced to swallow down those feelings? When he couldn't trust people not to let him down and hurt him?

Cupping her chin, Conrad tilted her face up so their eyes met. 'You are such an amazing person.'

She nodded, her vision swimming, because meeting Conrad had given her hope for the future. Not that her future could include him. But could she really find someone willing to love both her and Zach? Could she risk being that vulnerable, knowing the pain of possible rejection, knowing it could hurt her and her beloved little boy? The alternative was to live her future the way she'd lived the past six years, by just surviving.

'Don't let that fear hold you back for ever,' he said. 'You can't swear off relationships at the age of twenty. You deserve to be happy, too.'

He brushed her lips with his and euphoria flooded her body, that happiness he said she deserved. She wanted to step into the picture he painted. But when she lowered her guard enough to think about dating, she always pictured Conrad—them working together, romantic dates followed by intense love-making, her, Zach and Conrad laughing together the way they had the day of the snow.

But that was crazy, naive, the kind of dream younger Zara would have entertained, and look where that had led. To heartache and loneliness. Conrad was still caught up in the past and not even thinking about relationships, and she'd always known this would be temporary and that he'd go home. She'd most likely never see him again. If she wasn't careful with her wild imaginings, if she made another mistake, allowed another man close enough to hurt her, the consequences would be bigger, because Zach was old enough to understand and remember and feel rejected.

When she pulled back from his kiss, Zara deliberately changed the subject so she could dismiss the fear that it might be too late to protect herself where he was concerned. 'What about you? What will you do when you go back to Australia? Do you have a consultant job lined up?'

'No,' he said, stiffening slightly. 'I've applied for more locum work in Brisbane.'

'Why?' she asked, confused. 'Isn't it time you became a consultant?' Conrad was an experienced senior registrar. She understood why he'd wanted to locum in England—

a temporary post that had allowed him to gain some distance from his complicated relationship with Tessa, and to grieve. But more locum work in Brisbane made no sense.

'I'm just not ready,' he said, sounding defensive. 'I don't know where I want to settle.'

Zara's heart sank. If she'd needed more confirmation that he was still struggling with the past, still running away from his feelings of betrayal, this was it. If he wasn't ready to settle in Australia, he was even less likely to be thinking about relationships, whereas naive Zara was getting carried away again.

'But surely you'd stay where your family are,' she said sitting up and drawing the sheet over her body. 'Where James is? Brisbane?'

Ever since he'd told her of his and Tessa's history, she'd tried valiantly to ignore her jealous imaginings of them fixing their relationship and maybe getting back together one day. Who Conrad dated in the future, who he fell in love with, was none of Zara's business. She had no claim to him. But clearly, she was already way too emotionally invested.

'Yes, that's the plan,' he said, cagily. 'But, I don't know… I've really enjoyed my time working in the NHS. It's made me think about the kind of consultant post I want.'

Zara froze, her breath trapped in her lungs. He couldn't mean he'd considered moving to the UK, could he? She was too scared to ask. But her reaction to the idea, the elation that hijacked her pulse, spoke volumes. She was already in deep. If Conrad lived in England, if he wanted a real relationship, she'd want to continue to see him, to build on what they had and see where it could go. She would even, albeit slowly, allow him and Zach to get to know each other, because she trusted him and liked the kind of man he was.

But none of that could be.

'What about James?' she whispered, terrified and torn to shreds by her conflicted feelings. Part of her, that newly awakened part that clearly had feelings for Conrad, wanted him to stay. But she couldn't ask him to, nor could she rely on her instincts, her feelings, not when they'd steered her so wrong before.

'Yes. That's where I always end up, too,' he said, his voice quiet and thoughtful. 'I owe it to my brother to make sure James is okay, to patch up things with Tessa so I can be the uncle he needs. So I'll go back to Brisbane, and just... see how things pan out, I guess.'

Zara's dangerous excitement drained away, leaving chills behind. How stupid was she to get her hopes up like that? Had she learned nothing from Lorenzo's rejection? No amount of waiting patiently or staring at the phone would make it ring, just as no amount of naive wishing would make someone care when they didn't, or *couldn't* because they'd been hurt before too.

'Speaking of James,' he said, 'I wanted to ask you something.'

Her pulse accelerated again, but this time she shut down the foolish hope.

'There's a steam train exhibition at the weekend I thought Zach might like,' he said, his stare full of boyish excitement the way it had been the day they'd built a snowman. 'I'm on call Saturday, but we could go Sunday. You can ride on the train, and they serve high tea on board. We could make a day of it.'

Zara swallowed, her head all over the place, knowing she'd have to decline. It sounded innocent enough, and, like James, Zach loved trains. But exposing her son to any more of Conrad when he was already pretty smitten with 'the Aussie lodger' and when Conrad was leaving soon was too risky. If she spent another day with Conrad, watching him interact wonderfully with Zach again, she'd never be able to keep her volatile feelings in check. She couldn't let him any closer. If she did, she might not survive him leaving.

'Um…can I think about it?' she said, her eyes stinging. 'I usually catch up on housework and laundry at the weekend,' she finished lamely. But there was no point wishing for the impossible. She'd learned that the hard way while waiting for Zach's father to have a change of heart and seek a relationship with his son.

'Of course,' he said, his voice flat, pricking at her guilt.

This time it was Zara who got up from the bed first and locked herself in the bathroom. She faced her reflection, resolved to protect herself better, given their time was running out and Conrad would soon be gone. The only sure-fire way to safeguard her emotions as resolutely as she protected Zach was to end this now. To stop sleeping with him and part as friends.

She glanced at the closed door, her heart banging away painfully under her ribs as she imagined him on the other side—sexy, confused by her caginess, emotionally vulnerable because he was as susceptible to rejection as Zara. She couldn't imagine she possessed the strength to work with him and not want him with the same burning ferocity she'd always felt. Maybe she could hold on for one more week. Lock down her confusing feelings, take as much of him physically as she could get in the time they had left and face the emotional consequences when he stepped on the plane.

CHAPTER FOURTEEN

LATER THAT WEEK, Conrad was on his way to the delivery ward after a morning of surgeries, when he received an urgent call from his SHO, Max. He rushed to the ward, his adrenaline pumping. When he entered the delivery suite, Zara, Sharon and Max were with the patient, an anaesthetist and paediatrician standing by in the corner of the room.

'What's the situation?' Conrad asked, meeting Zara's concerned stare as he quickly pulled on some gloves.

'Shoulder dystocia,' Zara said, valiantly keeping the alarm he saw in her eyes from her voice. 'The baby's head was delivered three minutes ago. Mum's name is Gail.'

Zara appeared understandably panicked as the labouring woman gave a moan to signal another contraction. But there was no time to comfort either of them. Shoulder dystocia, a serious birth complication with consequences for the health of the mother and baby, meant the baby's shoulders were trapped in the mother's pelvis, delaying the birth of the body.

Conrad took the position beside Zara in place of his SHO, too focussed on the emergency to wonder why Zara had called Max and not him. He quickly examined the patient, glancing at the foetal heart rate monitor for signs that the baby was in distress.

'Okay,' he said, taking charge. 'Let's try the McRoberts

manoeuvre. Zara, you take the right leg, Max the left. Gail, the baby is a little stuck. We need to shift your position to help deliver the shoulders.'

As another contraction began and at Conrad's nod, his assistants flexed the patient's hips, bringing her knees up towards her armpits while Conrad placed his hand on her lower abdomen and applied pressure to the front of the pelvis. 'Push now, as hard as you can,' he instructed the patient.

With everyone present seemingly holding their breath, willing the situation to resolve, the baby moved slightly, but then retreated back into the birth canal.

As Gail collapsed back onto the pillow, clearly exhausted, Conrad looked up and made eye contact with a worried-looking Zara. A week ago he'd have seen respect and faith and encouragement in her stare, but now he just saw doubt. He wanted to reassure her that, together, they could safely deliver this baby, to ask her to believe in him, but even if there was time, even if they'd been alone, he was no longer as sure of Zara. Things had changed between them, as if they were both protecting themselves for the inevitable end of their fling, which was, of course, eminently sensible.

'One more push now,' Conrad said as the next contraction started. 'We're nearly there.' They performed the manoeuvre again, and this time, the shoulders were successfully delivered to a collective sigh of relief around the room.

Conrad completed the delivery of the newborn, placing the baby onto Gail's stomach before he quickly clamped and cut the cord and noted the baby's Apgar score.

'Well done, Gail,' he said. 'He seems fine, but the paediatrician will give him a quick check over, okay? Then he's all yours. Congratulations.'

He glanced up at Zara, yearning for that closeness he'd grown accustomed to whenever they worked together, but Zara seemed distracted. He couldn't help but recall how she'd withdrawn from him the other night when he'd suggested an outing with Zach. He understood that she was choosing to protect her son, and maybe herself, too. And he couldn't blame her. After all, he was making her no promises. In fact, ever since their fight, he too was desperately trying to protect himself.

But ever since the snowman, since the night he'd told her about Marcus and Tessa, he'd also started to imagine a different future for them, one where, instead of ending their fling when he left for Australia, he returned to England and they picked up where they'd left off. Dated for real. A serious relationship. But just because he was trying to manage his own confusion and doubts by selfishly blurring the lines, didn't mean Zara owed him anything. She'd admitted to always relying on herself, and he could understand why, given how she'd been hurt.

Despite the crazy ideas spinning in his head, the ways they could continue to see each other, he repeatedly came up against the same brick wall: Zara wasn't ready to take that risk for a relationship. If Conrad allowed her any closer or pushed for some grand gesture where one of them shifted their entire life to the other's country, he might discover that it was *him* she didn't want. Better to keep any promises off the table, to fly to Australia next week as planned and sort out his personal life. Maybe then his head would clear and he could think straight.

With all the excitement over and with his stomach still

twisting with doubt, Conrad washed up and headed for the office to make a note in the patient's file. That complete, he went in search of Zara, finding her in the ward kitchen.

'What happened?' he asked, trying and failing to keep the accusation from his voice. 'Why didn't you call *me*?'

She looked up at him and sighed, her fatigue obvious. 'It all happened so quickly. Everything was progressing normally until it suddenly wasn't. Max was already on the ward.'

She ducked her stare from his and busied herself making toast. Reluctant to cause another argument, Conrad bit his tongue. He wasn't doubting her story, but there was something off with her. She couldn't look at him. A sickening sense of déjà vu took him back to that first week, when they hadn't really known each other at all. When she'd been prickly, keeping him at arm's length, locking down any need for feelings as she'd done since she'd been hurt by that last guy.

Conrad sighed, terrified that the intense feelings he couldn't seem to contain, ones that fuelled those fantasies of uprooting his life and moving to the UK on the off chance that Zara might be interested, were his alone. He'd rushed into things before, with Tessa. From the way Zara seemed to be pulling back, reluctant to expose Zach to Conrad, reducing her professional reliance on him, Zara was obviously still happy to go it alone.

'Are you okay?' he asked, concerned because obstetric emergencies took their toll on everyone concerned and shoulder dystocia, which was fortunately relatively rare, could alarm the most experienced midwife.

'I'm fine,' she said, finally looking his way. 'It's been a long shift, that's all. I'm tired.'

He was just about to reach out and touch her, the urge automatic, when Sharon bustled into the kitchen. The older midwife paused, shooting Conrad a peculiar look before she moved to the sink and filled a water jug.

'How are you, Sharon?' Conrad asked. 'That was a bit of a shock for us all, I think.'

'I'm glad for the outcome,' Sharon said, catching Zara's eye before she looked Conrad's way. 'A great team effort.'

While Zara finished making the toast, Sharon discreetly made her exit, but something in the older woman's manner flushed his body with uncomfortable heat. The hairs on the back of Conrad's neck stood on end. Was he being paranoid? He sensed they'd talked about him behind his back. But surely Zara wouldn't do that after everything he'd confided in her and after she'd insisted on secrecy?

When they were alone again, he lowered his voice. 'Does she know about us?' he asked, his paranoia spilling free.

Zara shook her head, looking insulted. 'I haven't told her, but she suspects I'm seeing someone.' She looked up and met his stare. 'I'm rubbish at hiding my *post-sex glow*, apparently.' She rolled her eyes, her humour returning for a second. But the smile was tinged with sadness, as if she too sensed this disconnect between them and had no energy to fix it.

As he recalled her obvious fatigue, a surge of compassion welled inside him. He knew first-hand how shift work could mess with your sleep patterns and she also had Zach to care for.

'Listen,' he said, lowering his voice. 'I know it's Friday.' He paused, knowing she would understand he was speaking about their standing late-night arrangement when Zach was sleeping over at his grandmother's. 'But why don't you get an early night tonight?'

He would miss her, ache for her, but maybe he was being selfish. Maybe a bit of distance would help them both gain some perspective. After all, by next weekend this would be over and he'd be on a plane back to Australia. Then, touching her, kissing her reaching for her in the night, would be physically impossible.

She placed a steaming mug of tea on the tray and looked up. 'That's not a bad idea, actually. I could do with an early night.'

Conrad nodded, his pulse whooshing through his head. He wanted to kiss her, to ease her burden somehow, to care for her the way she cared for everyone around her, but he wasn't her boyfriend. She didn't need or want one of those and he was leaving anyway.

'About this weekend...' Zara's mouth flattened into a frown, her stare darting away. 'I'm sorry, but I don't think it's a good idea.' She looked up, something in her expression hardening, reminding him of the woman he'd first met, a woman who'd needed no one. 'Ever since the snowman, Zach has been asking about you non-stop. You made quite the impression on him. I'm scared that if he spends any more time with you, when you're gone, he'll be sad. I don't want to make it worse for him, no matter what I want for myself. I *have* to put him first.'

Conrad nodded, his stomach sinking. 'Of course, you do. I understand. I wouldn't want him to be sad either.' Of course she was protecting Zach. Her priorities were what they'd always been. Conrad's hadn't changed either. They'd always been on this trajectory, their fling temporary. He'd just got carried away by his feelings, lured by the idea that if they lived in the same country, it could be more than temporary. And that vulnerable, irrational part of him that had let her closer than he'd let anyone in six years couldn't help but feel a moment's bitterness. He'd been useful for a sexual adventure, but could never be anything serious, not when she was still dead set on holding men away.

She nodded, picking up the tray as if the conversation was closed. 'Thanks for understanding.'

'Just out of curiosity,' he said, before she could leave, his heart leaping in his chest, 'and because I clearly like to torture myself, if I wasn't flying to Australia next week, would your answer have been any different?'

Hypothetically, had they ever stood a chance of something more than just sex?

'I don't know,' she whispered, looking down. 'But I do know that I'm always going to choose to protect Zach. I'm his mother, so it comes with the territory.' She shrugged, sadly.

Conrad nodded, unable to argue with her inevitable and admirable choice, but crushed all the same.

'I'd better take this tea to Gail, before it goes cold.' She moved past him with the tray.

'Zara,' he said, before she'd gone too far. 'I'll miss you tonight.'

'Me too,' she said, walking away anyway.

But then they both needed to get used to doing that, because time was running out.

CHAPTER FIFTEEN

LATER THAT NIGHT, Conrad's door opened and Zara rushed into his arms out of the cold. 'I tried to stay away, but I couldn't do it. I know it's only going to make it worse when you leave, but I can't seem to care. I just want you until I can't have you any more.'

She stood on tiptoes, raised her mouth to his, kissing him deeply, passionately, her heart soaring when he returned her kisses, like for like.

'Thank goodness,' he said, kicking closed the door.

Even before she heard it slam, she was tugging at his clothes. 'Hurry,' she urged, needing him with terrifying desperation. 'I need you.'

She gasped as one of his hands grasped her backside and the other cupped her breast, his lips caressing the ticklish spots on her neck. She'd spent the entire rest of the day trying to justify this rendezvous, telling herself that as long as she kept Conrad away from Zach, only *her* feelings were at risk. Telling herself she could handle the emotional danger if she focussed on the sex. Telling herself she'd deal with any fallout when he was gone, just as she'd always relied on herself.

'I was sitting here, staring at the door, willing you to change your mind.' He kissed her again, stripping off her jumper and jeans before scooping her from the floor and carrying her into the bedroom with her legs wrapped around his waist. 'I'm so glad you did.'

He tumbled them onto the bed, his hips, the hard jut of his erection, between her legs, where she wanted him. But there were still too many layers between them and not enough skin-to-skin contact.

'Conrad,' she moaned, caressing his erection through his jeans as she pushed her tongue into his mouth. When he stood to remove his clothing and reached for the bedside drawer and the stash of condoms he kept there, she shimmied off her underwear.

'Will it stop?' she asked as he joined her on the bed, pressing kisses all over her body. 'This burning need? Tell me it will stop when you go,' she begged, needing to hear that she'd go back to normal, even if it was a lie.

He looked up, confusion and lust slashed across his handsome face. 'I don't know. I hope so. For both our sakes.' Then he buried his face between her legs, kissing her deeply with a tortured groan.

Because his touch, this wild passion, were the only things that could block out the loud ticking of the clock in her head, Zara lost herself to the oblivion of pleasure. While she was focussed on the way he made her body come alive, she didn't have to think about how, but for the fact he wasn't the right man to risk her heart with, she could so easily fall for him. She'd let him close, closer than anyone else, ever, and one day soon, she had to pay the price for that recklessness. But not yet. For a few more days she could hold off the inevitable sadness that would come when he left.

When he reared back, covered himself with the condom and pushed inside her, she clung to him, all but wrecked by the force of their uncontrollable need for each other. But this had always been too good, intense, a thrilling and passionate risk. 'Yes,' she cried as he gripped her hand and moved his hips, slow and deep.

'I can't stop wanting you,' he said, his face a mask of dark desire as he raised her thigh over his hip so he sank deeper, his body scorching her every place they connected. 'I can't stop counting the days.'

'Don't,' she said, shaking her head. 'Let's just enjoy every second, no regrets.' This had started with sex. Only fitting that they should keep it about sex, until the very end.

She'd had a minor wobble there for a few days, allowed her imagination to run wild with impossible what ifs, but her head was back on straight now.

'Zara,' he groaned as their bodies moved in unison, his thrusts pushing her higher and higher towards the release she'd come for. As the rhythm of their bodies built to a crescendo, Zara focussed on the pleasure, her orgasm ripping through her in powerful waves until all she could do was hold him as he crushed her in his arms, burying his face against the side of her neck, groaning.

When his body stilled, Zara closed her eyes and breathed him in, trying to memorise his unique scent, already certain she was falling for Conrad Reed. But that was okay. She'd come to terms with it, compartmentalised it the way she'd done for so many other parts of her life since becoming a mother. When you had a child you needed to put first, your own feelings didn't really matter.

Conrad raised his face from the crook of her neck, his eyes stormy. 'Part of me wishes I could stay,' he whispered, kissing the palm of her hand, and Zara's heart clenched.

She nodded and pushed his hair back from his face. 'Part of me wishes you didn't have to go. But we always knew it was temporary. I'll never forget my wild sexual adventure with you.'

Witnessing the doubt her words caused, she shifted under his weight. Their wishes made sense. Their relationship had always been intense, even when it was just fun. But wishes weren't reality, and when she was finally ready to fully open up her heart to a real adult relationship, she needed to be a hundred per cent certain it was with the right man, preferably one who lived in the same country. She wouldn't risk confusing Zach, nor would she expose her sweet little boy to any more rejection.

He rolled to the side and released her. Zara stood and hunted around for her scattered clothes.

'You don't want to stay?' he asked, his voice uncertain, so she winced with guilt. If only she'd possessed the stamina to resist him tonight, to start weaning herself off instead of selfishly taking every kiss and touch she could get.

'Just because I couldn't fight the temptation to be with you, I'm still tired.' Zara swallowed down the almost overwhelming urge to climb back into his warm bed and hold him all night long. 'I'll sleep better in my own bed.'

She pulled on her clothes, pressed one last kiss to his lips and hurried out into the bitterly cold night, where, finally, she was able to draw a deep breath. Only as hard as she tried to forget it, the look of confusion, doubt and hurt on his face as she'd left kept her awake for half of the night.

CHAPTER SIXTEEN

ON CONRAD'S FINAL day at Abbey Hill Hospital, Zara sat in the break room just outside the delivery suite with Sharon, feeling as if her world were about to implode. Zach had been sick all weekend with a cold, so she'd had to swap shifts with Bella. Since working three night shifts in a row, she hadn't seen Conrad since last Friday, when they'd made love as if preparing for the end of the world and then she'd fled. But with every day that passed where they didn't see each other, she felt a sick kind of triumph, as if she was already winning the battle of missing him, even before he'd left the country.

She picked at her salad, her head all over the place and her appetite non-existent. Now that the day of Conrad's departure was nearly upon them, Zara had a more pressing dilemma than fearing she might not get over the most intense relationship of her life—her late period.

'Two across,' Sharon said, breaking into Zara's reverie. 'A sudden attack. Four letters. Starts with an R.' Sharon was focussed on the crossword puzzle at the back of one of the magazines lying around the break room, as if this were just any other day. Of course, Sharon wasn't aware that Zara had slept with the sexy Australian locum, that she'd embarked on a foolish fling with him and developed deep feelings for him. That she might, if fate were cruel enough to throw not one, but two unplanned pregnancies her way, be having his baby.

'Raid,' Zara said absently, grateful to have something else to think about other than the fear burning a hole in her chest. She and Conrad had always used condoms, but they'd also had a lot of sex.

Sensing something was off with her friend, Sharon looked up from the magazine crossword. 'What's wrong? You've been off all morning.'

'I'm just tired,' Zara tried to bluff. But one look at Sharon's serious expression told her there was no point in trying to hide her concerns from the other woman. They were probably written all over Zara's face.

'I realised this morning that my period is a couple of days late, that's all,' she said with a sigh. Just saying the words sent her mind into a panic. What if she was pregnant? Would she have to raise this baby alone, too? She and Conrad weren't a couple. He was leaving tomorrow. And Australia was even further away than Spain…

But surely history wouldn't repeat itself…? Surely she couldn't have made another mistake? She swallowed, feeling queasy. How could she have been so reckless again? Yes, she'd practised safe sex and taken every possible precaution, but she should have known better than to take risks with a man who came from the other side of the world. A man who was emotionally unavailable because, like her, he was scared to rush into another relationship. A man she'd always known she couldn't have.

Sharon frowned, obviously concerned. 'Have you taken a pregnancy test?'

'I've been busy today, delivering other people's babies,' she said lamely, shaking her head and pushing away her lunch.

Part of her had wanted to stay happily in denial, hoping that if she left it long enough, her period would start and there'd be no need to wait for those pink lines to appear. No need to tell Conrad of the possibility. No need to know that it wouldn't make any difference to their readiness for a relationship. Just the possibility of a pregnancy had reopened feelings from the past—shame at her own stupidity, guilt that she might be about to mess Zach's life up even more, a resurgence of Lorenzo's cruel rejection—feelings she'd thought she'd conquered, but obviously hadn't.

'Busy having sex, by the sounds of it,' Sharon said. At Zara's sharp look, her friend turned sympathetic. 'Is your mystery man our sexy Australian locum by any chance?'

Zara gaped, her jaw slack as she ducked her head away from Sharon's expression of pity. 'How did you figure that out?'

'I have eyes,' Sharon said, closing the magazine. 'Perhaps you're too close to see it, but he looks at you with this kind of feral hunger. He seems devastated when you're not on the ward and smiles more when you're around. It's kind of obvious. We've all noticed.'

Zara blinked away the sting in her eyes, feeling stupid and naive. Could everyone she worked with also see how close she'd come to falling hard for Conrad? And now she might be having his baby…

'Yes, well, so much for "getting back out there" and "having a good time".' She threw two of Sharon's favourite arguments for why Zara should date back at her. 'Now look where I've ended up.'

Sharon tilted her head in sympathy. 'It might be negative. You won't know until you take the test.'

Zara nodded, feeling sick and imagining it was down to morning sickness. Of course, her practical friend was right. 'I'll grab one from the hospital pharmacy on my way home. Take it tonight,' Zara said, glancing at the clock, her stomach twisting as she packed away her uneaten lunch. Their break time was over.

'What if it is positive?' Sharon cautiously asked. 'I'm guessing he's still planning to leave tomorrow?'

'Of course he is. It was nothing serious. Just a sexual fling, the kind you've been telling me to have for the past six years.' Time to put to bed any naive notion that she and Conrad could possibly have a future. She had Zach to think about. Conrad had his own life to lead, grieving to do, his nephew to support.

'Unless it *is* positive,' Sharon pushed, 'which might change things...'

'It won't.' Zara shook her head, cutting Sharon off. She refused to think of that possibility. 'I'm almost certain it will be negative, and even if we wanted a relationship, which neither of us does, because we've both got trust issues, we're from different continents. We both have jobs and lives and commitments. Real life doesn't always work out.'

She swallowed, aware of the sickening similarities between her holiday fling with Lorenzo and her fling with Conrad. She'd known going into both that neither of them would last.

'Then I'll say no more.' Sharon stood, picked up her bag and eyed Zara with compassion that set Zara's teeth on edge. 'But please text me when you know the result of the test or I'll worry, too.'

'I will. And please don't tell anyone else about me and Conrad. I forced him to keep it a secret, because it was nothing serious and always temporary. I didn't want you lot teasing me, and I knew I'd never hear the last of it, having put off dating for so long.' She couldn't bring herself to say the word sex now, not when what she and Conrad had been doing felt bigger than just sex. It felt like a relationship. A *real* relationship. But of course, it wasn't.

'Of course I won't,' Sharon said, looking worried.

'And please don't look at me like that,' Zara pleaded. 'Everything is going to be fine. The test will be negative. Conrad will leave tomorrow. And life will go back to normal around here.'

As they left the break room together and headed back to the delivery ward, Zara wondered how many times she'd have to repeat the last point until she believed it.

Later that afternoon, Conrad had just finished discharging some patients with Max, when an alarm sounded outside the delivery ward. He took off running, aware of footsteps behind him. At the lifts, a flashing light told him some sort of emergency was occurring inside. He skidded to a halt, glancing around, relieved to see that Sharon and Zara were there too.

But there was no time to talk. A second later, the lift doors opened. A couple in their twenties were inside, the man supporting his heavily pregnant partner from behind. The woman clearly in second-stage labour.

'The baby's coming. Now!' she cried in a state of panic.

'I can't walk any further.' With that, a contraction took hold and she bared down, her weight supported by her partner.

'We'll get supplies,' Sharon said, grabbing Max and running back to the delivery ward.

Conrad pulled some gloves from the pocket of his scrubs, passing Zara a pair before pulling on his own. Together, they crouched side by side in front of the woman, blocking the lift doors from closing.

'What's your name?' Zara asked.

'Jessica,' the woman panted, moaning as another contraction began.

'We can't move her.' Zara shot Conrad a look.

'I agree,' he said as Sharon and Max returned with medical supplies and extra pairs of hands. Sharon unfolded a mobile privacy screen across the opening of the lift behind Zara and Conrad, blocking the view of anyone who happened to walk past.

With the screen in place, Conrad raised the woman's dress to her waist and Zara removed her underwear and quickly examined her. 'I can feel the head,' Zara said, meeting Conrad's stare. 'She's fully dilated.'

He nodded, grateful that she was there. Her calm manner was exactly what they needed, because, whether they liked it or not, they'd be delivering this baby in the lift, any second now.

'Jessica, you need to listen to us,' Zara said, fitting the cardiotocography or CTG sensors around Jessica's abdomen to pick up the baby's heart rate. 'When we tell you to stop pushing, we need you to pant, okay?'

The woman nodded, her eyes wild with fear and pain. Conrad laid the towels and a sheet that Sharon passed to him on the floor of the lift. Jessica's moan heralded the start of the next contraction. While she pushed, crouched in front of and supported by her partner, Conrad and Zara held their hands out at the ready to catch the baby if things happened quickly.

'Okay, pant now, Jessica,' Zara instructed the patient as the baby's head emerged.

Conrad quickly loosened the umbilical cord from around the baby's neck, while Sharon passed in more clean towels. Zara had just managed to spread them over her lap, when the rest of the baby was delivered into Zara and Conrad's waiting hands.

'It's a girl, Jessica,' Conrad said with a smile of relief, noting the baby's Apgar score. He and Zara held onto the newborn who'd been so eager to arrive, smiling at each other, laughing now the adrenaline rush was over.

While the parents laughed and cried and peered in wonder at their daughter, Zara cleaned up the baby with a towel and then handed her over. Conrad injected Jessica's thigh with syntocinon to help the uterus contract down to deliver the placenta and then he clamped and cut the umbilical cord.

'We're going to move you to a delivery suite now, Jessica,' Conrad said as Sharon wheeled in a wheelchair. 'So you can deliver the placenta.'

He glanced at Zara, hoping to see the same euphoria he felt in her eyes. That they'd delivered this baby together, practically hand in hand, made him feel closer to her than ever. But to his utter alarm, she looked close to tears. She wouldn't look at him. What was going on?

In a flurry of activity, Jessica was helped into the wheelchair by Zara and her husband, while Sharon and Max collected up the equipment.

'Do you want me to help with third stage?' Conrad asked Zara, reluctant to just walk away after such an emotionally fraught delivery. He wanted to wrap his arms around Zara and kiss away her frown.

'I've got it,' she said, barely looking his way. But perhaps she was simply focussed on the patient, on completion of the third stage of labour and performing the baby's neonatal checks after such an unorthodox delivery.

As Zara whisked Jessica and her newborn to a nearby delivery suite, ward orderlies started the clean-up, wheeling in a laundry bin and removing the screens. A hospital security guard appeared to lock the lift doors open while the cleaning was carried out. Concerned about Zara, Conrad wheeled the portable oxygen cylinder they fortunately hadn't needed and followed Sharon onto the ward and into the utility room.

'Well, that was a first,' Sharon said with a chuckle, disposing of the used syringe in the sharps bin.

Conrad nodded, parking the oxygen cylinder against the wall. 'Is Zara okay? She seemed…upset.' He knew the two women were close. Perhaps Zara had confided in Sharon about him leaving tomorrow.

Sharon ducked her head guiltily as she busied herself with the clear-up, and Conrad immediately knew that she knew about their fling.

'She'll be fine…' Sharon said, busying herself and not looking at him. 'Births can be an emotional experience, as you know, and she's probably just distracted. I told her to get a pregnancy test as soon as possible, that way she'll know for certain, although—' She broke off, finally realising that she'd maybe said too much.

Conrad froze, his blood chilling. Zara was pregnant?

Sharon turned to face him, clearly horrified that she'd let it slip. 'You didn't know, did you?' she said, her hand covering her mouth. 'I'm so sorry. I just assumed... It just slipped out. She's not certain,' she rushed on. 'In fact she's adamant it will be negative. She's going to buy a test on the way home... Perhaps she didn't want to tell you until she knew for sure.'

Conrad's stomach rolled. Not only did Sharon seem to know all about him and Zara and their fling, Zara had also confided in her friend that she might be pregnant. And yet she hadn't confided in *him*? Not even when he was the father. She obviously didn't trust him.

Sharon sagged in defeat, resting her back against the edge of the sink. 'What will you do?'

Conrad scrubbed a hand over his face, his mind racing with possibilities. 'Talk to her, of course. Make sure she's okay. I had no idea.' He'd always wanted a family of his own with the right woman, someone he loved, who loved him back and wanted him in her life...

Sharon nodded. 'I think that's a good plan. The two of you obviously have some stuff to sort out.'

Just then, Max poked his head into the room. 'There's a woman with an ectopic pregnancy in A & E.'

Conrad nodded and moved towards the door on autopilot, glancing back at Sharon. 'I have to go. Clearly it's going to be one of those crazy days.'

Sharon tilted her head, concern in her eyes. 'Want me to pass on a message to Zara?'

Conrad shook his head, feeling sick. The waiting emergency meant he had no time to think and no idea what he wanted to say to Zara anyway. 'Thanks, but I'll catch her later.'

Shelving his sense of betrayal that Zara had gone behind his back to her friend before coming to him, he hurried down the stairs to A & E with Max.

CHAPTER SEVENTEEN

THAT NIGHT, AFTER an evening spent operating on the ectopic pregnancy case, Conrad took his usual seat on Zara's sofa, his chest hollowed out with a sad sense of inevitability. So many times this past month he'd sat in this very seat, laughing with this woman, talking to her, kissing. He'd poured his heart out, told her about his brother, his grief, his shameful feelings of betrayal. Now he wasn't sure that he'd really known her at all. Because the pain he'd felt earlier at the hospital when he'd realised she'd kept a secret and gone behind his back to her friend had burned him alive. It was as if he'd never meant anything to her.

'Sharon said she'd let slip that my period was late,' Zara said, taking the seat beside him. 'I told you there was no privacy at work.'

'Is that all you care about? Secrets?' he asked, because, as far as he was concerned, an unplanned pregnancy with this woman wouldn't have been the worst thing in the world. He cared about her and her son. He trusted her. He'd assumed she'd trusted him. That they were moving in the right direction. That, but for his departure to Australia, they'd both want to continue their relationship. Before he'd found out that there might be a baby, he'd even been plotting ways he could return to the UK so he could see her again and take what had started as something casual and fun as the foundation for a real relationship.

But now, he was almost scared to find out how she felt. For some reason, maybe because he was reminded of the last time he'd cared about a woman and she too had gone behind his back, it felt that Zara was about to break up with him. But there was no need. They'd never been an item.

'Of course not,' she said, her frown turning to an encouraging smile. 'But it's okay. I'm *not* pregnant.' Her face lit up. 'I took a test when I got home from work this afternoon and it's negative.'

He met her stare, seeing nothing but relief and that distance she'd worn for the past week, whereas Conrad felt crushed. His heart, which had been pounding, plummeted to his boots. He hadn't properly had time to think about how he felt about Sharon's revelation, but with Zara's confirmation that there was no baby, all he felt was desolate disappointment.

'That's a relief,' he mumbled automatically, picking up on Zara's feelings on the matter. No point missing something that had never been. And now he knew exactly how out of sync his feelings were with Zara's.

'Yes.' She looked down at her hands in her lap. 'So you can leave tomorrow with your mind at rest. There's no reason to feel obligated or to stay in touch.'

She was practically pushing him out of the door. Obviously Zara's feelings for him were nowhere near as strong as his for her. He'd moved too fast again. Judged it wrong. Poured out his heart to a woman who could never need or want him because she still wasn't ready to let him, or any other man, close.

'I'm sorry that you had to find out from Sharon,' she

said, meeting his stare. 'I didn't intend to tell her, but she knows me so well. She knew I was worried about something.'

'You could have told *me*,' he said, hating that, for a few hours, he might have hypothetically fathered a child and been the last to know, just as he'd been the last to know when his brother had fallen for his ex. 'Especially when you knew that the last woman I cared about also went behind my back.'

'You're right,' she admitted, looking shamefaced. 'I'm sorry. But after Zach being sick all weekend and after my night shifts, I only noticed the date this morning. I didn't want to text you and there was no point worrying you if I wasn't pregnant, which as it turned out was the right call, because I'm not.' She smiled brightly then, and he shrank inside a little more.

'And more importantly, you don't need me or my emotional support, right? You never have, not when you can go it alone, same as always.'

She was so terrified of trusting the wrong guy, and she clearly didn't trust *him*. Whereas he'd been looking for more locum work nearby, taking Sharon's advice and wondering if there'd soon be a consultant job available in Derby and wondering how quickly he could return to the UK.

'That's not fair,' she said with a frown. 'I didn't set out to tell Sharon first, but she *is* my friend. And I didn't tell her that we've been having sex. She'd already figured it out by herself.'

Conrad nodded, glancing away, his doubts so acute, he wondered if he was once more overreacting. It wouldn't surprise him. His feelings were out of control, after all.

One minute he was convinced he had to leave as planned, the next he was plotting ways to stay.

'So that's all I am to you still? Just sex?' he asked, the panicked thudding of his heart intensifying. He and Zara could only work if they were on the same wavelength. For over a week, he'd tentatively tried and failed to draw out her feelings.

She blinked, opened her mouth to answer but no words emerged.

'I'm leaving tomorrow,' he pushed, needing to hear her declare herself before he walked away. 'I've been trying to give you space and not put pressure on the situation, because I've done that before and it didn't work out well for me. But I can't leave without at least raising the possibility of a relationship between us.'

She frowned, her eyes darting away and he had his answer. 'I'm not sure what you expect me to say to that, Conrad.' She dragged in a shaky breath. 'That I don't want you to leave tomorrow? That I *have* thought about us trying to have a real relationship?'

'Have you?' he asked, his chest tight. 'You haven't brought it up. Perhaps you were just going to wave goodbye without a backward glance.' Whereas he'd never felt more torn in two, even before the pregnancy scare.

'Of course I've thought about it, and I can't see how it could work,' she whispered, her stare imploring so he wanted to hold her. 'You live in Australia. Your family is there. James. And mine is here. With Zach to consider, I'm not free to just think about myself and my own wants.'

He knew all of that, but, for him, those reasons weren't permanent obstacles. Unless it wasn't that she didn't want a relationship, she just didn't want *him*.

'You're still not over the last serious relationship you had,' she said, 'otherwise you'd have no doubts about what you want. You'd be able to forgive your brother and move on. But you're stuck, Conrad, and the worst part is that I can understand why, and I don't blame you.' She sagged, as if exhausted.

He'd nodded along as she'd spoken, unable to argue with a single word. He *did* have doubts, because he'd felt Zara slipping away. He *was* stuck, but he'd started to feel that he could move on. For Conrad, the many obstacles she'd just articulated perfectly had seemed, for a moment, surmountable. But only if they felt the same way about each other, which obviously wasn't the case.

'When I want something serious,' she went on, 'I need a man who is sure about me *and* about Zach. Even if you lived here, even if you'd worked through your betrayal and grief, that would still be a big commitment. This, us, began as nothing serious. Trying to turn it into something else just feels…too hard.' She looked up, her eyes shining with emotions but her chin raised resolutely. She'd made up her mind.

'I understand,' he said, his insides hollow. 'I've been trying to change the rules, I know that.' Because she'd changed *him*. She'd made him see that he could let go of the past. 'I just hoped you might want more than a good time.'

'I'm not sure what I want in terms of a relationship,' she went on, reaching for him and then thinking better of it, her hand falling to her lap. 'But I know I can't afford to make another mistake like last time. I have to put Zach first.'

'So I would be a mistake?' She put him in the same category as Zach's father. She didn't want him. Couldn't trust him. Wasn't willing to take a risk for him.

She shook her head violently. 'No, of course not. I don't

know. This is the first time I've had to think about relationships since I became a mother. I'm just trying to do the right thing, for me and Zach, because I don't want either of us to be hurt.' She shook her head in defeat.

'It's okay, Zara. Maybe you're right—it *is* too hard. I'm leaving and I'm not making you any promises. I don't have all the answers. I just knew how I felt—that I'd do almost anything to try and make us work. But now there's no baby, I guess we don't have to worry about it.'

He stood, needing to get away. How could he have been so wrong about her? Yes, they both still struggled with trust, but while he'd been thinking of moving his entire life to be with her and Zach, to build a relationship with her, she'd been preparing to walk away, to push him away and keep her feelings safe.

'I'm sorry,' she said, sadly, looking up at him.

'So am I.' Conrad nodded, his stomach in knots. He wanted to throw out a glib comment like, *If you ever make it to Australia, give me a call*. But he'd never felt less like smiling.

'Take care, Zara,' he said instead. 'Of Zach and yourself.' And then he left.

CHAPTER EIGHTEEN

THE NEXT DAY, with her heart torn to shreds, Zara walked past the doctor's office on the postnatal ward and automatically glanced inside. Of course, there was no chance now of a clandestine glimpse of Conrad, just as there was no point hugging her secret close as she'd done every other day of their fling. It was over. He was gone. By the time she arrived home from her early shift, his flat would be empty and he'd be on the train to London for his evening flight to Brisbane. And it was for the best.

Seeing again his relieved expression when she'd confirmed there was no baby, Zara swallowed down the vicious pang of longing in her chest and shuffled towards the nurses' station. What had she expected? That he'd want to make a family with her and Zach? That he would move his entire life to be with them?

Their final conversation spun sickeningly in her mind. How had it gone so wrong at the end? And why, when it was always meant to be temporary, when he'd always planned to return to Australia, did she feel guilty and scared that she'd made a horrible mistake in refusing to talk about a future?

'Where's the new registrar?' Sharon said in an impatient voice as she shuffled items on the desk and then located a pen. 'I need them to prescribe some painkillers for the woman in bed ten.'

Zara shrugged, making some non-committal noise as she wiped two patient names from the whiteboard behind the desk. What did she care for the new registrar? The only thing that mattered was that the new doctor wouldn't be Conrad. She swallowed convulsively, her eyes stinging.

'What are you doing?' Sharon asked, snapping Zara's attention back to the present.

Zara looked up to see that she'd wiped the whiteboard clean of every name. Defeated and close to breaking down, she replaced the whiteboard eraser, her shoulders slumping. 'I'll write the names back up,' she muttered.

'I don't care about the names,' Sharon said, taking Zara's elbow and ushering her inside the vacant nurses' office, clearly sensing something was very wrong. 'What's going on with you today?' Sharon demanded, closing the door. 'Is it Zach?'

Mention of her son made things worse. Because she'd not only let Conrad down, let herself down because she was scared to admit the depth of her feelings, she'd also taken something from Zach. Her son didn't need a mother who moped around, living a half-life. And now that Conrad was gone, she saw so clearly how her fling with him had brought her back to life. But if she tried to explain the entire situation to her friend, she'd definitely break down, the well of emotion rising in her throat almost overwhelming.

'No, Zach is fine.' Zara shook her head, trying to reassure her friend that it was nothing serious. 'I just got distracted,' Zara said feebly.

'I'm not talking about the whiteboard.' Sharon fisted her hands on her hips. 'You look close to tears. I've never seen you cry.' Sharon urged Zara into a seat, taking the one opposite. 'It's Conrad, isn't it? You weren't just having sex—

you've fallen in love with him, haven't you? And now he's going back to Australia.'

Zara spluttered, mortified. 'No! Don't be silly.' Although she'd come pretty close to falling. Why else would she feel so...bereft now that he'd left?

'Are you sure?' Sharon pressed, her expression somehow both stern and sympathetic. 'Because you've been walking around like a zombie all morning and the only change is that he's flying back to Australia later this evening.'

Feeling weak with hypoglycaemia—she had zero appetite—Zara collapsed back into the chair. 'I told you: it was just sex, but obviously it's over now. I'll be fine. I'll get over it. I'm just...adjusting, that's all.'

But now that the 'L' word was out there, she couldn't ignore it. Could Sharon be right? Had she actually fallen deeply in love with Conrad? Could that explain the frantic panic making her desperate to rewind time and handle their final conversation differently? How stupid would she be if it were true? She wasn't having his baby, but Australia was even further away than Spain, and even if she was in love with him, Conrad could never love her back, could he...?

'How did he take the news about the test being negative?' Sharon asked, her voice cautious.

Zara shrugged. 'Fine, obviously. He was relieved.'

'Was he?' Sharon frowned. 'Are you sure?'

Zara looked up sharply. 'Of course he was. We were never in a relationship and he lives in Australia. Why? What do you know...?' Fear snaked down her spine.

'Nothing,' Sharon said, her expression serious. 'It's just that yesterday when I mentioned you were going to take a test, I thought he looked...excited for a second. But maybe I was wrong.'

Zara dropped her face into her hands, her mind reeling. She'd been so caught up in her own emotions—panic that she'd made another mistake, guilt that she'd told Sharon and hurt Conrad, fear that he'd reject her, just like Lorenzo, and she'd be devastated—that she'd taken Conrad's relief at face value. She'd told him a relationship with him would be too hard and as good as shoved him onto the plane.

But what if Sharon was right? What if he'd been trying to say he wanted a relationship and she'd finally and definitively pushed him away out of fear?

Closing her eyes, she saw his face as it had been last night, his expression flat with disappointment, his stare hollow with betrayal, because she'd not only let him down, she'd also clung to the safety of her independence and kept him out emotionally. How could she have been such a coward? He'd wanted to talk about the possibility of a relationship and she'd refused, dismissed him and the idea, let him believe she didn't want him enough, when, in truth, if Conrad wanted a real relationship with her, she'd move her and Zach to the ends of the earth for him.

With a sudden gasp, she looked up. It hit her like a blow. Sharon was right. She'd fallen in love with Conrad and she'd run scared from him and from her feelings. Why, in the cold light of day, with Conrad gone, did it now seem so obvious?

Seeing the moment of realisation on Zara's face, Sharon nodded and placed her hand on Zara's knee. 'What happened after you told him about the negative test?' she asked, her voice tinged with sickening sympathy that turned Zara's veins to ice.

'I told him I was scared to make another mistake. And then to make certain I'd killed it stone dead, when he wanted to talk about the possibility of a relationship between us, I pointed out that it was too hard and pushed him away.' She hung her head in shame.

Sharon said nothing, which was somehow worse than a stern lecture or an *I told you so*.

'Oh, no…' Zara moaned, feeling sick. 'I was so terrified of making a mistake again that I've actually gone and made the biggest one of my life, haven't I?' She looked up and lasered her friend with a stare, as if demanding a denial would fix it.

But just as they had with Lorenzo, her actions had consequences. Only this time, with Conrad, those consequences were more devastating. She was in love with a wonderful man she'd sent away without telling him of her feelings.

His words from the night before returned to haunt her.

I just knew how I felt—that I'd do almost anything to try and make us work.

He'd obviously been trying to tell her he wanted more. What if he *was* ready to have a serious relationship again and wanted one with her but she'd pushed him away because she'd still been scared to risk her heart? He wouldn't likely declare his feelings and move his whole life to England on the off chance that she might one day wake up and want to date him for real. Could he forgive her? Could he possibly love her back one day? Because now that she was thinking about it, she was pretty certain that was what she felt for Conrad. That over the past few weeks, despite every barrier she'd put up against it, she had fallen in love with him.

Sharon pressed her lips together in a stubborn line. 'Could you back up a bit? Call him and tell him you want to try and do long distance, maybe tell him how you feel about him? Maybe you could visit him in Australia and see how it goes?'

Zara shook her head. Would Conrad want to hear it? 'I think it's too late,' she said, tears threatening. She'd hurt Conrad because she was scared to hope for a real relationship. She'd convinced herself she just wanted sex, nothing serious, but Conrad had been right: she'd spent years punishing herself for the mistake of Lorenzo and denying herself romance and sex and love. And she'd found all of those things with Conrad.

'Even if he wasn't leaving tonight,' she went on, 'neither of us has been in a serious relationship for years. What if he won't give me a second chance?' Conrad had so much to work through—forgiving Marcus, reuniting with James and reconciling with Tessa, looking for a consultant job. But now that she'd woken up to the fact that she was in love with him, that serious relationship she'd put off for so long while she punished herself and lived in fear was suddenly the *only* thing she wanted.

'That sounds like the old Zara talking,' Sharon said softly. 'The one who seemed to be going through the motions of her life, not needing anyone else. The one whose smile was rare. If I'm honest, that Zara was a bit uptight.' Sharon smiled apologetically and reached for Zara's hand. 'You've come alive this past month.'

Zara nodded, her smile wobbling and her eyes smarting with tears. 'I know. It's him.'

'It's the two of you together,' Sharon stated. 'You complement each other. That's when the magic happens, when sex and connection turn into love.'

Zara sniffed, trying to pull herself together. They were at work, after all. And just because she loved him, didn't mean he had the same feelings for her. Could he want her and Zach? Because they came as a pair. She needed to apologise for running scared and find out.

Suddenly energised, Zara stood. 'I'll call him when my shift ends. Before he gets on that plane.' She glanced at the watch pinned to her uniform for the time. She could tell him how stupid she'd been. Confess that she had feelings for him and ask if there was any way they could make a real, serious relationship work. No more secrets. Should she also tell him she was in love with him? Or would he think that was too much, too soon?

'There's the Zara I've wanted to see all these years,' Sharon said with a smile of encouragement. 'We're quiet today and overstaffed. Why don't you finish up early? Call him now? I'll cover you.'

'Really?' Zara asked, her eyes filling with tears.

'Of course,' Sharon said. 'I've been rooting for you to find someone for years. Don't keep me hanging. Go.'

'Thanks. I'll let you know how it goes.' Throwing her arms around Sharon, Zara rushed to the doctor's office, where she'd left her bag, coat and phone.

CHAPTER NINETEEN

FROM THE DERBY to London train, Conrad opened his emails in an attempt to forget about the devastating final conversation he'd had with Zara. Last night, after leaving Zara's place, he'd messaged his parents to tell them he'd be leaving as planned and would see them soon. Until that very moment, he'd agonised over the decision of whether to leave or stay. But what was the point in delaying his departure from the UK when Zara had made it clear that she'd had her fun and that their fling was over?

Hollowness built inside him at the memories of their fight. Not that they'd raised their voices. It had been more of a quiet acceptance that they'd finally arrived at the end of their journey. Only for him, it hadn't been over. Before they'd become distracted by the possibility of a pregnancy and by Zara's explanations about Sharon, he'd wanted to force Zara's hand. To confront her with the idea of them seeing each other again, either in England, or Australia.

But he'd soon realised there'd been no sense pushing it; she didn't want *him*. She was scared to risk her heart, scared to make a mistake, scared to expose Zach to a man who might not stick around. And Conrad couldn't blame her. It wasn't as if he even lived in the UK. Not only did Zara have to think about Zach, just as Conrad needed to look out for James, but their situation was also complicated by a whole world of distance.

With a sigh of inevitability, and to distract himself from the pain gnawing a hole in his chest, Conrad opened the email reply from his mother. He scanned the message, reaching the last paragraph.

In other news, Tessa called. It seems she's turned a bit of a corner and is feeling up to being more social. She brought James to visit yesterday, asked about your travels and then asked if Dad and I can help out with school pickups when she goes back to work...

Conrad tried to focus on the words his mother had written, but the news didn't fill him with the relief he'd imagined. He was happy for his parents, for Tessa, for James. Families needed to pull together, especially in times of grief. But as something shifted from Conrad's shoulders, a weight he hadn't known he'd carried easing, he realised with a start that the mess he'd run away from wasn't his responsibility. Maybe because ever since the night he'd told Zara about Marcus's betrayal, he'd also started talking to his brother in his head. He'd taken Zara's advice and begun to properly work through forgiving Marcus. He still had much grieving to do, of course. But that was no reason for him to be alone, to pass by a relationship with an amazing woman who'd brought *him* back to life.

Zara had been right—he *had* been stuck and hiding from his feelings. She'd helped him to see that he was still clinging to that sense of betrayal, because he was scared to let anyone close again or to fall in love. Scared that he'd lose another person he cared about or be betrayed or rejected.

Only he hadn't been able to keep Zara out. She'd found a way under his guard anyway.

But at the first sign of trouble, he'd run again. He'd allowed her to push him away when he'd wanted to fight for them, to tell her his feelings and how he wanted a serious relationship. How he wanted her *and* Zach.

Sending a hurried reply to his mother, Conrad fought his rising sense of panic. Life was too short for regrets. He might have said that a hundred times, but it was only with Zara that he'd truly believed it. He saw now, with crystal clarity, that he'd been going through the motions before he'd met Zara. He'd called her out on hiding behind the mistake she'd made, on punishing herself, when he'd been hiding too. For all his talk of embracing the good times, the best times he'd had in years had been with Zara. Only a complete idiot would walk away from that before making sure there was no way in hell he could make it work.

Zara's reproach resounded in his head, as if she were in the train carriage with him, hurtling towards London.

I'm not sure what you expect me to say to that, Conrad. That I don't want you to leave...? That I have *thought about us trying to have a real relationship?*

Did that mean that if he lived in England, or if she lived in Australia, she'd want a serious relationship with him? Didn't he owe it to himself, to them both, to find out? Now!

Fresh panic seized him by the throat. He couldn't leave England like this, sloping off with his tail between his legs, scared to tell her that he wanted more than a fling. Scared to know if she wanted the same. He wasn't ready to give up on them just because they had commitments and lived in different countries. There must be a way to make something so good work. He'd move heaven and earth to enable them to be together if that was what she wanted. But first, he had to tell her what *he* wanted.

With his mind working properly for the first time in what felt like days, he typed a few extra lines to his mother.

Change of plan this end. Might not make flight today after all. Will keep you posted.

He pressed send, jerked to his feet and grabbed his bag. Then, manhandling his suitcase from the luggage rack, he positioned himself in the exit, so when the train stopped at the next station, he could get off and swap platforms.

His heart galloped with yearning and possibility. It wasn't over, not when he'd neglected to tell her that his feelings for her were no longer casual or *nothing serious*. And he needed to do that in person. Zara was at work. She wouldn't answer her phone if he called. There was only one way to make her understand how he felt about her and that was to head back to Derby.

CHAPTER TWENTY

WITH HER HEART THUNDERING, Zara ducked into the doctor's office on the postnatal ward and fished her phone out of her bag. With trembling fingers, she held her breath as the phone powered on, willing time to stand still or go backwards so she could make this right. What if he couldn't wait to get back to the Sunshine Coast, where he would easily forget about her and their brief fling? What if he got on the plane before she could tell him she was sorry and that she loved him? What if she missed her chance to be happy because she'd made the massive mistake of pushing him away?

With her veins full of icy panic, the screen of her phone lit up. She was just about to unlock it and dial Conrad, when several alert sounds came in, one after another.

Ping, ping, ping.

She opened the most recent text, elated to see it was from Conrad.

Phone low on charge. Can't call again but we need to talk.

Zara sagged with relief. He wanted to talk. That sounded promising. Seeing she also had three voicemails from him, she grabbed her coat and bag and put the phone to her ear so she could listen to the message as she walked to the car.

Hopefully Conrad would have recharged his phone somewhere by the time she called him back.

She'd just stepped from the office, his voicemail playing in her ear—'Zara, we need to talk...'—when she looked up to find Conrad striding down the ward towards her pulling his suitcase.

Dropping the phone to her side, she gaped at the wonderful sight of him in person. 'What are you doing here?' she said, her throat raw with longing, her mind foggy with confusion. 'Did you miss your flight?'

He shook his head, dropped his bags to the floor and cupped her face between both his palms. Then his lips covered hers and he dragged her into his arms.

Zara dropped everything, including her phone, which clattered to the floor with its voicemail from Conrad still playing. She tunnelled her fingers into his hair and parted her lips, kissing him back with everything she had, as if it were her last chance ever. She was too high to care that the other midwives might see, not to mention the patients. He was here. He wanted to talk. He was kissing her. Nothing else mattered.

She clung to him, yelping in protest when he tore his mouth from hers. 'I need to talk to you,' he said, panting hard, his stare flicking wildly between her eyes.

She nodded, dragging him into the doctor's office and closing the door, her hand in his. 'Conrad, I'm so sorry about last night,' she said, launching into her apology. 'Are you okay? What happened?' She swept her gaze over him, still doubting he was real.

Conrad shook his head. 'I'm fine. I got off the train. I came back to tell you I've figured everything out,' he said, gripping her hand as if he'd never let her go. 'I'm in love with you, Zara.'

Zara frowned, her heart clenching with wild longing. His words made no sense. Had she heard him right? He loved her?

'I realised it on the platform in Kettering,' he went on, scrubbing a hand through his hair. 'Wherever the hell that is.'

Despite the confusion and euphoria ransacking her body, Zara laughed and Conrad cupped her face with an indulgent smile.

'I was sitting on the train,' he rushed on, 'and I realised that I'd run away again, without telling you how I feel about you.'

'Me too,' she cried, gripping him tighter. 'I'm so sorry that I pushed you away. That I made you doubt. I want you to know that I *do* trust you. That you could never be a mistake. That I don't care how hard it is, I want to make us work.'

He cut her off with another kiss. 'I know you're scared,' he said when he pulled back, 'and I am too. But I love you, harder than I've ever been in love before.'

She tried to interject but he shook his head and continued. 'You were right about me. I *was* hiding from the past, running away from it, shielding myself with casual relationships so I didn't have to face the risk of anyone else betraying me or finding out that no one could ever love me. But my fear isn't enough of a reason to walk away from you, from the most real relationship I've ever had. I want you, Zara. You *and* Zach.'

'Conrad,' she said, trying to get a word in, to tell him that *she* loved him, too, but he rushed on.

'I'm ready to let go of the past, Zara, and actually build a real, serious relationship with you, if you'll let me.'

'Conrad, I want that, too. But what about your job in Australia? Your family? James?' Tears stung Zara's eyes, his words were so wonderful, but she'd still have to let him go, at least in the short term.

'Yes.' He nodded, his stare softening. 'I still need to address all of that, but that shouldn't stop us being together. I don't know how exactly—I'll move here, or you and Zach can come to Brisbane or we'll alternate. The point is, I want to be with you. I love you, Zara. That's what I want—us. You, me and Zach. But…what do you want?'

Zara laughed, her tears finally spilling free. 'Well, if you'd let me get a word in, I'd have told you that I want to be with you too. That's why I was leaving early just now, to call you and tell you how I feel. I didn't want you to get in the plane without knowing.' She looked down from the joy sparkling in his beautiful eyes, ashamed. 'I'm so sorry about last night. The way I pushed you away.' She looked up and met his stare. 'You're right: I was scared. Terrified, actually. For a moment, I thought history was repeating itself with that pregnancy scare. I thought you could never love me. Never want me and Zach. But this, with you, has been the first real, grown-up relationship I've ever had.'

'I know it's moving crazy fast.' Conrad frowned, his stare so intense, she gasped. 'But we owe it to ourselves to see where this could go. I know you're scared to make another mistake, but I won't let you down, Zara. You or Zach.'

She nodded. 'I know you won't. And it's *not* too fast.

I've waited six years for this, for *you*. We could never be a mistake, because I finally know now what love truly feels like. Real, grown-up love. I love you too, Conrad.'

His brows pinched together as hope bloomed in his eyes. 'You do?'

'Yes.' Zara laughed, cried, threw her arms around his neck and pressed her lips to his stunned mouth. 'I didn't properly realise it until today when Sharon helpfully pointed it out. But somewhere along my wild sexual adventure, I fell in love with you. I think it might have been when I watched you build your first snowman.'

Conrad grinned, kissed her and then pulled back, falling serious. 'About Zach. I know he's your top priority, but I want you to know that I love him too, because he's yours. I want to help you raise him and one day, when you're ready, I want him to be *ours*.'

Zara blinked, her throat aching. 'You are so wonderful.' Joy burst past her lips in a wave of laughter he kissed up as he wiped the tears from her cheeks.

They stared at each other with goofy grins on their faces for so long, Zara felt guilty for hogging the office. 'What shall we do now?' she asked, her hands caressing his face as if committing him to memory, knowing that she couldn't keep him, because he still needed to go back to Australia. 'Can you still make your flight?'

She would miss him. But she was already planning to apply for some annual leave so she could take Zach to visit him in Brisbane.

'There's more snow due, apparently,' Conrad said, drawing her into his arms once more. 'I saw it on the news before my phone died. If you'll have me, I'll come home with you tonight and take another flight to Brisbane in a few days.'

She smiled. 'I think that could be arranged. You can't fly anywhere if you're snowed in, maybe even trapped in my bed.'

His smile widened, his stare loaded with sensual promise. 'How soon before you could visit me in Australia? I need to tie up loose ends back home, to see James and my parents, but then I want to come back here, to be with you. To make this work. This time our relationship will be out in the open and *very* serious, so I hope you're prepared.'

Zara smiled, laughed, pressed her lips to his. 'I'll only come to Australia if you promise me a tour of the Sunshine Coast. It's been a long time since I've worn a bikini.'

'I think that could be arranged,' he replied, throwing her words back at her. Then he dragged her close for another deep and passionate kiss.

Neither of them noticed the office door being pushed open or Sharon stepping aside so anyone within peering distance could see them kiss. It was only when the applause and cheering started that Zara broke away from Conrad, and they turned, blushing to see their audience of teary-eyed midwives and mums cradling their new babies.

'Let's get out of here,' Zara said to Conrad, once her laughter had died down. 'We can pick up Zach from school and make plans for our visit to Australia. He'll be so excited.'

Conrad reached for her hand and they left the ward to more whoops and cheering, the loudest from Sharon, who yelled, 'Go get him, Zara.'

Zara met Conrad's beaming stare, her heart ready to explode. 'I fully intend to,' she said, slinging her arm around his waist.

He pressed a kiss to her lips, smiled that killer smile and winked. 'I'm all yours.'

EPILOGUE

One year later

THAT JANUARY IN BRISBANE, summer temperatures reached record highs. So the only sensible place for a wedding was on the beach. North of Brisbane, on a white sand cove on the island of K'gari, Zara and Conrad stood under a white linen awning, making their vows before a small gathering of friends and family.

Zara curled her bare toes into the sand and gripped Conrad's hands tighter in hers, certain that for the rest of her life, she'd hold him close—her best friend, her lover, her husband. Love and passion and devotion shone from his grey eyes, all but melting the simple strapless wedding dress she wore clean off. She couldn't wait to get him alone, couldn't wait to start this new adventure with him: their marriage. But first, she planned to enjoy every second of their wedding day.

'As Zara and Conrad have exchanged their vows of togetherness and exchanged rings, symbols of for ever,' their wedding celebrant said to their small congregation of guests, which included Pam, Zara's mother, and Sharon and Rod, who'd also made the journey, 'they move forward, their lives entwined as husband and wife and as parents to Zach.'

Their loved ones cheered and clapped as Zara surged up on tiptoes, her lips clashing with Conrad's in their first kiss as husband and wife. As always, she lost herself to their chemistry, holding him tight, kissing him hard, laughing against his smile, because falling in love with Conrad Reed had brought her endless joy.

'I love you,' he said, pulling back to peer down at her with desire and something close to adoration. And the feelings were very much reciprocated.

'I love you too,' she said, laughing through her tears as she reflected on the past year, where they'd bounced around between Australia and England, finally settling in Brisbane where they now worked in the same hospital.

Her lips found his once more and everything slotted perfectly into place. But she could only enjoy kissing her new husband for a few seconds, as two little boys, their two ring-bearers, Zach and James, pulled them apart with embarrassed squeals.

Conrad laughed, his hands resting on Zach's and James's shoulders. Zara's heart burst with love for him. He was such an amazing father and uncle, and the boys had become close friends.

As their guests surged forward to offer congratulations, hugs and kisses, Zara counted herself the luckiest woman alive. She had everything she could possibly want.

'Congratulations,' Sharon said as she hugged Zara close. 'I told you that you needed to live a little, have a little fun, didn't I? And look how it all turned out.'

Zara laughed at her smug friend, her stare meeting Conrad's. 'You're right. It's been the best time of my life.' Not that she regretted a single second of the journey that had brought her to Conrad, the man she loved.

Later, after photos on the beach, her husband snagged her hand and held her back as their guests wandered back to the lodge where their wedding party would take place.

Stepping into his arms, she raised her lips to his kiss. He cupped her face, that secret smile in his eyes as he peered down at her. 'Any regrets?' he asked playfully, secure in her love because she showed him what he meant to her every day.

'Just one,' she said, slipping her hands around his waist. 'Our celebrations are going to be way too long. I have to wait hours before I can get my hands on all this.' She slid her palms up his chest, over his white linen shirt, caressing his defined pecs.

'I know what you mean,' he said, his stare full of sensual promise as he gave her body a heated glance. 'But that's what a honeymoon is for. I love the boys, dearly,' he said about James and Zach, 'but I can't wait to have you all to myself for an entire week. Brace yourself for another wild sexual adventure, Mrs Reed.' He grinned and brushed her lips with his.

Zara melted into his arms, grateful to Conrad's parents, who would watch Zach for the week they'd be away in Fiji.

'So you think you're the man for the job, do you?' she teased, sighing into another kiss. She wasn't going to be able to keep her hands or her lips off him today.

Playfully, he cracked his knuckles. 'I'll certainly give it my best shot.'

They smiled, kissed again, this one turning heated enough to make Zara's breath catch.

'Mum…stop kissing,' Zach called from across the beach.

Zara and Conrad laughed and headed after their friends

and family, arm in arm. 'I'm not sure I can make that promise,' she said, looking up at the love of her life.

'Me neither,' Conrad said, pausing to press his lips to hers. 'But I can promise that I'll always love you.'

'Me too.'

* * * * *

If you enjoyed this story,
check out these other great reads
from JC Harroway

Forbidden Fiji Nights with Her Rival
Secretly Dating the Baby Doc
Nurse's Secret Royal Fling
Her Secret Valentine's Baby

All available now!

FLIRTING WITH THE FLORIDA HEART DOCTOR

JANICE LYNN

MILLS & BOON

To Kimberly Bradford Scott.

You're amazing.

CHAPTER ONE

DR. HAILEY EASTON didn't like the cold. Tired of northern Ohio winters, her past life, and the toxic relationship she'd left behind, she welcomed Venice, Florida's sunshine. However, when she'd moved south, she'd been thinking of warm weather and new beginnings, not her heated reaction to Dr. Cayden Wilton.

Having never experienced such awareness, Hailey's instant attraction to the cardiologist coming down the hallway wasn't something she could have foreseen, especially not after the drawn-out ten-year destruction of her belief in the opposite sex. Sometimes life threw in surprises. Her surprises had rarely been good ones, but things were going to be different in Florida.

Things were already different.

With a complete head-to-toe makeover, *she* was different. It was more than just her outer appearance that had changed. She was lighter, freer, and determined to shake her past. In her new sunshine-filled life she planned to erase the wasted years of John demolishing her already miniscule self-confidence and making her believe she hadn't deserved anything better than what little he'd given. Since she'd stayed for so long in the relationship, hoping he'd change, maybe she hadn't. Either way, with finishing medical school and acknowledging that it was now or never, she'd said goodbye to her old self, Ohio, John, and to silly dreams. Hello, Florida and the improved Hailey.

"I see who you're looking at and you're wasting your time." Her coworker Renee confirmed what Hailey had known. Dr. Wilton was way out of her league.

No, stop that, she scolded herself.

She wouldn't let John's voice reign any longer.

Being realistic wasn't being negative, though. Hailey was no beauty queen, but she had a good heart, loved people, and as far as looks, well, she had nice teeth and had always liked her eyes. They were her best feature, in her opinion, which was fitting as one's eyes were the window to one's soul. Thanks to the corrective eye surgery she'd gifted herself as a finishing-residency present, her thick glasses no longer obscured that window. Even with her radical revamping, she was more along the lines of an average, slightly overweight person, and not someone who turned heads. Cayden Wilton must be a leading cause of whiplash. The man was gorgeous.

"He's taken," Renee continued, glancing from the cardiologist to Hailey.

Just as well; she'd made her move to work on herself, to find her inner happiness, not to jump into another relationship. When she was ready to date again, it would be light, fun, about her, and she could play in any league that valued the things that mattered most.

"Taken?" Asking was way outside the old Hailey's comfort zone, but she couldn't hold back her curiosity, so maybe all those self-help books she'd been devouring were working. Dr. Wilton hadn't been wearing a wedding ring, but that didn't mean he was single. Of course, he wasn't. Like John, Dr. Wilton was one of the beautiful people of the world—everyone flocked to them with no effort on their part.

"Claimed would be a more accurate description," the charge nurse clarified from where she sat next to Hailey in the small open office cubby behind the nurses' station. The hospital walls were a light gray and were offset with stark white ceilings and trim. White tiled floors added to the calming, clean feel. The unit boasted a fresh clean linen scent that was a positive testament to housekeeping. "When he is ready to settle down, everyone expects him to marry Leanna Moore, especially Leanna. They're the hospital's very own 'celebrity' couple. We refer to them as Caydna."

Caydna? Venice General Hospital's drama was on a whole new level. She couldn't recall any couple name combos at her Ohio hospital other than someone occasionally referring to "Bennifer," "Brangelina," or "Tayvis" celebrity couples.

Hailey had seen Dr. Wilton three times. Once from across the hospital cafeteria during her orientation, yesterday during her first shift as Venice General's newest inpatient physician, and right now. Each time, she'd wondered if she was hitting menopause prior to her thirtieth birthday as she instantly flushed hot.

Dragging her gaze from the scrub-wearing cardiologist walking down the med-surg unit's hallway was impossible. Tall, athletically built, gorgeous hazel eyes, and brown, slightly wavy hair, he commandeered her attention and refused to let go.

As Cayden passed, Sharla Little rushed from her

husband's room, calling out to him. Melvin Little had required an emergency appendectomy for a ruptured appendix the previous night. After Hailey rounded on him at his transfer to the medical/surgical floor that morning, she had entered the cardiac consult to keep close tabs on his significant history of congestive heart failure. Now, fatigue and worry etched upon her face, Mrs. Little swiped at the tears that had started. Whatever she said had Cayden placing his arm around her shoulder and giving a hug. His unabashed show of compassion surprised Hailey. Good-looking, smart, and kind.

"Leanna Moore?" Why had Hailey spoken on his personal life? She did not want to get caught up in hospital gossip. As she said the name out loud an image of a pretty blonde on a billboard popped into her mind. "The radio personality?"

"The one and only."

Embarrassed she'd voiced an interest, Hailey forced her gaze to the computer screen where she should be addressing messages—she had a ton of new employee ones filling her inbox.

"It doesn't surprise me that you know who Leanna is despite having just moved to the area a few weeks ago. Born and raised here, she's Venice's darling. She wants Dr. Wilton and doesn't care who knows it. After they met at a charity event, she convinced him to do a weekly heart health segment during her morning show. He doesn't go out with any woman more than a few times, but Leanna lasted several months and they've kept in touch since, which makes her different from all the rest. Of course, their continued relationship may just be that he's a softie for raising money for the needy or promoting a good cause. I think he sits on every volunteer committee the hospital has."

"That's admirable."

Watching where Dr. Wilton still spoke with Mrs. Little, Renee nodded. "He's admirable. In lots of ways that go beyond that fabulous smile of his. Despite his playboy reputation, we all adore him and most of us have crushed on him."

Hailey arched a brow at the nurse who'd claimed to be happily married when they'd been chitchatting the previous day. "Even you?"

"Touché." Renee leaned back in her chair and grinned. "Not crush, per se, but my eyes can see. Mmm-hmm. He is fine."

Hailey smiled as the fifty-something woman fanned her face.

"So, what you're saying is that for a fun, no-strings-attached evening I should invite him to check out that tiki bar in Manasota that you were telling me about?" She had no intentions of doing so, had never asked out a man, but teasing Renee was fun. Even thinking that someday she might be so bold was mind-boggling. She'd always been demure, letting John dictate their relationship, and doing her best to keep the peace. That hadn't worked out well.

Renee's eyes widened as did her smile. "I tell you what, new girl, you forget everything I said and you have your fun. Just keep your heart in check so it doesn't get broken."

Her heart had already been broken. Just once, because she'd only had one romantic relationship. It had been a long and painful breaking, piece by shattered piece.

Taking a deep breath and forcing a smile, Hailey shook

her head. "I was joking, but like you, my eyes appreciate beauty. Dr. Wilton looks as if he belongs on a television medical drama rather than in a real hospital. He'd be an instant heartthrob." Ha ha. Look at her making a pun with his being a cardiologist. As far as her own heart, when and if she dated again, she'd keep it locked up tighter than Fort Knox. "Now, tell me about these volunteer committees and charities. I want to get involved in my new hometown."

She wanted to do more, to give back more, to focus on things beyond just remaking herself, but to also contribute to making the world a better place. In Ohio, John hadn't wanted her to have a life outside of residency and their relationship. Looking back, she was ashamed of how she'd let him rob her of so much joy. She had gifts to give and wanted to do just that. That volunteering was a great way to meet people and make friends was an added bonus.

Eyes twinkling, Renee turned toward where Cayden was stepping behind the nurses' station counter. "Good morning, Doctor Wilton. Saw you talking with Mrs. Little. Do I need to enter new orders?" She jerked her thumb toward Hailey. "Also, Dr. Easton wants to volunteer with Venice Has Heart. Can you help her?"

Hailey's jaw dropped. *That* was not what she'd meant when she'd asked about the charities. She never should have teased Renee.

Cayden's gaze shifted toward them, going first to Renee, then settling on Hailey. An amused light shone in his gorgeous eyes. His lips curved, digging dimples into his cheeks that matched the one on his chin. The man had a strong, yet friendly facial structure. From what

Hailey could tell, he had great everything, but she'd been wrong before.

"You want to volunteer for Venice Has Heart?" he asked.

She didn't even know what Venice Has Heart was, but that didn't stop her from saying, "Renee thinks I should and suggested I talk to you about doing so." Hailey glanced toward the charge nurse who looked all innocent although she was far from it, then returned her attention to him. "Where do I find out more?"

"That's great. We're always looking for more volunteers." His phone dinged and he glanced down at the message that appeared on his watch face. "Sorry, one sec." Brows veeing, he typed out a quick response, then smiled at Hailey, causing a major rhythm hiccup. "As far as where to find out more, I'd love to tell you about Venice Has Heart. I've got to round on a few patients, then get back to the clinic, but maybe we can meet this evening, I can give you the lowdown then."

Hailey's face heated. Meet that evening? How long was giving her the "lowdown" going to take? Unless he was using her volunteering as an excuse to make plans with her and if so, how did she feel about that? She'd just moved to Florida a few weeks before. She'd intended to focus on building a life, not a romantic relationship.

Drastic makeover or not, she knew Cayden was just being kind as he had been with Sharla Little. She shouldn't read anything into his invitation other than at face value he wanted to tell a new colleague about a beloved charity.

Beside her, Renee elbowed her arm. "Hailey was just saying she wanted to try out that fabulous tiki bar in

Manasota and check out some of our Florida nightlife."
Her coworker smiled big at Dr. Wilton. "Maybe you could
have dinner, listen to the band, watch the sunset, tell her
about Venice Has Heart, and all the reasons why moving
to our little sunny part of the world was a great decision."

The hospital floor could just open and swallow Hailey,
chair and all. The sooner, the better. But Cayden didn't
seem to mind. If anything, he seemed intrigued by Renee's comment.

"That sounds like a great idea." He looked directly
at Hailey, making her forget to breathe as she stared
into eyes that were a deep green with golden flecks and
rimmed with an intense blue. "Shall I pick you up at six?"

Feeling panicky, she reminded herself that it was just
an innocent meeting between colleagues to discuss a volunteer opportunity and shook her head. "My shift ends at
six, Dr. Wilton, but I'll meet you there at seven." Look at
her taking charge with the time suggestion. Such a small
thing, but after years of following John's dictates, pride
filled her that she hadn't just said yes.

"It's Cayden. Thought I mentioned that yesterday," he
said, his smile revving up her heart rate even more. His
phone dinged a second time, and, glancing down at his
watch to view the message, he sighed. "Sorry. Duty calls.
I'm going to see Mr. Little and the other cardiac consult."
He shot one last smile toward her. "Looking forward to
seeing you at seven, *Hailey*."

"Okay." She didn't say *Cayden* back, couldn't even
wrap her brain around doing so, which was silly. She'd
been on a first-name basis with coworkers in the past. But
saying Cayden's name out loud felt as if it would be more

than something casual and not something she should do in front of Renee.

What is wrong with me?

He moved to leave the nurses' station area to head down the hospital hallway. Renee grabbed her arm, giving an excited squeeze, and mouthed, "Girl!" However, the nurse rapidly straightened when Cayden turned back toward them, standing just to the other side of the counter separating the nurses' area from the hallway but still in close proximity of the office cubby along the back wall. A fresh heatwave infused Hailey's face because no way had he missed Renee's theatrical shimmy.

His gaze dropped to where Renee's fingers wrapped around her arm, then lifted to Hailey. A twinkly light shone there, making the golden flecks glisten. "We should exchange numbers in case something comes up and one of us is running late."

"Or if one of us needs to cancel."

His brow lifted. "Changing your mind already?"

"I meant in case you were too busy to meet and just wanted to call."

"Why would I do that?" He made it sound as if the idea was preposterous.

Taking a deep breath, she cleared her throat. "You're a cardiologist. I can think of a few scenarios that could prevent you from meeting me."

"A few," he agreed, grinning as he handed her his phone to punch in her number. "But I'm not on call tonight, so we should be good. I was more concerned that you might get hung up here at shift change." A realistic possibility, she thought as she typed in her number with shaky fingers. He took the phone, glanced down at what she'd input, then hit Dial, causing her phone to vibrate in her scrub pocket. "Now you have my number, too. I'm looking forward to a relaxing evening of a good food, music, sunset, and great company. See you at seven."

This time when he turned to leave, it was a stunned, wobbly-legged Hailey grabbing Renee's arm.

"I thought you weren't on call tonight," Hailey reminded Cayden from where she sat catty-corner from him at an outdoor table at The Manasota Mango. After he'd pulled out her chair and waited for her to sit, she'd thought he'd move across from her. Instead, he'd chosen the closer seat to where they could both easily see the band on the far end of the outdoor patio. When the hostess had seated them, he'd requested to be in easy line of vision, but not so close that the music would be too loud for them to hear each other when talking. The young lady had chosen the perfect spot.

"I'm not." Cayden slid the phone back into his pocket. "But, as you could tell, that was the hospital. You know how it is. In our profession, you're always working on some level. I like to keep up-to-date on any changes in my hospitalized patients."

Taking a sip of the fruity nonalcoholic drink she'd ordered, Hailey nodded. She did know how it was for many in her profession. With solely overseeing inpatient care as a hospitalist, she didn't get a ton of after-hour calls. At least, she hadn't in Ohio as a resident and wasn't expecting to in Florida.

Although she'd been nervous when she'd first arrived at the restaurant, she'd mostly relaxed as they'd eaten their meal and chatted, assuring herself that Cayden's invitation had been nothing more than a casual one of convenience for telling her about Venice Has Heart. His easy laughs, frequent compliments, and seeming fascination with whatever she said was enough to make a woman's head spin, though.

"That was Dr. Bentley who came on at the end of your shift," he continued. "Melvin Little has increased shortness of breath. Dr. Bentley ordered a chest X-ray and additional labs. He questioned if there were any other tests that I'd like done prior to my rechecking Melvin in the morning."

"Sorry to hear that his breathing has worsened." Neither Melvin nor his wife had mentioned anything when she'd rounded prior to the end of her shift. "I'll be there in the morning."

"Ah, so if you completely avoid me, I'll know I failed miserably tonight." His eyes twinkled.

She made a noise that was a somewhat embarrassing cross between a snort and laugh. "You already know you're a success. Your passion for educating our community on heart health through a fun event completely wowed me. All you're missing is my name signed on the dotted line to have me locked in for a full day of providing medical consults with anyone who has an abnormal screen."

"I'll bring the ironclad contract in the morning," he teased. "My grandfather died of a heart attack when I was young. I've often wondered how different things would have been if he'd just known how to take care of himself, things like a proper diet and lifestyle habits." His expression had gone momentarily serious, then he smiled. "But you're right. Tonight is a success because I got to spend time getting to know you."

Remember what Renee said. Have fun, but don't take him too seriously.

"Yes, since we'll be seeing each other with the Venice Has Heart event." Cheeks burning, she took another sip of her pineapple and coconut drink, thinking maybe she should have gone for the real deal for liquid courage. She'd not wanted to dull her senses while talking to him in hopes that she would be less likely to say or do silly things. But, being with him, knowing people were looking their way and likely wondering why he was with her, twisted her stomach into knots.

Quit, she reminded herself. *Quit. Quit. Quit. Cayden asked you here, is smiling at you, and seems to be enjoying himself. Being with him was great practice for if you ever do risk dating again.*

Just like her "as friends" Saturday night plans with a neighbor was great practice. She'd bumped into Ryan several times at neighborhood events and the gym. His offer to introduce her to his friend group had been kind and she looked forward to the cookout. When ready, she'd need all the help she could get she'd not been on a first date in ten years. Although she and John had officially called their relationship quits with Hailey moving into their guest bedroom three months prior to leaving Ohio, she'd not dated. Having done so in Ohio would have antagonized an already bad situation. Not to mention that she'd had zero interest. Apparently, the Florida sunshine was thawing something inside her, though, because her body was logging all kinds of interest where Cayden was concerned.

"You'll definitely be seeing me with Venice Has Heart." His smile deepened his dimples.

"Um, yeah." Hailey gulped. She was a novice when it came to men, but good grief, what she saw in his eyes. His gaze burned so hot it was a wonder she didn't spontaneously combust. "I look forward to volunteering. I love that you have the local nursing programs involved to take blood pressures and random blood sugar readings."

Could she sound any cornier? She wasn't used to having dinner with gorgeous single, flirty men. The emotions hitting her and having to deal with them weren't things she could learn about from her self-help books, that was for sure.

"It's a great experience for them on a lot of different levels as they get real-world experience. Their instructors always provide positive feedback that the students have shared."

"Anytime one can get hands-on experience is a good thing. The band is good."

His brow arched. "Do you like classic rock?"

Although somewhat familiar with it, she didn't even know the name of the song that was currently being sung. "I like most music," she answered honestly. "But even if not my favorite genre, I appreciate the band's musical skills. They're talented, don't you think?" She smiled. Wasn't that what her books said to do and to do frequently? Smile because a smile went a long way to making most situations better.

"They are." Something in the way that he said it made her wonder if he had paid any more attention to what song was playing than she had. "What's your favorite genre?"

For years Hailey had listened to rap because that had

been John's favorite. Her favorite hadn't been something she'd thought much about, maybe ever. For far too long she hadn't thought about what her favorite anything was. No more. In her new life, she was finding herself, her likes, and her dislikes. She'd never be purposefully oppositional, but she wasn't going to be a doormat ever again. She considered what she'd listened to while she'd been unpacking her few belongings into the house she'd bought not too far from where they currently were. "I listen to a variety of music, but when alone, I tend to listen to pop. I'm going with that as my favorite."

"When you're not concerned about whether or not someone else is enjoying what is playing, you listen to pop." His observation was so on the money that she blushed. He took a drink from his bottle, then placed it back on the table. "Who is your favorite artist?"

"Elvis," she said without hesitation, smiling as memories assailed her of listening to the Memphis crooner with the couple who'd rescued her from bouncing from one foster family to another. He'd been her adopted parents' favorite and she'd grown up listening to him and other iconic performers from the sixties and seventies. She'd been eleven when she'd been adopted by the older couple who'd never had children of their own. Hailey equated the singer with having a home and a family because she never had prior to being introduced to his silky voice.

Cayden chuckled. "Not what I was expecting you to say. As the known King of Rock 'n' Roll and not a pop artist, I have to ask, why Elvis?"

"Why not Elvis? After all, like you said, he is the 'King of Rock 'n' Roll.' But if you meant a more modern artist or band, I'll go with Ed Sheeran."

"Nice. I saw him in concert back during my early college days," he surprised her by saying, although she wasn't sure why she was surprised. No doubt Cayden had an active social life that had included numerous concerts over the years. "He is a super-talented musician. My friends and I had a great time."

"He did a show in Columbus at the beginning of my freshman year. A group of classmates sold a kidney or two to come up with enough money to go see him and invited me to tag along." She smiled at the memory, trying not to question herself too much on why she'd let John systematically cut her off from everyone in her life. With moving from one foster home to another and her adopted parents opting to homeschool her, she'd never had any close friendships. She had been thrilled when her classmates had asked her to go with them to the concert. She'd thought she was on top of the world—making friends and having a boyfriend for the first time ever. The concert had been one of her few friend outings. John had thrown a fit. He'd thrown a fit for her breaking things off and moving to Florida, too, telling her she'd regret leaving and come running home, lonely and begging for his forgiveness for her "stupidity." There was no level of loneliness that would send her back to him. Being with John the past ten years had been some of her loneliest and with her childhood, that was saying something. Thank God she'd had her lifelong dream of being a doctor to focus on and keep her from sinking into despair.

"Willing to sacrifice body parts for great music—making a note of it," Cayden teased, taking a sip of his drink and pulling her back to the present. A present where she had achieved her greatest goal and now planned to heal the holes in who she was, to get to know that person, and learn to love herself completely and know that she was enough and didn't need anyone else in her life. "You went to school in Columbus?"

"I had a scholarship to Ohio State for my undergraduate studies. Staying for medical school made sense." John had been there. After her parents died, without him she would have been completely alone in the world, as he'd pointed out on a regular basis. Looking back, she wondered what her life would have been like if she'd left Ohio. Better in many ways, but she had learned powerful lessons. She hadn't been a fast learner, but she had eventually caught on. She'd never wear that in-a-serious-relationship cage again. "What about you? Are you originally from Florida?"

Cayden took another drink from his bottle. "I grew up around Gainesville, did residency in Kentucky and a fellowship in Kansas. I missed the ocean enough to know I didn't want to live anywhere that didn't offer a sunset over the water."

Having already fallen in love with being near the sea, Hailey understood. She ran her finger over condensation forming on her glass. The moisture was cool beneath her fingertips and as welcome as the breeze cutting the evening's heat. "Because sunsets are what you like best about being near the ocean?"

"More that I wanted to remind you that Renee mentioned our watching the sunset." He grinned in a way that had Hailey gulping. His smile was lethal. Maybe he couldn't help himself and just naturally flirted with every woman. Not that she'd seen him do so with anyone else, not even the hostess who'd definitely given him the eye. "I'm fine with staying here, listening to the band," he continued. "Or we could walk across the street and watch the sunset from the beach. There are just enough clouds in the sky that the colors should be spectacular."

A spectacular sunset over the water with a gorgeous man sounded surreal. Scary, too. But Hailey had moved to Florida to be different, to step outside her comfort zone, and to create the life she wanted. That life should include spectacular sunsets.

"Watching the sun set while sitting on the beach would be great and something I've not done since moving here."

He feigned horror. "What? How is that even possible? That should have been one of the first things anyone who moves here does."

"It's not that I haven't wanted to." She glanced toward the band who'd started singing a Lynyrd Skynyrd classic. "But I wasn't sure how safe it would be for me to be on the beach and walk back to my car by myself after dark. I've not heard of any safety issues, but I'm new to the area and trying to make good choices, not put myself in compromising situations."

Unlike the past. She'd made a terrible choice with John and compromised for almost a decade. Had she stayed so long because she'd been grieving her parents, in school, then in residency, and she just hadn't had the energy to break free? Was that why she'd turned a blind eye and forgiven so many things? Or had the fear of being alone kept her there?

"I doubt you'd have any problems, but it's always best to be safe." Cayden finished his drink, placed the bottle on the table, then motioned for their waitress to bring their check. Hailey reached for her purse, pulled out her wallet, but Cayden shook his head. "Tonight is my treat."

Clutching her wallet, she met his gaze and hoped her face wasn't as rosy as it felt. "I don't expect you to pay for my meal."

His brows scrunched together. "When a man invites you to dinner, you should expect him to pay. My advice is that if he expects you to pay, next time, tell him to hit the road."

"Duly noted." She was so used to paying for everything with John that she'd just automatically planned to do the same. John's thoughts had been that she should just be grateful for the opportunity to support him. If she'd let him, he would have broken her financially the way he had her heart. Fortunately, most of her parents' estate had been tied up until a few months back. Acid burned her throat, and she took another sip of the virgin drink, letting the cold liquid glide down her throat to ease the heat. The fruity sweetness did little to dissolve her bitterness at her own foolishness that she'd once again let John into her head. Maybe it was natural for him to pop into her mind since tonight was the first time she'd ever had dinner with a man who wasn't John.

"To be fair, though, Renee instigated our dinner tonight."

Cayden shook his head. "Renee might have made the initial suggestion, but I asked. Dinner is my treat."

"In that case, thank you." She slipped her slim wallet back into her cross-body and assured herself that it was okay that she was letting him pay even though doing so felt awkward. The new her did not pay when she met a man for dinner. Okay, got it. "For the record, what about if I ask someone to dinner? Who should I expect to pay then?"

Not that she'd probably ever be so bold, but this new Florida Hailey was a work in progress. She refused to be boring, walked-all-over Ohio Hailey ever again. Talking with Cayden was insightful and wonderful and reinforced that she'd been right to start fresh in a place of her choosing. The hospitalist position in Venice had been a godsend.

Cayden shrugged. "That one is okay either way. If he insists, its fine for you to let him pay. But he doesn't lose points if he lets you since you asked." He paused, then added, "Not the first time. If there's a second, call me old-fashioned, but he needs to man up."

It was difficult to think of the charming man sitting across from her as old-fashioned, but there was something about him that made her think he had an old soul. She liked whatever that something was.

"Tonight is enlightening." And an unexpected bonus to her new Florida life. "You're easy to talk to and seem quite the expert. Being new to the area, I should come to you for all my dating advice."

Hilarious. Unless one counted tonight, which she didn't since it wasn't one, she hadn't been on a first date in years. With the way John had shredded her heart, she might never risk letting someone in to mess with the woman she was working to become.

Certainly, she'd fight to protect the new her and would

steer clear of anyone who threatened her hard-won peace. There were worse things than being alone.

She didn't need Cayden's, or anyone's, advice to know that.

Life had taught her that painful lesson well.

CHAPTER TWO

CAYDEN AND HAILEY crossed the street, paused at his SUV long enough to grab a blanket, then headed to the beach. When they reached the sand, he took off his shoes and Hailey did the same. Hot pink covered her toenails and her big toes each had a palm tree emblem in the middle of the polish. Liking the glimpse at her whimsy, Cayden grinned.

The Gulf's breeze whipped at her long blond hair, dancing the strands about her lovely face. She'd had her hair pulled back at the hospital. He loved that she'd loosened it for their dinner. She'd also changed and wore white capris, a bright blue top, and plain white canvas shoes.

Her heavily lashed eyes were cloudy with uncertainty, as if she was trying to decide if he'd really been eyeing her toenails. That he understood. He wasn't a feet guy, or at least, he never had been. But those brightly painted toenails were downright sexy. Of course, looking at her curvy figure, he couldn't name one part of Hailey that he didn't find attractive. She fascinated him, which explained why he was on the beach with a coworker. He liked women and wasn't shy about it, but he didn't spend personal time with women he worked with. Doing that was much too complicated when it didn't work out and it never worked out. He no longer wanted it to. He'd been cured of that ailment. He had a great life, was never lonely when he wanted company, and was completely happy with lifelong bachelorhood. He only spent time with women with an exit plan already in place, and never coworkers. Apparently, Hailey was the exception to that rule because none of that had kept him from asking her to dinner to discuss her volunteering with Venice Has Heart when he could have just sent her to their website.

"I'd thought it would be more crowded," Hailey mused as, their shoes dangling from their fingers and the blanket folded over his arm, they made their way across the warm sand.

"It's later in the day on a weeknight so not too busy, but it can get crowded at times." When they were about halfway to the water, he stopped. "This okay?"

She nodded, watching as he spread the blanket, then sat to face where the sun was making its descent toward the horizon. A seagull squawked in the distance and a couple of sandpipers darted to and fro at the edge of the surf. The golden light reflected off the water, casting a picturesque view for what was in many ways the most interesting evening he'd had in a long time. So long, in fact, that he couldn't recall having felt the excitement that buzzed through him when he looked at the woman next to him. He'd felt the buzz the first time he'd seen her and each time since. While grabbing something to eat with a colleague, he'd noticed the smiling blonde chatting with the hospital administrator. Yesterday, he'd practically tripped over introducing himself to her.

Hailey stared out at where small waves were racing

ashore. She hugged her knees and appeared to relax to the calming sea sounds. He'd always found peace in being near the water and was pleased she seemed to do the same.

Hailey twisted toward him. The sun's setting rays cast a hue to her face, making the blue of her eyes seem almost electric. "Are you always this nice?"

"Nope." Take this moment for example. He felt more naughty than nice. "Why did the phrase, 'Nice guys finish last,' pop into my head?"

As he'd hoped, she smiled. "I can't imagine that you ever finish last."

"There have been times I've finished last." But not because he hadn't given his best effort.

"Look at you. You're a successful cardiologist and gor—" She paused. Her cheeks glowed brighter than the setting sun.

Suspecting what she was going to say and pleased that she thought so, he grinned. "Go on, Hailey. Finish what you were about to say."

Odd, as he wasn't one to fish for compliments, but he craved hers.

Her lips twitched. "I was going to say that you're easy on the eyes, but I stopped because I didn't want to give you a big head."

Her compliment did funny things to his chest, like make his heart jerk. What was it about her that made him feel as if he'd morphed back to high school days?

"You think I'm easy on the eyes?" he teased, but deep down, he admitted that he was encouraging her to elaborate because he still wanted to hear more.

"Don't pretend you're not aware. You've looked in a mirror. You know how blessed you are."

Interesting that her tone almost held accusation.

"I could say the same in regard to you," he said. She was a beautiful woman who took great care with her appearance, although he suspected that beneath the makeup she was just as stunning. Beneath the powder and paint, she had a natural beauty that shined through.

She rolled her eyes in a way that made him wonder if, when looking in her mirror, she saw the same person he did. He didn't think so. Which might explain why her cheeks turned such a rosy shade each time he complimented her, and she seemed so unaccustomed to the praise. Could she really not know how beautiful she was?

"Looks fade, Hailey. Mine, yours, everyone's. It's what's on the inside that matters."

"I agree with you, of course. But, in the real world, most people never look to see what's on the inside unless it's nicely packaged on the outside." Her words held too much hurt for them to be a casual observation point. Who had punched the holes in her? And why did the urge to patch those holes hit so hard? Not just repair the broken pieces, but to kintsugi them with the finest gold so that the new was better than the former version? They'd just met and he was not a white knight and didn't want to be.

"I'm not most people, Hailey." When her face remained serious, he added, "Just ask my mother and she'll gladly tell you all my finer points."

Her expression lightening, Hailey snorted. "Hmm, not sure I trust your mother to give an unbiased opinion. But I don't need to ask her because, surprisingly, I believe you."

"Thank you, I think." He chuckled, wondering if his

own cheeks now matched the streaked sky. "I'm torn on whether that was a compliment or a backhanded insult."

"Compliment." She smiled a big, real smile that stole his breath, then turned to look at the water. The fading sunlight highlighted her features, showcasing her beauty that far outshone their surroundings.

"Then thank you," he told her.

She stared at where the sun was inching beneath the horizon's edge. Cayden couldn't drag his gaze from her. The breeze coming in off the Gulf ruffled her hair, and the sun's glow cast her in a golden hue that gave her an ethereal appearance, as if she couldn't possibly be real. Maybe she wasn't because she sure triggered other-worldly reactions.

"I can't believe I've not been coming out here in the evening when I'm so close. This is so peaceful, and feels safe." Cayden wouldn't call sitting next to her watching the sun go down "safe." *Dangerous* was the description that came to mind.

"You've ruined me," she continued. "I'm going to want to come back again and again."

"We can anytime you want. Being near the water is my thing and I don't mind company." At least, he didn't tonight. Usually, he preferred being at the beach alone.

"Ha, after so many years of being landlocked, I may want to be out here day and night, but I promise I wasn't implying that we come together." She laughed. "There's something mesmerizing about the sound of the water, isn't there?"

There was something mesmerizing about the sound of her laughter, something that should have him leery of further developing a friendship with her. "Just let me know whenever you want company for a beach sunset or walk," he offered anyway. "Or we can go to Caspersen Beach to look for shark teeth. It's just down the coast and something a lot of folks around here enjoy."

Her eyes widened. "Look for shark teeth?"

He chuckled at her expression. "Did you not realize you moved to the shark tooth capital of the world?"

"The hospital forgot to list that in their job description. Does that mean there's more sharks here than anywhere else?" Her face squished. "For the record, that would not be a selling point for me. Although, I guess it's too late now since I'm here."

"Not sure about the number of sharks compared to other places, but the number of shark teeth has to do with the area having favorable conditions to fossilize the teeth. If you've never been shark tooth hunting, you're in for a treat."

"Ohio girl. I've never found a shark tooth, much less been shark tooth hunting. I didn't even know that was a thing or that there was a shark tooth capital of the world."

He tsked. "You can't live here and not ever go shark tooth hunting."

She eyed him. "You say that as if you're confident I'd find a shark tooth."

"I am."

Her expression grew suspicious. "Am I missing something? Are they just lying around on the sand or something?"

He laughed. "Sometimes you can find them lying on the beach. Here, too, for that matter, especially after a storm. But the best ones are in the water at Caspersen, even the occasional megalodon tooth can be found."

"You want me to hunt shark teeth *in the water* after you just told me the beach is the shark tooth capital of the world and that there are sharks?" She gave him an I-don't-think-so look. "No, thank you."

He couldn't resist teasing. "You'll be fine so long as you stay away from the teeth still attached to the shark."

She snorted and made a funny face that had him liking her more and more. "No worries there. I'm not knowingly going anywhere near a shark."

"Lucky for you then that the teeth we would be hunting aren't attached." He chuckled, thinking the lightness in her tone was more beautiful than any sunset he'd even seen.

"But they once were, so maybe shark tooth hunting isn't my thing. Although, I'll admit you have me intrigued that you're so confident I'd find one. I've never been that lucky on those types of things. I've never even found a four-leaf clover my whole life."

"Then your luck is about to change."

Her smile was slow, innocently seductive, as she said, "I'm tempted to say yes simply from curiosity, but then I recall what they say about curiosity and the cat."

"Fortunately, you're not a cat."

"Ha! When it comes to sharks, I admit to being a big scaredy-cat. I mean, I know they are just animals doing what nature intended, but nature also dictates my survival instinct to stay away."

"I promise to protect you."

Her humor faded, as did his, and his assurance felt like more than just part of their fun banter.

"I can protect myself." Her chin tilt dared him to say otherwise even as he recognized the forced gusto in her eyes. Wondering what, or who, had made her so prickly, Cayden longed for the return of lightness.

"Even from sharks?"

Taking a deep breath, she swallowed and relaxed a little. "I'll defer dealing with sharks to you."

"Good idea. You're acing this listening to advice thing." Too bad he wasn't listening to the warning bells going off in his own head about what he was doing with her, a coworker, watching the sunset on a beach, and flirting with her despite all the reasons he shouldn't.

"Being a good student was never a problem. It's the rest of life that I've struggled with." She sighed, then with a soft smile back on her face she rested her chin atop her knees and stared at the sunset with deep appreciation. "This is so much better than when I watched while sitting in my car."

Cayden wanted to know more, to know what struggles she'd faced, but sensed she wouldn't tell him, so kept his questions to himself. The thought of her sitting in her car, watching the sunset by herself, tugged at his insides.

Her gaze cut to him and after a moment, she smiled. "I...thank you, Cayden. For dinner, the expert dating advice—" her smile widened when she said that one "—for the sunset, for asking me to go shark tooth hunting, for making me feel happy, for, just, well, for an enjoyable evening with someone who I feel is a new friend. It's been really nice."

"Seriously, anytime you want to watch the sunset from the beach, just call. I'll meet you so you don't have to worry about being alone." For safety reasons. That was why he kept offering. To keep her safe.

Who was going to keep him safe from his growing attraction to her was another matter completely.

"Are you going to tell me about last night?"

Even prior to arriving at the hospital, Hailey had known Renee would ask about her evening with Cayden. What she hadn't known was what she wanted to share. How could she explain what she didn't understand. Despite his "playboy reputation," Cayden had been a perfect gentleman. She'd had a great time, even agreeing to go shark tooth hunting with him, because why not? The new her was supposed to be adventurous and open to new experiences. Shark tooth hunting, from the beach as she wouldn't be going in the water, would certainly be that. She wanted to make friends, to have a social life, and be involved with her community. Going with Cayden just made sense, right? So, why did butterflies dance her in her belly at the thought that she'd be spending more time with him?

Knowing she couldn't ignore Renee, she smiled. "We ate dinner, listened to the band, and discussed Venice Has Heart. Thank you for suggesting that. Venice Has Heart sounds like an amazing community outreach program."

"It is." Renee literally rubbed her hands together. "Now, tell me more. Being happily married as I am, I have to live vicariously through you when it comes to Cayden."

Attempting to look casual, Hailey shrugged. "There's nothing more to tell."

Renee jerked her head back in disbelief. "Oh, come on. You were with the hospital's most notorious bachelor and I saw how he looked at you yesterday like he wanted to devour you in one bite. There has to be something more to tell."

Hailey fought gulping at Renee's assessment. Cayden hadn't looked at her that way. Sure, there had been moments the night before when she'd swear his flirting went beyond friendliness and making a new coworker feel welcomed. But she couldn't convince herself that her makeover was so good that Cayden would be interested in her, and yet...no, his offer to meet her for future sunsets and to take her shark tooth hunting weren't date offers. As surprising as it was, Cayden had been easy to talk to, had made her smile, and was hopefully destined to be a friend. That he was the sexiest man she'd ever met had no bearing on how much she'd liked him other than to make her uncomfortably aware of her body's reaction to his hotness.

"I see you stalling. Tell me." Renee wasn't going to let up. Hailey's silent mulling had made it seem as if more had happened than what had, so she glanced up from where she'd been charting a note on the patient she'd seen first thing that morning.

Looking her coworker directly in the eyes, she smiled as big as her plumped-up lips would allow. "As you know, we met at the bar you recommended. The food and music were wonderful. He told me about Venice Has Heart. I'm volunteering for the event."

Renee frowned. "What about drinks and a sunset with our favorite cardiologist? Please tell me you didn't waste that fabulous opportunity by just talking shop all evening."

"You are who told me that he's already claimed for whenever he tires of being a bachelor." Did he have an emotional involvement with the radio deejay beyond friendship? Hailey hadn't gotten that impression. What she had gotten was the impression that he liked the shiny new her. Absently, she reached up to touch where she had her hair extensions pulled back. He'd sounded so sincere in his claim of outer beauty fading that she wondered what he'd think if he knew just how much she'd done to enhance her appearance. Would he have noticed Ohio Hailey? What was she thinking? She didn't want him to notice Florida Hailey. She wasn't in the market for a relationship. She wasn't ready for one. Only, she couldn't deny that his flirting had made her feel...good.

Renee's brows scrunched. "Yes, but Cayden is way in the future. No reason you can't have fun in the here and now."

"He seems like a great guy to be so involved with the event. I enjoyed dinner and talking with him, but I'm just coming out of a long and unhealthy relationship. I'm really not interested in anything more than friendship with any man." There. Maybe that truth would appease Renee because Hailey did like her and hoped their working relationship would develop into friendship. To say anything further was setting herself up for gossip. "I need to check on Melvin Little. Is Sharla with him this morning?"

Frustrated that Hailey wasn't telling her more, Renee sighed. "She barely leaves his side. She tells me they've been together for over fifty years."

"He's fortunate to have her." What would it be like to have someone who cared that much about you for that long? Sharla adored her husband and the sentiment seemed to be mutual. In many ways they reminded her of her adoptive parents. The Eastons had loved each other and given Hailey the only real affection she'd ever known. Prior to them, she'd been bounced from place to place from the point her birth mother had died from an overdose and if her birth mother had known who Hailey's father was, she'd not listed it on her birth certificate. When her adoptive mother had died from breast cancer, her father hadn't lived a year before succumbing to a heart attack. All the old feelings of being alone in the world had hit and she'd clung to John no matter what he did. As unhealthy as it had been, his was the longest relationship of her life. Maybe she could forgive herself a little for trying so hard to make things work.

"I was told that Dr. Wilton would be by this morning to check on him and the sick sinus syndrome patient in Room 204." Renee looked at Hailey as if she expected some type of reaction. If she got one, it would be over Hailey falling down memory lane, which felt more like nightmare street.

Meeting Renee's gaze was her only reaction to her coworker's comment.

"Great. With Mr. Little's ruptured appendix then surgery putting a toll on his body, his heart needs to be watched closely." She didn't mention that she already knew Cayden would be by. "Are you going with me to see him, then?"

"Do you need me to?" Renee crossed her arms, pouting a little that Hailey wasn't revealing what she wanted to hear and that, perhaps, Hailey truly had "wasted" the opportunity. What had Renee expected her to do? Make out with Cayden under the stars?

Knowing her color was rising and her coworker was sure to notice, Hailey shook her head. "No, I was just checking."

Yikes. Her voice had broken a little.

"Then I'm going to stay here to do paperwork, maybe scribble notes on how you should have taken advantage of who you were with last night. Just because I told you to guard your heart didn't mean you couldn't have fun. Life is short. Sometimes you have to live a little." Renee waggled her brows. "Or a lot, if you get my drift."

Face aflame, Hailey grimaced. Yeah, that had never been that much fun for her. Maybe because it had always been about her trying to please John, doing whatever he wanted to try to make him so happy that he wouldn't want anyone else. Her best efforts hadn't worked, so maybe neither of them had been having much fun.

Knowing she had to get away from Renee's watchful eyes, Hailey headed to check on Melvin. Some of the medical floor rooms were doubles and some were private. Whether by luck or design, he was in a private room. Hailey knocked on the open door before stepping into the pale gray room with its white tiles. Although he was still on a liquid-only diet, the room smelled of oranges and Hailey noted peels on the wheeled bed tray that was pulled closer to Sharla than her husband. As long as his exam was okay, she planned to start him on bland soft foods that morning and would have Dietary bring breakfast.

"Good morning," she greeted as she took in the pale man lying in the hospital bed. He had the head of the bed raised and a couple of pillows stuffed behind him, propping himself up farther. He was in his midseventies, had thick white hair, and was too thin. All except his feet and ankles, which were swollen. They weren't weeping through the compression hose that she'd put on him the previous day, though. He hadn't been thrilled but hadn't had the energy to refuse. "How are you feeling today?"

"Like I'm starving and want to go home." He coughed. The cough had been wet, as if he'd needed to clear phlegm from his throat and struggled to do so.

"I'm hoping to do something about the starving part," she assured him, smiling. "As far as the going home, the charge nurse informed me that you had chest flutters last night and the night staff consulted with your cardiologist." Recalling where Cayden had been, who he'd been with during that consultation, Hailey's heart fluttered, too. "No symptoms since last night?"

Grunting as he cautiously scooted up farther on his hospital bed, Melvin shook his head. "I think it was just indigestion but after what happened with my stomach, I wasn't keeping quiet."

"Understood." His ruptured appendix had required his lower abdomen to be surgically opened and "cleaned" because he'd ignored his pain. Sepsis had quickly set in, increasing the criticalness of his situation. "How's your surgical site?"

He adjusted the white cotton hospital blanket covering him. "Okay, I guess. Just aggravating I had to have my appendix taken out. I thought that was something that happened to kids, not grown men."

She shrugged. "A bad appendix can happen at any age."

"Apparently," he muttered. "Too bad I didn't realize

that was what was causing my pain. I thought I was trying to pass another kidney stone."

"Since both are painful, I understand how you could make that assumption. Besides my planning to let you eat, I've got more good news this morning. Your white blood cell count is trending downward so going home is getting closer."

Although he looked relieved, he grumbled, "No wonder with as much medication as you people have pumped into me."

"All those medications seem to be working." Hailey shifted her gaze to the tired-appearing woman sitting in the chair beside her husband's hospital bed. Had she eaten anything other than the orange? Hailey made a note to request Dietary bring an extra breakfast tray, if available. When Hailey had entered the room, Sharla's fingers had paused in the crocheting she was doing on making an afghan. The colors reminded Hailey of the previous night's sunset with its mix of warm red, orange, and golds. Her fingers itched to reach out to see if the yarn was as soft as it appeared. "That's beautiful."

Brightening at the compliment, Sharla held up the piece for Hailey to better see what she had done. "It's all my favorite colors. Working with my hands helps me not be so nervous at being here." Arranging the piece back into her lap, she chuckled. "I found that crocheting was good therapy years ago when we lived up north. I usually make several a year."

With med school, then residency, Hailey hadn't had time for hobbies since high school other than occasionally losing herself in a book. She hoped to find a few interests that would fill her with passion. Her adoptive mother had painted, and Hailey had dabbled with that on occasion during her teens. Wanting to please her talented mother who'd hoped Hailey would possess artistic ability, she'd never been able to relax enough to truly enjoy what she was doing, though. Hailey's talent had been reading, studying, and making excellent grades. She'd been great at doing those, but not so much on anything creative that she'd tried thus far in life. Maybe she'd try her hand at some new creative ventures, but for now, she was excited to learn more about her new hometown, to meet people, volunteer, and get involved in the community.

She wanted to have a life, because she'd not had one since…since before her parents died, since before John, and residency. Only during those few years after the Eastons adopted her up until they'd passed had she belonged anywhere and had a life.

With her move to Florida, she was changing that.

She examined Melvin, taking care with his surgical site as she checked the incision, and was glad that he continued to progress. "Let's see how you do with soft food, then we'll advance your diet as tolerated. If you don't have any reoccurrence of chest symptoms and your labs continue to improve when I review them in the morning, we will discuss a discharge plan."

Hailey made notes in his electronic record, putting in for the dietary order changes and the tray for Sharla. She also ordered labs to be drawn the following morning. She spoke with the couple a few more minutes, making sure to address questions, then went to check on another patient. Hopefully, Larry Davis would be able to be discharged that day or the following morning.

After disinfecting her hands with the wall sanitizer

pump just outside his doorway, Hailey entered the gentleman's room, expecting to see him watching old Westerns as he'd been doing the previous two mornings. Instead, he appeared to be sleeping.

"Good morning, Mr. Davis," she greeted, not wanting to startle him as she approached his bed. His chest was rising and falling, but when he hadn't roused when she reached his bedside, nervousness set in. "Mr. Davis? I'm going to touch your arm."

She placed her hands on his arm and gave a gentle shake. He didn't react to the stimulation. She did a quick pulse check. There, but thready.

"Mr. Davis, this is Dr. Easton. I'm going to listen to your chest," she told him in hope that he was aware of her presence. She placed the diaphragm of her stethoscope on his chest. Grimacing at what she heard, she pulled out her phone to call for assistance.

CHAPTER THREE

"CODE BLUE. CODE BLUE," the announcer blared over Venice General Hospital's PA system then proceeded to give the location of the emergency, citing the medical floor and patient room number. Cayden recognized the number as the one he'd been headed to. Larry Davis had been admitted with sick sinus syndrome earlier in the week and had been improving. He'd been transferred out of the at-full-capacity cardiac care unit to the medical floor two days prior. He'd been somewhat better the previous day and Cayden had planned to recommend he be sent home that day or the next. What had changed?

The man's vital signs, apparently.

Having been in the medical floor hallway, Cayden rushed to Mr. Davis's room, not surprised to see part of the code team in action. That Hailey led the code had his stomach buzzing with excitement the same as it did each time that he saw her. He'd enjoyed their evening together and was looking forward to introducing her to shark tooth hunting. As a friend, he assured himself, despite his attraction to her. Friendship worked with their being co-workers. Being lovers did not. He needed to remember that. You'd think with the beating Cynthia had given his heart he wouldn't need to remind himself. Then again, she hadn't been the first to trample on his affections. Fortunately, she was the last and would remain so as he'd permanently taken his heart off the market.

"Dr. Wilton," Renee said, noticing he had entered the room. While Hailey did chest compressions, the charge nurse delivered oxygen via a bag valve mask.

At his name, Hailey's blue gaze lifted from where she'd been observing Larry, met Cayden's for a millisecond, then returned to her patient, all without her palms pausing from where she rhythmically compressed the man's chest. That brief meeting of their gazes had Cayden sucking in a deep breath before he hit the ground from lack of oxygen himself.

"You want me to take over compressions?" He moved beside her, knowing the lifesaving actions quickly wore out one's arms. Depending upon how long she'd been doing the hundred-plus compressions per minute routine her arms might already be trembling. They'd just called the code, so probably not long, but he wanted to help.

"Either that or you can lead the code until the compression nurse arrives to take this over."

Cayden had been so close he wasn't surprised he'd beat the rest of the code team to the room. His gut instinct told him to let Hailey run the code. Today was her third day on the floor. He'd assist and jump in where needed. He leaned in next to her, clasped his hands, and held them just above Larry's chest. "On the count of three, I'll take over compressions. One. Two. Three." His hands replaced hers in pushing in Larry's chest just over two inches with each downward push. "Fill me in on what happened."

"I came to check him. He looked to be asleep and wouldn't rouse," Hailey told him. "He was breathing, just, but pulse was thready. Systolic blood pressure was in the low sixties. Oxygen saturation was upper seventies then and now."

A nurse rushed in with the crash cart and, while Cayden continued to compress Larry's chest, Renee continued to deliver oxygen via the bag valve mask ventilator. Hailey and the nurse who'd arrived with the supplies dug into the cart, one going for medication while the other opened the defibrillator.

A documenter, security guard, and a respiratory therapist rushed into the room, along with another nurse. The respiratory therapist took over the bag valve mask delivering air. Renee shifted to the crash cart, taking over opening the defibrillator leads and freeing Hailey to assess the situation and direct the code.

A nurse cut Larry's gown out of the way, and Renee pressed the defibrillator leads to the man's chest. Glancing toward the display, Hailey waited the few seconds while the machine assessed Larry's heart's electrical activity.

The defibrillator didn't recommend a shock and Hailey advised, "Keep doing CPR."

"Trade on compressions." The code team's compression nurse leaned in to take over Cayden's role. On the count of three, Cayden shifted back as the nurse immediately started pressing the man's chest.

Stretching out his arms, he stepped back, then moved beside Hailey to assess the situation, his gaze going from the telemetry to the defibrillator's display. The machine screen changed, flashing its new recommendation. She was on top of it, immediately reacting.

"Prepare to deliver shock," Hailey said, then warned, "All clear."

Everyone who'd been administering care stepped back, making sure they weren't touching the patient. First glancing to check that everyone truly appeared all clear, Hailey pushed the button that administered the electrical pulse that would hopefully jolt the patient's heart back into rhythm.

Immediately, Cayden and the others were poised, ready for whatever was needed, all the while holding their breath as they waited for the machine's analysis of Larry's heart rhythm. He was in ventricular tachycardia where his heart was essentially quivering without pumping sufficient blood to supply his body with oxygen.

"Give epinephrine," Hailey ordered, not glancing up as an anesthesiologist entered the room. Good. If the patient warranted intubation, the specialist would be the one to do so. Efficiency of time was of the essence since compression would have to be stopped for tube placement. Cayden could do it, as no doubt could Hailey, but neither of them had the experience the specialist did.

Everyone performing their roles, they continued giving lifesaving measures. As soon as the defibrillator monitor advised to do so, Hailey ordered everyone to step back so she could administer another electrical shock.

"All clear," she said, then pushed the machine's button for a second shock in continued hope of restoring a normal rhythm.

Holding his breath, Cayden watched the screen. There. A normal beat, then another. Another. And another. *Yes.*

"Equipment is showing a normal sinus rhythm," Hailey informed them, her voice calm, but relieved.

A collective sigh went up around the hospital room. Not that Larry was out of the woods, but he was alive, and his heart was currently pumping oxygen out to his body. How long that lasted was another matter. His heart could stay in rhythm or jump right back out. Or worse. His heart could completely stop beating.

"Let's get him ready to transfer to the Cardiac Care Unit," Hailey ordered.

Within minutes, Larry was being transferred to the CCU and would soon thereafter be in the cardiac lab for testing to find out what had triggered his dangerous arrhythmia. Cayden and Hailey traveled down the hallway with the team as they rolled the patient's bed and equipment. Once their patient had been handed off to the CCU, Hailey took a deep breath.

"What a morning, huh?" Cayden asked from where he stood beside her, watching as the CCU team took over Larry's care. "Not even working on the floor a week and you've already saved a man's life. Congratulations."

Hailey gave him a *Yeah, right* look. "Some third day on the job. Not counting orientation, of course." Her gaze going back to their patient, she let out a long sigh.

His heart went out to her. Having a patient to code was never easy. To have one happen so quickly into starting a new job was diving in headfirst. "You did good."

Looking surprised at his compliment, she smiled, but it was a weak one. "Thank you. I'm just glad he didn't die. For so many reasons, that would have been terrible."

"You saved him."

She didn't look convinced, instead shaking her head. "The team saved him."

"The team under your lead," he reminded her, surprised at just how rattled she appeared. Thinking back, he'd probably been rattled on his first few codes, as well.

"Honestly, I was hoping to send him home. I'd thought possibly today." She eyed where the CCU team was setting up Larry's equipment in his new high-intensity care room that was really more of a three-sided area open to the hallway with a large sliding glass door that could be pulled closed for privacy. "Thank goodness I hadn't."

"I'd planned to recommend he go home today, too. The reality is that one's health can change in a heartbeat." He nudged her arm. "Some things can be predicted. Some can't." She knew that but with her so fresh out of residency, he understood why she was being critical of herself. As far as things that could and couldn't be predicted, take his reaction to her, for instance. Because his simple nudge had him intensely aware that he'd touched her. Given where they were, what they'd just experienced, he wouldn't have predicted the zings shooting through him. Yet, there they went. *Zing. Zing. Zing.* He swallowed, then added, "Pun intended, and you have to smile that the heart specialist has jokes."

"Thanks." She smiled and it was a little more real. "The whole team showed up quickly and worked well together. Plus, we had you there. Not every code is lucky enough to have a cardiologist to give a hand." She cut her gaze toward him and surprised him with a nudge of her own, eliciting another flare of zings. "I appreciated you being there, Cayden. To have you and Renee in the room definitely made me feel better just because you were familiar and friendly faces."

Her admission had his stomach flopping. Familiar and friendly. That's what they were destined to be. Not that those zings felt familiar or friendly, but more of an attack on logic and good intentions. "Then I'm glad I arrived when I did. But I have no doubt that you would have been just fine. You ran the code exactly the way I would have done."

Giving an appreciative smile, she stood a little taller and nodded. "You're right. I worked plenty of codes during residency. However, this is my first one while not a resident, the first one at a new hospital, the first one during my first week on the job, and that made it feel different," she admitted, brushing a strayed-from-her-ponytail lock of hair back behind her ear and meeting his gaze. "I'm not sure if that makes sense, but like I said, it was nice knowing I had you there. Is the med-surg floor always this exciting?"

He was glad she'd had him there, too. Not because she'd needed him, but because she'd said his presence had comforted her. He liked that she felt that way, that she'd viewed his presence as a plus. What he wasn't sure of was how much he liked those things or how much he liked the way she was looking at him with more than a little awe mingled in with appreciation.

"Med-surg has it's days, but most are relatively calm compared to the other hospital units." He grinned. "Apparently, despite having never found a four-leaf clover, you're just lucky that way."

She snorted. "The cardiologist really does have jokes. However, that we got him back into rhythm makes me feel lucky." She glanced around the busy CCU room where Larry was being attended to by the nurses, respiratory therapist, and anesthesiologist. "No one wants to lose a patient, but especially not during your first week on a new job." Hesitating a moment, she stared directly into Cayden's eyes, making him feel as if he needed to loosen his collar and his scrub top didn't have one. "I'm no longer needed here and should head back to the medical floor. I've got a few more patients to see for my morning rounds."

She turned to go and had taken a few steps before Cayden caught up to walk beside her. "Me, too. That's why I was so close when the code was called."

She continued toward the elevator bank. "You being so close is something else that makes me feel lucky. Maybe four-leaf clovers are overrated."

"Maybe." He was glad she seemed to have gotten her composure back and was making jokes. "We should celebrate."

Now where had that come from? They didn't need to celebrate her doing her job. Yet he wanted to take her out to do just that. To celebrate her because his gut instinct said Hailey wasn't used to being celebrated. He probably wasn't the guy who should be doing so, since he was deeply attracted to her physically and they were co-workers. That wasn't a good combination. Just look at the messy situation he'd been in when Cynthia had cheated on him. He'd been ready to promise his future to her and she'd not been faithfully committed to him in the present. Which shouldn't have surprised him. His own parents hadn't been faithful to each other.

Hailey looked at him with confusion. "Celebrate?"

"Life should be celebrated." None of his meanderings of the past made that any less true. "And especially when it's the result of a successful code during one's first work week."

"Ah, I see." Her lips twitched. "In that case, what did you have in mind, Dr. Wilton?"

"Dinner and a toast to the unnecessity of four-leaf clovers for good fortune?"

She hesitated, waiting until they'd reached the elevator bank and she'd pressed the up arrow prior to turning toward him. The elevator door opened. No one was in the car and they stepped inside.

"Dinner two nights in a row?" Her eyes flickered with uncertainty as they met his. "I'm not sure that's a good idea."

Cayden couldn't argue. Somehow, though, he suspected her reasons ran deeper than them working together. "I asked so I'm paying. A free dinner could be called good luck, too."

Her lips twitched, hinting that she was fighting a smile. Good. He wanted to make her smile. "Hasn't anyone ever told you that there's no such thing as a free dinner?"

She was probably right. There was always a price to be paid, but that didn't keep his insides from lighting up like the Fourth of July when she agreed.

Incoming waves lapped at Hailey's feet as she walked along the shore. She and Cayden had eaten dinner on the same blanket he'd had from the previous night. When they'd finished, she'd said she'd like to walk, and he'd immediately stood. Spending time with a man who didn't purposely do the opposite of whatever she suggested was such an oddity that she'd caught herself staring at him for much longer than she should have. He hadn't seemed to mind, just smiled at her as if it was the most normal thing in the world. The light breeze coming off the water and the temperature felt perfect after a long day spent inside the hospital. The company was perfect, too. Too perfect.

"Tell me about Leanna Moore." What was she doing? Trying to prove to herself that he wasn't perfect? She knew he wasn't. No one was, including and especially her. Or maybe she was trying to sabotage the sense of contentment that being with him filled her with. Contentment? That wasn't the most accurate way to describe how she responded to him. Besides, there was no reason for Cayden to tell her anything about the woman he'd once dated. He and Hailey were just friends...right?

But Cayden didn't seem upset by her inappropriate and out-of-the-blue request. "She and I hit it off for a while. We worked when neither of us was interested in anything long-term. She started wanting something more." He squinted at how the evening sun hit his face. "She's a great person. I was upfront with her that I wouldn't ever want more and we ended the physical side of our friendship before things got too messy for us to remain friends."

Hailey walked closest to the water, and a fresh wave lapped at her feet.

"It's good you remained friends." She and John sure weren't. The unfriendly sentiment was mutual except when he was trying to convince her to return to Ohio. He'd called the night before, but not wanting her enjoyable evening with Cayden spoiled, she'd let the call go to voicemail. "Renee mentioned that you do a weekly segment during her morning radio show."

"I'm flattered that you were talking about me with Renee and curious as to why she would mention Leanna. Not that I go around broadcasting my personal life, but it's no secret that I've been involved with women."

Involved. Hailey mentally gulped at what he likely meant by that. "Renee must have gotten the wrong impression that you were more serious."

"That we've remained close friends may confuse some." He shrugged. "But, to be fair, at one time Leanna had hoped for a proposal, but that was never going to happen. Not from me. I've no desire to ever get married."

The water pulled back toward the sea, causing the sand to shift beneath Hailey's feet and she fought to keep from stumbling.

"Me, either." Heat infused her cheeks the moment the claim left her lips and she felt compelled to rush on. "Marriage is overrated." Not that she knew firsthand, but by some standards she'd been John's common-law wife due to how long they lived together. Ten wasted years. She wouldn't be risking that again. Relationships never lasted in her life, anyway.

Just as another wave rushed around them, this one climbing midway up Hailey's calf, Cayden stopped walking. "You continue to surprise me, Hailey. Why is it that you agree with my sentiments on marriage?"

"I was in my last relationship for almost a decade." Her *only* relationship. "Between that, school, and residency, I've missed out on a lot in life, you know?" Which was true and easier to admit than going into the details of just how hollow that relationship had been. "I want to do things with friends, the things most people did during their teens and university days, but I didn't. I was too busy making sure I made good grades and working." Next to her, he was quiet, and she wondered if she'd admitted too much. "I'm not sure if that makes sense, but it's where I'm at in my life journey and for the first time in a long time, I feel at peace."

As she said the words, she acknowledged their validity. Not that she'd achieved all or even most of her self-improvement goals, but because she'd taken control of her life and was making steps in the right direction. That she was telling him those things was further validation of how far she'd come. How could he make her so jittery inside and yet be so easy to talk to that she told him things that were so personal? Things that she was just realizing as she was saying them?

"As I said, you surprise me." He met her gaze and she fought to keep from looking away. "Being near the water gives me that sense of peace. I run here most mornings because my day goes better when I've spent time near the water."

Staring into his eyes, she wondered if diving in would bring further peace or throw her into complete turmoil. "If being near the water is what brings peace, then I should have moved long ago."

Concern shone on his face. "I take it your life in Ohio wasn't that great?"

"It led me to here so I'm not going to complain." Because, right here, next to this delicious and kind man who she was pouring her most inner thoughts out to felt like a marvelous place to be. She could tell that he wanted to ask more, but he just nodded. Maybe that was part of why he was so easy to talk to. He seemed to instinctively recognize her comfort zone and didn't push beyond it.

"I'm glad you're here, Hailey." It was probably just how the sun shone, how it hit his gorgeous hazel eyes, how the soft waves lapped at her feet that had her feeling more in sync than she'd ever felt with another person. What was it about him?

"Why?" She couldn't believe she'd asked. Even after all the time they'd lived together, having such an open, honest conversation with John would have been difficult. Impossible even. He hadn't been one for deep conversations. Or conversations at all unless the topic was something that interested him.

"Why not?" Cayden gave a sheepish grin and reached for her hand, entwining his fingers with hers. They were warm, strong, firm, full of electricity that zapped from him to her. Hailey was completely stunned.

Why is he holding my hand?

Heart pounding, she gulped. Taking a deep breath, she reminded herself that she was the new Hailey. The new Hailey could hold a gorgeous man's hand if she wanted to. It didn't mean anything. Maybe this was what friends did. Or maybe he wanted to be more than friends. What was it Renee had said about guarding her heart but still having fun? Being with Cayden was fun. How long had it been since she'd been more than an inconvenience and wallet? Since she'd felt attractive? Wanted? Feminine in all the best ways? Had she ever? When Cayden looked at her, she felt those things. Those scary, wonderful, addictive things.

Why not?

Yeah, she could think of a million reasons, but none of them had her pulling her hand from where it was clasped with his.

Later, orange and red hues painted the sky. Hailey sat on the blanket they had left spread during their walk and Cayden had gone to his car.

"Dessert and our toast to good luck," he proclaimed when he returned, holding up a small bag cooler and wine holder.

She eyed them with mixed feelings. "If I keep hanging out with you, I'm going to gain back the progress I've made in losing weight and will never reach my goal."

His forehead wrinkled. "You're dieting?"

"For my whole life it seems." Mainly, she'd just gotten a bit down after her parents died and the resulting extra pounds had added up over time. Food comforted her, making her feel better in the moment. She didn't like the trait but recognized it as her reality. It was a wonder she hadn't gained a lot more than she had over the last ten years.

Cayden ran his gaze over her, which should have made her want to suck everything in as tightly as she could, but she sat still under his scrutiny.

"The only diet you need is one where you eat healthy."

She snorted. "Says the man who brought appetizers and dessert in addition to the side salad, asparagus, and salmon I ordered for dinner."

"I didn't know I was sabotaging something that was important to you. Fortunately, you're perfect as you are. Besides, I chose fresh strawberries. They're a great source of vitamin C and good for you." He handed her the plastic champagne glasses, then removed the bottle's foil cover.

"No cork?" she asked, having imagined that he'd pop the top. Or was that just something that happened in movies?

"No cork." He grinned mischievously. "You may fault me for a technicality."

Wondering what he meant, she arched a brow. "Uh-oh. What have you done?"

He turned the bottle so that she could read the label.

"Sparkling apple cider?" She tsked as he poured bubbly liquid into one glass and then the other. Why did her insides feel just as bubbly? "You're right. I may deduct points from your celebration skills." Although, not really. She was blown away that he'd brought the bottle.

"I should get an A for effort since I noticed you didn't drink anything alcoholic last night and so I opted for an alternative, just in case." He twisted the top onto the bottle, then slid it back into the cooler bag. She held out one of the plastic glasses. Grinning, he took it, then clinked it to hers. "Here's to your first code's success."

He'd noticed that and adjusted what he'd bought to accommodate what he'd thought she'd want? Gulping back the emotions hitting her, Hailey raised her glass, touching it to his.

"And to points not deducted."

CHAPTER FOUR

ALTHOUGH THEY TEXTED, Hailey didn't see Cayden again until Sunday morning for their planned shark tooth hunt. At least, not outside of her mind, she hadn't. How could she think so much of someone she'd just met? How could she miss him? She'd been off from the hospital on Thursday. It was her designated self-care day. She exercised, got a massage, had her lashes, hair, and nails done on rotation in Sarasota, had her weekly online mental health therapy session, and furniture shopped. She'd not had a lot of things to move as most of her parents' things had been auctioned off after they'd passed. She'd been eighteen and had agreed with what the estate trustee recommended.

With the exception of a few mementoes and a painting of her mother's that John had never liked and insisted stay in the closet, she'd left most things at the apartment she'd shared with him, including the majority of her clothes. She'd wanted very little from her former life, just a few books and things from school, and had taken off from Ohio with what fit into her car. Upon arrival, she'd unpacked at the house she'd bought with only having seen it online, but knowing it was the right one. Next, she'd traded her boring sedan for the shiny blue convertible that had caught her eye when she'd driven by the lot in Sarasota. Her new life would be filled with things she'd picked, things she liked, starting with a bright, airy home, lots of whites and turquoise colors making up the sea theme she'd chosen. With initially focusing on her physical appearance and mindset, her new job, and attending neighborhood events, she'd not had much time for home decor shopping. When she had gone, she'd been picky so the process was slow. The week she'd arrived, she'd bought a bed, chest of drawers, nightstand, and an oversized amazing reading chair. She'd made a department store run for bedding, bath linens, and odd and ends. The following week, she'd found a four-person dining room table and chairs to put in the window nook off her kitchen. For a sofa, she'd been willing to wait until she found just the right one. Happily, she'd found the one today, along with a comfy chair, and bleached wooden coffee and end tables. She made arrangements for the items to be delivered the following evening, so, despite how she couldn't stop thinking of Cayden, she'd declined his phoned invitation to listen to a band playing at a nearby community village shopping area.

On Saturday, she went to the cookout with Ryan. He'd been fun, a gentleman, opening the car door and introducing her to his friends. Even though the evening was "just as friends," his attention had made her feel good, but in such a different way from how she felt with Cayden that she'd not been able to prevent comparing the outing with when she was with him. Unfortunately, she'd also not been able to stop wondering what Cayden was doing. Had he gone to listen to music the night before, only with someone as a date rather than friend? Perhaps with Leanna Moore. The green in Hailey's veins didn't bode well for someone who wasn't ready to date and, although innocent and arranged prior to meeting Cayden, was with another man.

Cayden muddied the waters of her somewhat clear vision for her future. She was more attracted to him than she'd known possible. After the horror of her relationship with John, the last thing she should be thinking about was a man. But Cayden was never far from her mind. Had she truly only known him a week?

Was that the real reason she'd not gone with him Friday evening? Fear of how he'd already gotten beneath her skin? After all, she could have invited him to wait with her on her furniture delivery and they could have gone to listen to the music afterward. Was she scared of how he made her feel? And if so, wasn't being afraid letting John still wield control over her life?

On Sunday morning, a beach-adventure-ready Hailey watched for Cayden's arrival and rushed to meet him before he'd much more than gotten out of his car. Her home was still too bare for her to let him in, which didn't make a lot of sense since she'd gotten the new pieces Friday and she'd let Ryan come in when he'd retrieved her for the cookout. It hadn't seemed to matter so much what *he* thought of her bare walls. It shouldn't matter what Cayden thought of her home. It was hers and as long as she loved it, that was what mattered. She didn't have to please anyone else.

"You're very quiet." Cayden glanced her way from the driver's seat of his SUV. As Ryan had, he'd opened the passenger door for her, something John never did. Of course, they'd been very young when they'd first gotten together and that probably made a difference. Maybe. Either way, she'd felt giddy inside like a silly schoolgirl at the gesture. How low were her standards if it took so little to impress her?

Something else to work on—have higher expectations from everyone she let into her life.

"I was thinking about needing to shop for my apartment." The truth, just that she'd had several other thoughts, too. "I've been to several places, but not found what I'm looking for. My walls are very blah." Other than in her bedroom where she had her mother's painting that she cherished. She'd have hung it in her apartment with John if she hadn't feared that he might do something to it if she'd left it in plain sight. "Not that I want clutter, but I hope to find a few special pieces to give the place a splash of me."

"A splash of you?" Cayden chuckled, glancing her way briefly as he maneuvered his vehicle through the light traffic. "That sounds intriguing and possibly painful."

"Ha. Ha. You knew what I meant." She'd wondered how things would be between them with her saying no to going with him Friday. She'd explained about the furniture, but she half expected him to be upset that she'd not done as he wished. His smile and nature were so relaxed that any uncertainty over saying no had quickly dissolved.

As silly as it was since she was similarly dressed, he'd caught her completely off guard with his bare legs as she'd only seen him with scrubs or rolled-up casual slacks. For their shark tooth hunting adventure, he wore a Venice Has Heart T-shirt complete with various local sponsors listed on the back and a pair of yellow with little pink flamingos swim trunks that came to just above his knees. He'd opted for leather sandals. Casual Cayden was just as hot as Dr. Cayden. Maybe more so as he seemed more approachable in his "play" clothes.

More approachable? Ha! If he'd been any more approachable she'd have been pushing him back on the sand after their "celebration" toast and strawberries. That he had a playboy reputation and hadn't made any moves on her should clue her in that, despite his occasional flirty comment and the spark she saw in his eyes that she'd swear was desire, ultimately, he wasn't interested in anything more than friendship.

"What are you needing? Maybe I can help," he offered, fortunately oblivious to her mental ramblings.

"You have spare lamps, pictures, and such lying around to give my house personality?" She didn't know exactly what she wanted, just knew she'd recognize the right additions when she came across them.

"You wouldn't want what's in my house." He tapped his thumbs against the steering wheel. "My condo is the ultimate bachelor pad, right down to the bicycle and surfboard in my living room. But I'm game to changing our plans to going shopping instead of to Caspersen."

Fighting a smile, she eyed him with suspicion. "Afraid you won't be able to live up to your promise of helping me find a shark tooth?"

"I keep my promises." His gaze cut to hers, emphasizing his point with its intensity and having her swallow. "We've plenty of time for finding shark teeth. Just say the word and we'll save that for another time and go shopping today."

That Cayden was willing to change their plans so readily, that he was willing to go shopping with her, had her eyeing him with renewed awe. John would have complained and only have agreed if she'd begged and they'd been shopping for him. He'd do all kinds of things when there was something in it for him.

"I'm not going to be contacted by a home makeover show anytime soon," his grin widened, "but I have decent taste. Plus, having two spare arms to carry things would be helpful."

"Or I could just use a shopping cart," she teased trying not to let her gaze go to where his arms were on display. He looked as if he could carry a lot of things. He wasn't bulky muscled, just really fit, as if he took his role as a cardiologist and promoting good heart health seriously. Hailey swallowed. Yeah, he looked like the poster child—man—for good heart health. Or maybe a poster for a heartthrob, because he was certainly that, too. Take her heart for instance. It was throbbing so hard that she was surprised it didn't drown out the music he had playing.

He chuckled. "You could, but where's the fun in that?"

"We're not dressed for shopping." She had on her bathing suit beneath her loose shorts and baggy T-shirt. They definitely had a we're-heading-to-the-beach vibe.

"You're in Florida. Beach attire works for most occasions."

She twisted in the passenger seat to more fully look at him. "You would skip going to the beach to go shopping with me?"

He nodded.

"Okay, you may regret this, because I'm going to take you up on your offer." Not that she didn't want to go to the beach with him, but she would like to find a few things for her house and she was curious about shopping with Cayden.

"Just point me in the direction you want to go and that's where I'll drive." He didn't seem the slightest fazed by their change of plans.

"Yeah, that's not a good idea. I'm still learning where things are so you may have to help. Plus, I've searched around here and haven't found what I want. I'm looking for lamps, pictures for my walls, a few cool knickknacks, that kind of thing. As cliché as it may seem, my home theme is the water."

"I'm impressed you have a home theme."

"Other than 'bachelor pad'?" Had she really just batted her lashes when his gaze was on the road, anyway?

"Yeah, I don't see that one working for you." He grinned, then glanced her way. "If you don't mind the drive, there's a place just outside Sarasota that might have what you're looking for."

"I'm good with Sarasota. It's less than an hour and where I purchased my living room furniture." She made the drive every Thursday for her big makeover maintenance.

"To Sarasota it is, then."

Cayden drove her to a large warehouse-type store that offered a variety of new and locally made items. Shopping with him was an adventure. He was funny, made hilarious suggestions, and yet, fairly quickly homed in on her taste preferences. When he pointed out two lamps that had been made by a local artisan, excitement hit.

"Those are amazing." She ran her fingertip over the intricate piece of smooth bleached driftwood that made up the base and neck of one of the lamps. The artist had covered the lower portion of the base with seashells. "Do you think I'm going overboard with my beach theme?"

"You do recall that you didn't let me see your house so I've no basis to answer with any accuracy?"

She gave a sheepish smile. "Sorry."

"But, for whatever its worth, my thought is that if you like the lamps, and you obviously do, buy them." He shrugged. "If, down the road, you decide that you want to change them out, you can. You're not stuck with today's decision forever."

He made a good point and she suspected that she'd regret it if she didn't buy one. She could even envision the piece in her living room next to her new sofa.

"Which do you like best?" She knew which she preferred but was curious if he agreed. Part of her hoped he didn't as he seemed much too in sync with her thoughts.

He ran his gaze over each lamp, then pointed to the one that had originally drawn her attention. "That one. Both pieces are great, but I like how the artist seeped the turquoise into the variances in the wood. It's subtle enough that you barely see it initially, but is a testament to its connection to the sea."

"Sold." Because, seriously, how could she not choose that one since he'd picked the lamp she'd liked best? Or ever get rid of the piece when he'd described the design exactly how she'd seen it? The subtle hint of color inflected into the wood added just the right pizzazz. She suspected she'd never look at it without being reminded of him, which gave her a moment's pause. She didn't want her home to remind her of him or anyone. It was supposed to be about her, her safe place and haven from the world. Still, she had chosen prior to his description and truly, the lamp was perfect. "Let's put those 'spare arms' to use."

Grinning, he picked up the lamp. "While you finish looking, I'll take this to the cashier for them to hold until we're ready to check out."

Hailey didn't find anything else that jumped out at the shop, but she loved the lamp and paid for it. Cayden loaded the artsy light onto the back floorboard of his SUV. He placed the shade on the seat, then used the towels he'd brought for their beach excursion to protectively place around the lamp.

"I could sit back there and make sure it doesn't get banged around," she offered. Truth was, she was impressed by his thoughtfulness in how he arranged the lamp.

"And have me looking like I'm driving Miss Hailey?" He wrinkled his nose. After one last check to make sure the lamp was secure, he got into the driver's seat. "I prefer to have you up here next to me." He buckled his safety belt, then started the car. "Are you in a hurry?"

"Not necessarily. What do you have in mind?"

"The bigger farmers markets are on Saturday but there are some that carry over onto Sundays. They usually have a variety of vendors ranging from food to artisans. There's one not too far from here," he told her. "We could grab lunch, walk around to see if we can find any other treasures for your home."

Her home. Not her apartment, but her home. Because that was what she was making in Florida. A home for herself.

A home and a new life that she liked more and more.

* * *

A couple of hours later, Cayden watched as Hailey surveyed the ice cream selection with eyes as big as any child's. Rather than order, she turned to him and shook her head.

"I'm going to pass. Thanks, though."

"It's organic and made with all-natural ingredients," he said. They'd eaten a healthy lunch and he'd been the one to suggest ice cream. Ice cream was his weakness. Not that he did, but he could eat it every single day and not get tired of the cold dessert. He wasn't even picky on what flavor. He liked them all. Some better than others. In his book, there were no bad ice cream flavors.

"That's not it. You go ahead."

Then he remembered she'd mentioned dieting. How did he convince her that her curves were perfect without making her self-conscious or have her to think he was being a jerk? Because he really liked the ease in which they'd enjoyed their day and didn't want to do anything that jeopardized that comradery. It had been a good day. A great day. Surely, she must think so, too.

Sure, he'd been a bit prickly Friday evening when they'd been on the phone and she'd said she had to wait on her furniture. Her reason had felt as flat as if she'd said she had to wash her hair. That he'd been disappointed had bothered him. He had no right to be bothered that she'd said no, but he'd spent most of his on call day mulling over just how much it had.

He didn't want more than friendship with her, and yet…he did. Hailey was refreshing, with an air of innocence mingled with an irresistible feminine allure that sucked him right in.

"I'm not eating ice cream if you're not, Hailey." He would be a jerk if he did that when he knew she wanted ice cream, too. But he didn't want her to feel he was sabotaging her if he pushed. He wanted her happy with herself. If she could see herself as he saw her, she would be. He'd hoped that with their plans being to go to the beach that she'd have foregone the makeup, because he longed to see her without it, but she'd been fully made up. He knew she was just as stunning barefaced as she was with all the latest beauty aids. How much he longed to see what she didn't readily reveal to the world should have Cynthia's name flashing through his mind like a warning beacon, but instead was muffled by how protective he felt at Hailey's vulnerability. He suspected someone had done a real number on her body image and although it wasn't Cayden's place to clear her vision to her true beauty, he wanted to do just that. Seeing how she still longingly stared at the display, he suggested, "How about if I order a small bowl and share a few bites?"

"I—" She glanced toward him, a slow smile spreading across her lovely mouth. "Okay, but just a few bites."

That a girl. "Which flavor do you want?"

She pointed to his favorite and he grinned. Incredible how in tune they were. "Great choice."

He ordered two scoops in a small bowl, then paid the cashier while another employee prepared their order. He slid his money clip into his pocket and took the ice cream bowl. Hailey had walked over to where a wide ledge served as a bar top–style table at the base of the storefront window. She sat on a stool and stared out at the boardwalk. Yeah, she should see what he saw. She was so beautiful she stole his breath and yet, it was the pureness in her eyes, in how she looked through the glass with appreciation of everything she was seeing, in how she smiled when she glanced up and saw him. That sweet, genuinely-happy-he'd-bought-ice-cream smile got him right in the feels.

"Remember, this is guilt-free ice cream." He pulled one of the spoons from the ice cream and handed it to her. "Enjoy."

"I didn't see 'guilt-free' written anywhere in the description."

"It should have been. For real, this place is known for using all-natural ingredients, nothing GMO or processed." He pulled the other spoon from the ice cream, a large glob sticking to the utensil. He stuck the cold confection in his mouth and savored the fruity flavor. "Mmm. Good and good for you."

"Next thing, you'll be trying to sell me oceanfront property in Arizona." Watching him, Hailey toyed with her spoon. "It's not fair that men can eat whatever they want and still look like you."

He scooped a second bite. "That's not an accurate statement."

"Do you eat whatever you want?" she challenged, still not using her spoon for anything other than to point it toward him.

Fortunately, other than his ice cream addiction, he ate a healthy Mediterranean diet and was lucky that he preferred eating clean. Ice cream was his guilty pleasure, and even then, he sought ones made with natural ingredients.

"I exercise regularly," he defended.

"No doubt."

Her tone made him smile and he flexed a little. "You like these?"

Snorting, she rolled her eyes with great exaggeration. "It's mostly your modesty that impresses me."

"I get that a lot." Laughing, he gestured to the bowl. "Eat up before it melts and you have a strawberry milkshake instead of ice cream."

Hailey ate one bite to his every three, and her bites were tiny in comparison to his, but at least she did eat some of the dessert and seemed to savor each bite. He refrained from saying anything more for fear she'd stop eating altogether. He didn't want to be a stumbling block, but whoever had made her think she needed to diet deserved a hardy talking to.

When they'd finished their dessert, they headed back out onto the blocked-off street where numerous vendors were selling their wares. The smell of roasted cinnamon pecans and almonds from a nearby booth filled the air and lured several passersby.

"Admit it," he said, glancing toward where she was taking in the busy booths and their various goods. "The ice cream was worth it."

"Sure, it was." Amused sarcasm laced her words. "At the moment," she added. "However, if you ask me when I'm in the gym huffing and puffing and it takes me more than an hour to burn off what I just ate..." She let her voice trail off, then clicked her tongue. "I really shouldn't have."

"You know you look fabulous, right?"

Her cheeks went bright pink. "Thank you for saying so, but I'm well aware that I've always been a little pudgy. I gained extra weight on top of that during med school.

I want to get it back off. I've lost some since completing residency and I plan to keep working on the rest. I don't fool myself that I'll ever be thin, but I'd like to be healthy, you know?"

He ran his gaze over her and shook his head. "What you call pudgy, I call sexy."

"And my ex called fat." Her color heightened after her words slipped out, letting him know she hadn't meant to say them.

Right in the middle of the busy-with-pedestrians street, he stopped walking to look directly at her, letting the crowd weave around them. "For the record, your ex was an idiot."

Looking stunned, Hailey's blue eyes lifted to his, then her mouth slowly curved upward. "You're right. He was."

That smile... She obviously had no clue how seductive her mouth was, how the curve of her neck should be listed as lethal to a man's peace of mind because he was so wanted to nuzzle her there. How—*get yourself together*, he ordered. Where were they...oh, yeah.

"Good, we're in agreement. Don't let his lack of good sense influence how you see yourself. You're beautiful. Inside and out. Now, let's go check out those paintings at that booth just up ahead." With that, he grabbed her hand, lacing his fingers with hers, and took off walking as if it weren't a big deal that he was holding her hand.

But, just as when they'd been walking on the beach, Hailey's soft hand clasped within his felt as if touching her was a very big deal. Even more so than during their sunset stroll. Which meant he probably shouldn't be holding her hand. But he wasn't letting go.

Not when Hailey held on to his hand as if he'd offered

her a lifeline to lift her from some terrible place she'd been stuck for much too long.

"I love it!" Hailey exclaimed of the artwork Cayden had just hung on her living room wall. She'd been anxious about letting him inside her house, wondering what he'd think of what she'd done thus far. As he'd been helping her carry her purchases inside, she'd not had much choice short of turning him away at the door. The truth was, she'd enjoyed their day, enjoyed being with him. And, as nervous as she'd thought she'd be at his seeing her incompletely put together house, when he'd walked in, he'd glanced around and that he'd liked what he'd seen was obvious.

His approval shouldn't matter. She'd lived on edge trying to get John's approval. She sure didn't want to be in a relationship where that misery became part of her day-to-day existence again. A big difference, she reminded herself, was that no matter what she did, John never really gave his approval regarding anything that wasn't to his benefit. Cayden seemed to selflessly give his time and again. That made her smile big. How wonderful to be with someone who made you feel better about yourself?

With his hands resting on his hips, he stared at her new picture. "She's growing on me."

"Ha! Don't give me that. You were the one to point her out to me." Pulling her gaze from him, Hailey admired the mermaid with her soulful eyes, turquoise tendrils and tail, and the chaotic sea. Wild waves crashed about the mermaid, but she appeared at ease, her expression one of being at peace with the world. The artist had used broken shells to create the mixed media rock emerging from the sea that the mermaid perched upon and nacre to make a pearly bikini top. Hailey had immediately fallen in love with the piece and how well it would look with her living room decor. She'd been right.

"You thought that meant I liked her?" He clicked his tongue. "I was joking when I said you should buy her."

Unfazed by his ragging, she shook her head. "No, you weren't. You like her as much as I do." His poor attempt to look innocent of her accusation failed miserably. "That's why you insisted upon buying her as a housewarming gift," she reminded him, still stunned by his generosity after a lifetime of only gifts from her parents. John had come through with holiday gifts, but they'd always been generic types of things. Supermarket flowers on her birthday. A small box of chocolates on Valentine's. New department store gloves and scarf set at Christmas year after year. Thank God she had no need of his gloves and scarfs in Florida. She'd left them all. Not that there would have been anything wrong with his gifts if they'd come with feeling rather than an obligatory holiday appeasement and expectation that she'd have done something extravagant for him. Besides, how many gloves and scarf sets had she needed? None now, because she had finally stepped into the sunshine. She met his gaze and hoped he could see how much she appreciated him. "Thank you, again, Cayden."

His brow lifted, but after a moment in which he looked torn on what he might say, he returned his attention to the artwork. "There is something about her that latches on to you and won't let go, isn't there? And you're welcome. I'm glad you gave in to my gifting her to you."

She hadn't wanted to, but he'd insisted that he'd spotted the artwork first and called dibs, saying that it was the perfect housewarming gift for a friend who'd just moved to town. He was smooth with the lines. Yet she didn't doubt his sincerity or that she would always treasure the piece. "Even the colors are perfect. As if she was meant to come home with me."

He gestured to where she'd put her new lamp. "That looks great, like it was made for this room, too. Great find."

"You're an expert at this shopping thing, too." He really was, and she'd had tons of fun in the process. "Maybe instead of shark tooth hunting, we can look for big shells. I'd like to have one to put on the table there."

He looked at her in question. "A conch shell?"

She nodded. "I think that's what they're called."

"You don't need to buy one. We can find good shells around here, but if we don't find what you're looking for, then we can go to Sanibel Island."

Sanibel Island. She'd heard of it at some point but couldn't place where it was in her mind. "How far away is that?"

He shrugged. "Just a couple of hours drive."

She gave a horrified look. "A couple of hours is too far to drive to find a seashell."

He laughed. "Where's your adventurous spirit?"

"Hidden beneath my practicality that says driving a couple of hours to find a seashell doesn't make good common sense. Especially when there are dozens of tourist shops around here that sell shells."

"We could say that we're going to Sanibel Island for sightseeing, rather than for shell hunting. Or maybe we will find one when we go shark tooth hunting. The catch to finding great ones really is to either go early or to dive to find them, though."

She adjusted where the lamp sat on the end table. Happiness bubbled inside. The lamp and the painting truly were the perfect finds and she'd had the most perfect day. "Dive?"

"Snorkeling," he clarified. "Although, we could scuba, too. Truthfully, if you were game to learn, that would be the best way to find what you want."

She shook her head. She could wait on finding a shell. There was no rush. "Ohio girl, remember? I'm not used to the ocean. I'd never been prior to moving here and the idea of snorkeling or diving makes me feel claustrophobic."

He looked taken aback. "You moved here without ever having visited? Where was your practicality when you made that decision?" His teasing tone filtered out any real judgment in his question.

"It seemed like a good idea at the time." Glancing around her bright, airy house, which made her feel free and light by just being in it, then at him, she lowered her lashes and smiled. "It's early yet, but so far, I'd say moving here was a great idea."

His eyes crinkled with his return smile. "You're liking our subtropical climate and good-natured natives, eh?"

"Absolutely." Everyone she'd met had been kind, especially him. That he was also the hottest man she'd ever met…she fought fanning her face. "The sunsets are beautiful, too."

"Some say they're spectacular."

Had he just stepped closer? Oh, heaven above, she really was about to fan her face.

"Speaking of sunsets, last night's was amazing. Did you see it?" he asked.

"Not really," she admitted. "I was at a cookout with a friend, and after eating, we were playing games in a small fenced-in backyard where the view wasn't that great so I didn't pay much attention."

An odd look settled onto his face as his gaze met hers. "A male friend?"

"Yes. A neighbor offered to introduce me to his friend group. They were a fun bunch. You'd like them."

The cookout, meeting Ryan's friends, playing cornhole, terrible as she'd been, had been fun. She'd been a little giddy that she was checking another box of having her new life.

"Are you going to see this neighbor again?" Cayden's eyes darkened and even though the evening had been innocent, she had trouble holding his gaze. She took a step back.

"I'm sure I will." She'd bumped into Ryan each time she'd gone to the community room events and he was frequently in the workout room while she was there for her early morning torture sessions. He'd been sweet and she'd enjoyed meeting his friends. They hadn't made any specific plans, but he'd asked if it was okay to call, and she'd said it was. Making friends was a priority and Ryan was one of the first she'd met.

"Oh." Cayden's face blanched of color, then red splotched his cheeks.

His "oh" held so much disappointment and negativity that she couldn't let it pass. She'd dealt with both much too often. Fingers curling into her palms, she said, "Go on."

"What do you want me to say, Hailey? That I'm glad that you went out with this guy last night and that you're planning to see him again?" He harrumphed. "I can't do that."

"Ryan," she supplied prior to thinking better of it.

"That's his name?" Cayden asked. She nodded, and he continued, "Okay, you told me to go on, so I will." He flexed his jaw. "I'd rather you not go out with Ryan again."

She fought flinching. John telling her what she could and couldn't do echoed through her mind. He wouldn't have said "rather you not" but would have just told her that she wasn't going to. That didn't seem to matter though as she lifted her chin.

"The cookout was just as friends, but for the record, you don't get a say in whether or not I go on a date with someone." Even as she said it, she questioned the validity of her bravado. Disappointing Cayden bothered her. She didn't want to disappoint him and that irked. She'd spent ten years trying not to disappoint John. Ten years that she'd never get back. She needed to focus on not disappointing herself and not another man.

"It's just—" Cayden stopped, raked his fingers through his hair, and closed his eyes as if he was at a loss for words.

"Just what?" Barely able to breathe, she crossed her arms and stared at him.

"The truth is that I'm jealous you were with another man last night, Hailey." He appeared as shocked as she was by his confession. Shocked, and perhaps a bit self-disgusted. "How's that for a truthful admission?"

Hailey's knees threatened to give way. "Why would you be jealous?"

"I like you." He didn't sound thrilled by his admission, but he'd said the words without hesitation.

Her heart pounded. She was standing in her living room, staring at the most gorgeous man she'd ever known, and he'd just said he liked her. Was this what it felt like to have the most popular guy in school notice you when you were of the wallflower variety?

"I like you, too."

Cayden's gaze didn't waver from hers. "Yet you were with another man last night? Why would you do that?"

She hadn't done anything wrong. His questions made her feel like bringing up all kinds of protective walls. Her evening had just been "as friends," but if it had been a date, she was well within her rights to have gone. She was not wrong to want to experience life.

"I just met you this past week," she reminded him, trying to choose her words wisely because she didn't want to argue with Cayden. How surreal was it that she felt as if she'd known him much longer? In reality, she'd been to the beach with him twice, seen him at work, and spent today with him. They were strangers. And yet, they weren't. She felt as if she knew him better than the man she'd lived with for almost ten years. "I can't even believe we're having this conversation."

"You're right." Frowning, he worked his jaw from one side then to the other. "Does *Ryan* know about me?"

Stunned, Hailey stared at him. "Why would I have told Ryan about you? A week ago today, he invited me to the cookout so I could get to know people because I'm new in town. You and I are coworkers." She put her fisted hands on her hips. "Please explain why Ryan would need to know anything about you?"

Cayden stared at the woman glaring at him and thought her well within her right to do so. Everything she said was true. What was wrong with him? He was acting like a jealous boyfriend.

He didn't do boyfriend. Hadn't in years. Sure, he'd gone out, but he'd only been involved with women who knew the score and didn't have false expectations. He'd let his romantic involvement with Leanna go on too long as she'd started wanting more and losing their friendship would have been a shame. Cynthia had been his last real girlfriend where his heart had been involved and, after that had ended as disastrously as his previous attempts at being in a supposedly committed relationship, he'd given up on happy-ever-after and was quite content with his happy-right-now status. Why he'd ever thought such a mythical thing existed was beyond him. It sure hadn't been the example his parents had set. Great as they were individually, together they'd been malignant. As far as jealous? Yeah, he didn't do that, either. Why had he told Hailey he was jealous?

Because it was true. Right or wrong, for the first time in forever the thought of a woman being with anyone other than him had him seeing green.

"You're right." Because what else could he say?

Her jaw dropped. "I am? I mean, of course, I am. I'm just surprised that you're admitting it. That's a new one for me."

"I've said it before, but your ex was an idiot." He paced across the room, staring at her mixed-media mermaid and battling emotions that felt as tumultuous as the artwork's churning sea. "That you were out with another man last night caught me off guard, Hailey. That's all."

He couldn't call it cheating because that implied something that existed between him and Hailey that didn't. But he couldn't squelch his dislike of the idea of her with another man, even if only as friends. Years had passed since the last time he'd cared about what a woman did with her time away from him. He wasn't the jealous type. Yet he wanted to beat his chest and warn this Ryan guy to stay away.

What's wrong with me?

"Am I missing something, Cayden?" Hailey pushed.

He turned back, taking in the stubborn tilt to her chin, the just as determined glint in her eyes. How was he supposed to explain that he didn't want a relationship, but he didn't want her out with other men? He couldn't tell her that. She'd laugh in his face or tell him to get out or both. Rightly so.

"Cayden?" She came to stand a foot in front of him when he remained silent. "We had such a great day. I don't want to argue with you. I don't understand what's happening."

What was happening was that his gaze had dropped to her mouth, watching as her lips formed each word, and now, all he could think, feel, was how much he wanted to kiss her. Out of desire, but also, as a way of staking his claim.

Frustrated with himself, he shook his head. "Nothing. I just—it's time I go."

Because as easy as it would be to give in to what he wanted to do, to kiss her, how strongly that he didn't want anyone else doing the same, made his head spin. He did not want to stake a claim. He didn't care what women did when they weren't with him. He hadn't since he'd found out Cynthia had been screwing around with another man. Beyond that, hadn't he decided that he and Hailey were coworkers, and anything more than friendship would be complicated?

Friendship with Hailey was already complicated.

Even so, unable to resist, he leaned in, and kissed her forehead. "Good night, Hailey."

With that, he hightailed it out of her house. Denying just how much Hailey got under his skin had become impossible. That quick peck to her forehead had done little to appease the culminating burn within him.

Since she claimed to not want marriage any more than he did, and he saw how she looked at him, sometimes so innocently that he wasn't even sure if she was aware how hot desire burned in her eyes, maybe he shouldn't deny either of them.

But if they became lovers, could they remain friends after the fires died down?

He liked Hailey more than as just the woman he wanted to devour from head to toe. They may have only known each other for a week as she'd so sassily pointed out, but he was positive he'd miss her if he lost her friendship.

CHAPTER FIVE

"GOOD MORNING," a tired Hailey greeted Melvin Little and his wife the following morning. Mondays had always been just another day as during residency she was just as likely to work on weekends as weekdays. More so, usually. With her new Monday through Wednesday work schedule, she rotated out with other physicians and would cover one weekend a month. Had she not tossed and turned all night with thoughts of Cayden, of trying to figure out what that little kiss had meant and why he'd left, then she might feel rested. Instead, she'd used drops to try to clear her red eyes and applied extra powder to hide her dark circles. Maybe no one would notice. She smiled a little brighter at her patient. "I hoped you'd be recovered enough that you'd have been dismissed prior to my returning to work this morning."

The bushy white-haired man scooted up in his hospital bed, grimacing a little as he did so, but moving easier than he had the last time she'd examined him. "Hoping to not have to see me again, Doc?"

She shook her head. "Just wishing you well." She glanced at the blanket in Sharla's lap. "Wow. You've gotten a lot of your afghan completed. That's wonderful."

"Thank you." Keeping a tight hold on her needle and

yarn, Sharla proudly held up the sunset-colored piece. "I'll probably have it finished within the next couple of days if he doesn't go home."

"Is that a request to keep him here until you've finished?" Hailey teased, running her hand beneath a hand sanitizer dispenser, then moving beside where Melvin lay. He still appeared pale, but his color was better.

"Could you?" Laughing, Sharla shot her husband a loving look. "When I get him home, he's going to be his usual cantankerous self and thinking I'm supposed to wait on him hand and foot. Having him here is like a vacation for me."

Melvin grunted at his wife's poking. "Don't let her fool you. She lives to dote on me. She did the same with the kids and now the grandkids. They came by yesterday. The whole lot of them. This room was a madhouse for an hour or so. Be glad you missed the chaos."

Hailey couldn't imagine having a big family and what it must feel like to have them be there for you. Those too-short years she'd had with the Eastons had just given her a taste of family life and then it had been ripped away.

She cleared her throat and her thoughts. "That's good you got to see them, but I hope you didn't overdo it."

He shrugged. "Hard to overdo anything when I'm just lying in a hospital bed and waiting on this old body to heal."

"There are different ways to overdo it." After first gloving up, Hailey listened to his heart, his lungs, then checked his abdomen. Everything sounded, looked, and felt as it should other than his chronic heart issues. He seemed to be improving from his surgical emergency and was slowly getting his strength back. "I think I have bad news for you,

Sharla. His white blood cell count was completely normal this morning. His surgical site is healing with no redness, drainage, or other sign of infection from his ruptured appendix. His BNP, that stands for brain natriuretic peptide, is still elevated, but not so elevated that home management of his heart failure shouldn't be sufficient. His numbers may have come down enough to be at his baseline, even. But either way, the levels are safe to further address in an outpatient setting. Dr. Wilton—" her heart squeezed as she said his name out loud "—will be by this morning and will be able to give you more information regarding your outpatient heart failure follow-up. As long as he's in agreement, then you'll be discharged later today."

"That's wonderful." Sharla smiled at her husband.

"Doc, that's the best news I've heard since I showed up at this place," Melvin said, coughing as he did so.

Hailey hadn't heard any rattles in his chest, nor had his chest X-ray picked up on any fluid buildup in his lungs. His cough and continued elevated BNP concerned her, but when everything was overall so improved, those weren't sufficient reasons to maintain acute inpatient care.

She talked with the couple a few more minutes, then left his room to round on the remainder of her patients. The unit was full, but no one had anything too exciting going on. When Hailey returned to the office cubicle behind the nurses' station to make further chart notations, Renee glanced up from where she worked and grinned big.

"You just missed Dr. Wilton." The nurse manager eyed Hailey curiously as if she was expecting a reaction. Hailey did her best not to give one as Renee continued, "I think he was going to Room 211." Renee waggled her drawn-on brows. "If you hurry, you can catch him."

Catch Cayden. Hailey's heart sped up. She hadn't been able to quit thinking of him the night before. Mostly, she marveled that he liked her enough that he was upset that she had gone to the cookout with Ryan and had admitted that he was jealous. Even with the hair color, extensions, weight loss, and the rest of her big makeover, how was that even possible?

Struggling to hide how knowing he was near affected her, Hailey adjusted her stethoscope from where the tubing poked up from her scrub top's pocket. "Did he need to consult with me on a patient?"

Hopefully oblivious to the thundering in Hailey's chest, Renee shook her head. "Not that I'm aware of. I was just letting you know that he came by so that, you know, you could find a reason to bump into him, talk to him, maybe mention sharing dinner and another romantic sunset with him. That kind of thing."

"Not once have I said I shared a romantic sunset with Dr. Wilton." Not out loud, but they had been romantic. *Spectacular.* "Nor is there a reason for me to purposely bump into him, Renee." No reason other than she yearned to see him, to know if he was upset with her, to know if frustration would still shine in his gorgeous eyes when he looked at her. Maybe she didn't want to see him, because if he gave her a cold shoulder, how was she going to hide her disappointment? Why would he give her a cold shoulder when he'd kissed her good-night? A peck, but it had been a kiss. Plus, he'd said he was jealous. That had to mean something.

What do I want it to mean?

"Did he make any notes on Mr. Little? I'm planning to discharge him today unless Dr. Wilton prefers he be kept one more night for further observation."

"He hasn't yet." Renee gave a sly grin that hinted she wasn't buying Hailey's lack of forthcoming details. Her coworker would have a field day if she knew Hailey had seen him outside of work two additional times since their Manasota sunset and that Cayden's lips had touched her the night before. Her forehead. But they had touched her. Perhaps her coworker could see the scorch marks, because she was fairly positive her skin was branded from the simple caress. "He's in with Mr. Little now."

Hailey's belly churned. How would Cayden act around her? Would he be friendly or standoffish? If the latter, would it be from being professional or as a carryover from his displeasure at her having gone to the cookout with Ryan? Whatever Cayden's reaction, he'd be professional. He wouldn't cause a scene or purposely trigger hospital gossip.

"Oh, goody. You don't have to not purposely bump into him, because there he is now." Renee gestured to behind where Hailey stood. "Hello, Dr. Wilton. Your timing is perfect. Look who is back at the nurses' station."

Yeah, Cayden was professional and wouldn't cause hospital gossip. Renee, on the other hand, had no issue with saying whatever popped into her mind. Despite her warnings to guard her heart, her coworker had completely gotten on board with the idea of Cayden and Hailey. Maybe because she considered herself the cupid who had shot the arrow and felt invested in their relationship. Either way, Hailey believed Renee's intentions weren't malicious, but, oh, how she wished she wouldn't be so obvious.

Taking a quick breath, Hailey turned, met Cayden's gaze and attempted to read his mood. Instantly, she realized that he was doing the same. Had he been concerned that she'd be upset with him? In the entirety of their relationship, John had never cared if he'd upset her. If he had, she'd been expected to get over it and to not do whatever had caused him to upset her again. Even with his cheating, he'd blamed her, citing that she had been too distracted with medical school and residency to meet his needs.

Why did I forgive him time and again?

Swallowing at her own past follies, she smiled at Cayden and after only a moment's hesitation, his lips curved upward, too. Hailey's entire body lightened as her muscles released from the tension that had bound them.

No matter what happened, she wanted to end up as friends with Cayden. Maybe that's all they should be to preserve that future friendship and their working relationship. But how could she insist upon something that she wasn't sure she could do? Because the bubbles of giddiness filling her at his smile weren't bubbles of just wanting to be his friend.

"Good morning, Dr. Wilton." She kept it more formal for Renee's benefit, but knew he'd know why she had. He wore his standard hospital navy scrubs that pulled out the golden flecks in his hazel eyes and she had to fight the strong urge to hug him because he'd so readily smiled back. He didn't seem to play the games she'd come to expect.

Do not put him on a pedestal. You've only known him a week, she reminded herself.

Why did it feel as if she'd known him on some level her entire existence? Thinking she'd lost her mind, she cleared her throat. "What are your thoughts on Mr. Little?"

"He has high hopes of going home today." Cayden grasped the tip of the stethoscope he had draped around his neck, the muscles in his arms flexing as he did so and drawing Hailey's gaze. His teasing flashed through her mind and her belly clenched at the memory. It was too late to think of Cayden as just a friend. Maybe at some point in the future she'd be able to, but the man tangled up her nerve endings into a hormonal mess she hadn't known she was capable of being.

The real question was what was she going to do about how he affected her? He didn't want anything serious. She didn't want anything serious. Why couldn't they just have fun together? Why couldn't he truly impart some of his expert advice to guide her through her initial "dating" debut? She wanted to explore the joy he triggered within her, to flirt and revel in his attention for however long it lasted. As long as she kept her heart safely tucked away, what would be wrong with soaking up the deliciousness of time spent with him?

Biting into her lower lip, Hailey forced her gaze back to his face, realized Cayden knew exactly what she'd looked at, thought, and she gulped. "Are you on board with his being discharged today?"

Okay, so her voice might have been a slightly higher pitch than normal, but for the most part she'd managed to sound professional.

"His heart failure is chronic, stable overall, and had nothing to do with his initial admission. His surgical complications from his ruptured appendix are resolving." Cayden's gaze stayed connected to hers to the point where Hailey felt the conversation was something personal rather than purely professional, that there were two conversations occurring. One with words and another with their eyes. "From an acute cardiac standpoint, Melvin is safe to go home and will definitely be more comfortable there while he recuperates. His wife will keep close tabs and will get him back here if anything changes."

"Absolutely," she agreed, grateful his assessment had been the same as hers and even more grateful that he seemed as relieved that everything was okay between them as she was. They'd talk soon, away from the hospital. She'd figure out how to say she wanted to spend time with him, to date him, even. But that she would date other men, too, if the opportunity and desire to presented itself. The new Hailey wouldn't be bound by an exclusive relationship that could a man power to dictate her life the way John had. She wouldn't risk getting too close to Cayden and falling into old habits. Seeing other men would be a constant reminder not to get too attached because she and Cayden were casual. "I'll write up discharge orders and have a hospital follow-up appointment scheduled with his primary care provider. Do you want to see him in your office in a few days, as well? Or to just have him follow up with you at his regularly scheduled cardiac checkup?"

"Within the next two weeks would be best."

I'm sorry about last night. That's what his eyes were saying, what her heart was hearing.

"Have my office get him worked in on my schedule."
Me, too, she told him back.

At least she hoped her eyes were broadcasting as
clearly as his were. Were hers also transmitting the hesitation she saw in his? He wasn't his usual, teasing self,
making reading him difficult and she was far from an
expert at her best moments.

"I'll get it noted." Listen to them sounding all business.
Standing there, staring at each other, Renee watching
them with a Cheshire cat grin, Hailey felt self-conscious
because she wasn't sure what to say or do with their audience. She looked at the charge nurse. "What?"

"Nothing." But Renee was smiling when she turned
back to her computer screen. When the charge nurse
started humming, Hailey shook her head and gave
Cayden a *Sorry...* look.

"Don't forget that this Thursday evening is a meeting
regarding the Venice Has Heart event," Cayden continued. "It's at six in the Main Street Community Room. I
hope you're planning to be there."

"Of course." Avoiding looking directly toward Renee
in case her coworker glanced up, Hailey nodded. No way
would she be able to hide her thoughts if she met Renee's
gaze. "Thursday works perfectly as I'm off from the hospital. I truly do want to get involved in community events
and to be helpful wherever I can. I planned to volunteer
with some charities even before I moved to Florida. I
feel lucky to have done so this quickly thanks to Renee."

"That's great. We appreciate everyone who volunteers." Yeah, she doubted their conversation was fooling Renee.

"I'm looking forward to meeting the other volunteers."

She was. Making friends was high on her priority list for her big move to Florida. She'd been so isolated for so long. She was getting to know some of her neighbors via their HOA neighborhood activities and community gym, and she'd met Ryan's group at the cookout. Slowly, but surely, she'd make friends.

"We have the best volunteers at Venice Has Heart. I…" He hesitated then seemed to change his mind about whatever he'd considered saying. She assumed that Renee being able and eager to hear their discussion limited what he was saying as it did for Hailey.

There was a quiet pause where they just looked at each other, then Hailey gave a nervous laugh. "I should get Mr. Little's discharge started. He'll be excited that you're in agreement for him to go home. Sharla is going to have her hands full."

She'd hoped he'd say something more, but after a moment of obvious debating with himself that had Renee looking back and forth between them, he just nodded. "Sounds good, Hailey. Thanks for taking care of that."

She didn't see him again that day and considered texting him, but decided she shouldn't. No matter how many self-confidence podcasts she listened to while doing household chores and therapy sessions she attended, she wasn't sure she'd ever get over her insecurities. What if Cayden had realized he wasn't interested in anything more than friendship and being her coworker? Either way, she'd be fine, she assured herself. She did not need him or any man for affirmation of her value. She was enough. Just ask her therapist.

After work, Hailey stopped by a home goods store and purchased an outdoor patio set that included a propane-fueled fire pit and arranged to have it delivered early Thursday as she didn't have any self-care appointments until later in the day. She found an outdoor rug that matched and managed to finagle it into her new car by lowering the convertible top and buckling it into the passenger seat. If she envisioned having friends to come over to visit, socializing with them while sitting on her patio, it would happen, right?

The following two days, one of Cayden's partners was on call for the cardiology rounds. In his late forties, Dr. Brothers was polite, to the point, and there and gone in under fifteen minutes each morning. Having known the posted call schedule didn't keep Hailey from feeling disappointed as each day passed without her seeing or hearing from Cayden. On Wednesday evening, she started a yoga class and ended up with a coffee date for the following morning with another newcomer who worked as a nurse at an extended living facility.

After an hour at her community gym and her patio furniture delivery, she met Jamie, and had a low-carb protein smoothie that tasted pretty good. They ended up walking around the man-made lake near the shopping center, chatting away as they continued to get to know each other. Jamie had recently moved to the area and was as eager to make friends as Hailey. They promised to make their Thursday mornings a new tradition. Hailey would have to adjust the timing on her Sarasota beauty session trips, but that should be easy enough by planning ahead.

That evening, Hailey debated on what one would wear to a Venice Has Heart volunteer meeting. She ended up settling on a casual power-red skirt, white eyelet top, and comfy sandals from her new wardrobe. Not too casual and not too dressy.

When she arrived at the community center, she wasn't sure where to go, but met up with a very tan and fit late sixties couple. They claimed to be longtime volunteers and advised her to follow them. They were dressed casually in shorts, T-shirts, and sandals so she was glad she'd not chosen anything dressier. When they entered the room, there were already around thirty volunteers present, including Cayden and Leanna Moore. Most everyone was somewhere between the Krandalls' level of casual and Hailey's, but not Leanna. She stunned in white capris pants and a turquoise top that matched her eyes, chunky jewelry, and not a hair out of place. As beautiful as the radio personality had appeared on the billboards, the signs didn't do her justice. No wonder Renee had said they all believed Cayden and the woman would eventually end up together. They were absolutely fantastic standing next to each other, as if they'd both won the best of the best in the gene pool. Seriously, had she come there tonight hoping to invite him to spend time together? Why would he want to when he had someone as dynamic as the radio deejay vying for his attention. The woman looked at Cayden with pure adoration.

Perhaps sensing that Hailey had arrived and was staring at him, Cayden spotted her and smiled. The curving of his lips instantly sent her pulse upward. Seeing him, Leanna glanced toward Hailey. She smiled, too, but it wasn't nearly as bright as Cayden's had been. As if to stake her claim, Leanna placed her hand on his arm, saying something to recover his attention.

"Come sit with us," the Krandalls offered, oblivious

to Hailey having been put in her place by Leanna that had just occurred. "Just know that our plan in keeping you close is to have you signed up to help with the half marathon."

"I think I'm already signed up to help elsewhere. Although, to be honest, I really don't know specific details other than the event is in a couple of months." Confused, she smiled at the couple. "Venice Has Heart is a race?"

Mr. Krandall chuckled. "Venice Has Heart is much more than a race and will be here before we know it. The day starts out with the half marathon that Saturday morning," he said as they made their way toward a group in the corner. "Afterward, there are different booths, all geared to make people more heart healthy. There will be blood pressure checks, educational bits, relay races and bouncy houses for the kids, that kind of thing."

"There's a vegan cook-off competition. Some of the vendors will be selling veggie burgers and other vegan food options to broaden dietary palates and introduce things folks may not have ever tried so they can know how tasty healthy eating can actually be," Mrs. Krandall added, waving to someone as they passed a table. "There will be relay races for the kids, face painting, that kind of thing, too. It's just a great day all the way around with something for everyone. It's one of our favorite days of the entire year and takes about a year's worth of planning."

"It sounds wonderful." She smiled at the woman. "If you're signing me up to help with the race, I assume you're in charge of it?"

"This is the third year of the Venice Has Heart event," Mrs. Krandall explained. "Bobby and I have put together the half marathon portion each year. Usually, we get to meetings early, but we picked our grandson up from band practice and ran him home this evening. He's involved in so much that his mom and dad can't always get him to and fro. We're glad to come to the rescue."

Her husband chuckled. "Listen at her acting as if we're late when we still arrived on time despite picking our Robert up from middle school."

Hailey smiled as the couple bantered back and forth all the while introducing her to the other race volunteers. Their energy was impressive, as was how welcoming they were. This, she thought. This was exactly the sort of thing she'd been hoping to become a part of. She liked these people already and they strove to do good in the world.

"Linda, you aren't trying to steal away one of my medical volunteers, are you?" Cayden hugged the woman, then shook Mr. Krandall's hand. "Hello, Bob."

The older couple beamed at him with obvious affection.

"Hailey didn't tell me that she was one of your volunteers or I *might* have left her alone." Mrs. Krandall laughed. "Probably not, but maybe."

"No?" Cayden tsked his tongue. "Sorry, Linda, but I have other plans for Dr. Easton during Venice Has Heart."

"Doctor? Good for you." Linda glanced toward Hailey, admiration on her face. "You should have told me that there was little chance he'd let me have you."

"Sorry," she apologized at the woman's playful scolding. "I honestly didn't know what all Cayden had in line for me."

"He'll have you doing more than refilling water bottles and cheering on our runners," Linda chuckled. "But he could stick you in the medical tent that morning in case any of our runners have issues. We'd love to have you with us."

"For the record, I was going to let Hailey choose what time frame she wants to volunteer, but if she wants to come early for the half marathon, that works for me."

"I'd love to," Hailey assured them, earning smiles from the couple.

They chatted a few minutes. Then Cayden placed his hand on Hailey's back and steered her away from the others. "You came." Had he thought she wouldn't show? "I didn't know if you would change your mind or have other plans."

Had that been a dig at her possibly having gone out with Ryan or someone else? She straightened her spine to stand tall.

"We haven't known each other long." Yes, she was purposely pointing that out yet again. "But I do my best to follow through on things I say I will do. If I'm physically able to do something I've said I would do, then that's what I will be doing."

"Noted and good to know." His lips twitched, letting her know that her response had amused him. Perhaps because her hands had gone to her hips which she hadn't realized until that moment.

She ordered her tense muscles to relax. "You're in charge of the medical volunteers?"

"Darling, Cayden is in charge of the whole production. Venice Has Heart is his baby." In a waft of something that smelled absolutely fabulous, Leanna stuck out her hand. "Hi, I'm Leanna Moore."

Not surprised that the woman had soon followed Cayden, Hailey shook her hand. "I know who you are. I've seen your billboards, but they fail to do you justice." The woman beamed. "I'm Hailey Easton," she continued. "I work with Cayden at the hospital and offered to volunteer."

The woman glanced back and forth between them. "You're a nurse?"

Hailey greatly admired nurses, but that Leanna immediately assumed that must be her role irked.

"Hailey is a hospitalist at Venice General. The hospital was lucky enough to have her start a few weeks ago," Cayden supplied, then returned his gaze to Hailey. "And, really, although Leanna says I'm in charge, it's the people like her, Linda, and Bob, and so many others who put the individual pieces together who make the event such a success."

"He's much too modest." With a plump-lipped smile and her eyes conveying so much more than mere admiration, Leanna patted Cayden's cheek with familiarity. Her beautifully manicured hand lingered on the last pat prior to slowly gliding down his chin.

Was this what he'd felt when he'd said he was jealous that she'd gone to the cookout with Ryan? Hailey didn't want to feel jealousy. She'd known Cayden less than two weeks so how could such intense green be filling her veins? She was getting too caught up in Cayden. Especially with how much she'd missed him that week. How could she miss someone she'd only known existed for such a short time? Especially when he had never been hers to begin with?

"Dr. Wilton's modesty was one of the first things I noticed about him." Hailey hadn't been sure if he'd catch her reference to the teasing comment she'd previously made to him, but his grin said he knew exactly what she'd meant. He didn't call her out on addressing him so formally and Hailey wasn't quite sure how she felt about that. Despite what he'd said, was he glad she'd kept it formal when Leanna was around to witness their conversation? Enough dwelling on Cayden's relationship with the radio beauty. It wasn't any of Hailey's business and she needed to remember that. "Nice to meet you, Leanna," she automatically told the woman from a lifetime of good manners. Then she looked at Cayden, meeting his gaze. "Point me in the direction where I can be useful or at least learn what I need to know. I want to help."

Cayden introduced her to Benny Lewis, a gem of a woman who was a retired nurse and who headed up the event's medical volunteers. Hailey got the impression that Cayden might have stuck around, but Leanna called him to where she was now with another group, saying she needed his input.

"How long are you willing to volunteer, and do you have any special interests in the day's events?" Benny asked. "Knowing that will help me know best where to place you. We want to keep our volunteers happy, so they'll be back year after year."

"This is all new to me, so no special interests other than wanting to be useful. As far as how long—" she shrugged "—how long do you need me?"

Benny chuckled. "Honey, I'll use you all day if you're willing."

Hailey glanced toward Cayden. The group he was with spoke animatedly about whatever it was they were discussing, smiling and laughing as they did so. Leanna's hand rested on his upper arm, and she leaned in to tell him something, making him laugh. Hailey's heart hiccupped.

"If it's helpful, I can be there all day." Perhaps seeing him with the radio personality would be helpful to Hailey, ingraining just how out of her league he really was despite his attention the previous week. She did want to spend time with him, but it was just as well that she didn't want a happy-ever-after as she'd only get her heart broken again. "Linda and Bob mentioned helping with the race. If there's something I can do to be useful, I'd love to assist with that."

"You want to help from start to finish? That would be amazing." Benny hugged her. "It'll be a long day. But there are several of us who do just that and think it's one of the best days of each year. I'll start you in the medical tent for the half marathon, then transition you to volunteering in the blood pressure reading area. We have nursing student volunteers taking the pressures, checking blood glucose readings, that kind of thing. Any people with abnormal results are offered a brief consult with one of the provider volunteers on what they need to do to decrease their heart disease risk."

"What a wonderful event for the community," Hailey said and meant. Education was everything in living a healthier life. She knew that firsthand. Her adoptive parents had been wonderful people, but sedentary and she'd followed in their footsteps until recently.

"It is. By the end of the day, you'll be mutually exhilarated and exhausted." Benny motioned to a table where several other volunteers were gathered. "Come on. Let me introduce you to the rest of the medical crew. At least the ones who are here tonight. We have a few who couldn't attend. And, of course, you already know Dr. Wilton. He's there from start to finish. The man is tireless when it comes to getting the word out about having a healthy heart and living your best life."

Hailey had been living her best life since meeting him. Not that he was why, she assured herself, but because she was living the life she had envisioned and was creating for herself. Cayden was just one small part of her "best life."

After the introductions, Benny ran through items she had listed out on a clipboard, making sure their team would have all the necessary equipment for the day. Apparently, they'd be set up inside a large tent. A church was supplying tables and chairs and more volunteers. Another was supplying water and heart-healthy snacks. Home health, hospice, private ambulance services, and several other health agencies would have booths and activities for attendees. During the afternoon there would be a live band and a charity auction. According to Benny they'd start closing things down around six and hopefully be done between seven and eight. As she'd asked for the half marathon medical volunteers to arrive at around six that morning, Hailey agreed that it was going to be a long day. Most of the other medical volunteers were working in half-day or shorter shifts, but Hailey looked forward to being there all day. She really did want to be involved and give back to her new community and what a great way to do so. She'd even mentioned the meeting to Jamie that morning and her new nurse friend might volunteer, as well. How cool to have a friend who wanted to spend time with her?

The meeting lasted about an hour, then ended. Hailey enjoyed getting to know the medical team and said goodbye to them. Cayden made it over to them once but had quickly been summoned back to where Leanna had wanted his opinion yet again. Apparently, the woman still needed his attention as they were deep in conversation. Hailey had caught him looking her way a few times, but he'd not made it back to speak directly to her since right after she'd arrived. Not a big deal, she assured herself. The event was what was the big deal and why she was there, why they were both there. He was busy with making sure all the last-minute details were in place.

Hailey considered going to tell him bye, but decided it would feel awkward with the others around to witness her doing so. She said a few words to Benny, then to Linda and Bob, letting them know that she had volunteered for the medical tent, and would see them early on the Saturday morning of the Venice Has Heart event which was a month away.

Glad she'd gone, excited about volunteering, and conflicted about Cayden, Hailey had made it to her car when she heard him calling to her from where he'd apparently followed her out of the building.

"Hailey, wait up."

Fingers on her door handle, she turned and saw him jogging toward her. Her heart raced as if she was the one jogging. He'd come after her. That had to mean something beyond his being grateful she was volunteering, right? "Practicing for the race?"

Catching up to where she stood next to her car, he grinned. "Something like that. Are you in a rush to go?"

Her breath caught. "Not necessarily. Why?"

"I've not eaten. Do you want to grab something with me?"

She considered saying yes. She wanted to say yes. However, she forced herself to admit the truth. "I actually ate before coming to the meeting. Sorry."

He regarded her a moment. "Can I tempt you with a drink and a sunset, then? That seems to be our thing."

She was tempted. Oh, how she was tempted. But she shook her head because as much as she wanted to go, to talk with him, her emotions were running rampant after seeing him with Leanna and just how jealous that had made her. "Not tonight, Cayden, but thanks for asking."

He nodded as if he understood, but he failed miserably if he was trying to hide his disappointment and that boosted Hailey's courage.

She opened her car door, then paused. "If you're willing, I would take you up on the offer to go shark tooth hunting, still, though. If you aren't busy, maybe we could go this weekend?"

He regarded her a few moments, then arched his brow. "You don't have other plans?"

She knew what he was asking. She'd declined Ryan's offer to go to a concert in Tampa with others she'd met at the cookout. It had sounded like a fun outing, and yet, she'd made an excuse rather than say yes.

"I don't have plans on Saturday or Sunday morning and truly would like to go to the beach." Not that she had to have him with her to do so, but going with him would be nice and she didn't see herself shark tooth hunting without him. "Maybe I'll get lucky and find the perfect big shell for my table."

"We'd have better odds of that in Sanibel," he reminded her.

"It's okay if I don't find just what I'm looking for as I'm not in a rush. If I do find a great shell, well, that's just an added bonus to spending time with you." Heat flushed her cheeks. There. She'd been obvious in that she liked him. She might as well confess, at least to herself, that she'd turned Ryan's invitation down and purposely left her weekend open in hopes of spending time with Cayden. Which was okay, just so long as she didn't get too caught up in thinking time with Cayden was something more than just fun.

"I... Sure. I'd love to take you on your first shark tooth hunt. Does Saturday morning work? Around seven?" His eyes sparkled with the glittery gold flecks that fascinated her. Ha! Everything about Cayden fascinated her. He was a fascinating man. A fascinating man who was smiling at her in a way that had her cheeks flushing further because he made her feel pretty fascinating, too. How did he do that? When he was so fabulously gorgeous, how did he make her feel as if she were the one who was worthy of adoration? Would he have looked at her the same way if he'd met her pre-makeover? If he'd seen her prior to the hair and lash extensions, prior to the dull brown to blond, prior to the weight loss? Did it matter? She didn't even like that person she'd been. Not so much because of her outer appearance, but because of how timid she'd been on the inside, allowing John to take such advantage of her heart.

"Seven works great for me." She was used to getting

up early to exercise prior to having to be at the hospital. She tended to wake early even on her off days. She smiled up at him, thinking he truly was the most handsome man she'd ever met. "I look forward to finally finding a shark tooth, and maybe getting lucky and finding a shell."

"Then I'll see you Saturday morning. Don't forget to bring your water shoes and sense of adventure."

Before she chickened out, Hailey stood on her tiptoes and kissed his cheek. "Good night, Cayden. Sweet dreams."

CHAPTER SIX

"So, I take this sifter thing and I wade out into the water and just scoop up a bunch of sand and shells and whatever it picks up and I'm to hope I get a shark tooth?" Hailey eyed Cayden as if he'd lost his mind. Toes digging into the sand, her big straw hat with its tied strap beneath her chin, her baggy T-shirt and loose shorts over her bathing suit, she clutched the screened scoop. "As in, go in the water where the sharks who lost these teeth are?"

"The sharks who lost these teeth are long past," Cayden reminded her, wondering what it was about her that had him so tied up in knots, that had him thinking about her more often than not. She was beautiful, but he'd dated beautiful women in the past. It was something much more potent than physical beauty that had him so hooked. And that good-night kiss…yeah, his dreams had been sweet, all right. He'd barely thought of anything else day or night. With his work schedule not having him in the hospital Tuesday and Wednesday, and her being off Thursday and Friday, he'd missed her and considered texting her a hundred times. He should have. His reasons for not doing so had been petty. Even after her tentative smile on Monday morning, he'd let his jealousy over her going to the cookout with another man dictate that he put some distance between him and Hailey. The moment he'd spotted her with Mrs. Krandall he'd admitted to himself that he was behaving like a Neanderthal and was only depriving himself of the most fascinating woman he'd ever met. No more. "Besides," he continued. "You don't have to go out into the water that far. Just follow me, do what I do, and you'll be fine."

She eyed him skeptically, not budging from where she stood next to where he'd placed their things on the sand. He'd not unpacked their bag but would later if they decided they wanted to relax and watch the waves. He'd packed a blanket, sunscreen, the small medical kit that was always in his beach backpack, and even a small cooler with drinks and snacks in hope of extending their time together. Maybe she'd agree to lunch at one of the restaurants they'd drive past on their way back to her place.

A strong breeze whipped at them and she grasped hold of the brim of her hat, the other clasping the sifter. "What if I don't want to do what you do? What if I prefer to watch?"

"You want to just watch?" He arched a brow. "Do I need to remind you that you're the one who suggested we do this today? That you are here to find your first shark tooth? No sitting on the sidelines allowed."

She wrinkled her nose. "A woman has a right to change her mind."

He laughed at her dubious expression. "Come on, Hailey. You're going to have fun. I promise."

That's when he noticed the gleam in her eyes. "You big faker. You're already having fun."

Her lips twitched and her eyes danced with mischief. "Who says I'm having fun?"

If ever he'd heard a challenge, she'd just issued one with her flirty tone and lowered lashes.

"Me." Catching her off guard, he grabbed her at the waist, hoisted her over his shoulder, and headed toward the water.

"Cayden! Stop! What are you doing?" she demanded, laughing. "Oh, no, you're not," she warned as he waded into the water, his feet sluicing through the incoming wave. "Cayden, put me down. Seriously, you're going to hurt yourself. Put. Me. Down."

Enjoying having her in his grasp, Cayden walked farther into the water. "Don't worry. I plan to."

"Put me down on my feet while I'm not in the water," she clarified, squirming in his grasp. Her body was warm against his and she smelled good, like citrus blossoms. Probably an aftereffect of her sunscreen, but he wanted to breathe in and let her permeate every part of him.

"Why would I want to do that when the view is so great from where I'm at?" he teased.

"I wouldn't know. All I can see is your backside!"

He laughed. "Poor you."

"It's not that bad, but—"

"You trying to sweet-talk me by saying you like my bum?" He definitely liked the sweet curve of hers in his periphery as he had her draped over his shoulder, the feel of her in his grasp.

"No, I'm not saying I like your bum." She wiggled as he continued farther out. "I'm saying you're going to drop me. Seriously, Cayden, put me down before you do."

Cayden took another step, using caution to make sure

he had solid footing as another wave came in, hitting him just above knee level. He was far enough out now that the water would be midthigh if a bigger wave came in.

"Cayden, the water is going to knock you down."

"Then you should be still so I can keep my balance," he warned jokingly. Surprising him, she instantly quit wiggling. "That was quick."

"I don't want to end up in the water." She was still stiff in his hold.

"Now, where's the fun in going to the beach and not getting wet?" A wave came in and water splashed onto his shorts hem.

"That's what you're supposed to be showing me, how fun looking for shark teeth is, right?" Her voice held an edge and he tried to decide if she was playing him again. "Getting tossed into the water was not part of the plan."

He gave an exaggerated sigh. "I guess you're right." He slowly slid her down his body, keeping a tight hold until her feet were firmly planted on the sand with the water rushing around their legs. To keep her hat out of the way of his chest, she had to look up and she remained doing so when she was set upright on her own two feet. Whether from the coolness of the water or how she pressed against him, goose bumps prickled her skin. His, too, but he knew exactly what had elicited his reaction. It wasn't the water. As her body had lowered, she'd wrapped her arms around his neck and if he held her this way much longer, he'd have to dunk himself prior to heading back to shore to keep from embarrassing himself. He cleared his throat. "I must be getting soft in my old age because in my younger years you'd be swimming back to shore about now."

"You're wrong." Her arms clinging tightly around his neck, almost as if she were afraid to let go, she shook her head. "I wouldn't."

"No?" Something about her tone, the way she clung to him, had him looking at her closer. The teasing light in her eyes was gone and he knew the apprehension that shone there had nothing to do with their flush bodies. His stomach knotted. "Can you swim, Hailey?"

She shivered against him. "No."

He tightened his hold at her waist. "Why didn't you say so earlier?"

Pink tinged her cheeks. "It's a bit embarrassing to not be able to swim at my age."

"Nothing to be embarrassed about, but something we should rectify." As much as he was enjoying having her pressed to him, knowing she couldn't swim, he wanted her out of the water. He scooped her back up and began carrying her back to shore. Only this time, he didn't toss her over his shoulder, but rather, held her against him where he could see her face.

"We don't need to rectify anything, and I can walk, you know," she protested, but she wasn't trying to get down and almost seemed relieved that he held her. Although, probably it was more a relief that she would soon be back on the beach. Rather than immediately put her down when they reached the shoreline, he brought her beyond where the waves stretched to powdery dry sand, then he lowered her.

"I know and it's a lovely walk you have, too." He hoped to ease the twists in his gut. Whether the idea that he could have tossed her into the water without knowing she couldn't swim or from how her warm body had been

pressed to his had caused the kinks, he wasn't sure. Probably a combination of both. "If you're going to live in
Florida, you need to know how to swim."

Not that he had any say in the matter, but he wouldn't
let her not learn how.

From beneath her oversized hat, she stared at him.
"Is it a prerequisite or something? No one gave me that
memo when I bought my house."

"No, but it should be." He appreciated her attempt at
humor now that she was safely on ground, but he saw the
vulnerability in her gaze, the self-disgust that she couldn't
do something she thought she should. Heart squeezing at
her vulnerability, he brushed his fingertip over her chin.
"How is it that you never learned to swim, Hailey?"

Swallowing, she shrugged and stepped back from him.
"My parents were older and weren't interested in water
activities. As I reached an age where I could have learned
on my own, I was busy with studying and school stuff.
Learning just never came up."

"Until you decided to move to a state that is surrounded by water on three of its four sides," he pointed
out, missing the warmth of her body against his. To distract himself, he bent to pull the blanket from his backpack and spread it upon the sand and tossed his sandals
onto opposite corners to keep the wind from lifting them.
He'd changed into his water shoes earlier but didn't want
to wear them now as he didn't like the feel of wet sand in
his shoes. He'd switch to his sandals prior to their leaving. He put his backpack down on the other end to hold
the blanket in place.

"My moving to Florida shouldn't be a problem since I
plan to stay out of the water. I can enjoy living in Florida

without getting more than my feet wet. Well, except for perhaps when you're around." Her color had returned now that she was safely on the beach, but her teasing smile wasn't enough to dissuade him.

"You need to know how to swim, Hailey." He wasn't sure why her knowing seemed imperative to him. But it did. What if he'd tossed her into the waves? What if she went to the beach with someone else and didn't reveal her inability to them and they tossed her? What if something happened to her? His rib cage caved in around his chest, squeezing so tightly he couldn't breathe. Yeah, she needed to know how to swim.

"You want me to enroll in a class?" She furrowed her brows. "I'd be in there with all the little kids. No thanks. This has caused me enough humiliation for one lifetime."

Which sounded as if there was a lot more to the story.

"No need for classes with kids. I can teach you," he offered. He wanted to teach her. For lots of different reasons.

"You?" She eyed him through narrowed eyes.

"Don't sound so incredulous. I know what I'm doing. I worked as a lifeguard during high school. We offered swimming courses that I assisted in teaching."

She snorted. "Of course, you did."

"What's that supposed to mean?"

She shook her head. "Nothing."

He lifted her chin. "Tell me."

"It's just not surprising that you're an expert at swimming."

"I'm not sure I'd say I'm an expert, but I am qualified to teach you and you need to learn. The good news is that with me teaching you, you'll have private one-on-one instructions."

From where she stood on the other side of the blanket, she eyed him. The rise and fall of her chest was a little too rapid for her to be as indifferent as she pretended. "Just as you're teaching me to find shark teeth? Because so far, we're batting zero."

"The day has barely begun."

Her chin lifted, pulling free from where he touched her, but a smile played about her lips. "True, but all I'm saying is that I haven't found any teeth yet and you did promise that I'd find one."

How she went from vulnerable to using those big blue eyes to turn him inside out in a completely different way was testament to just how under her spell he was. That had nagged at him all week, but at the moment, basking in her smile, all that mattered was Hailey.

"You will, Hailey. Just as you will learn to swim."

Hailey did find a shark tooth. She found around twenty fossilized shark teeth of various sizes and breeds. Not that they'd looked them up yet, but Cayden had identified several of the teeth as makos and one as a sand tiger tooth. She'd sifted out several fossilized stingray bones and a horse tooth, too. Not that she'd have known what they were had Cayden not told her.

She'd not gone out beyond midcalf into the water. When she did so, she was fully aware that Cayden's return trips into the sea to dip out more sand and shells coincided with hers and that he always put himself out farther in what was a protective move in case she lost her footing. His automatic chivalry was sweet and something she wasn't accustomed to. John had teased her mercilessly about her inability to do something so "childish" as knowing how to swim. As she was making herself into the woman she wanted to be, she really should learn to swim.

Now they sat back on the familiar blanket that she'd become quite fond of, eating apples he'd stored in a small cooler. The cold juicy fruit was delicious.

"Thank you for bringing snacks. I wasn't expecting to be so hungry."

"Being in and around the water always works up my appetite." He gestured to the apple. "These are always a good option for a quick pick-me-up."

She nodded. "How long have you been coming out here?"

He shrugged. "All my life that I can recall. When I was a child, prior to their divorce, and separately after, my parents often rented a vacation house in Venice. It was always my favorite beach to visit."

"Because of the shark teeth?"

He grinned. "Probably. That was something different from the other places where we vacationed, and I was all boy."

He was still all boy. Well, man. In the water, his body pressed against hers had been all solid, strong man. She'd never been picked up and thrown over someone's shoulder. Cayden hadn't hesitated when doing so, making lifting her seem effortless. As apprehensive as she'd been of being in the water, deep down she'd known he wouldn't let anything happen to her and she'd been stunned at someone lifting her that way, that someone *could* lift her that way. He made her feel...dainty and feminine.

"Were you serious about teaching me to swim?"

His gaze cut to hers. "Absolutely. I want to teach you. I don't like the thought of you not knowing how to safely get yourself out of the water."

Her as in her specifically or just that he didn't like anyone not knowing how?

"Why?"

His grin was lethal as he said, "Because you never know when some man is going to toss you over his shoulder and throw you into the sea."

"You didn't throw me into the sea," she reminded him, swallowing back how being with him made her feel, with how just sitting on a blanket and eating fruit felt surreal and special.

"No, but I could have since I didn't know. Good beach advice would be to make whomever you're with aware that you don't swim."

"Now you're my beach expert, too?" At his look, she relented. "Fine. I should have told you. Like I mentioned, my parents were older and there were a lot of things I didn't do during my childhood that many would consider as standards, like learning to swim." Ecstatic to be out of the foster system, she'd been content to be in her room with a good book and her parents had never discouraged her from doing just that since they'd also been lifelong readers. She'd loved the peace, the stability they'd brought into her chaotic life, but maybe she should have stepped outside of the comfort zone they'd created for her. "In the future, I promise to make anyone I go to the beach with aware of my inability to swim."

He crunched into the last bite of his apple, put the core into a bag in his backpack, then wiped juice from his fingers. "In the future you won't need to since you're going to learn."

He sounded so confident that Hailey had no choice but to believe him. Why not? Thus far he had proved brilliant at all he did. Why should teaching her to swim be any different?

"Just when and where are these lessons going to take place?"

"My condo complex has a pool. I can teach you there or we can go—"

A scream sounded from down the beach, preventing Cayden from finishing his answer. Immediately to his feet, he took off down the beach in the direction the distressed cry had come from. Grabbing up his backpack where she'd noticed a first aid kit earlier, Hailey quickly followed.

Please don't be a shark attack, she prayed, hating that her brain immediately had gone there. *Please don't be a shark attack.*

Seeming paralyzed in the waist-deep water, a teenaged girl flailed her arms. Hailey didn't see any red discoloration the way it seemed to instantly appear in the movies when a shark attacked so maybe it was something else. But all she could think was that they were at the shark tooth capital of the world and there had to be a reason that it was the perfect environment for creating fossils like Cayden had told her.

Regardless of what it was, the other teens who'd been in the water with her seemed frozen, too, staring at their friend rather than going to where she was until finally one young man snapped out of whatever had taken over him and he began cutting through the ten or so feet that separated him from where the girl screamed in panicked agony. That Cayden reached her at about the same time the teen did said something about how fast he'd gotten there. Perhaps because of his lifeguard training, or maybe just because of his natural athleticism, the man could move. Again, there didn't seem to be much he couldn't do and do well.

"What happened?" he called as he closed in on where the girl was still thrashing her hands as if trying to shoo something away.

Scared to go into the water and knowing she shouldn't as she might create another emergency, Hailey hesitated at the shoreline, a cold wave lapping at her ankles and sending shivers over her body. What if Cayden needed the first aid kit?

What if whatever had hurt the girl hurt him?

"Something bit me. On my leg," the girl cried between sobs. "It burns bad."

Burns. That wouldn't be a shark bite, would it?

"Careful in case whatever got her is still around," he warned the teen boy who seemed as unsure of what to do as Hailey felt from where she stood. "Sounds as if it may have been a jellyfish. Let's get her out of the water so we can figure out what's going on."

A jellyfish. That was way better than a shark in Hailey's eyes, although with the way the girl was crying, perhaps she didn't think so.

Cayden was still talking, but the waves drowned out whatever he was saying. Feeling helpless as she waited, Hailey reminded herself that for her to go into the water would be more of a hindrance than a benefit. For her to go out as far as the girl was when she couldn't swim could possibly create a second crisis, so logic said to stay put and to just be ready to help once they got the girl to shore.

Logic also said to call for emergency help. Pulling her phone from where they'd put it into his bag earlier in the day, Hailey dialed the three-digit emergency number, all the while keeping her gaze on the trio in the water. Please, please, please be okay. The girl and Cayden.

"This is Dr. Hailey Easton. I'm at Caspersen Beach. A teenaged girl is injured and is currently being assisted out of the water. Not certain as to the cause or extent of her injuries at this point."

Cayden and the young man guided the sobbing girl to the beach. Once beyond the water break, they lowered her onto the sand.

"Good. You called for help and grabbed my bag," Cayden praised, noting what Hailey held and that she was on the phone with emergency services.

Hailey had zero experience in acute emergency care of aquatic animal attack injuries. Not that she was sure that it was a jelly that had injured the woman. Her knowledge of jellyfish was limited to books and movies. Beyond her inability to swim, she felt ill prepared to deal with the current situation and she didn't like it. She'd always aimed high, to be the best she could be, not incompetent. At the moment, she felt at a huge disadvantage.

"Definitely a jellyfish injury," Hailey informed the dispatcher as she grimaced at the girl's left leg where a clearish purple tentacle wrapped around her thigh and ran down her leg. The skin beneath the detached tentacle welted a deep red as did an area on the girl's right palm, probably caused from when she'd reacted to the jelly's tentacle at her leg and tried to remove it. Wanting to help medically if needed, she handed the phone to the teen boy who'd aided Cayden getting the victim out of the water. "Here, talk to the dispatcher and keep her informed of whatever we say."

The boy looked unsure, but took the phone while Hailey knelt next to where they'd laid the girl on the sand.

Rather than immediately check her, Cayden glanced around them on the sand. Quickly spotting a shell, he got it. "This isn't going to be pleasant for you," he told the teen, "but I need to get the tentacle off you immediately. Hold still."

Hailey's Ohio hospital and emergency room rotations hadn't prepared her for jellyfish sting injury. Inadequacy hit. She wasn't working in the emergency room and by the time an admitted patient made their way to her, any acute reaction would have been handled in the emergency department. But she needed to know basics of emergency care when living near the ocean. The girl was hysterical and going into shock, possibly even beginning an allergic reaction to the venom, and that, Hailey could assist with. So, while Cayden used the shell to scrap where the tentacle clung to the girl's skin, taking care to press with enough force to remove all bits of the tentacle to stop the release of more venom into her system, Hailey placed her hand on her inner wrist for the dual purpose of checking her pulse and in hopes of distracting the teen from what Cayden was doing. They needed to calm her down as her hysteria would only exacerbate her reaction to the jellyfish's venom.

"What's your name?" she asked, making mental note of the girl's tachycardic heart rate.

"Sasha," the teen boy answered when the girl continued to sob rather than answer Hailey. Her hysterics made getting a respiration count a bit trickier, but Hailey paid close attention to her breathing pattern.

"Hi, Sasha. I'm Dr. Easton and that's Dr. Wilton. We work at Venice General," she told the girl, keeping her voice calm and hoping to reassure both her, the boy, their other friends and the small crowd that were gathering around them.

The girl's panicked gaze cut to Hailey and her cries eased enough for her to ask, "Am I going to die?"

"No, you're not going to die," Hailey answered, even though it was possible if the girl had an intense enough reaction to the venom. Sasha was crying so profusely that it was difficult to tell if her runny nose and breathiness were from her sobs or if she was having a more intense than normal reaction to the sting. Hailey winced as blotchy red whelps that seemed to be multiplying while Hailey watched began covering Sasha's arms and legs.

"We're going to take good care of you and more help is on the way." She took the girl's uninjured hand into hers and gave it a gentle squeeze. She didn't want to alarm Sasha further but if Cayden had an antihistamine they could give her, then the sooner the better. "Cayden, Sasha has a rash. Do you have anything in your medical kit that I can give her for that?"

Apparently, he'd satisfied himself with the removal of the tentacle from her skin or decided that treating the rash took precedence. "Hand me my bag. I should have something to help."

She did so, and he pulled out the first aid kit, along with a water bottle. He handed the water bottle to a bystander.

"Pour out the water in this and fill it with sea water," he instructed as he unzipped the medical kit. "Sasha, have you ever had an allergic reaction to anything?"

"She's allergic to peanuts," the teen on the phone with the emergency dispatcher replied, answering for the girl again.

"Anything else?" Cayden asked, his gaze on the girl.

Tears streaming from her puffy eyes and down her face, Sasha shook her head, then swiped at her runny nose. She coughed and it had a wheezy sound.

"Sasha, I want you to open your mouth for me," Cayden instructed. "I need to look at your throat."

The girl did so. Cayden didn't say anything as he looked, but his gaze flicked to Hailey's for a millisecond and she knew what he'd seen, what she'd already suspected was happening.

Sasha's throat was swelling.

Why didn't it surprise her when Cayden dug into his medical kit and pulled out an epinephrine auto-injector? Was the man ever not prepared?

"You're not allergic to a medication called epinephrine?" he asked yet again, wanting to be sure the girl didn't have an allergy to the adrenaline.

"Not," the girl said, coughing again. "Just peanuts."

"She used a pen like that when she reacted to peanuts on a school trip once," the young man supplied.

"Sasha, most people don't react to jellyfish stings so intensely, but unfortunately, you are," Cayden told the girl whose brows lifted above her puffy eyes. "I'm going to give you the injection into your leg to slow, and hopefully stop, the reaction you're having to the jellyfish venom."

He didn't give the girl time to protest, just popped the

injector against her injured leg in the thigh, delivering the possibly lifesaving medication in the process. When done, he tossed the device by the backpack, then took the water bottle from the bystander who'd done as he'd instructed. Cayden poured the seawater over the area the jelly fish had stung, then gently patted the area dry with a towel from his bag. Digging through his medical kit, he pulled out a tube of steroid cream and squeezed some onto the girl's leg, gently spreading a thin layer over where she'd been stung.

Hailey noticed the red line across Cayden's hand and winced. "You're stung, too."

"Got that when we were still in the water." He didn't look up from where he worked on Sasha's leg. When satisfied that the sting on her leg and hand were coated, he squirted a bit of the cream on his own hand.

In the distance, sirens blared and Hailey sighed in relief that the girl would soon be on her way to the hospital. She'd be treated in the emergency department, and the determination would be made of whether or not she needed to be admitted for overnight observation based upon how she responded to the epinephrine, any additional medications the paramedics administered, and how she did after a few hours of being watched.

Within minutes, the girl was loaded into the back of the ambulance and on her way to the hospital.

"Thank you," the teen boy told them, taking off so he could follow the ambulance to the hospital with his friend.

Clapping erupted around them. Hailey joined in, clapping for Cayden and what he'd done for the girl. His cheeks turned pink, and he tried dismissing what he'd done. "Just doing what anyone else would have done."

Hailey's heart squeezed at his humility. She didn't want to keep comparing the two men, but she couldn't help herself. John would have been calling every media outlet in the area, expecting to be heralded a hero on the nightly news. Cayden on the other hand, got a phone number from one of the teens who'd been with the girl so he could call and check on her progress.

As the bystanders dissipated, Hailey gathered his things, putting them into the backpack and waited for him to finish talking with the girl's friends. When he had, they headed back to where they'd left their things farther down the beach.

"What just happened made me realize I need a living-near-the-sea emergency medicine crash course," she admitted as they made their way over the sandy beach.

"You'd have been fine if I hadn't been here."

She shook her head. "I wouldn't have. Beyond the fact that I couldn't have gotten her out of the water, not once have I ever treated a jellyfish sting. I mean, what other living on the Gulf of Mexico things do I need to know?"

"Other than how to swim?"

"After what just happened you may never get me to agree to go in the water again." But even as she said it, she acknowledged that she did want to learn. She'd hated knowing that if Cayden had needed her that she'd have had to stand ashore and helplessly watch, that if he hadn't been there, she wouldn't have been able to help Sasha to shore.

"What happened with Sasha is a rarity when you consider how many people get into the water. Beyond that, most who encounter jellyfish and do have the misfortune to be stung, don't have anaphylactic reactions." He held up his hand. "Like me for instance."

"True, but I don't think I'm going back in beyond where I can walk and see all around me." She winced at the red mark on his hand. "I'm sorry you got hurt. Is there anything I can do?"

"Kiss it and make it better?"

Hailey's breath caught. "If you think that would help."

He held out his hand. "Only one way to know for sure."

Swallowing, Hailey touched her lips to his hand, taking care to avoid the steroid cream by kissing just to the side of his injury.

"Better already," he assured her, smiling at her in a way that could almost convince her that her kiss truly had made him feel better. "For the record, I plan to teach you to swim in a pool, Hailey. Not in the open sea."

"I… I do want to learn." Because she didn't want to limit herself. Not ever again. "However, learning to swim isn't likely to change how I feel about getting into the ocean. But we'll see."

Because if she truly didn't want to limit herself then she had to be open to the possibility that she might change her mind.

"We'll start with learning to swim. If, after you've mastered swimming, you want to venture outside the pool, then we will. No pressure."

She didn't comment on his "we will." Who knew what the future held? For now, she was just going to appreciate that she got to spend the day with an amazing man who was kind and patient and had acted heroically with his only motivation being to help the teenager. Plus, he acted as if own injury was no big deal rather than milking it for all it was worth. Since she'd asked if there was anything she could do, she didn't count his request for her to kiss his hand and make it better. She'd been so fearful for him and the girl when they'd been in the water, she wanted to wrap her arms around his neck and kiss him for real in gratitude that he was okay, that he'd saved Sasha, both in the water and on land.

"I'm quite impressed that you had an epinephrine pen in your medical kit. I wasn't expecting that level of preparedness."

"No?" The corners of his eyes crinkled with his smile. "My sister is allergic to bees. I always keep a pen handy, just in case."

"You have a sister?" Did she sound as envious as she felt? How often had she wished for siblings?

He nodded. "Casey is older than me by a couple of years. She and her husband live in Atlanta, where my mother now lives, too, so she can be close to the grands. Dad lives in Tampa, so not too far away. During a visit a few years ago, Casey forgot her emergency medication injector and had to go to the emergency room to get treated. Since then, I keep one on hand."

"Amongst the many things I'm grateful for, I'm glad you had one today."

"Me, too." As they reached the blanket they'd abandoned in a rush, he asked, "You want to sit here a while, walk, or look for more shark teeth?"

"Ha, that's a trick question, right? We have already established that I'm not going back into the water."

"I'd be willing to scoop for you if you want to search for more shark teeth. Maybe you'll find a megalodon."

He would do that. But the truth was, she didn't want

him back in the water, either. She was being a total wimp, but she preferred all of his body parts being where she could see them.

"As cool as finding a fossilized prehistoric shark tooth would be, I think I've had enough beach time for the day." Sasha's jellyfish encounter had been a great reminder of all the reasons she needed to be cautious with water activities beyond her inability to swim. "If you're not in a hurry, we could grab something to eat. My treat. Something took off with the rest of my apple. When Sasha screamed, I'd tossed it onto the blanket, and now it's gone."

He chuckled. "Some seagull or crab thought it was its lucky day."

Being with Cayden had Hailey thinking it really was *her* lucky day.

CHAPTER SEVEN

CAYDEN GRINNED AT how excited Hailey looked when she glanced up from where she was reviewing a patient's chart on the small office alcove behind the medical floor's nurses' station and saw him. She'd gone from calm professional to sparkling. Spotting him had given her joy and he liked the thought of his being able to make her happy. Over the past month, she'd certainly made him happy.

"Hello, Dr. Wilton," she greeted, sounding all businesslike as she glanced around to see if any of their co-workers were close by. There weren't. Keeping her voice to barely above a whisper, she asked, "Would you be interested in going on a double date with my friend Jamie and her boyfriend? She's my nurse friend from my yoga class. Remember that I mentioned she plans to volunteer at the Venice Has Heart event, too?"

"Hello, Dr. Easton." The bluest sea had nothing on Hailey's eyes. He wanted to dive in and lose himself. "Are you asking me on a date?"

Glancing around again, letting him know that despite their having seen each other numerous times outside of work, she preferred to keep their personal relationship just between them. Since neither of them wanted anything serious, it was honestly for the best that she preferred their coworkers not in on the time they were spending together outside the hospital. He doubted they were fooling many, though, especially Renee.

"Before you say yes," she warned, brushing a hair back behind her ear, "it's a working double date."

Intrigued, he leaned against her desk. "A working double date? You'll have to explain that one to me as I have no idea what you're talking about."

She laughed. "Probably not, but no worries. It's not anything too strenuous. I'm not putting you to doing landscaping or some other type of tough manual labor."

"I wouldn't be opposed to helping you with your landscaping or any other manual labor that you need to have done." He enjoyed the time they spent together.

"Good to know and something I'll keep in mind. But this is much better than that. It's a restaurant that my friend wants to try." She sounded so excited that he couldn't help but smile. He did that a lot around her. "You pay to learn how to cook a particular meal and do so with a chef guiding you through each step. Afterward, everyone sits down to eat the meal together. Someone Jamie works with mentioned to her how much fun they'd had when they went, and we agreed it sounded like something interesting to try." The term puppy dog eyes came to mind with how she looked at him. "Say you'll go with me."

"You know I'm not going to tell you no, right?"

Hailey grinned. "I'm hoping you're not because she's already made reservations for this Saturday night. We were afraid to wait because the only reason we got an opening on such short notice is that we were the first to reach out after they'd had a last-minute cancellation."

Saturday night. Cayden's excitement tanked. "I'm the cardiologist on call for the hospital this weekend."

Her excitement visibly fizzled.

"Sometimes I only get a few calls. Sometimes I'm there the whole weekend." He'd never really minded too much, but the disappointment on Hailey's face had him wishing he could assure her he would be able to be there the entire time for their double date. "But I usually don't make any big plans because my time isn't my own and I should be prepared for whatever the shift throws at me."

"I forgot about you being on call," she admitted, her disheartenment palpable. "I definitely understand that you have to work. Actually, that will be me having to be at the hospital next weekend for my turn on the weekend work rotation."

Which meant his seeing her would be limited to whether or not she wanted to go out after her shift ended rather than spending an entire day with her as they'd done the past two weekends.

"Just because I usually keep my schedule clear doesn't mean I can't go with you, Hailey. I just can't guarantee that I won't have to bail last minute if I get called in to the hospital." He looked directly into her big eyes, wanting to see the sparkle back in them. "I'm willing to chance it if you are."

Because he didn't want her to ask someone else to go on the double date. She hadn't mentioned the Ryan guy and Cayden hadn't asked. What had been the point when he and Hailey had been together more often than not? Either of them were free to see someone else if they chose. Neither wanted forever and eventually, they would go to just being friends.

"I'm not sure how much fun it would be to take a couples cooking class by myself if you got called away, but…" She seemed to be considering and for a moment he thought she was going to say she'd just ask someone else, and despite his previous thoughts, his breath caught as he waited for her to continue. "Let's try," she suggested, "and I'll keep my fingers crossed that you don't get called in."

Yeah, he would keep his crossed, too. She'd understand work-related things came up. The past two weeks had been fun.

"Perfect. It's a date." As he said the words, he realized what he'd said. A date. He didn't date.

"A double date," she corrected, then smiled at him so brilliantly that his heart did a funny flip-flop. Did she have any idea how much she dazzled him? He really didn't think so as most of the time she seemed to question herself. She was such a sweet contradiction, one moment exuding bold confidence and another completely blind to how great she was.

"It's been a long time since I've been on a double date," he mused from where he still leaned against the desk. Not since Cynthia. Double dating felt more serious than just going out as a couple having fun. He wouldn't back out on Hailey. He didn't really want to. But perhaps it wouldn't be a bad thing if he got called in to the hospital.

"I've got you beat." She made a soft snort sound. "For me, it's been a lifetime."

"Meaning you have never been on a double date?" That surprised him. She'd been in a long-term relationship prior to moving to Florida. Then again, he'd already deduced that her ex was a loser who was responsible for a lot of her insecurities. Cayden would have a hard time not punching the guy if he ever had the displeasure of running into the jerk.

"That's correct." She averted her gaze, looking embarrassed and as if she regretted her admission. The vulnerability on her face had Cayden retracting his thoughts on getting called in to the hospital. Hailey deserved double dates and whatever else she wanted.

"Then I'll have to make sure this first one is a good one." Which he wouldn't be able to do if he was at the hospital. She was an amazing woman and Cayden did not want to let her down the way her ex had.

"I...uh... I'm sure it will be." Her cheeks still a little pink, she lifted her gaze to his and changed the subject. "Have you been in to see Room 208 yet? The patient was admitted for a bacterial urinary tract infection that was resistant to oral antibiotic options. He's here so he can receive intravenous medication that his culture and sensitivity test showed should resolve his infection. He doesn't have a cardiac disease history other than controlled hypertension, however, when I listened to him this morning, he threw several partial beats. The EKG I ordered only showed numerous pre-ventricular contractions so that's likely what I heard. But my gut instinct was that I should have you take a look at him so I entered the consult."

"Maybe you just wanted me to have an excuse to stop by so you could ask me out," he teased, pushing himself up from where he'd been half sitting on the edge of her desk.

Her eyes widened. "No. I didn't enter the consult for personal reasons. I wouldn't do that."

She looked so horrified that he relented rather than tease her further.

"I'm joking, Hailey. I know you wouldn't. Just as I didn't stop by here just to see you, but I admit that getting to see you is an added bonus to making my rounds these days."

She regarded him a moment, then keeping her gaze locked with his, bestowed him with the sweetest smile. "Thank you. Seeing you is an added bonus, too."

Cayden's heart threw a few wild beats, thudding against his ribcage. Reminding himself that they were at work, that someone could return to the nurses' area any moment so he shouldn't pull her to him so he could kiss her plump lips, he cleared his throat. "You want to go with me to examine 208?"

She clicked a button to close the electronic medical record program, then stood. "I'd love to, Dr. Wilton."

Later that day at Cayden's office, Dr. Pennington knocked on Cayden's office door while he was at his desk, dictating his last patient's consult note. He motioned for his coworker to come in while he finished the section he'd been working on, then paused the dictation program on his phone.

"I know it's last minute," his colleague began from where he'd sat down across from Cayden's desk, "but would you swap call weekends with me? I'm on for next weekend and Layla's parents have decided to come visit."

"You want to swap call for you to take this weekend and me to cover next weekend?" Him be off during the double date and be on call next weekend when Hailey would be working—could he be that lucky that his partner was asking to do that?

"I completely understand if you can't," the cardiologist continued. "I started not to ask because of how last-minute it was, but thought I would at least check on the off chance that you didn't have anything going on. I'd asked Rob and he already had plans so he couldn't."

Excited, Cayden leaned back in his chair. "Swapping works great for me as it's this weekend that I have something going on that I was concerned I'd get called away from."

"Seriously?" Dr. Pennington looked relieved. "That's fantastic. I owe you big, pal."

"Ditto." Cayden liked it when life worked for the better for all concerned. It seemed it rarely did, but this time he'd certainly lucked out.

That evening, he and Hailey tried a restaurant in Punta Gorda and she agreed to go to dinner with him the next evening after her shift as well, but they stayed close, choosing a seafood place that had open seating next to the water. She ordered a salmon appetizer that she insisted was some of the best fish she'd ever eaten and insisted he try. She was right.

He'd have spent every evening with her, but the following evening she had her yoga class and on Thursday evening she'd said she had other plans and hadn't elaborated. He'd offered to come by on Saturday so they could do her first swim lesson, but just as she'd done each time he'd mentioned doing so over the past few weeks, she'd put him off yet again.

He wasn't used to women putting him off when he wanted to see them. He wasn't used to caring. With Hailey, he craved every moment with her. He wasn't thrilled by that truth and assumed the excitement of being with her would soon wear off. Only, he'd never experienced the excitement he felt with being with Hailey. She made everything feel new.

On Friday evening when he arrived at her house to pick her up for their cooking date, the scent of sunshine and the sea met him. Whatever air freshener she used, he liked the clean, nonperfume fragrance. It fit the crispness of her white walls and furniture with their turquoise and sea-themed accents, including the pieces they'd picked up in Sarasota that first weekend together. The place felt homey, relaxing, and an extension of her, especially the mermaid mixed-media painting he'd gifted her. He looked at the piece and saw Hailey. It's what he'd seen from the beginning, calm amidst chaos. She did calm him. She also made his world a bit chaotic.

She confused him, had him behaving in ways he didn't understand and that were completely out of his norm. For instance, why hadn't he seduced her? He wasn't blind. She wanted him. But there was something so innocent about her sexuality that, despite knowing she'd lived with a man, he'd held himself back from taking what he wanted. Maybe he even worried that sex would change things between them in ways that would be the end.

He wasn't ready for the end. Not yet.

"These are for you." He handed her the brightly colored bouquet of assorted flowers that he'd swung into the hospital gift shop to buy when they'd caught his eye on his way out of the hospital. He'd liked the yellows and bright pinks mixed in with the daisies and other flowers. The colorful bouquet had made him think of her.

"Aw, thank you. They're beautiful." She went to the kitchen and pulled out a shell-encrusted vase they'd picked up the previous weekend at a shop they'd stopped at on their drive back from Sanibel Island. She placed the flower vase on the end table beside her driftwood lamp and the shell she'd selected from the bounty they'd found. "When I bought this and said it would be perfect for flowers, I wasn't hinting for you to buy me some."

"I didn't think you were," he assured her. "I'm glad you like them."

"I do. Tonight is going to be fun," she promised, walking to the back patio door to check to make sure she'd locked it. He imagined the enclosed area's outer door stayed locked, but he was glad she took the extra precautions even with living inside a gated community. The thought had him pausing. Had he ever considered whether or not a woman in his life locked her doors?

"If I have to cook my own meal, at least I get to do it with you." Not that he minded cooking his own meal. He'd been doing so pretty much from the time his parents divorced. Casey had helped, but Cayden had definitely surpassed his sister's cooking skills.

"You say that, but you've never cooked with me to know whether I'm more of a hindrance than a help." She grabbed her purse from the kitchen bar and turned to him, smiling big as she did so. His chest did funny things when Hailey smiled at him. Things like make up beats of its own rather than follow the usual *lub-dub* normal sinus rhythm. Her face powder didn't hide the pink tinge to her nose and cheeks.

"You got too much sun today." Which surprised him as she'd diligently protected her skin during their outings.

"Yeah, it's not too bad, fortunately, but I should have reapplied my sunscreen sooner." Moving toward her front door, she smiled at whatever ran through her mind. "I was sweating it off faster than I could have reapplied, anyway."

He'd not noticed anything different outdoors, but he'd not really been paying attention, either and she might really have worked on her landscaping. "What were you doing? Lawn work? I was serious in that I'd help you."

Not that it was any of his business, but everything about her fascinated him and he wanted to do things to make her life easier.

She'd been heading toward her front door but turned to look at him and grin. "Would you believe that I was playing pickleball?"

She sounded so proud that he did believe that's what she'd been doing.

"I didn't know you played."

"A more accurate statement would have been if I'd said that I was learning to play pickleball." She gave a self-deprecating laugh. "Unfortunately, I have the athleticism of a slug so it's slow going, but I'm enjoying learning and am already better than when I started."

She moved with such grace that he couldn't imagine her not being able to do anything she wanted, but he wasn't going to argue. What he would do is take advantage of something else they had in common. He'd been playing for years as it was something he and his buddies had enjoyed since college days.

"What you're saying is that if we play, I currently have a decent chance of winning?"

She snorted. "Oh, you're pretty much guaranteed to

win. I've never been good at sports, but I'm determined to up my game since it's a popular activity at our community center. Barry says I keep getting better each time we play."

Barry. Cayden's insides withered into green mush. How could she be so nonchalant about seeing another man? He bit back an expletive.

"Barry is a neighbor, by the way. He's married and I'd guess to be in his seventies."

Had she sensed his reaction? Or maybe he'd just thought he'd held back his frustrated curse. He and Hailey were just casually dating, not moving toward anything serious, so he shouldn't care who Barry was and he sure shouldn't feel such relief that the man was nothing more than a friendly neighbor.

That he did was concerning, but not something he wanted to delve into too closely.

To do that might be having to admit things he didn't want to admit and tonight was about making Hailey's first double date dream worthy.

Later that evening at the Be the Chef cooking venue, Hailey tossed a piece of rice at Cayden, not surprised that he deflected her playful throw. He had been the perfectly attentive date. Jamie had been wowed by him. Hailey's heart was full of pride at sharing them with each other. How blessed was she that she got to have such a fun new friend like Jamie and a great date like Cayden?

"Hey, quit wasting our dinner," he ordered, but with a mischievous gleam in his eyes that warned he was already plotting his playful revenge.

From the time they'd arrived at the venue, he'd been

all smiles. Mostly he'd been that way since he'd gotten to her house other than a short moment where he'd been moody when they'd been discussing her playing pickleball. She'd guessed what had been bothering him. He didn't need to know every detail of her life, but she'd quickly enlightened him, anyway. The thought that he already knew so much, that she thought of him all the time, first and last thing each day, terrified her. Being so wrapped up in him, in spending time with him, was scary as she wondered how they'd proceed when things ended. That he was still friends with Leanna gave her hope that maybe they'd find a way to be friends, too, as she couldn't imagine her new life without him as a part of it. That was what was the scariest. How had he become such an integral part of her new life when she'd meant to never let any one man dominate her time?

"I think we have a few grains to spare," she assured him. She'd be skimping on the rice, anyway, and having more of the grilled vegetables. Amazingly, she'd dropped another five pounds over the past month. Each one had required a lot of work and discipline as she was dining out with Cayden so frequently.

"You say that as if I'm not a starving man." His words lacked conviction as he tossed a grain of rice back at her.

"Hey, the both of you quit that," Jamie warned from where she and Doug worked at the meal prep station next to Hailey and Cayden. "Act your age."

Hailey and Cayden exchanged looks, grinned, and simultaneously tossed rice grains at her friend. Snorting, Jamie rolled her eyes and started to join the fun, but their chef instructor cleared her throat, putting a stop to their shenanigans.

Not surprisingly, Cayden was an excellent slicer and dicer of their vegetables, which Hailey appreciated because he distracted her to the point that her wielding a knife while standing close enough she could feel his body heat wasn't smart. She'd never been a great cook. At least, not to hear John tell it. She'd worked long hours and still prepared their meals, but her best attempts had failed to impress him. Nothing she'd done had impressed him. She'd never had great self-confidence. After spending so much of her life with John it really was no wonder that she'd spiraled downward and believed she hadn't deserved better. Other than school and residency, he'd isolated her then consistently chipped away at her self-worth. Glancing over at the man working next to her, his gaze lifted to hers. Grinning, he winked, then went back to stirring the food mixture in the cooker, completely oblivious to how his simplest gesture set off an emotional tsunami.

Happiness bubbled. She was out on a double date with the most gorgeous, wonderful man and her new friend whom she adored and seemed to adore her back. All evening, she caught herself looking his way, shocked really by how quick his smile was, how desire *for her* shone in his eyes. Concern ebbed away her happiness.

She hadn't planned to date anytime soon after her move but meeting him had changed that. When things ended, how could any man ever measure up? She was spending more and more of her spare time with him. If she wasn't careful her new life was going to revolve completely around Cayden. That terrified her. She and Cayden weren't forever. Even if she wanted them to be, which she didn't, she wouldn't be able to maintain her shiny new facade indefinitely, and eventually her new life would collide with her old and he'd see the real her, the version that never would have caught his attention.

Fake it until you make it, right? With her hair and lash extensions, facial treatments, and so forth, she had the faking it down pat.

Or maybe not as she dreamed of kissing Cayden, of doing much more than kissing him but, other than quick pecks and lots of hand-holding, she had pulled away each time. Some things couldn't be faked. What if Cayden found her as lacking as John had? What if their becoming physically involved was the catalyst to revealing what no amount of makeup and self-help books could hide?

Yeah, she was getting way too attached to Cayden, was way too caught up in what he thought of her, and as lovely as their evening was, she needed to take control of her new life back and quit planning everything around him.

CHAPTER EIGHT

"GIRL, YOU'RE NOT looking so good."

Hailey hadn't needed Renee's assessment to know that. She'd gone to bed not feeling well and had awakened feeling worse. Still, she'd headed to the hospital. She'd only been on the job a couple of months. She wouldn't miss work unless she was literally unable to move. She was moving. Barely. So, she'd work and stay masked to keep from spreading germs to her patients and coworkers. "I'll be okay."

Maybe.

Cayden didn't have any direct admissions and wasn't on call so Hailey didn't see him that morning. Just as well as she didn't want him to see her so subpar. Makeup couldn't hide her putrid color. By lunch, she gave in to Renee's demand that she reach out to the hospital administrator to see if someone could cover the remainder of her shift. Not once during med school or residency had Hailey missed a single day, but she was miserable.

Fortunately, the hospitalist coming in for the evening shift was available, allowing Hailey to head home and to bed. By evening, she admitted defeat and called out for the following morning.

She slept, woke several times, forced fluids, then fell

back into fitful sleep. About dawn, she settled into a decent rest and didn't wake until almost noon. Unfortunately, she was still running a temperature and had body aches that rivaled being hit repeatedly by a baseball bat.

"Got. To. Drink." With the fever on top of her stomach issues, she was going to get dehydrated. She shuffled to the kitchen, opened her cabinets and saw nothing appetizing, then went to stand in front of her refrigerator. Nothing there appealed, either.

She got a glass of water, then headed onto the patio. Maybe just sitting there where she could see the sunshine and the lake would help. Maybe it did as she couldn't say she felt any worse. No better, but not worse. Feeling worse might be impossible, though.

"Quit feeling sorry for yourself."

Eventually, she went back to bed. She didn't recall falling asleep, but she must have as her phone ringing startled her awake. She reached for it and realized she'd missed several calls and texts from Cayden.

"You left work early yesterday and haven't responded to any of my texts. If you hadn't answered this call I was headed your way and not leaving until I put eyes on you," he told her. "Are you feeling better?"

She shook her head, grimacing as pain stabbed through her head.

"Hailey?"

Her lips stuck together as she tried talking. "Not better."

"You sound terrible."

"Thanks," she managed, opening and closing her dry mouth.

"Do you need anything?"

"To feel better. Going to sleep now." Except she needed to drink something with electrolytes, first.

After disconnecting the call, she opened a delivery app and placed an order. Drinks, crackers, soup. She had this sick thing down.

For fear she'd dose off and not wake up when her supplies arrived, she made her way into her living room, blanket, pillow, and all, and crashed onto her sofa.

Picking up the grocery bags and a package of sport drinks from Hailey's front porch, Cayden rang her doorbell again. After a minute or so, her deadbolt clicked, and the door opened.

She blinked, her long lashes sweeping across her cheeks. Dark circles and makeup rimmed her eyes. Her hair was disheveled. She wore an Ohio State sweatshirt and a pair of loose pajama pants and had a blanket wrapped around her shoulders.

"You look terrible." The moment the words escaped his mouth he longed to take them back because he'd swear her already pale skin blanched a few more shades.

"Sound terrible." She coughed, emphasizing her point. "Look terrible. Feel terrible." Her puffy eyes met his. "What are you doing here?"

He held out her groceries as if that somehow explained why he was there. "I came to check on you."

"I'm fine."

She didn't look fine. If it was flu season, he'd think she had the flu. "Is it okay if I carry these to the kitchen?"

She moved aside. "Enter at risk of catching whatever I have."

"I'll take my chances." He generally didn't get ill, but

he'd use caution, making sure not to touch his face and would wash his hands well.

"Okay." She looked lost for a moment, then appeared overcome with exhaustion. "I need to go to bed." With that, she turned, stumbled, and righted herself just as he reached her, groceries still in tow. "Just need sleep."

"Have you eaten today, Hailey?" He placed the groceries on the floor to free his hands and followed her, not touching but close enough he could catch her if she started going down.

She paused in her slow shuffle. "No."

"Once you're in bad, I'm going to cook you something." He wasn't leaving her side until she was safely in bed. Like the rest of her home, the room was done up in whites and turquoise. Throwing off the color theme was a shelf loaded down with books. She'd been telling the truth about self-help books. There were dozens of them. The thing he liked most was a painting of a young girl staring off into the blurred distance. Had she gone to one of the markets without mentioning it to him?

"I bought soup." He had to strain to hear her mumbled words.

"I'll get one of the sport drinks. You could use the electrolytes. Then, I'll heat the soup."

She didn't argue, just crawled into her bed and pulled the covers over her body. Eyes closed, she grunted something that sounded like thanks.

With one last worried glance, he left her room, grabbed the groceries, and proceeded to her kitchen. He should have come over when he hadn't heard back from her the previous night. He'd tried texting and calling but had just thought she'd gone to bed early. When she still wasn't responding by this evening, he'd had to know she was okay. She wasn't okay.

He found a metal straw, poured some of the sport drink into a cup, then brought it to her room.

"Hailey, let me help you sit up long enough for you to sip on your drink."

She roused, raising a little, and taking the smallest drink in history prior to her head returning to her pillow. He placed the cup on a painted mermaid coaster on her nightstand, then headed back to her kitchen.

He unpacked her groceries, putting them away, with the exception of the soup and saltine crackers. He heated up the chicken noodles, spooned out a small bowl, put a few crackers on her plate, then headed to her room. She'd gone back to sleep. Did he wake her or let her sleep? If not for the fact that she'd not eaten or drunk much, if anything, all day, he'd let her rest. But if he couldn't get liquids inside her orally, she would need an intravenous infusion.

"Hailey, wake up. You need to eat."

She mumbled.

"Hailey." He shook her shoulder. "It's time to eat and drink. If you can sit up, I'll feed you."

Her eyes opened and she peered at him. "Why are you in my bedroom?"

"Not for the many reasons I'd like to be. Actually, that's not true. With you ill, this is right where I want to be, taking care of you." His words stunned him, but he assured himself that's what friends did for each other. "Let's get you scooted into an upright position."

"May not stay down. Or in." She winced. "Not been a good twenty-four hours."

"Noted. You still need to eat and drink. If you can't keep anything in, you're going to Venice General for intravenous fluids."

"I—thank you." She attempted to push herself off the pillow but failed. Cayden helped her to sit with her back against her headboard.

"Take a drink." He held the cup for her while she sipped through the straw. "Can you feed yourself or do you need help?"

"I'll try." She took a few bites then seemed bored with her food.

"Try or I'm bringing you to the emergency department to get fluids." Seeing her so weak was wrecking him and he needed to be doing something, anything, to make her feel better.

"No ER." Grimacing, she took another drink, then let him feed her half of the soup, watching him with hooded eyes with each delivered bite. She held up her hand. "No more. Need to sleep."

"Okay, sleep. I'll wake you for more fluids after we see if you're going to keep this down."

He wasn't going anywhere until she was improved. A lot improved.

Hailey woke with a start, having heard a noise in her bedroom. There, in the low light streaking in through her windows, Cayden stretched out in the oversized reading chair. He'd pulled it next to the bed and didn't look nearly as comfy as she felt when curled up there.

Why was Cayden in her bedroom? Why was his hand holding her forearm as if he was afraid to let go? Then the former night's events came rushing back. Cayden had come to her rescue. She had vague memories of his waking her throughout the night to drink.

She glanced at the clock, then pulled free from Cayden's touch. Oh, no. She should be at work. She was new and had no-showed. Would they fi—?

"I called last night," Cayden interrupted her panic, "and let the hospital know you wouldn't be in today."

Part of her wanted to protest at his high-handedness, but gratitude filled her. How had he known to? Not that he wasn't aware of her work schedule, just that she was surprised he'd thought to call in for her. "Thank you."

"You may not be thanking me if word gets out that I called in sick for you. That might be difficult to explain to Renee."

Hailey rubbed her temple. Yeah, Renee getting wind wouldn't be good.

"How are you feeling this morning?"

"Alive," she mumbled. "Alive seems an improvement from yesterday."

"You were pretty rough when I got here."

She reached for the drink he had by her bed, took a sip, then nodded. "I'm embarrassed that you saw me like that." Grimacing, she touched her hair, then covered her face with her hands. "And like this."

"You're beautiful, Hailey. No makeup required."

Mortified that he'd seen her without makeup—no, that wasn't right. He was seeing her with two-day-old makeup she'd slept in. She probably looked like a clown. "You've obviously caught whatever I have. Delirium is setting in."

Looking much too serious, he shook his head. "No delirium, just good taste. Are you hungry?"

She nodded.

"Do you feel up for toast? When I was putting away your groceries, I noticed you had purchased bread and oatmeal, too. I'll gladly make you whatever sounds good."

Embarrassed that she was just lying there while he was offering to prepare food, she scooted up, meaning to rise, but dizziness hit.

"I can make it," she said anyway, hoping the room stopped spinning so she could stand.

"I'd rather you let me."

She pressed her fingers to her throbbing temples, thinking maybe it was her head spinning rather than the room. "Don't you have to be at work?"

"My office manager rescheduled my appointments."

Guilt hit. He was a busy man and had things to do other than nurse her back to health. He had stayed with her all night, had awakened her to drink, had helped her to the bathroom and held a washcloth to her forehead when she'd gotten ill.

"I don't want your appointments canceled because of me." She'd inconvenienced him enough.

"Already done, Hailey. I'm not going anywhere today other than staying right here so I can take care of you."

"I—okay. I'm going to go to the bathroom. Toast and a drink sound wonderful."

Having someone to take care of her was wonderful. She'd gotten sick when she'd been twelve. Her mother had held her most of the night. That had been the only night someone had held her while she was ill. Her mother, and now, Cayden.

Gratitude filled her. He truly was a kind man. And, hopefully that really was just gratitude she was feeling and not anything more because falling for Cayden would be all too easy. She couldn't do that.

Not if she didn't want to end up with a broken heart that no amount of nursing back to health would heal.

The following Saturday, Cayden eyed the sunscreen-coated woman from where she sat on the edge of the swimming pool. She swirled her toes in the pool water. Her nails were flamingo pink and her big toes each had a tiny palm tree with sparkly leaves. He wasn't a feet man, but Hailey's never failed to catch his attention. Probably because they were attached to her toned legs that were glistening in the sunlight.

"This is probably a waste of time as I've no plans to swim."

"Spending time with you is never a waste." He liked being with her. "Besides, we're focusing on floating, not swimming,"

"Show me how floating is done again." She obviously stalled, making him question again if something had happened to make her so leery of learning. She wore the same black one-piece bathing suit with a pair of shorts that she'd worn to shark tooth hunt.

He moved closer to where she sat, placing his hands to either side of her hips on the pool edge. He looked directly into her eyes. "Are you afraid of the water, Hailey?"

She moistened her lips, then took a deep breath. "Yes."

"You're afraid because you can't swim? Be assured that we're going to change that. It may take us a few days or a few weeks, but you will learn to swim."

She eyed him, then stalled further by saying, "Maybe

I'm afraid because there are living things in the water that can hurt me."

"There are living things outside the water that can hurt you," he reminded her, not buying her excuse, especially as the pool water was crystal clear. "You obviously function just fine."

She feigned shock. "You're right. There are. I should go inside and cover myself in bubble wrap."

"Bubble wrap would make for an interesting swim lesson and might help you float."

Sighing, she ran her fingers along where she'd braided her hair. "You think I'm being silly, don't you?"

Silly wasn't one of the adjectives he'd use to describe her. Beautiful, brilliant, mesmerizing, frustrating, but not silly.

"What I think is that you aren't going to get past your water hang-ups until you are confident in your ability to swim. I'm sorry about what happened with Sasha, but that isn't something that happens often, Hailey. Nor does learning to swim mean that you have to go into the open sea if that's not your thing. Prior to what happened with Sasha, you wanted to learn."

"I do. It's embarrassing that I can't. It's just that…" She hesitated. "I tried to learn once before. It didn't go well."

"You didn't have me for a teacher." He'd taught numerous kids over the years he'd worked as a lifeguard. Teaching Hailey would be his pleasure.

"Maybe I'm not someone who is meant to swim."

Eyeing her, seeing the holes in her self-confidence, he yet again wanted to hurt her ex. "Work with me, Hailey. We will get you there."

She still looked hesitant. "I don't want to upset you if I'm not able to do the things you want me to do."

"I'd never be upset with you for not being able to do something, Hailey." Surely, they had spent enough time together that she realized that. "I'd be disappointed if you didn't try at all, but never upset that you tried and failed. It's the trying part that I count as the most important."

She stared into his eyes, her gaze holding fast as his hands went to her waist. Seeming to know what he wanted, she nodded and slid forward as he guided her into the water and against him. The water only came to his waist but, with their height difference, came in just beneath her breasts. Cayden gulped.

"See, this isn't so bad." Holding her felt good, just as it had when he'd lowered her into the water at the beach. Hailey against him felt right.

"Only because you're holding me," she pointed out with a self-deprecating smile. "If you hold me like this the entire time, I'll be fine."

Cayden wouldn't mind holding her the entire time. However, he wanted to help her overcome her fears and he especially wanted her able to safely navigate in water. "I won't let anything happen to you, Hailey."

He meant in the pool, and yet, with her in his arms, how protective he felt of her gave him pause. He wouldn't let anything happen to her. Anywhere. Not if he had any say in the matter.

Clinging to him, she seemed to sense that his mind had gone deeper than the surface of what he'd said. She squeezed where she held on to his arms. "Then, let's get this over with."

"Such an enthusiastic student," he teased.

"It's not that I'm not grateful that you're spending your Saturday trying to teach me. I am appreciative. It's just that," she hesitated, seeming to not know how to express her concerns as she shrugged.

Unable to resist, Cayden leaned in to kiss her temple. Once again, her citrusy scent assaulted his senses, making him deeply inhale. But it was how the feel of his lips pressed to her, how zings of awareness shot through him that had his legs threatening to buckle. He cleared his throat. "We'll stay where you can stand up at any time you feel you need to. Just relax and trust me to keep you safe."

Too bad he didn't trust his ability to keep himself safe from how his emotions were getting so tangled up with Hailey.

"I do trust you." Seeming surprised by her admission, she stared at him with eyes so blue they shamed the pool's bright color. After a moment, she tentatively smiled and loosened her death grip on his arms. "Tell me what to do."

Cayden told her, and as she attempted to do as he asked, he kept his hands at her midsection, keeping her afloat. "We're going to keep practicing this, Hailey. We'll go from one side of the pool to the other for as many times as needed."

"As many times as needed? I hope you have all day."

"I do." His hand beneath her abdomen, Cayden guided her through the water. They made the trip several times. "You did great," he praised, helping her to her feet.

"I didn't do anything except lie there."

"That's what floating is all about. Just lying on the water."

"Without sinking," she added.

"Not sinking is an important component of successful floating." Just as keeping his gaze locked with hers was an important component of keeping his mind off how her wet suit clung to her body.

"Maybe I'll eventually float without you having to hold me."

He had mixed feelings about that. As much as he wanted her success, he liked the excuse to touch her. "Practice makes perfect."

"It'll take a lot to convince me that you weren't born perfect."

Her comment surprised him. "You think I'm perfect?"

"As close as I've encountered." Sunshine reflected off the water and her eyes, creating a surreal, almost mystical look.

"I'm far from perfect, but you make me wish I was."

She blinked. "Me?"

"It's no secret that I'm attracted to you, Hailey."

She hesitated, then, a small smile on her full lips, she placed her hands against his chest. "I'm attracted to you, too, Cayden." Her hands trembled. "How about we finish and get dried off?"

Cayden didn't need water to float. She was enough to have him soaring.

CHAPTER NINE

STARING AT HER reflection in her bathroom mirror, Hailey rubbed her plumped lips together, evenly spreading the shiny gloss. After they'd gotten back to her place, she'd showered to wash off the pool's chlorine, donned a sundress and sandals, and carefully reapplied her makeup. She'd applied lotion, styled her hair, and changed outfits twice. Butterflies danced in her belly as she stared back at her image, barely recognizing herself as the same woman she'd been just a few months ago. What would Cayden have thought of that woman? Would he have noticed her with her dull hair and her ineptitude with anything to do with beauty? Would he have looked at her the way he had while they'd been in the pool? Like he'd wanted to kiss her? To do much more than kiss her?

Hailey gulped. No doubt he had finished in her guest bathroom long ago and was waiting for her. She could hear where he'd turned on the television in the living area.

With one last look in the mirror, she left the reprieve of her bedroom's ensuite bath. Only, when she went into her living room, Cayden wasn't there. For a moment, she thought he'd tired of waiting and had left. The shade to the glass patio doorway was pulled back. He must be on the covered patio.

She was quite proud of the comfy outdoor area she'd created. She'd spent many an hour out there already and it was one of her favorite things about the house. That and looking out at the little man-made lake and watching birds come and go. Fortunately, she'd not seen any alligators, but was told that one occasionally sunned along the banks. She was no more a fan of alligators than she was of sharks or jellyfish so if she never spotted one, she'd be just fine.

His back to her, Cayden was sitting on the comfy over-sized lounger with his feet propped up. Going around to join him, she realized he'd fallen asleep. How cliché that she'd taken so long getting ready that he'd dosed off? The irony of it had her smiling.

With the freedom granted by his closed eyes, she studied him, taking in each of his features. His dark hair was still lightly damp from his shower. His thick lashes spread out long over his cheekbones. His chest rose and fell rhythmically with each breath. He was so handsome that he made her question why he was really there, with her, saying things like that he was attracted to her. Had her drastic makeover really been that successful? That the new her could attract someone so wonderful?

He looked so peaceful that rather than wake him, she sat down beside him, snuggling close enough that she leaned against him and closed her own eyes. She wasn't one for naps and couldn't imagine falling asleep when she was near someone as dynamic as Cayden, but being next to him, letting herself relax against him, was nice.

Only, it didn't take long for his breathing pattern to change, hinting that if he'd been asleep, he no longer was. She shifted to glance at him and met his half-lidded hazel gaze. Had any man's eyes ever been more beautiful? More mesmerizing?

He didn't say anything, just brushed his fingers along her face, skimming her hairline, then gliding along her chin ever so gently. Goose bumps prickled her skin. Her heart quivered. All of her did. His touch was reverent, as if he couldn't believe he was there *with her*. Surreal. Maybe she had fallen asleep and was dreaming.

"Cold?" he asked.

Hailey shook her head. She wasn't cold. Quite the opposite. Her insides burned. Her gaze lowered to his mouth and temptation hit so strong that she longed to know what it would feel like to kiss him for real and not the light touches they'd been playing around with for weeks. Breathing was more and more difficult. Maybe that was why she scooted so close that his breath became hers.

He didn't move, just waited to see what she was going to do. Hailey wanted to know her next move, too. She was no seductress, no siren to lure men. Yet she'd have to be blind not to see that, for the moment, Cayden was under her spell, and his breathing was as ragged as her own at just her lightest touch. His reaction had her heart racing and her body aching, and made her crave him enough that resisting temptation was impossible.

She stretched the tiniest amount, pressing her lips to his tentatively with her eyes wide open. She didn't need to watch him, though. She could feel his response, could hear the low half growl, half moan that escaped him when she lingered, tasting his mouth.

"Hailey." The way he said her name emboldened her. She placed her palms against his cheeks, marveling that she touched him, that she threaded her fingers into his hair, then pulled him to her.

"Hmm?" she whispered against his mouth, so close she could feel the warmth of his breath. "Tell me what you want."

"You know what I want." His hands were on her now, her shoulders, her back, her bottom as he lifted her to lie upon him and molded her firmly against him to show her just how much he wanted her.

She'd never quite envisioned this moment when she'd bought the lounger, but she'd never be able to see it again without thinking of Cayden beneath her, his hands cupping her bottom as they kissed. Oh, how they kissed.

Hailey wasn't sure how long they kissed. An eternity could have passed, and it wouldn't have been enough to fully savor him. She wasn't sure how much time passed prior to her fingers sliding beneath his T-shirt, removing his T-shirt so she could run her hands over his chest and shoulders. She loved touching him, experiencing his responses. Soon, she couldn't think about his responses for her own, though. All she could do was feel.

"You're sure?" he asked.

Hailey wasn't sure of anything except that he best not stop the magic he was wielding over her body. She wasn't sure what words came out of her mouth, but they must have been the right ones because his smile was so beautifully perfect as he caressed her face.

"Hailey," he said, kissing her and forever changing her, winding her so tightly that she had no choice but to explode into tiny bits of colored confetti that floated back to earth from some heavenly place.

* * *

If there was really such a thing as grinning from ear to ear, Cayden imagined he was doing exactly that as he marveled at the woman he held close to his sweat-slickened body. Marveled because she was marvelous. As his coworker, his friend, and his lover.

His lover. Because he loved her? Right after the most amazing physical experience of his life was not the time to be contemplating his feelings for Hailey. Delirium had obviously set in, because when he looked at her he couldn't help but think that he wanted to hang on to this feeling forever.

Forever was a life sentence he'd not planned to endure.

So why did forever feel like it wouldn't be nearly long enough if Hailey was by his side?

"Anyone ever tell you that you're an amazing kisser, Hailey? An amazing everything."

"No. But then, until today, I'd only ever kissed one man."

Cayden's eyes widened. "You're kidding?"

Taking a deep breath, Hailey rolled so that she was lying next to him rather than on him. "I wish I was," she half mumbled, not looking at him. "John was my first and only boyfriend prior to, well, um, you."

"You'd never kissed anyone other than your first boyfriend?" He'd known she wasn't overly experienced. Had liked that, even. That innocent air about her had been one of the reasons he'd not rushed their physical relationship. Had he known the intensity of what they just shared, nothing would have held him back short of Hailey herself.

She shook her head.

"How is it that you've only kissed one man other than me?"

"Men weren't exactly beating down my door."

He scooted to partially sit up and stared at her in such shock that, had her skin not still been flushed from what they'd done, she'd have blushed. "Were the men in Ohio idiots?"

She snorted. "I've mentioned that I made a lot of life changes beginning just prior to and continuing after moving to Florida." She reached up and touched her hair. "My appearance was one of those major changes. New hair, new eyelashes—" she batted them "—corrective eye surgery to lose my glasses, eyebrows, extreme diet and exercise, facials, fillers, and makeup consults with how-to classes, manicures, pedicures, the list goes on." She grimaced, then reached for her shirt. "Honestly, it's exhausting and things I'd never bothered with before. I wouldn't have had time even if I'd wanted to, not with med school and residency and John. Trying to improve one's looks is time-consuming and expensive. I started in Ohio, and my first week here I was at appointments every day, some days two or three. Now I spend my Thursdays and some Fridays doing maintenance appointments."

"You don't need to improve your looks, Hailey. You're gorgeous."

"You didn't see me before," she reminded him, putting her shirt back on.

"Doesn't matter. I'd have still found you attractive." His attraction to her went way beyond her hair and nails.

Hailey laughed a hollow sound that held more pain than humor. "You say that, but that's because you're looking at the new me. The me that, short of going under the reconstructive knife, has maximized her looks. No one found me attractive. Just John and he—" She stopped. Her gaze lifted to his, seeming horrified at what she'd just told him.

Idiots, he thought. John and every man who'd ever made her see herself in any way other than beautiful.

"He what?" Cayden prompted from where he sat next to her on the lounger.

Not looking at him despite his willing her to, she shrugged. "I prefer to think he liked me in the beginning, but honestly, he may never have. I was his meal ticket and security blanket. To put it bluntly, I was basically his sugar mama."

Her confession shocked him. Little things she'd said and done that he'd put down to feminine independence now took on a new slant. He furrowed his brows. "As a resident?"

"My parents weren't wealthy, by any means, but they had done all right for themselves. I inherited a decent chunk when their house was auctioned off as it was on a nice piece of land in a popular area in Cincinnati. Fortunately, Dad had set up a trust with his life insurance policy and the trustee rolled most of the estate sale into that investment account that I couldn't access until recently. I got a monthly living expense payment from the trust but I couldn't access the bulk of it until finishing graduate school or my thirtieth birthday—whichever came first. Thank goodness he did that as otherwise, I'm not sure I'd have anything left because John spent every penny he could get his hands on."

Whatever amount her inheritance was, Hailey was the real treasure.

"I'm on record as saying the man was an idiot." How could the man have been in a long-term relationship with Hailey, have had her vying for his love, and been more interested in things?

"It could be argued that I'm the one who was foolish, because it was me who let him take advantage of me for so long."

"You obviously cared about him."

She nodded. "I thought I loved him and vice versa. Now, whether from time away from him or my therapy, I recognize that I was so desperate for love and attention that I was easy prey for him to swoop in and convince me that he was all I deserved."

"You deserve good things, Hailey." Everyone did. Cayden hugged her, not liking how she remained stiff in his embrace. "The best things."

"So my therapist keeps reminding me." Not seeming comfortable with his holding her, she reached for her underwear and sundress, putting them on prior to continuing. Once dressed, she walked over to stare out at the man-made lake that bordered her backyard. "I didn't date in high school. Not a single date. It wasn't because I didn't want to, but that no one asked."

The pain and embarrassment in her voice had Cayden's insides aching for her. That she'd felt the need to move away from him after what they'd just shared had his insides aching, too. Surely, she knew there was no reason to feel embarrassment with him?

"Apparently, you've been surrounded by idiots your whole life."

She turned, met his gaze with her sad blue eyes that ripped at his heart when they'd been so happy, so full of desire, just minutes before. "I was an introvert and wasn't involved in much during my school years. At first due to bouncing from one foster home to another, but then, after my parents adopted me, because I was happy to have a family and wanted to be with them. I met John early in my college freshman year around the time my mother died from breast cancer. My father died less than a year later from a broken heart. John was the only person in my life."

"I'm sorry, Hailey." He wanted to hold her, to wrap his arms around her until she felt so loved that loneliness could never take hold again, but when he stood to go to her, she shook her head. Sensing she needed to say whatever was in her heart, he grabbed his clothes and got dressed while she continued.

"Even after I acknowledged that our relationship was over, I went with the status quo rather than making the break." She took a deep breath. "Ending things meant being completely alone in the world. That scared me."

"You've obviously overcome that fear." At her look of doubt, he pointed out. "You moved to a state where you didn't know anyone. That takes guts."

Her expression remained dubious. "Or a really strong desire to start over where no one knew the old, boring me."

"You were never boring, Hailey." Unable to stay away a moment longer, he crossed the patio to where she stood and placed his fingertip against her temple. "What's up here is completely fascinating."

"I'm glad you think so." A tear slid down her cheek, gutting him.

"Don't you?"

She swiped at the tear, waving him off and taking a few steps away from him. "I'm working on that, too."

"As part of this big makeover you've done?"

She nodded. "I'm creating the life I want."

His brow lifted. "That sounds like a line from a self-help book."

"That's quite possible. There's a bunch of them on the shelf in my bedroom and I've read them all at least once." Glancing toward him, she didn't quite meet his eyes. "Now you realize I'm a messy work in progress and we shouldn't have done what we did a few minutes ago, not with the baggage I carry."

"Who doesn't have baggage, Hailey?"

Hailey's gaze lifted to his. "You."

He harrumphed. "You think I don't have baggage? I must put on a good show, then, because I've enough to fill an airport. We could start with the girlfriend I dated through high school and my first two years of college. I planned to marry her the summer prior to starting med school."

"What happened?"

"She got pregnant by some random guy she met on a girls' trip to Miami. I might have forgiven her, except apparently it wasn't the first time she'd cheated."

"I'm sorry."

"It gets better," he admitted, wondering how such an amazing day had turned into a confessional. "Hurt, I jumped into another relationship, which started off great. I was planning to propose, but that time it was my roommate who Cynthia cheated with. After that, I quit believing in love as I realized that when it came to women, I prefer being friends with benefits, like my relationship with Leanna was, rather than anything with promises of fidelity and forever."

Which had him circling back to his earlier thoughts about Hailey. Because no matter how much bringing up the past might make him want to recant those earlier thoughts, he couldn't. Hailey was unlike anyone he'd ever met. Beautiful in ways the eyes couldn't see, in addition to wowing him with her eyes and infectious smile. Smart, funny, trustworthy.

Fidelity and forever not only didn't feel impossible with Hailey, but rather, his heart's inevitable destiny.

Stunned by the women who had been in Cayden's life, Hailey stared at him, thinking she could toss his own words back at him. His exes had been idiots. How could any woman have had his love, have had him wanting to spend his life with her, and her to have treated his heart so callously?

Hailey just couldn't fathom it.

She also couldn't fathom how she was going to move past what they'd done earlier. They'd had sex. Good sex. Phenomenal sex. Sex that had blown her away. Sex that he'd enjoyed, too. He had been right there with her every touch and moan along the way. Not because she'd been worriedly trying to make sure he liked what they were doing. She'd been so caught up in what he was doing to her body that she hadn't been thinking, just feeling and touching and basking in such unexpected pleasure. He'd given that to her so selflessly, had made her feel so good.

Just looking at him, she wanted to grab hold and never let go. Which was foolish and why he'd just reminded her that he preferred being friends with benefits and didn't do commitment. No doubt he wanted to make sure that, in her inexperience, she didn't mistake what they'd done to mean anything more than what it had been. Sex.

Her heart squeezed in protest. What was wrong with her that despite all her big plans and goals she'd fallen for the first guy she'd become involved with? She'd not even planned to date, had known she needed to focus on herself and not a relationship. He'd been so deliciously tempting that she'd been unable to resist, had convinced herself that she was just dipping her toes into the dating world by spending time with him. Ha. How foolish was she? Would she never learn?

"I—you're right." She stood a little straighter, needing all her strength to do what needed to be done. Self-preservation demanded she take control of her life and fortify the miniscule barriers he'd blown through to reach her vulnerable heart in such a short time. No way could she recover from a heartbreak at Cayden's hands. Her heart was much too fragile from where she'd pieced it back together after John's crushing it. No way would she go back to the weak, clingy woman she'd been, begging for John's love and attention. "I'm glad we can discuss this like adults and that we're in agreement. Promises of forever and fidelity would ruin our friendship." She didn't want to hear fake promises. She wanted...no, she did not want that. She couldn't want that. To want that would bleed her heart dry. "I owe you the biggest thank-you for what happened between us, because sex was never like that with John. Now I'm curious as to what all I've been missing out on and look forward to fully jumping into the dating world."

That she'd shocked him was obvious. His eyes had

widened, then narrowed. "You plan to jump into the dating world?"

She nodded. "I haven't learned all the things I should have learned by this point in my life. Thank you for helping me realize how fun sex can be when it isn't bogged down by emotional entanglements. Is it always that good? I mean, with other people?" Realizing he could take what she'd said as her fishing for a compliment, she quickly added, "Oh, never mind. I'll find out for myself."

Nausea gripped her stomach at the thought of anyone touching her other than Cayden, but she kept her tone and expression light.

Cayden continued to stare at her in disbelief. Had his previous involvements been clingy afterward? She wouldn't cling. She knew doing so would be futile. Just look at how long she'd clung to John. She'd never do that again.

But if she continued seeing Cayden, would she remain as determined? Or would she fall into a lifetime of desperately wanting to be loved and end up devastated?

Look at how passionate she was about him after just a few months. She had to put herself first, to preserve her new life, and not let anything or anyone steal that from her. Not even herself.

"But I think what happened between us shouldn't happen again. With us being coworkers, continuing the benefits part of our friendship would be too complicated."

"You don't want to see me again?"

Only during every waking moment.

She hated herself for the thought, for her weakness, her foolishness.

"Not outside of work and Venice Has Heart."

He raked his fingers through his hair, paced across the patio, then turned to her. "Did I miss something, Hailey? Something I did wrong?"

She shook her head. He'd done everything right and that was the problem. "It's best if we don't do this again, and we need to see other people. I've spent so much time with you that I haven't gone on dates with anyone else. I want to experience all life has to offer that I've been missing out on."

A cold look settled onto his face, erasing the warmth he'd always looked at her with. "Fine, Hailey. You have fun experiencing all those things you've missed out on in life."

With that, Cayden left.

Crumbling with sobs that wracked her body, Hailey sank onto a chair, cradling her head in her palms. Just look at what a mess she'd made of her new life, falling for the first man to smile her way.

Fortunately, she'd stepped up to the plate and done what was right for her self-preservation.

Surely, her heart would forgive her when it realized how much pain she'd saved it down the road.

CHAPTER TEN

A MONTH HAD passed and a tired-from-tossing-and-turning Hailey arrived at the Venice Has Heart event's medical tent. She'd not seen Cayden yet that morning, but not doing so before the day ended was unavoidable.

Not seeing him made it easier to deceive herself about how tangled up she'd become in the fantasy of being the recipient of his attention.

Her heart had yet to forgive her. So had her body for depriving it of Cayden's magic. She missed him more than she could have imagined. Not that she didn't see him or that he wasn't polite. He was. But he didn't look at her the same. He never met her eyes. Never smiled at her. Never laughed with her. Never texted her funny memes or messages to have "sweet dreams" as she drifted to sleep. Never…never anything because whatever had been between them, they were now only coworkers.

It was what she'd needed to happen, but was still slowly killing her.

Which reinforced that their ending sooner rather than later had been the best thing that could have happened, even if only her logic and self-preservation instinct agreed. Even her friend Jamie had thought Hailey was nuts when she'd revealed that she couldn't be involved with Cayden. Her poor heart wouldn't have survived if she and Cayden had grown any closer. Whether it was going to currently was debatable.

Had anyone ever died from a broken heart? What was she asking? Her own father had died from his broken heart over grieving his wife. Having Hailey in his life hadn't been enough for his will to live to press on. How sad that even for her father she hadn't been enough?

After the change in their relationship, Hailey had briefly considered bailing on the Venice Has Heart event, but she wanted to volunteer and be involved in the community. That had nothing to do with Cayden. She met with the group the previous week, enjoying reconnecting with the Krandalls and Benny, but seeing Cayden smiling and laughing with Leanna had been pure torture. That he'd avoided speaking with Hailey completely had been for the best because she might have burst into tears at how hollow she felt without him in her life.

"Looks as if we've had a great turnout for the run." Having been rushing around helping check runners in and making sure everything was in order, Linda sat down in a folding chair and fanned her tanned face with the torn-off side of a cardboard box. She smiled at Hailey. "Bob and I ran the half marathon this morning before daylight. We didn't want to be slackers."

Hailey didn't think anyone would ever accuse the couple of that.

"How long have you been married?"

"Since I was sixteen and we eloped."

"Sixteen? Was that even legal?" Hailey stared at the women in astonishment. "That's so young."

Linda laughed. "Didn't feel too young and my daddy

probably could have forced the issue if he'd wanted. He didn't because he knew I'd been wanting to marry Bob since I was five." Linda's expression brightened with her memories. "He wrote me one of those check yes or no boxes letters asking me to being his girlfriend."

Hailey couldn't help but smile. "I take it you checked the yes box."

Bob stepped up behind his wife and grinned. "That would have been too simple for my Linda. She wrote back asking if I wanted babies and puppies. When I marked yes, she wrote back saying she was going to marry me." He gave his wife an indulgent look. "Who was I to argue with the prettiest girl in class?"

Hailey stared at the couple. "You only dated each other?" When they nodded, she added, "Didn't you ever wonder if you missed out by not dating anyone else?"

"There was no need to date anyone else when I met the best in kindergarten," Bob assured. "Linda's the only date I wanted. Still is."

Linda patted his cheek. "Ditto, darling."

Hailey watched them with more than a little envy. What would it have been like to have loved and been loved from such a young age? To have grown up knowing that your someone was always there?

They chatted for a few minutes then Bob left to check on where the vendors had set up their booths.

"Isn't he a sweetheart?" Linda asked, watching as he left the tent.

"I'll admit I'm a little jealous."

"He's definitely a keeper." Linda's gaze cut to Hailey. "Is there no one special in your life?"

Face aflame, Hailey fought picking up the cardboard

piece Linda had fanned herself with earlier. "I... There was, but we're not involved anymore. It was never going to work. I mean, I miss him, but—" What was she doing? Linda didn't want to hear her pathetic love story. "Yeah, it wouldn't have worked out."

"What makes you think it wouldn't have worked out? Bad temperament, bad finances, bad breath, or bad sex?"

Hailey's jaw dropped, then managed to say, "None of the above."

"Then, if you miss him as much as it sounds you do, you need to do something to make it work out. Flirt with him a little or something to let him know you're still interested."

"I've never been one of those girls who were natural-born flirters." Not that it would matter if she was. Cayden barely acknowledged she existed these days.

"Just smile and bat those pretty eyes. If it's meant to be, things will work out," Linda advised. "Now, let's double-check our supplies before heading to the main stage for the kickoff. You don't want to miss that."

Yeah, missing Cayden was more than enough.

They were just finishing their check when, clipboard in hand, Cayden walked into the tent.

Hailey's chest tightened. Linda's question echoed through her mind. How had Hailey known it wouldn't work? It just wouldn't have. He was him and she was her. To have continued would have just been delaying the painful inevitable. The only real question had been at what point had she wanted to accept her heartache and refocus on her self-healing and being the best her she could be.

Wearing navy shorts and a Venice Has Heart T-shirt

and baseball cap, Cayden was gorgeous. But then, he was no matter what he wore. How could she readily argue his inner beauty was his most stunning attribute when he was so gorgeous on the outside?

What if your best self had been the you who had been with him? her heart whispered before she could hush it.

His gaze went to Linda and didn't budge, almost as if Hailey weren't there. "Anything you ladies need before we officially get started?"

You. For a brief moment, she worried that she'd said her thought out loud. Neither Cayden nor Linda were gawking at her, so she must not have.

"We're good," Linda told him. "No one has needed our services, yet, but that will change once the race gets started. Do you recall last year when those men ran into each other and the one was knocked out cold?"

Hailey was glad Linda continued to chat with Cayden, because it allowed her to try to tamp down her silliness. She did not *need* him. That the thought had entered her head annoyed her. She missed him, a lot, but that didn't mean she needed him.

"Isn't that right?"

Hailey blinked at Linda. Having no idea what she'd just said, she took a cue from her self-help books and smiled. That must have been an okay response. Linda went right back to talking with Cayden until he took off to head back to where Leanna was deejaying the event live on the radio station where she worked.

"Maybe you should try your flirting skills on Dr. Wilton," Linda suggested, causing Hailey to choke on air and have to cough to catch her breath. "He's a great catch."

He was a great catch, but he didn't want to be caught.

Hailey coughed again, searching for the right response. Fortunately, Linda laughed and nudged her arm. "Don't look so horrified. It was just a suggestion. Come on. They want us all there for the official kickoff and it's almost time."

Leanna introduced Cayden to the group of volunteers, participants, vendors, and spectators and as with everything, he gave a dynamic motivational pep talk to everyone there. Next, a heart transplant patient who was walking the event said a quick prayer. Cayden wished them all luck and to always have heart.

The official buzzer sounded and the runners were off.

Hailey and Linda made their way back to the medical tent, where Hailey would be most of the day. The first fifteen minutes were slow, but then Cayden arrived on a UTV with one of the runners sitting in the truck bed–type back. Another volunteer drove and, from where he rode beside her, a gloved-up Cayden pressed a bloody gauze pad against the injured woman's knee.

"This is Aimee. She fell and has a pretty nasty gash on her knee from where she hit the pavement," Cayden informed her as he helped the forty-something woman out of the golf cart. As Hailey gloved up, he helped Aimee get settled onto the exam table that had been set up in the tent.

Hailey expected him to leave, but he knelt next to where she had to examine the woman's wound. She pulled off the gauze and winced. "You took a nasty tumble."

"Oh, I'm one of those people who never does anything halfway." Aimee sighed. "I'm not sure what I tripped over. My own feet, I guess, as there was nothing on the pavement."

While Cayden swapped out his gloves, Linda asked questions to fill out a medical encounter form, then had Aimee sign a release.

Apparently planning to assist, he handed a squirt bottle of sterile solution to Hailey. "Saline?"

Did he know it was all she could do to keep her hands from shaking as she took the bottle? Could he hear the thundering of her heart at how near he was?

"Thanks." Taking the bottle, she rinsed the bleeding wound, clearing out a few stray bits of gravel and wishing she could clean out the wounds of her heart as easily. "The cut is deep and needs sutures to close it."

Aimee winced. "I figured. This isn't my first bout of clumsiness."

"I can send you to the emergency room or I can do the sutures. Your choice," Hailey offered, grateful she'd noted the suture kits in their supplies.

"If you can do it here, then please do." The woman looked relieved that she wasn't going to have to travel elsewhere. "My husband was running ahead of me and doesn't know I fell. He wouldn't complain, but I'd like him to finish the race."

"Gotcha." She glanced toward Cayden. She caught his eyes unexpectedly and her heart ached when her gaze met his and saw a glimmer of something before it disappeared. Her eyes stung with moisture. Not now, she scolded herself. Now was not the time to be dwelling on Cayden. Recalling why she'd glanced up, she asked, "Since Aimee told Linda that she's not allergic to anything, could you draw me up a couple of milliliters of lidocaine, please?"

Cayden did so and handed the syringe to her, taking

care for their hands not to touch. *No worries, Cayden*, she thought. *Our touching might have rendered me a heaping mess and you'd have had to sew Aimee's knee without me.*

Changing her gloves over to the ones in the suture kit, Hailey kept her gaze focused on Aimee. She injected the area to anesthetize the skin, activated the needle safety device, then handed the syringe back to him. "I'll close her with the Ethilon number four, please."

Cayden had already pulled out the suture material and dropped it onto the sterile field drape.

Once Aimee was numb, Hailey used the curved needle to put in nine sutures.

"Great job," Cayden praised when she was finished.

Instantly, her eyes prickled with tears again. He was the most positive, uplifting person she'd ever met. Not once had she gotten the impression that he wanted to take over. He was confidently content in her abilities, had been cool with assisting, and had vocalized his appreciation for her skills. He hadn't pointed out that she'd struggled to get that first knot in place because her hands had been shaking. Shaking that hadn't been from lack of belief in herself, but from his nearness. Cayden shook her whole world. He had from the moment she first noticed him from across the hospital cafeteria. If only she'd known then what she knew now, she could have avoided him completely and saved them both a lot of trouble. Only... only, her patient was eyeing her sutured knee.

"Unfortunately, no matter how great of a job, you're going to have a scar, Aimee," she warned the woman, then gave instructions on home care and the need to follow up with her primary care provider for a wound check and suture removal.

When finished, aware of where Cayden was talking with Linda, Hailey disposed of her gloves, then took the medical encounter form that Linda had started to record care provided. Before Hailey finished, the golf cart driver arrived with another runner. Hailey started to stand, thinking she'd finish the simple notation of what she'd done on Aimee's knee later, but Cayden stopped her.

"Linda and I will triage him while you finish your note."

So, willing her hand to be steady, she documented the basics of suturing Aimee's knee, stealing a few glances to where Cayden knelt next to the man sitting on the table Aimee had recently vacated and which Linda had wiped with disinfectant. Kind, gentle, caring, compassionate, all those descriptions and more ran through her mind as she watched Cayden interact with the newcomer, watched him laugh at something the man said when Linda placed a cooling towel on the back of his neck and handed him a sports drink.

Cayden glanced at his watch, then toward her, catching her watching him. His smile faded. He had no smile for her, instead quickly looking back toward the runner, then standing to say something to Linda. Having finished the chart, a wrecked but determined to trudge forward Hailey joined them.

"Roger, here, just needs to cool down. He started out too hard too fast and got overheated. I don't think he's going to need intravenous fluids, but you can keep an eye on him. Leanna messaged that she needs me to join her for the broadcast."

Leanna. Because although Hailey was an emotionally tangled mess, Cayden was used to moving from friends with benefits to just friends or whatever it was they currently were. Maybe eventually they'd be friends like he and Leanna were. Or were he and Leanna in the friends with benefits category? Maybe he'd even eventually prove right all those who believed that when he settled down, it would be with the beautiful deejay.

When he settled down? He had no plans to ever settle down. If he had—she'd what? His willingness to settle down didn't mean he'd have ever chosen Hailey, that he could have ever loved her.

Sighing, she met his gaze and her breath caught that he hadn't moved, but was looking at her with a sad longing that he failed to hide.

Oh, Cayden. Could you have ever grown to love me? Was that even possible, when she'd barely started loving herself and he'd said he no longer believed in love?

Was she truly so gullible, so desperate to be loved, that whatever had been in his eyes made her want to believe in the seemingly impossible?

Cayden had stayed late into the previous night working with his team leaders to make sure they had everything set for the event. With only a few snafus, everything seemed to have gone smoothly. Definitely, the day had been a success, raising needed funds and awareness of heart disease and ways of preventing it within their community. The official activities had ended, and the breakdown and cleanup process had started.

"Cayden?"

Recognizing Hailey's voice, Cayden braced himself. At the hospital he could compartmentalize his interactions with her, could draw upon his professionalism as a shield from the slaying being near her gave him. But, here, he'd lost that edge and had slipped more than once, asking himself over and over what had led to her pushing him away after they'd shared such an intimate connection. What they'd shared had been different, special, addicting. At least, to him. She'd shut him out almost immediately. *Why?*

Had she sensed his growing feelings for her? Sensed that he'd been leading up to telling her that she'd changed his mind—his heart—about so many things and so had pushed him away?

"I know it's been a long day, but are you busy after all this is done?"

Knowing he couldn't just keep standing with his back to her, he sucked in a deep breath and turned to face her. She looked as tired as he felt. He hadn't really anticipated her staying from start to finish, but she'd jumped in to help wherever needed all day. He shouldn't have expected less, not from Hailey.

Maybe she'd been trying to be kind by ending things, afraid she'd hurt him further if they continued. She didn't have to worry. Her reminder of why he didn't get emotionally involved had served its purpose. He'd keep his heart locked away for good this time.

He nodded. "I have plans."

For a moment he thought she was going to turn to leave, but instead, her gaze met his, full of a tumultuous mixture of resignation and forced courage. "With Leanna?"

He nodded. She'd asked him to go eat with her to go over the day's events and to make notes on what worked well and what they could do to improve for next year's event while it was fresh on their minds.

"I... Okay." Why was she looking at him that way? She was the one who'd insisted they end their relationship. "Have a good night then."

Disappointment on her face, Hailey turned to leave. The urge to stop her hit him hard. But he wouldn't. The past month had been difficult. How much harder would it be if he gave in to the urge to beg her to give them another chance? To let him continue with her in the new life she said she was creating for herself?

How crazy was that when she'd let them go so easily? When he'd been about to hand her his heart and she'd shoved the door closed before he could? Three times and he was out. Only, Hailey was nothing like his previous two heartbreaks. Even calling them that felt wrong when they barely registered in comparison to the world-shattering pain Hailey's cutting him out of her life had unleashed. He needed to just let her go.

"Was there something in particular you needed, Hailey?" he asked anyway, causing her to turn back.

She stared at him a moment, then shook her head. "Nothing. Have a good night and thanks again for involving me in today. It was truly a blessing to be here."

She'd been busy in the medical tent with Linda and then with doing heart health consults. She'd taken a few breaks for grabbing something to eat and he'd seen her strolling around to watch the kids playing in the bouncy house, a faraway smile on her face that made him wonder what she was thinking. He'd bet it hadn't been about the things seeing her watching those children had elicited within his bumfuzzled brain. He blamed lack of sleep.

Last night and for the whole of the last month. He was physically, mentally, and emotionally exhausted.

"Thank you for volunteering," he found the will to say, even adding, "We hope you'll be back next year."

Her lower lip disappeared into her mouth for a moment, drawing his gaze and eliciting self-disdain at how her tiny gesture twisted him into knots.

"I'll always be there if you need me, Cayden."

Her wording seemed strange and he continued to mull it over while he watched her leave, and he struggled to keep his mind on task during his and Leanna's dinner. She was quick to point that out to him, and when she asked him to her place for drinks, he was quick to say no.

He only wanted one woman and she no longer wanted him in her life.

Grateful for her shower to wash away the day's grime and the tears she'd given in to on her drive home, Hailey towel dried her hair, then put on shorts and a T-shirt to sleep in. It had been a long day, and one with extreme emotions. She'd loved volunteering but being with Cayden outside the hospital setting had highlighted her downward spiral ever since she'd ended their relationship.

Since she'd pushed him away. That was what she'd done. She even knew why. Because he scared her. The way he'd held her, kissed her, touched her, looked into her eyes as he'd made love to her, that had terrified her. Because he made her believe that he cared and she hadn't known how to deal with that. The only two people who had truly cared for her had been gone so long that she'd forgotten how wonderful it felt. It's what she'd craved with John, but never gotten. But Cayden, despite the

words he'd said, hadn't held back. He'd nurtured everything good inside her.

Then.

Now he'd cut himself off from her emotionally and
was unavailable to her in every way.

Calling herself every kind of fool, she headed to the
kitchen, got herself a glass of water, and headed out to
her patio. Her gaze immediately went to the lounger. She
needed to get rid of the thing because she couldn't look at
it and not recall how she'd boldly kissed Cayden, how he'd
kissed her back, then made love to her. She'd set her fears
aside that night, kissed him and made love to him without any past doubts getting into her head despite there
being so many and Cayden had been why. He'd nurtured
her confidence, lifted her up to discover the things she
hadn't previously learned about herself and life.

She'd moved to Florida to start over from past mistakes and had ended up making the biggest mistake of her
life. Because she'd not trusted in what she'd seen happening between them, not trusted in what she saw when he
smiled at her, not trusted in her ability to decipher what
was real and what she wanted to be real.

Too late she was seeing clearly what she'd had and lost.
Question was, what was she going to do about it? Be-
cause Florida Hailey refused to go down without a fight.
Sure, that she thought she could compete with someone
of Leanna's caliber might seem deluded to some, but
Cayden hadn't loved Leanna. Not like he had with her.
Because she was lovable.

She was. Whether it was months of being away from a
man who'd emotionally abused her or doing her therapy
and self-healing, she finally realized she was lovable be-

yond whether or not Cayden ever chose to risk his heart with her again. She was lovable.

Or maybe she was so exhausted that she was delusional. One or the other.

Either way, she had to find Cayden and tell him everything in her heart. He'd always been easy to talk to, but telling him how she'd let fear hurt them both wouldn't be easy. Could he ever forgive her?

Her doorbell rang. Heart racing, she walked into the house, then peered through the front door's peephole. Cayden! Without thought, she flung the door open and barely prevented herself from flinging herself into her arms.

"You're here." Did he think her strange that she was grinning at him? Why was she grinning? Just because she'd had an epiphany did not mean that he felt any different.

"Can I come in?"

She moved aside, allowing him into her house, watched him automatically start to go out to the patio area, but he changed his mind, stopping in the living area instead.

Mind racing, Hailey followed him there, sitting down on the sofa since he'd taken the chair. "Why are you here, Cayden? I thought you had other plans."

"Leanna had suggested we meet to discuss things we'd do differently or the same at next year's event while it was fresh on our minds. We finished early."

"It wasn't a date?" Happiness filled her. More than it should. Just because his plans with Leanna hadn't been a date didn't mean he was going to forgive and forget that Hailey had been too afraid to let him love her.

"I've not been on a date since with you. I have no interest in dating."

"Oh." Then, sucking in a deep breath and reminding herself that she would be okay no matter what happened, she bared her heart. "Me, either."

His brow lifted. "How are you going to experience all the things you've missed out on in life? The things you couldn't wait to experience?"

Hailey grimaced at the pain she'd caused him. If he'd give her the chance, she'd make it up to him. "I was wrong about what I had missed out on. Dating was never the life experience I was missing out on. Not really."

"No? You'll understand that I find that confusing since that was the reason you gave me for why we couldn't be together."

"Yes, I imagine you do find it confusing." But she was going to lower every wall around her heart and present it to him. Hopefully, since he'd came to her house, that meant all hope wasn't lost. "What I had been missing and never experienced was you, Cayden."

Shock registered on his face, and he swallowed. "Me?"

She nodded. "I gave a decade of my life to a man who was emotionally and mentally abusive. I allowed it to happen. I'd forgive him for doing me wrong, but it never stopped him from doing it again. Probably as a defensive mechanism, I convinced myself that I didn't want to be in a relationship again, that I wanted to be single and free. In reality, it was another relationship like the one I had with John that I didn't want."

"Understandably so." He stared directly into her eyes, making her feel very exposed.

"I know you didn't understand, probably could never

understand," she continued, "why I said the things I did on the night we made love." She refused to call it sex ever again. "How could you when you grew up in a loving home where you were always wanted? That wasn't my life. Between foster homes, John, and even with my adopted parents to some degree, I was never necessary." Sweat popped out on her skin and she walked to stand next to where he sat on the sofa. "I convinced myself that in my new life, I was enough, that I didn't need anyone to be complete."

His gaze didn't waver from hers. "You are enough, Hailey. You always were."

"I am," she agreed, kneeling beside him. "From the beginning, I recognized how different you were, Cayden. Just, everything about you. You were so handsome and wonderful that I never gave myself any confidence that you could truly be mine. I didn't think a makeover existed that would allow someone like you to fall for someone like me."

That's when it hit her that she'd washed away all the powders and creams, leaving her face as exposed as her heart. He'd seen her with smudged makeup that she'd replaced the moment she'd felt up to it when he'd taken care of her when she'd been sick. She fought the urge to cover her face with her hands as he studied her face. She needed to do this, to let him see her.

"You're beautiful, Hailey. With or without makeup."

His sincerity warmed her heart because, bless him, he meant what he'd said. She had to reveal everything to him, who she had been along with this new woman she had become and would continue to blossom as.

"You're seeing the makeup-less version that still has

lash and hair extensions and fillers. I'll be right back."
She went to her bedroom, got a box down from the top
of her closet. She carried it into the living room and set it
down on the coffee table. Her hands trembled as she lifted
the lid to reveal the contents of her former life. The last
photo she'd taken with her adoptive parents was on top
and her heart ached with missing them. They had loved
her and for that she'd forever be grateful. They'd given
her a home and family, even if it hadn't lasted nearly long
enough. She picked up the photo and handed it to Cayden.
"This is me. The real me who didn't believe you could
ever love her and so she convinced herself she didn't want
love or forever. The me who was so scared of what was
happening between us that I destroyed the most precious
gift I've ever known."

Still reeling that he'd driven to Hailey's rather than going
home, reeling at the things Hailey was saying when he'd
wondered if she'd even let him into her house, Cayden
took the photo, stared at the pretty young woman staring
back at him, and wondered what all the fuss was about.
Sure, Hailey's hair and lashes were different. Her lips
weren't as full, and her beautiful eyes were hidden behind
a thick pair of glasses. Reaching into the box, he pulled
out other photos, mostly school pictures which were never
the most flattering, but even with those, her beauty came
through. He glanced through the stack, coming across
only one that was of her and a man who must be her ex.

He tapped the photo. "How old are you here?"

Her gaze was glued to the photo. "Eighteen. I thought I
was the luckiest girl alive that John was interested in me.
I got rid of the other photos of us. There weren't many

considering how long we were together. I kept this one as a reminder that once upon a time, I thought he loved me and that I'd never be alone again. Clinging to that is what led to me staying in a bad relationship. I kept the picture to remind myself to never let anyone close enough to me for them to hurt me ever again."

He fought the urge to crumple the photo, but tossed it back into the box. "Maybe I should have kept pictures."

"It didn't work, anyway."

Knowing she meant him, Cayden flinched. "Hurting you in any way was never my intention."

She shook her head. "You didn't hurt me, Cayden. My holding on to the past that I came here to put behind me is what hurt me." She gave an ironic laugh and swiped at her watery eyes. "I changed my outer appearance because I wanted to be different. Sure, I was doing the therapy sessions, but I was still prisoner to the inner me who didn't feel lovable and so if I convinced myself I didn't want to be loved, then I could pretend my shiny new outer appearance was lovable."

He gestured to the photo. "You were never unlovable, Hailey. The woman in those photos is you and, of her, your lovability, I have no doubts."

Her smile was offset by her tears. "Thank you. You're the kindest person I know."

He snorted. "You think I'm being kind?" He shook his head and stood, bringing her up from where she'd knelt with him. He lifted her chin so he could look directly into her eyes. "Saying that you are lovable isn't me being kind. It's me telling you the truth."

More tears slid down her cheek and this time when she went to wipe them away, he caught her hand with his and laced their fingers. Bending, he kissed her wet cheek. "Don't cry, Hailey. I never want you to cry."

"I'm sorry, Cayden. About everything. I've messed everything up, haven't I?"

He shook his head. "The fake lashes and hair will eventually all fall out and you'll be back to yourself."

Confused, she stared at him. "That's not what I meant."

"Nor maybe what I should have said. I want you happy. I want you to look in the mirror and see the most beautiful, wonderful woman in the world. If those things help you to see what I see, then by all means, keep them. Do them for *you*, because they make you happy, but not because of your perception of anyone else's standards."

"I—okay. Now you sound like my therapist."

"What does your therapist say?"

"That I should use whatever tools necessary to rebuild my inner power and once I've rebuilt it, then I get to choose which tools I keep and which I toss aside."

"Smart therapist." He studied her, taking in every feature, every nuance of her face. "You embracing your inner power is going to a beautiful thing to behold, Hailey."

"I—when that happens, will you be a part of my life, Cayden? Not just at work, but in all of my life? I was wrong to push you away when all I really wanted was to hold you so tightly that you'd never leave. I've regretted doing so every moment since, no matter how much I tried to convince myself I'd done the right thing."

Hope had been building in Cayden from the moment she'd opened the front door and smiled at him. Hope that demolished the makeshift walls he'd put around his heart.

He could never defend his heart from her, not when she owned it.

"Haven't you figured it out yet, Hailey? I know how lovable you are because I love you. Completely, thoroughly, and to utter distraction. It's not anything about your outer appearance, but about what's in here." He lifted their laced hands to where he could press his finger to her heart, then grazed his knuckles across her temple. "And about what's in here. So much so that no matter how much I tried to keep my heart locked away, reminding myself of past betrayals, I fell for you anyway because you are unlike any person I have ever known. My heart knew that long before I acknowledged how I felt." He took a deep breath and looked straight into her eyes. "I love you, Hailey."

Hailey could barely believe what she was hearing. Was it even possible that he loved her?

"I didn't know." Staring at him in awe, she started over. "Maybe, I did know, Cayden. Because I felt safe with you, enough so that I told you things I'd never told anyone. Enough so that I showed you those photos and deep down, I knew it was okay to show you, that you wouldn't be repulsed."

"The only photo that did was the one with you next to the wrong man."

Happiness filling her, more than she'd once dreamed possible, she asked, "Are you the right man?"

"For you? You better believe it."

Wrapping her arms around him, Hailey hugged him, so grateful for the strong beat of his heart against her cheek. "I do."

"I should warn you that someday I'm going to want to hear you say those words to me again. We'll wait until you're ready, until you see forever in the way you've made me view it, but with you, Hailey, a lifetime will never be enough."

Hailey's heart might explode with joy from what she saw in his eyes. Love. Forever. That fidelity he'd mentioned. It was all there and more. She knew because all those things had to be shining back at him as he looked into her eyes. "Someday, I'd like to say those words to you again. You and you alone."

Then Cayden was kissing her, and all Hailey could think was that this must be what happy-ever-after felt like, because she was positive that was exactly what it was.

* * * * *

If you enjoyed this story,
check out these other great reads from
Janice Lynn

Risking it All with the Paramedic
Breaking the Nurse's No-Dating Rule
Heart Doctor's Summer Reunion
The Single Mum He Can't Resist

All available now!

MILLS & BOON®

Coming next month

HEALING THE BABY SURGEON'S HEART
Tessa Scott

'Well, let me at least walk you back.'

'I'm fine, really.'

'Well, if you get bored and want someone to talk to over the next few weeks, I'm here every Tuesday evening with my fellow louts.'

'I'll keep that in mind,' Claire said, truly appreciative of his offer.

Kiernan's lips curved into a slight grin. 'Oh—and one more thing. If you decide to hit up the usual tourist spots, you might want to spray down the Blarney Stone with a strong antiseptic before kissing it. Just saying.'

Claire chuckled quietly. 'That's good advice.'

Kiernan smiled and nodded. 'Well, you take care.'

'You, too.' Claire said as she walked past him.

Once outside, she took a deep breath and allowed the cool night air to seep into her lungs. For a split second, she questioned her decision to close the door on any further interaction with Kiernan. But she had no choice. She had come to Ireland to make a difficult decision that could potentially alter the course of her life from hereon in. The last thing she needed was to tempt another complication that would only create more heartache. She had had enough of that for a lifetime already.

Continue reading

HEALING THE BABY SURGEON'S HEART
Tessa Scott

Available next month
millsandboon.co.uk

COMING SOON!

We really hope you enjoyed reading this book.
If you're looking for more romance
be sure to head to the shops when
new books are available on

Thursday 16th January

To see which titles are coming soon, please visit
millsandboon.co.uk/nextmonth

MILLS & BOON

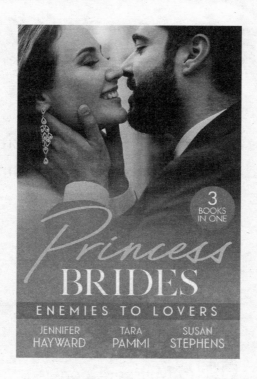

LET'S TALK

Romance

For exclusive extracts, competitions
and special offers, find us online:

⬤ MillsandBoon

𝕏 @MillsandBoon

◉ @MillsandBoonUK

♪ @MillsandBoonUK

Get in touch on 01413 063 232

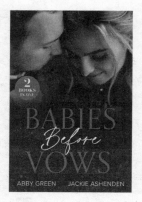
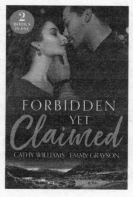
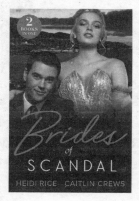

Afterglow Books is a trend-led, trope-filled list of books with diverse, authentic and relatable characters, a wide array of voices and representations, plus real world trials and tribulations. Featuring all the tropes you could possibly want (think small-town settings, fake relationships, grumpy vs sunshine, enemies to lovers) and all with a generous dose of spice in every story.

♪ @millsandboonuk
◎ @millsandboonuk
afterglowbooks.co.uk
#AfterglowBooks

For all the latest book news, exclusive content and giveaways scan the QR code below to sign up to the Afterglow newsletter:

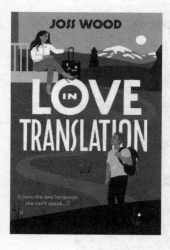
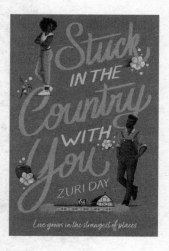
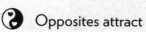
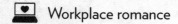
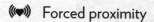

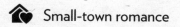

OUT NOW!

REBECCA
WINTERS

ANNE
OLIVER

DONNA
ALWARD

3 BOOKS IN ONE

A *Mistletoe* CHANCE ENCOUNTER

Available at
millsandboon.co.uk

MILLS & BOON

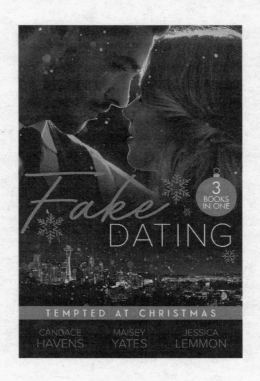